WESTERN

Rugged men looking for love...

An Uptown Girl's Cowboy
Sasha Summers

Hill Country Home
Kit Hawthorne

MILLS & BOON

AN UPTOWN GIRL'S COWBOY
© 2023 by Sasha Best
Philippine Copyright 2023
Australian Copyright 2023
New Zealand Copyright 2023

First Published 2023
First Australian Paperback Edition 2023
ISBN 978 1 867 29821 2

HILL COUNTRY HOME
© 2023 by Brandi Midkiff
Philippine Copyright 2023
Australian Copyright 2023
New Zealand Copyright 2023

First Published 2023
First Australian Paperback Edition 2023
ISBN 978 1 867 29821 2

® and ™ (apart from those relating to FSC®) are trademarks of Harlequin Enterprises (Australia) Pty Limited or its corporate affiliates. Trademarks indicated with ® are registered in Australia, New Zealand and in other countries.
Contact admin_legal@Harlequin.ca for details.

This is a work of fiction. Names, characters, places, and incidents are either the product of the author's imagination or are used fictitiously, and any resemblance to actual persons, living or dead, business establishments, events, or locales is entirely coincidental.

MIX
Paper | Supporting
responsible forestry
FSC® C001695
www.fsc.org

Published by
Harlequin Mills & Boon
An imprint of Harlequin Enterprises (Australia) Pty Limited
(ABN 47 001 180 918), a subsidiary of HarperCollins
Publishers Australia Pty Limited
(ABN 36 009 913 517)
Level 19, 201 Elizabeth Street
SYDNEY NSW 2000 AUSTRALIA

Cover art used by arrangement with Harlequin Books S.A.. All rights reserved.

Printed and bound in Australia by McPherson's Printing Group

An Uptown Girl's Cowboy
Sasha Summers

MILLS & BOON

Sasha Summers grew up surrounded by books. Her passions have always been storytelling, romance and travel—passions she's used to write more than twenty romance novels and novellas. Now a bestselling and award-winning author, Sasha continues to fall a little in love with each hero she writes. From easy-on-the-eyes cowboys to sexy alpha-male werewolves to heroes of truly mythic proportions, she believes that everyone should have their happily-ever-after—in fiction and real life.

Sasha lives in the suburbs of the Texas Hill Country with her amazing family. She looks forward to hearing from fans and hopes you'll visit her online: on Facebook at sashasummersauthor, on Twitter @sashawrites or email her at sashasummersauthor@gmail.com.

Dear Reader,

Welcome back to Granite Falls. The little town has seen quite a population boom since book one. We're not done yet. You've visited the McCarrick brothers and their cutting horse ranch in previous Texas Cowboys & K-9s books. This time, Angus McCarrick is our leading man. He likes his life as is and swears he's not the marrying type, but our heroine, Savannah Barrett, might change that.

As the daughter of one of the wealthiest and most influential families in Texas, Savannah has grown up trying to live up to her father's expectations. Having a one-night stand with a dreamy mystery cowboy is the most out of character thing she's ever done. But that one unforgettable night leaves her with lifelong consequences. Pregnant. With triplets.

Angus wants to do the honourable and right thing for the babies, but Savannah wants more. Can her pregnancy lead to real love, a family and the whole package? Or are she and Angus destined to co-parent their triplets from two very different worlds?

I hope you enjoy Savannah and Angus's story and that you'll come back to Granite Falls soon!

Happy reading,

Sasha Summers xoxo

DEDICATION

**Dedicated to those willing to fight for
their happy endings. Keep up the good fight!**

CHAPTER ONE

"IT'S MY BIRTHDAY, TOO."

Savannah stared up at the starry sky, blinking furiously. "I know, Chelsea." Her twin sister didn't have the best track record for keeping plans but this was different. At least, it should be. A sisters' night to celebrate their birthday. An evening at Gresham Hall. Some yummy dinner while The Rustler's Five, their favorite band, played, then spending the night at the elegant West Mill Inn and getting spa treatments tomorrow. "Chels...this was your idea." An idea they'd agreed to months ago. It *was* their birthday.

"I know. I know. Rain check, okay? I'll make it up to you, so don't be mad, okay?" Chelsea pleaded. "Please, please, please."

Savannah could never stay mad at her twin for long—they both knew that. But she wasn't ready to forgive and forget just yet. "Can you blame me?"

"You'd understand if you met him." Chelsea's swoony sigh had Savannah shaking her head.

Her sister loved falling in love. Staying in love, however, was a different story. And, though Savannah never said as much, Chelsea's relationships were more about attraction than real love. It was a long shot, but she had to try. "What about taking a rain check with him? Asking him—"

"Damien."

"—Damien if he can wait one night?" Savannah waited. And kept waiting. The longer Chelsea stayed quiet, the more frustrated Savannah became. If her sister did delay things with Damien and go ahead with their plans, she'd be sullen and pouty and the whole evening would be ruined. Basically, the evening was ruined either way. "Never mind." She took a deep breath. "Have fun with Damien and I'll see you later."

"Oh, Pickle, you're the best." Chelsea squealed. "There isn't a better sister in the whole wide world, I know it. Why don't you try to have some fun tonight? It'd be easy to do. Just smile and laugh and be charming—you're a hottie, too, y'know? Take a page from my book and find yourself some hottie of a cowboy eager to give you a *really* happy birthday."

"Yeah, sure." Savannah had never and would never.

"I'm serious, Pickle. You need to learn to cut loose a little. Orgasms are good for you."

Savannah's sigh was all irritation. Twins or not, they were two entirely different women.

"Your loss. Okay, I'll bring a big cake home and we can eat it all when you get home tomorrow, okay?" But she hung up before Savannah could answer.

"Happy birthday." She turned to head back inside the dance hall—and slammed into a wall. Her phone fell, hitting the wooden porch with a thud. But the hands resting on her shoulders informed her she'd collided with a very broad chest—not a wall. Even if it was rather wall-like—as chests go. "Sorry." She stepped back, mortified.

"Excuse me, ma'am." A deep voice. Smooth and warm.

Savannah looked up. The tan felt of his cowboy hat cast a bit of a shadow on his face, but she could make out a strong jaw lined with a close-cut auburn beard.

"My fault." He touched the brim of his cowboy hat before stooping to pick up her phone and offering it to her.

"No, it was mine…" She took her phone. "Thank you. I

wasn't watching where I was going. Distracted… I mean, I was distracted."

"Bad news?" He nodded at her phone.

"Um…" She shrugged. "Yeah." But she wasn't going to let Chelsea stop her from enjoying her night.

"Sorry to hear that." He sounded sorry, too. Which was sweet.

"Thanks." She blew out a slow breath, trying to rally. "Not really bad news. Not in the grand scheme of things. My sister. She just… We had plans for tonight and she canceled. She does that—a lot. At the last minute. I don't know why I'm surprised. It's our birthday. We're twins, so I guess I thought… Hearing it out loud, I sound pretty selfish." She stopped, realizing she'd just shared way too much information with a complete and total stranger. "Anyway."

He tipped back his hat then, giving Savannah a clear view of his handsome face. The first thing Savannah noticed were his eyes. Warm and brown with just the right number of lines at the corners to imply he was good-natured. Beyond that…well, he was ridiculously handsome. Very…manly. One might even say sexy. Well, *Chelsea* would say it. Chelsea would get that look, that *He's mine* look. Savannah never thought about a man like that. Until now.

Get a grip. With an awkward smile, she headed rapidly toward the door before she could make things worse.

Inside Gresham Hall, the low rumble of the crowd and blast of air-conditioning cleared her brain. She was upset. Emotional. Irritated. Disappointed. Heck, mad even. Her reaction to the bearded cowboy was fueled by *all* of *that*. Not that there was anything wrong with her appreciating a good-looking man. He was. She did. And that was that.

She made her way to the table they'd reserved along the edge of the dance floor. Chelsea had insisted on paying for the premium table. She'd wanted to be up close to see the band. Now Savannah squirmed in her seat. Alone. Up front. She'd never felt more exposed in her entire life.

"Ready for a drink?" The waitress was young and perky, her cleavage dangerously close to spilling out of her low V-neck T-shirt. "Or are you waiting for the rest of your party?"

"It's just me." Savannah forced a smile. "I'll take a white wine."

The server's brows rose. "Sure." She eyed the empty chair. "Can I take this? We're expecting a full house."

"Of course." Maybe having the empty chair gone would make this less awkward?

"Great." The server lifted the chair. "I'll be back with your wine."

Savannah nodded, watching the chair and the server disappear into the crowded room. Was this really what she wanted to do for her birthday? Sit here, alone, drinking? Wasn't that plain sad? She could go. If she left, she could go to the hotel, put on her comfy pajamas, watch *New Girl* on Netflix, and order room service. She should go. Except she really wanted to hear The Rustler's Five. *Dammit, Chels.* She tapped her manicured nails across the wood-top table as she started making a mental pros-and-cons list. Bottom line, if she left, she might not get a chance to see her favorite band live again—at least not anytime soon.

"I couldn't help but notice you, darlin'." The words were slurred. "You're too pretty to be sittin' here alone."

Savannah glanced at the man leaning a little too far into her personal space. Unlike the handsome cowboy she'd encountered on the porch, this man was an overt creeper—his focus entirely on her chest. Ugh. This was one of those times when she wished she was as good a liar as Chelsea. "I'm not alone."

He smiled, using his thumb to point back over his shoulder. "Then why did I see your chair get carried off?"

She frowned. "I'm not interested."

"Well, that's because you haven't given me a chance." The man rested both hands on her table. "Give me five minutes and I can change your mind."

Savannah considered the man. He was handsome enough. He was groomed and pressed, with a fresh shine on his boots. Appearance wise, there was nothing wrong with the guy. "While I appreciate your enthusiasm, you can't change my mind."

"No?" He chuckled. "I'd hate for you to miss out. Hell, I'd hate for us both to miss out. How about I go get myself a chair and we talk about this?"

"No. Thank you." She stopped drumming her nails, sending him her most glacial stare. It normally did the trick. Normally.

"I never back down from a challenge, darlin'." He winked. "You're all feisty and I like that."

Was he serious? It's not like she was using big words. She glanced around the room, looking for a quick exit. She didn't have the patience for this. But her gaze landed on the hottie cowboy from outside. He was watching her. Correction, he was watching the sleazy cowboy talking to her. And hot cowboy wasn't happy. When his eyes met hers, he stood and headed her way and all Savannah could hear was Chelsea's advice ringing in her ears. "Cut loose. Have some fun."

But then sleazy cowboy was taking her hand and, ick, rubbing his thumb along the inside of her wrist—and what happened next was mostly a blur.

ANGUS HAD NEVER liked Jason Tilson. He was a fast-talking, self-inflated piece of shit that lived for the hunt and loved to talk all about his conquests. At the moment, Jason was laying it on thick with the sad-eyed woman who'd almost knocked him on his ass not ten minutes ago. And it bothered him. Something fierce. He didn't know the woman from Adam, but he couldn't sit there, knowing it was her birthday and she was alone, and leave her prey to a sono-fabitch like Jason Tilson.

That was why he slipped off the barstool, grabbed a spare chair from a table he passed and headed toward where she sat. He didn't know what the hell he was doing, but Jason was taking her hand and the look on her face told Angus everything he needed to know. He was too far in to stop now.

"Jason." He grabbed the man's shoulder and spun him around.

"Gus?" Jason shook off Angus's hold. "You mind?"

"Yep." He set the chair down with a resounding thud. "She does, too."

Jason looked at the woman, who was watching them with wide eyes, and then back at him. "You and her are... together?"

"Maybe. Maybe not. What's it matter?" Angus stepped closer.

Jason bowed up. "It matters 'cause you're interrupting our conversation."

Angus gripped the front of the man's shirt. "The conversation is over."

"Gus." The woman was up, her hand resting on Angus's arm. "I don't need anyone fighting for me."

Angus released Jason.

"Bye, Jason." She waved, then sat.

Jason smoothed his shirtfront and snapped, "You coulda said something."

"I did, several times, but you were having a hard time understanding the concept of no." The woman crossed her arms over her chest. "*No* should have been enough. Gus shouldn't have had to step in to make you listen."

Angus couldn't sit. He was glad she was getting the chance to speak her mind but even more pissed by what he was hearing. He couldn't help but say, "You owe her an apology."

Jason didn't like that one bit.

"Go on." He gripped the chair back.

"I'm sorry." The words were dripping with sarcasm, but Jason turned on his heel and made his way back to the bar before Angus could do or say anything more.

"This birthday just keeps getting better and better." The woman sighed. "Thanks for that." She was studying him.

He nodded, uncertain what that look meant.

"You want to sit?" She nodded at the chair he'd carried over. "Ward off any more unwanted advances." There was a ghost of a smile on her full red lips.

He sat, doing his damnedest not to stare. Here he'd tried to be chivalrous and chase off that scumbag Jason. She likely wouldn't appreciate him giving her a once-over. But she was beautiful. As soon as she'd walked into him, he'd been a little starstruck by just how pretty she was. In a soft way. Fragile. Classy and elegant. Untouchable for a man like him. "We'll have to come up with a signal so I know what's wanted and unwanted."

She did smile then. "Oh, good point. Don't want the welcome ones scared off." She leaned forward to rest her elbows on the table, meeting his gaze. "Thank you. Gus?"

"You're welcome." His chest felt tight. Damn, but she was something to look at. "You know my name. What's yours?"

A strange expression crossed over her face. It was no more than a handful of seconds but whatever she was thinking looked like a weighty decision. "Chelsea." She twisted her long hair and pushed it back from her shoulders. "My name is Chelsea."

The server arrived with a big glass of white wine. By the time he'd placed his order, Chelsea had already knocked back a third of her glass. Maybe the whole thing with Jason had upset her more than she was letting on.

An awkward silence hung over the table until the server came back with his beer. She kept looking his way, blushing, and sipping her wine. And he didn't know what to make of it.

"Happy birthday, Chelsea." He toasted her.

She had a blinding smile. "Thank you. Here's to having a fun evening." She tapped her glass to his beer bottle.

"Cheers to that." He took a healthy swig of his beer.

Her phone chirped so she pulled it out of her purse. One look at the screen, her smile disappeared, and her phone was shoved back into her purse.

After a long stretch of silence, he asked, "All good?"

She finished off her wine. "Family. My father." She took a deep breath, her eyes traveling over his face before she went on. "He's on the controlling side of things. Okay, he's very controlling. My sister and I planned this without telling him and he's not happy about it."

Angus could understand a father being disappointed about missing his daughters' birthday. "Did he have something special planned?"

She shook her head, her long brown hair swaying. "Oh, yes—but not for our birthday. He's hosting some dinner party for his big important friends tonight. Momma has a migraine—she gets them a lot when Dad has a dinner party—so he needs me to come play hostess. You know, smile and nod and refill drinks." She peered into her empty wineglass. "I'm very good at it, too. Being charming."

"I'm sure you are." Angus got the feeling she had some talking to do. Surprisingly, he wasn't against listening.

"My sister has managed to ensure he'll never call her for help—they don't get along. At all. My twin does what she wants, when she wants, no matter what."

"Like tonight?" He couldn't help but be hurt on her behalf.

"Yes. Like tonight. Sometimes, I envy her. You know? What would that be like? To do what you wanted?" A new glass of wine appeared and Chelsea took a sip. "The thing is, I get how lucky I am. I've never wanted for a thing in my life. Material things. It's my parents' way of showing us they love us, I guess. By buying us things. Sometimes I wish they'd carve out some time for us—just the family." She took another sip. "Of course, my sister says the four of us together for more than an hour would lead to disaster, so..." She shrugged.

He and his brothers hadn't grown up with a bunch of stuff, but they'd had loving and affectionate parents. Family dinners and chores, supporting each other's football or baseball or rodeo events, and working the horses at the ranch. They were all in it together. He couldn't imagine growing up any other way—especially not the way Chelsea was describing.

"I'm sorry, Gus. You're being so sweet to me. If Ch— my sister was here, she'd tell me I was being a real downer and to lighten up, so..." She smoothed her hair back from her shoulder and looked at him. "I'm going to try that. So, I'm going to say something a little uncomfortable now." She swallowed. "I just have to get up the nerve."

Angus sat up, his curiosity piqued.

"You're single?" Her gaze met his.

"Lifelong bachelor. That's the plan."

"I think you're incredibly attractive." She took a sip of wine.

"The feeling is mutual." Which didn't do her justice. "But I'm not so sure if the wine might be clouding things."

"No." She drew in an unsteady breath. "I thought so on the porch. I thought so before the wine got here. I do think the wine gave me the courage to say it out loud." Her gaze was glued to his mouth. "I'm not drunk, Gus. I know what I'm doing and saying."

His grip tightened on his beer bottle. "That's good to know."

The music started but he didn't move. As long as she was looking at him like that, he had no interest in anything else. He'd never been so drawn in, so eager to burn in the fire she set deep inside of him. She was mesmerizing. Beautiful. And she wanted him. There was no denying or pretending otherwise.

"Dance with me?" She held her hand out to him.

The moment his fingers threaded with hers, he knew he was done for. He wouldn't be driving home tonight or in any rush to get on the road in the morning. As long as Chelsea wanted him around, he'd stay. Holding her close on the dance floor set his every nerve on end. He lost himself in the feel of her. Her sweet softness. The scent of her. The way she fit against him.

"Gus?" she whispered.

"Hmm?" With her head resting against his chest, he suspected she could hear his heart pounding away.

"Thanks again." She sighed and looked up at him. "I think this is going to be the best birthday ever." Invitation burned in those dark eyes of hers.

His hand pressed flat against her back and he drew in a slow breath. If he didn't do something to diffuse the tension between them, he was going to kiss her in a way that might not be acceptable for a public dance hall. "I don't have a cake and I left all my birthday candles at home, but you can still make a birthday wish, if you've got one?"

She smiled broadly, her hands sliding up his chest to wrap around his neck. "My birthday wish? That's easy." She stood on tiptoe and pulled his head down to hers. "You."

"Don't waste your wish on that." He murmured against her lips. "You've already got me."

Her lips clung to his and Angus forgot about the music and the band and the other people on the dance floor. Kissing her was all that mattered. And when she made a little groan of pleasure, dammit all, he didn't want the song to end.

CHAPTER TWO

Four Months Later...

"I CAN'T MARRY YOU." Savannah loosely tied the snowflake-print apron around her vanishing waistline.

"Before long, you're not going to be able to hide...that." Greg, her closest friend, pointed at her stomach.

"My stomach? Is it that bad?" She ran a hand over the swell, sighed, and tugged the apron in place.

"Of course, it's not bad." Greg hugged her. "I don't think it's bad. But you know your parents aren't going to see it that way."

"Tell me something I don't know." Savannah turned. "Where are the sprinkles?"

"Here." Chelsea handed her the jar with red, white, and green sprinkles. "You could do worse than Greg, Pickle. He's cute. And rich. And he loves you." She picked up one of the cookies Savannah was decorating and took a bite. "These are so yummy."

"And for the fundraiser." Savannah wiped the back of her forearm across her forehead. "So, stop eating them. Unless you plan on helping me bake?"

Greg eyed Chelsea. "I can't tell if you were just insulting me or supporting me?"

Chelsea shrugged. "Me neither." She took another bite of cookie. "I'm only eating one more."

"Chels, I'm serious. For every one you eat, you have

to decorate." Savannah frowned as her sister devoured a perfectly decorated gingerbread man.

"You know you don't want me to decorate cookies." Chelsea wiped her hands together. "I'd traumatize the children."

"Whatever." At least they were done talking about her pregnancy. Every day for the last month, Chelsea or Greg would bombard her with questions she had no answers to. Namely, what was she going to do? It was a question she had asked herself multiple times daily since she'd learned she was pregnant. She wasn't supposed to be able to get pregnant. Ever. She'd grown up with irregular periods and been diagnosed with polycystic ovary syndrome. Her obstetrician had told her the only way she'd ever get pregnant was with reproductive therapy.

Yet, here I am. Pregnant.

"Your new hair. Did I miss the big reveal?" Greg asked, eyeing Chelsea's shock of white-blond hair. Greg was one of the few people that dared to go toe-to-toe with her twin sister. His father handled her father's legal affairs—which meant he'd been a fixture in their home for as long as Savannah could remember. They'd practically grown up together. Once Greg passed the bar exam, he worked for his father—which meant he worked for her father, too.

"Did you see a mushroom cloud over the house on your way here?" Chelsea grinned. "No worries, you'll get to be here, front row, for the fireworks." She adjusted her oversize elf hat. "Maybe I should show them my hair right after you tell them you're pregnant?"

"Dad would have a heart attack." Savannah pressed the snowflake cookie cutter into the last little bit of dough. "I know you two don't get along, but you don't want him to drop dead."

Chelsea's eyebrows rose. "Where is daddy dearest?"

"In the barn." She put the cookie cutout on the cookie sheet and carried the tray to the oven. "The new horses are here."

"The overpriced horses we have no use for?" Chelsea reached for another cookie.

"Stop!" Savannah snapped, slamming the oven door. "Not another bite. I mean it."

Chelsea held up her hands. "Pregnancy sure has made you grumpy. You should eat a cookie. Depriving those babies."

"It's definitely babies?" Greg asked, eyeing her stomach with renewed concern.

"You mean, it hasn't changed since she found out a month ago? Yep." Chelsea held up three fingers. "She'll be as big as a house in no time."

Savannah shot her sister another look and set about making another batch of cookie dough. Every year, she made take-home treats for A Night with Santa. It was a fundraising event for the No Child Hungry charity that her family cosponsored. It was a charity close to her heart, one she'd advocated and worked with during her time in the pageant world.

"You know Daniella and Becky will make the rest tomorrow." Chelsea was eyeing a star cookie. "That is what they get paid to do, Pickle. So why are you in here slaving away?"

"Because having the cooks make the cookies doesn't feel, I don't know, homemade? Besides, it's the one thing they will let me cook. And I need some holiday spirit." But really, it was because she was restless. If she didn't keep herself occupied, she was overwhelmed. Her future was rushing toward her, and she couldn't come up with a plan that worked. She always had a plan. Always. This, she hadn't planned for.

It wasn't like she could pretend this wasn't happening. So far, she'd managed to camouflage her slight baby bump with layers, but that wouldn't work for much longer. The house they all shared was massive, and they were all pre-occupied with their own lives, but even her father would eventually notice she was the size of a whale. From the way it was going, that would be sooner rather than later. She could already feel the babies moving. They were real. Busy. Growing inside her. And, ready or not, they were coming.

"Hey." Greg took her hand. "I'm serious about this. Marry me."

It was sweet, very sweet. That was Greg. One of the good guys. Which was why she couldn't marry him. "And if you meet your one true love?" Savannah fanned herself and leaned against the kitchen counter.

"Unless pigs start flying and Hell freezes over, there's nothing to worry about." Greg's one love had left him at the altar and turned him into a cynic. He said love was the first step in a marathon of torture and pain. "I'd rather spend the rest of my life with someone I respect and like."

"And you'd win major brownie points with Dad." Chelsea took the star cookie. "Last one, I promise."

Savannah threw a pot holder at her sister.

"I've never pretended I didn't have ambition." Greg shrugged. "He'd help me get into the DA's office, it's true. But, if you marry me, I can make sure he goes easy on you."

"Maybe I should marry you. I need more help in that department than Savannah." Chelsea wiped some of the frosting off with her finger. "Is this a new recipe? I want to bathe in this stuff."

Savannah let the two of them carry on. While they picked and prodded at one another, Savannah stifled a yawn. She was so tired. One of the things she was having trouble with was fatigue. Like bone-deep exhaustion. She'd always been a doer, but now one of her favorite things to do was nap. Or take a bath. The clock said it was almost six, so there wasn't time for a nap before their standing seven o'clock dinner. But a bath...

"Can I count on you two to keep an eye on those?" She pointed at the oven. "The timer's set." She couldn't stop the yawn this time. "I'm going to take a bath."

"We got this." Chelsea gave her a thumbs-up. "I won't eat them all."

"I've got this." Greg squeezed her shoulder. "Try to relax, Savannah. Stress is bad for you."

She nodded as she left them in the kitchen. Her parents wanted to make sure that there were no illusions about their status, so her family home was big and audacious. Momma came from old oil money, and Dad was part of the Austin Cougars pro football family dynasty. But Dad wasn't satisfied with riding on his family's coattails. No, Richard Barrett had been a mayor and judge and, if he had it his way, in two years he'd land himself a prestigious position in government. From the custom leather furniture to the big game hunting trophies he'd had mounted and displayed throughout the home, the Barrett name represented wealth and excess, and her father was proud of that.

By the time she'd climbed the grand staircase and headed down the east wing to her suite, she was dragging. She turned on the oversize bath, poured in some citrus bath salts, and turned down the overhead lights to a nice, soothing glow. But once she was chin-deep in bubbles with her head resting on her bath pillow, her brain started throwing out questions.

What was she going to do?

One night. One mistake. And now everything had changed.

There was no way to find Gus. It was impossible to track the name Gus—nothing else. And even if she could, would he want to have anything to do with her or the babies? They'd talked enough to know that they were from different worlds. Chances were, her father wouldn't let Gus within five feet of her—let alone his Barrett grandchildren. It was probably for the best that Gus wasn't a factor.

She closed her eyes and, for a few minutes, let herself think about the night she'd had with her sexy bearded cowboy. Never in her wildest dreams could she have imagined anything as pleasurable and intense as what they'd shared. But, more than that, they'd talked. She knew how close he was with his brother. That his father had passed on and his mother lived with her sister in North Carolina. She knew he loved horses more than just about anything. And she knew he had a big, barrel-chested laugh that had made her smile until her cheeks hurt. His big, rough hands had made her feel loved and cherished. How could she consider that, her time with him, a mistake?

"He was a good guy." According to the pregnancy book she had hidden under her bed, talking to the babies was good. "Your dad. He was a cowboy. A big, sweet, tender giant who made all my birthday wishes come true." Her fingers traced along the swell of her stomach before she pressed her palms flat. "There you are." She smiled at the flutters and twists she felt in her belly. "Enjoying our bath?" She rested her head back and sighed. "Let's enjoy a few more minutes of peace and quiet before your aunt Chelsea starts tonight's dinner off with a bang."

Her parents, specifically her father, were ridiculously

overprotective. Dad couldn't handle not being in control of a situation—or a person. Momma had tried to explain it was his love language, but Savannah knew that wasn't a thing. Over the years, she'd learned to pick her battles. It was easier to live at home than move into an apartment of her own and have his round-the-clock security trailing after her and tracking her every move. She took after her mother, preferring to avoid her father's temper. Chelsea, on the other hand, lived to make their father's blood pressure skyrocket. Like now. Bleaching and chopping off her hair? Dad was going to flip. She took a deep breath. "Maybe I should listen to your aunt? And tell them all about you three tonight?" But the last time she'd listened to Chelsea, she'd wound up spending the night with her hottie bearded cowboy. And that hadn't exactly worked out the way she'd expected. "Maybe not."

ANGUS WASN'T A FOOL. He'd donned a freshly starched shirt and jeans, polished up his best boots and trimmed his beard so it was respectable. It wasn't that he didn't always take pride in his appearance—he did. But the Barrett family was old money and having them as a client would open doors for McCarrick Cutting Horses. If he needed to put on his Sunday best to impress Richard Barrett, he would—the man was Texas royalty.

"They're fine-looking horses." Richard Barrett was a talker. "The best. I won't settle for anything less."

Angus had noticed that for himself. Since he'd driven down the long, tree-lined drive leading toward the Barrett home and beyond, to the barns, every detail screamed *money*. Which, for someone like Richard Barrett, likely equated to the *best*. "I wouldn't bring them to you if they weren't." Angus rested his arms on the top rung of the impressive pipe corral. He wasn't blowing smoke, though. He wouldn't sell a horse if it wasn't in peak shape; his reputation hinged on it. "They're the best. Sharpest. Agile. Instinctual. They'll serve you and your herd well."

"I'll hold you to that." Mr. Barrett clapped him on the shoulder. "How about you come up to the big house for dinner? We could put you up in one of the guest rooms while you're training us on commands."

"I don't want to inconvenience anyone." It would be a lot nicer staying here than some motel for the next two nights. Besides, it'd be nice to see how the other half lived. Getting to rub it in his brother Dougal's face only sweetened the deal.

"I wouldn't have asked if it was." Richard smiled. "Tonight will only be a small family dinner. A few close friends, is all."

Angus kept stride with the older man as he led them from the barn. The Barrett homestead was more like a mansion. In truth, it resembled a fancy hotel more than anything. With staggered pitched rooflines, a turret or two, columns along the front, and windows lining both floors. What made it more daunting was the amount of white Christmas lights framing the home. An illuminated wreath hung from every window and several Christmas trees were strung with white and blue lights along the drive to the house. "You've an impressive home, sir." Which seemed nicer than saying it was a little much.

"I do." Mr. Barrett chuckled. "Only the best." He opened one of the heavy wooden doors and stepped aside. "Come on in, son."

Angus took a quick look around and almost tripped over his own feet. If he thought the outside was a little much, the inside was…well, it *was* too much. First thing he noticed were the hunting trophies. A lion. An-honest-to-goodness lion was stuffed and mounted, midleap, onto the back of a running big-horned animal. "Is that a—"

"Kudu." Richard pointed at the animal. "*That* was a good hunting trip. You like hunting?"

He wasn't a fan of trophy hunting, but he'd keep that to himself. "I don't have much time for it." Angus hoped that was a neutral enough answer.

"You should make time." Richard pointed up. "That one was hard getting out of the mountains, let me tell you."

Angus glanced up at the bighorn sheep mounted on a clump of decorative rocks jutting out of the wall of the massive room. "I bet." How much did that cost? Not only to have the animal stuffed and mounted, but to have a fake mountain built into your wall to display the animal? The McCarricks were comfortable, but this? Well, this was another level of money—one he couldn't wrap his mind around.

"Richard?" a woman called from the bottom of the stairs. "Who is that, dear?"

"Lana, this is Angus McCarrick, of McCarrick Cutting Horses. He brought our new horses all the way here himself, to train us and make sure we were happy. Angus, this is my beautiful wife, Lana."

"It's a pleasure, ma'am." There was an air of frailty about the woman that had Angus gently shaking her hand.

"You're most welcome." She smiled. "You're staying for dinner?"

"We will put him up while he's here. Two or three nights," Mr. Barrett added. "I'll get Savannah to tell Mary to get him a room ready."

"I'll tell Mary." Mrs. Barrett argued. "Savannah's having a moment to herself."

"What's the matter with her?" Mr. Barrett was frowning.

"Nothing is the matter, Richard." Mrs. Barrett sighed.

"But *I* can tell Mary." She smiled at Angus then. "Excuse me, won't you."

"Drink?" Mr. Barrett led him through two iron-in-laid wooden doors. "It's not easy living in a house full of women, let me tell you."

Angus didn't respond, inspecting the room with interest. There was a fireplace on the far rock wall. The snap and pop of the fire echoed in the cavernous room. Even with the holiday decor, abundant white lights, and a towering Christmas tree decorated in all white and silver, the room felt cold. "Whiskey? Scotch?" He glanced at him. "Beer?"

If he was going to play with the big boys, he needed to drink like the big boys. "I'll have what you're having." Which could be a big mistake.

While Mr. Barrett was pouring the drinks, others arrived. Pete Powell and his son, Greg. Pete, it turned out, was Richard's oldest friend and lawyer. Greg was following in his father's footsteps. Lana returned to assure Richard that she'd taken care of things with Mary, whoever that was, and Angus's nerves were starting to relax when Richard Barrett's eyes bulged out of his head and he yelled, "What the hell did you do?"

Angus froze, as did everyone else. A quick sweep of the room saw Mrs. Barrett and the elder Powell were staring over his shoulder in shock. Greg Powell, on the other hand, looked like he was trying not to laugh.

"Let me guess, you don't like it?" This, from a voice behind Angus.

"No, I don't." Richard Barrett's face was an angry shade of red. "You look—"

"Like Pink? The musician? You know who that is, don't you, Dad? That's what I was going for." There was amusement in the woman's voice. "Oh, we have company? Isn't anyone going to introduce me?"

Angus turned slowly, avoiding any sudden movements. Whatever was happening, he wasn't about to get sucked into any drama. This deal was too big—too important. But the moment he saw what—who—was causing the commotion, Angus froze.

No breathing.

No heartbeat.

Nothing.

Because it was her.

"Chelsea Barrett." She was walking toward him, smiling, like she'd never laid eyes on him before.

Angus was reeling. Was this a joke? Did she really not recognize him? His pride stung something fierce. For him, their night together had been anything but forgettable. He swallowed. Hell, she'd tempted him to consider something more—and that never happened. After an hour of sleep, he had woken to the sound of the motel room door shutting. He had wrapped the sheet around his waist and pulled open the door to see her climbing into a cab and driving away. He had stood there, like a damn fool, willing her to look back. As if that would have somehow changed something. It had been a one-night thing. That was all. But it had been one hell of an unforgettable night. Or so he'd thought.

"And you are?" Chelsea was smiling up at him—still *no* sign of recognition on her face.

But, up close, she didn't look exactly the way he remembered her, either. Besides the super short, white-blond hair, there was something *different*. "Angus McCarrick." He shook her hand. Something was definitely different. It had to be her, didn't it? She was so familiar. But she wasn't as soft. Not her body, her eyes. That was it. Her eyes were different.

"Sorry I'm late." Another voice.

Angus was too busy studying Chelsea Barrett to care.

"You missed Dad's freak-out." Chelsea pointed at her father, wearing a familiar smile. "He's still red, but I don't think we need to worry about a heart attack or calling the paramedics."

"Chelsea." Lana Barrett scolded. "That's not funny. You know your father needs to be careful of his blood pressure."

"You okay, Dad?"

"Yes, Savannah." Richard Barrett took a deep breath. "I'm fine. I should be used to your sister's antics by now." He sighed. "Angus McCarrick, of the highly recommended McCarrick Cutting Horses, meet my other daughter, Savannah. Also known as Miss Fort Worth, Miss Texas, and Miss Southwest."

"Obviously she's the good twin," Chelsea added.

Then it clicked. Chelsea was a twin. Every single inch of him tightened as he turned. He knew it before he saw her. But once their eyes met... It was her. Exactly as he remembered her. Beautiful and willowy and right there— triggering a barrage of memories from their night together. And just like that, he was aching for her. Not good. Not good, at all.

But, damn, it was a relief to see her react. She recognized him. Boy, did she. Her fleeting smile, so sweet, before her expression shifted to sheer panic. All the color drained from her face so quickly, Angus found himself moving toward her. Too bad Greg, the clean-cut junior lawyer, beat him to it. Angus didn't miss the way lawyer boy protectively draped his arm across her shoulders. Or the way he murmured something for her alone. If that wasn't staking a claim, he didn't know what was.

"I'm fine, Greg," Savannah whispered, her spine stiffening enough to have lawyer boy's arm slip from her shoulders. For one second, she looked directly at him. The message was loud and clear.

Keep your mouth shut.

He got it. He did. He wasn't about to make things awkward by announcing they knew each other. No way, no how.

"It's nice to meet you." He took a very deep breath. "Savannah." He didn't miss the slight tremor in her hand as she took his.

Sonofabitch. The jolt was there—as strong as he remembered. From her sharp indrawn breath, she felt it, too. Good, dammit. He'd spent the last few months trying to convince himself that their night together had been nothing special. One touch, taking her hand, and it was clear he'd been lying to himself.

"Welcome, Mr. McCarrick." She let go of his hand, flexing her fingers.

"Angus will be staying with us the next few days." Richard Barrett clapped Angus on the shoulder again, his voice booming. "Showed up with three of the prettiest horses I've ever seen. Being the professional he is, he's staying until the boys and I've mastered the commands and such. Make sure the horses are a...good fit."

It was the reminder he needed. This was an important business deal for him and his brother. Angus wasn't worried about the horses. Richard Barrett, he wasn't so sure about. Now that he knew who the man was, everything Savannah had told him was enough for Angus not to like the man. But this was business and he needed to set that aside if he wanted to have the all-important Barrett name endorsing McCarrick Cutting Horses. Business was business.

"I know you, Dick. It won't take long." Pete Powell

chuckled. "You're more stubborn than a mule. Once you make up your mind about something, it's done."

Angus nodded, doing his best to tune out Savannah—of how close she was. Yet not close enough. *Dammit all.*

"It's time for dinner," Lana announced.

This is gonna be a hell of a long dinner. He followed Mrs. Barrett from the big room down the hall to what Angus suspected would be another big, impressive and intimidating room.

"I don't envy you." Chelsea trailed behind the group, watching him and Savannah. "*Training* Richard Barrett? Yeah, no. Good luck with that."

He had no response for that. Savannah smoothed her hair from her shoulder and he could almost feel the silky strands sliding between his fingers or falling forward, over his chest and shoulders.

"Whatever this is, you need to cool it," Chelsea whispered, making sure only the three of them could hear her.

Angus paused, frowning. *What the hell?*

"Don't say a word. Twin thing." Chelsea tapped her temple. "You two, cool it." She pointed back and forth between them. "Come on, Pickle." She took Savannah's hand.

Savannah nodded and headed into the room without a backward glance. It left a familiar hollowness in the center of his chest. He didn't like it. He didn't like any of this. Except for finding Savannah again. That part was good. Or was it? She didn't exactly seem happy to see him. Then again, it had to be awkward to have her one-night stand showing up on her doorstep, hobnobbing with her father. That was all it had been. A one-night stand. And that night was long over.

And yet, risky or not, he couldn't help but wonder what would happen if the two of them wound up alone. Would she acknowledge the spark between them? Would she want to experience even a sliver of the pleasure they'd shared that night? He sure as hell did. One thing was certain, Savannah Barrett was worth the risk.

CHAPTER THREE

SAVANNAH PUSHED THE apple pie around on her plate. To-night's nausea had nothing to do with her pregnancy and everything to do with the fact that her gorgeous bearded cowboy was sitting directly across the table from her.

He was here. Here. At her family dinner table. Gorgeous and bearded. Flesh and blood and 100 percent untouchable.

Thankfully, she had years of practice at being a hostess. Smile. Nod. Act interested. Read the room. Keep conversation flowing. Laugh—but not too much or too loudly. In general, be charming. She was good at it, normally. But tonight, she couldn't seem to get her footing.

Gus—Angus—was doing just fine. He was completely unfazed by her presence. While she sat there thinking how ridiculously handsome he looked in his tan button-down oxford, he was laughing and chatting and eating his dessert as if he hadn't made her cry out from orgasm.

Chelsea kicked her, again, under the table.

Because I'm staring.

"Done?" Chelsea asked, nodding at Mary, who was hovering at Savannah's shoulder.

"Oh, yes, thank you, Mary." She leaned back so Mary, the evening maid, could clear her dessert plate.

"No problem, Miss Savannah." Mary smiled as she took the plate, her voice low as she added, "You didn't eat much. If you want anything later, just let me know."

"That's kind of you." Her stomach churned at the idea of food. All she wanted was the peace and quiet of her room.

"How long have you been in the cutting horse field?" Greg asked Angus.

Savannah knew this already. Angus's family had been raising and training cutting horses since his family settled in Texas, generations ago.

"My family's been raising horses since they came over from Scotland. It's in our blood. My grandmother used to say we had kelpie blood." Angus shrugged. "My grandmother loved Scottish folklore."

"Have you ever been to Scotland?" Her mother was charmed.

Because he is charming. The thick, tousled auburn hair. The well-groomed beard. The flashing eyes. *Oh, give it a rest.*

"No." Angus shook his head. "I hope to, one day."

"What's a kelpie?" Chelsea propped herself up on an elbow, fluttering her eyes at Angus.

It was Savannah's turn to kick her sister under the table.

"Ow—um..." Chelsea shot Savannah a death glare and shifted in her chair, out of Savannah's range. "I'm not familiar with the term."

"A water horse." Angus's warm brown eyes glanced at her. "Most of the legends are meant to warn children away from water and single women away from charming strangers out to trap you."

"Good advice." Her father seemed louder than normal. "Advice you two should heed." But he seemed to be talking directly at Chelsea. "It's not easy being the father to daughters, let me tell you."

Chelsea rolled her eyes. "But, Dad, how else am I supposed to meet my soul mate and have a bunch of grandbabies to carry on the family line?"

Her father wasn't amused. "If you were interested in finding your soul mate, I'm sure your mother and I would come up with some decent candidates."

"Gosh, thanks, Dad, but I'm not sure that's how you meet your *soul mate*." Chelsea sighed and sat back in her chair.

"There's no such thing." Richard Barrett nodded. "A partner. A reliable, loyal, like-minded partner is better than some romanticized ideal. You're old enough to realize that and stop wasting your time on men that would never make a good husband."

"According to you," Chelsea pushed back.

Mr. Barrett grumbled something under his breath, then said, "According to anyone with half a brain—"

"Do you have siblings, Mr. McCarrick?" her mother cut in.

"I do. My brother, Dougal. We're partners in the family business." Angus's smile made Savannah's insides go soft. "We butt heads now and then. As families do, sometimes."

Dougal was Angus's best friend—someone Angus loved dearly. Like she loved Chelsea.

"Hear, hear." Pete Powell chuckled. "At the end of the day, family is all that matters."

"It is." Angus nodded. "Family first."

He said it with such conviction, Savannah's heart clenched. Family first. His family. She resisted the urge to cover her stomach. *His* family.

Savannah glanced at her father. Though he liked to say he worked as hard as he did to provide for his daughters, that was more an excuse. Her father was an ambitious man. He wanted the name and power and money. He needed it. The Barretts were already in that top 1 percent, but it still wasn't enough for him. That had nothing to do with making sure she and Chelsea were financially secure.

"And carrying on the family legacy." Her father tapped on the edge of the table. "You girls have quite a mantle to carry. Responsibility and prestige and hard work. Whoever you pick will have to toe the line. I know my girls won't let me down."

"On that note, Savannah and I have a podcast to listen to." Chelsea stood. "'Night, Mr. Powell, 'night, Greg. Mr. McCarrick." She waved.

Savannah stood, too, grateful for her sister's out. "It's been a lovely evening. Good night." She couldn't resist taking a last look at Angus. His warm brown eyes were waiting for her. His smile had those just-right crinkles at the corners of his eyes in full force.

If they'd been alone, she'd have gone around the table and climbed into his lap. *Wait, no.* She wouldn't. Surely... Yep, she totally would. Not exactly the most reassuring realization to make, but there it was. The way his focus shifted to her mouth, she suspected he'd let her climb onto his lap and use his big strong hands to hold her in place.

"Come on." Chelsea slipped her arm through Savannah's and tugged her from the dining room.

Savannah waited. Her sister wasn't one for keeping her thoughts to herself. But they made it all the way to Savannah's room before Chelsea opened her mouth.

One word—that said so much. "Gus?" Chelsea leaned against the closed bedroom door.

Savannah nodded.

"Shit." Chelsea pushed off the door. "You okay?"

Savannah shook her head. Okay was not how she was feeling.

"You going to tell him?" She flopped onto Savannah's bed. "I mean, I won't blame you if you don't but..."

She sat beside Chelsea, smoothing her cream silk blouse over her stomach. "I should. He is the father." Telling him would turn an already complicated situation into an impossible one. "But Dad…"

"Would probably castrate him." Chelsea sighed.

"Gee, thanks, Chels." Savannah pressed her hands over her face. "That makes everything easier."

Chelsea took one of her hands. "Sorry. You know me, I can't help it." She squeezed her hand. "He seems like a really nice guy. Like he might be dad material, you know? And he's so *hot*."

"You noticed?" She nudged her sister. "I noticed, you noticed." She lay back on the bed beside her sister.

"What?" Chelsea glanced at her. "He *is* hot. But he's yours."

"He is not mine." She rested her hand on her stomach and concentrated on the fluttering, rolling movement there. He was *theirs*. Their father.

Gus—Angus was a nice guy. A sweet, hardworking, family-loving, beautiful manly-man. A man who was the father of her babies. She drew in an unsteady breath, tears stinging her eyes. What sort of person would keep a father from his children? Could she live with that? She knew the answer before she'd finished thinking the question. "I have to tell him."

"You want me with you?" Chelsea asked, squeezing her hand again.

"No." She squeezed back. "I can do it."

"You're not worried about getting…distracted?" Chelsea rolled onto her side. "You know." She bobbed her eyebrows. "'Cause he's hot. I'll keep my fingers crossed for you. You know, working off some stress would be good for you."

"Oh, Chelsea." Savannah couldn't help but laugh. "Hot or not, learning he's going to be a father isn't something I'd consider foreplay." And, no matter how hot or tempting he was, she had to tell him about the babies. Climbing into his lap or falling into his bed was not an option. No way, no how, no matter how much she might want otherwise.

ANGUS HAD SPENT an hour pacing his room before he'd given up and taken a shower. She wasn't coming. Unless he wanted to spend the night going door-to-door, he couldn't exactly go find her. He was pretty sure that was the fastest way to get his ass kicked out of the Barrett household.

The shower was stocked with fancy bottles of shampoo and body wash, exfoliating cream and foot scrub. He read the back of the bottles and used them all. His feet had never been officially scrubbed before but it felt damn good. *Who knew?*

He stepped out onto the bath mat, wrapped a towel around his waist, and wriggled his toes. "I'm going to have to get some of that." He took the bottle of foot scrub out of the shower and headed into the bedroom.

"Hi." Savannah, in a white nightgown with her hair falling down her back, was sitting on his bed.

He stopped. "You're here." *No shit, genius.*

She nodded, her gaze bouncing from his chest to his face and back again. "I… I wanted to talk."

She was here, that was all that mattered. "Not to stop me from stealing this?" He held out the foot scrub.

Her smile was worth it. "No. Feel free. Have it." There was laughter in her voice.

He eyed the bottle. "Now I don't have to feel guilty."

"Guilt-free foot scrub." She laughed then.

"Question. Why does your sister call you Pickle?"

"Oh. She had a speech thing when we were little. She used to say dill instead of deal, stuff like that. She went around telling people that we were twins and that made me a big deal. My speech therapist would ask, is Savannah a big dill pickle or a big deal? She thought it was funny so it's become my nickname."

"Huh. Well, okay then." He shrugged. "So, you're not here to talk about this." He set the foot scrub on the side table and sat beside her on the bed. "What are you here to talk about?"

"Um…" She cleared her throat and took a deep breath. "You and I… You're naked."

And she was pretty damn distracted by his chest. He didn't mind. He kinda liked the way she was looking at him. A whole hell of a lot. "I just got out of the shower."

"Right." She forced her gaze up. Dammit. The hunger in her eyes had him gripping the bedcover. "The foot scrub," her voice was soft and husky.

"Screw the foot scrub." He leaned forward, cradling her face in his hands. "I was hoping you'd come."

She leaned into him. "I had to."

His lips brushed over hers, pulling a groan from deep inside his chest. "You taste as sweet as I remember."

She was up on her knees as she slid her arms around his neck. "You remember?"

"Every damn thing." His lips sealed with hers, parting her lips and breathing her in. He felt it the minute she melted into him, her hands sliding up and into his hair and holding him close. He moved, sliding his arms around her waist and lifting her up and onto his lap.

He couldn't get enough of her mouth. Full and soft lips moving over his with a frenzy he understood. Her fingers twined in his hair, tugging him closer still. Her breathing picked up as she straddled him.

The crush of her breasts against his chest had him groaning again.

As hungry as he was for her, he wanted to slow things down. Some little voice in his head told him she'd wanted to talk… Talking wasn't going to happen as long as her nails were sliding down his back.

Her hands gripped the towel around his waist. She wriggled, an impatient grunt slipping from her lips and into his mouth. They could talk later.

His hands slid up the silky softness of her thighs, sliding her nightgown up as he went. The gown needed to go. She leaned back for him to pull it up and off and toss it aside. His memories hadn't done justice to her lush curves. The slide of her bare breasts against his chest had him throbbing against her. The curve of her ass fit his hands as he settled her close against him.

"Gus." She stared down at him, nodding. "Please."

"You're sure?" he rasped, barely able to hold back.

She arched her hips against him. "Please."

They came together suddenly, both of them moaning at the depth and force of the fit. He loved her moan. He loved the way she clung to his shoulders as she thrust against him. It was hard and hot and fast—without control or hesitation. That was what haunted him. How free she was. Savannah had no inhibition. She gave him pure pleasure, holding nothing back.

It didn't take long for his release to build. He wanted to hold on and make things last, but one look at her face, driven and clouded with desire, made that impossible. He gripped her hips and thrust into her, the power of his release emptying his lungs and draining his body. She bit into his shoulder, arching into him until she was shaking. He held on to her as her soft, broken cry rolled over him.

He lay back on the bed, pulling her gently beside him and tucking her against his side. He needed a minute to calm his heart and steady his breathing. Hell, he needed more than a minute. Loving Savannah wrung him out— and he had no complaints.

"I… I'm sorry," she gasped.

"I'm not." He turned his head, burying his nose in her hair.

She laughed softly. "No…me neither."

He hugged her close. "Happy to hear that."

She sighed, going soft against him. "Angus."

"Savannah." He ran his hand down her back. "Savannah suits."

"Chelsea didn't?" She looked up at him.

"Savannah is a better fit." He smoothed one long strand of hair from her shoulder. "I didn't imagine it."

"Imagine what?" Her clear eyes searched his.

"How beautiful you are. Or how good we are together." He kissed her.

She blinked, slowly stiffening in his arms. He felt it, saw it—the way she was withdrawing from him.

"What's wrong?" He ran his finger along her jaw.

"Nothing." Even her voice was distant.

"I call bullshit."

Her smile was reluctant, but she didn't relax.

"You can tell me." He tilted her chin up until their eyes locked. "I'm a good listener."

"I know." She blinked rapidly, then pressed her eyes shut. "I should go." She looked the way she had when she'd told him her name was Chelsea. Like she wasn't sure what to say.

"You can be honest with me." He hoped she would be.

She opened her mouth, then closed it. She was really struggling. "What if it's hard to hear?"

Were those tears in her eyes? "I can handle it." At least, he hoped he could handle it. He wasn't so good with tears. He propped himself up on an elbow.

"Angus…" She tugged his towel up to cover her. "I…"

She stood, stooped for her nightgown, and tried to put it on without dropping the towel.

He stood. "Let me help."

"No…" She stepped back. "I can do it." The towel fell and her hands dropped to her stomach.

Angus watched her cheeks go red, but couldn't understand why she was fumbling with her gown or acting so jumpy. It wasn't like he'd never seen her naked before. He had—and thoroughly enjoyed every inch of her. She had a beautiful body.

There was a soft knock on the door. "Angus?" It was Chelsea.

Savannah shook her head and held her finger up to her lips.

He picked up the towel off the floor, waited for Savannah to hide in the bathroom, and cracked his bedroom door. "Hi."

"Hi." She shook her head. "I know she's in there." Her words ran together. "I'm a little tipsy. I'm also hoping you two have finished your business because my dad is up and drinking, and he's been known to poke around. Because, you know, he's an ass."

"Seriously?" Angus knew Richard Barrett was a dick, but this was still a surprise.

"Yep. Wait, are you telling me it's unusual for a father to do bed checks on his adult daughters?" Chelsea feigned surprise. "Anyway, I've come to rescue my sister. Don't you know Savannah is a perfect child? I, on the other hand, know ways of sneaking around undetected by our self-important father."

"I'm here." Savannah slipped past him into the hallway. She looked more frazzled than ever.

"Look at how messy your hair is." Chelsea giggled. "Let me guess, the talk didn't happen?"

"You're drunk, aren't you?" Savannah was frowning at her sister.

"A little." Chelsea held up her thumb and forefinger to illustrate.

Savannah looked horrified. "We should go."

"I told you." Chelsea gave him a head-to-toe look. "You got distracted—not that I blame you. You're going to have to tell him eventually."

What the hell does that mean? "Savannah—"

"Will be here tomorrow." Chelsea tugged Savannah's hand. "And he'll be dressed, so talking will be more likely to happen."

"Chelsea, could you please shut up," Savannah all but hissed. "Angus, tomorrow... We need to talk."

"I got that," he murmured, beyond confused. "Just answer one question. You *are* okay?"

Chelsea nudged Savannah. "You're right, he is sweet."

He didn't know what to make of the look on Savannah's face.

"Just tell him." Chelsea nudged Savannah back. "He can sleep on it and it'll give him time to calm down."

That didn't help the mounting pressure in his chest. "Okay, tell me."

A loud thump caused all three of them to jump.

"Hurry up. It's easy, Pickle. You say, I'm pregnant, and that's that," Chelsea whispered. "And, yes, *you* got her pregnant. Savannah is like a sex camel—she can go a long *long* time without sex. Excluding you." She grabbed Savannah's arm and pulled her stunned sister after her. "Close your door," Chelsea called back.

Angus closed the door and stood, frozen in place. Pregnant. Savannah was pregnant. Sonofabitch. With his baby. His. He slid down the door to sit. A baby. He was going to be a father. Him. It was a lot to take in.

And then there was Savannah. She was worried—so worried she'd hesitated to tell him. It ate at him. What exactly was she worried about? That he'd want nothing to do with the baby? Or that he would? How the hell was he supposed to sleep without knowing that?

CHAPTER FOUR

As FAR AS long nights go, Savannah was pretty sure last night had been the longest night in the history of long nights. Not only had her sister dropped her news on Angus, she'd had to take care of Chelsea. She'd had to press a cold washcloth to her sister's forehead as Chelsea heaved up what must have been a bottle of whiskey before they both crawled into Savannah's bed to sleep. Rather, Chelsea slept. Savannah tossed and turned and tried to come up with something to ease her panic. So far, she'd had no luck.

The sun was streaming into her bedroom when Chelsea finally moved, groaned, and pressed a hand over her eyes. "Don't hate me," Chelsea murmured. "I know I screwed up, big-time."

"You did." She was too tired and frustrated to sugarcoat things.

Chelsea rolled to face Savannah, moaning. "You look awful."

"If you're trying to make amends, maybe start with something kind or flattering or not rude." Savannah turned her head on the pillow to look at her sister. "You look pretty rough yourself."

"You're gorgeous... But your eyes are all puffy and dark." Chelsea frowned.

"Surprisingly, I couldn't sleep."

"It's my fault." Chelsea scooched closer, draping her

arm around Savannah and resting her head on her shoulder. "I'm sorry. I'm so, so sorry. It just came out."

"You were drunk." Savannah patted her sister's arm. Drinking was something Chelsea did. Like their dad. And neither of them handled their liquor well.

"I was." Chelsea nodded. "But still. I… I just blurted it out."

"I know. I was there." And she'd replayed the look on Angus's face most of the night. He'd been shocked, which was expected, but they hadn't stuck around for much else. Chelsea had been right, their father—also on a bender— had checked in on them not five minutes after they'd collapsed in Savannah's bed.

"Poor Angus." Chelsea moaned again. "Can you imagine how he feels? First, seeing you again was a surprise— but a good one, I'm sure. Then finding out you're pregnant with his kid—kids. I mean, talk about a hell of an evening."

Savannah couldn't stop the tears from coming then.

"Oh, Pickle." Chelsea hugged her tighter. "I'm not helping."

"No," Savannah sobbed. "You're not."

"Breakfast," Momma's cheery voice rang out as she backed into Savannah's bedroom. "Oh, goodness." She stood, breakfast tray in hand, staring at the two of them. "Whatever is the matter?"

"N-nothing." Savannah sat up, wiping at the tears, and hoping her mother hadn't heard anything. "I have…a migraine." Her mother was a frequent sufferer of migraines and would be instantly sympathetic, not suspicious.

Chelsea sat up, too, gripping her head and mumbling several expletives.

"That's not nothing." Their mother put down the tray and sat between them. "That's horrible. Would you like me to draw you a bath? That helps me sometimes."

"A bath would be great." Savannah kept wiping at the tears.

Momma smiled as she reached up to tuck Savannah's hair behind her ear. "I'll pull the curtains, too. Light doesn't help. And I'll make you some ginger tea. I swear it'll settle your stomach." She swallowed. "I mean, I always get nauseous when I have a migraine so—"

"Me, too." Savannah had a hard time meeting her mother's eyes.

"I'm here." Chelsea leaned against their mother. "I need attention. I feel bad, too."

Their mother laughed. "Migraine?" Momma disapproved of drinking. She felt so strongly about it, their parents now had separate bedrooms. Admitting to a hangover wasn't going to earn Chelsea a bit of sympathy from their mother.

"Let's go with that..." Chelsea sighed as their mother draped an arm over her shoulder.

"I think you two are too big to take a bath together, but I can get one going in your room if you like, Chels?" With a kiss on each of their foreheads, Momma stood, pulled the curtains closed, turned on one lamp in the far corner, and headed into Savannah's bathroom.

"We have the best mom." Chelsea sort of collapsed on her side, her head in Savannah's lap. "You're going to be just like her," she whispered.

Savannah ran her fingers through her sister's short do. "I hope so."

When it came to mothering, she was the best. She'd been hands-on when they were little and she made a point to have special time with them now. From afternoon tea in town to shopping trips and spa days, she always made them both feel loved and cherished. If, however, their father was in the mix—she seemed to fade into the background. Chelsea said it was because Mom knew he'd talk over her and ignore what she said, so she didn't try anymore. It hurt to see Momma diminish herself for him.

"There's toast there." Momma pointed at the tray, wiping her hands on a towel. "Might not hurt you to have a piece before you get in the bath."

Savannah didn't argue. She nibbled on the dry corner and hoped her stomach would behave while Momma was still in the room.

"I'll be back with the tea in a bit." Momma held her hand out. "Come on, Chels, let's get your bath going, too."

"Oh, goody." Chelsea moved in slow motion as she stood. "Then, a nap?"

"Hopefully you two will be up for having lunch." Momma slid her arm around Chelsea's waist and, carefully, led them to the door. "Your father has a few of his Rodeo Board pals coming over. He wants to show off the new horses and give that nice young man, Angus McCarrick, some introductions."

Angus would appreciate that. In all their hours talking that long-ago night together, he'd mentioned his desire to grow their operation. He had a real passion for horses. He'd been animated when he'd talked about that moment of connection with a difficult horse or seeing a horse in sync with their rider and precipitating what came next. She couldn't remember ever feeling that way—about anything.

"Try to rest, Pickle." Momma blew her a kiss as she pulled the door shut behind them.

Sitting alone in a dark room didn't do much to brighten her mood. She lay back on her bed and rested her hands on her stomach. "I'm going to have to face him, you know?" She closed her eyes to concentrate. The flutters and rolling were faint and unpredictable. She was looking forward to more reassuring concrete solid kicks and movements.

Whether or not this pregnancy was expected, she was happy she was going to be a mother. It was the rest of it that had her so terrified and uncertain. Her parents. Angus. What her life would look like once the world knew.

Dad might actually have a heart attack.

Her whole life, she'd gone out of her way to make her parents proud of her. Her father, especially. To earn one of his real smiles, a rarity, had filled her with such pride. The older she got, the fewer and more far between those real smiles became. He seemed to get harder and more jaded with each passing year. He stopped caring about their school events and birthdays—unless someone he deemed important or influential was going to be there. Her pageants were important, giving him exposure and more connections. He was disappointed that she wanted to give them up. *Now there's no choice.*

It was foolish to think that she could bring out the father of her childhood, but she couldn't let go of the idea that, somehow, someway, he was still inside. Chelsea told her to get over it and accept that their father was now an outright asshole. But trying to win his smile and approval had turned into a habit she didn't know how to break. Finding out about her pregnancy would probably take care of that.

Then she remembered. "The bath." She pushed off the bed and hurried into the bathroom. The bubbles were piled high, but the water wasn't spilling over the sides yet.

The smell of lavender and eucalyptus should have been soothing, but instead her stomach flipped and Savannah ran for the toilet to throw up her dry toast breakfast.

CONSIDERING ANGUS HADN'T got much sleep, things with Mr. Barrett and his top ranch hands went well. He had no choice but to set all thoughts of Savannah and the pregnancy aside and focus on work—for now. Richard Barrett might be a proud sonofabitch, but he was smart enough to understand that learning the commands would make him look good in the saddle. Once the older man's well-dressed friends started showing up to watch, looking good was of the upmost importance to Mr. Barrett. It helped that the horses were well trained and responsive. He'd handpicked these four horses for that reason.

Angus spent the morning rubbing shoulders with a judge, a congressman, an investment banker, and others who served on the board of the Fort Worth Rodeo Board with Mr. Barrett. They weren't all ranchers but most of them liked to pretend they were—and they had the money and inclination to buy the tools of the trade even if they didn't really need them. That included cutting horses—which Angus would be all too happy to provide.

He'd planned on staying with the horses and working through any questions or concerns the ranch hands might have for him, but Mr. Barrett steered him in the direction of the big house, along with his guests.

"Y'all go on ahead into the den. Barb has some snacks and drinks set up, and Lana will be along shortly, with the girls." He pointed the way.

Girls as in Savannah? His chest collapsed in on his lungs as he glanced toward the stairs.

"I figure we should settle our accounts before we settle down for lunch? I like to get the money out of the way." Mr. Barrett clapped Angus on the shoulder. "If that's agreeable with you?"

Business. He took a deep breath. *This was business.* Whatever was going on with Savannah could wait another ten minutes, surely. "Yessir."

"Good. Then let's head to my office."

As soon as he crossed the threshold of Mr. Richard Barrett's office, Angus understood what it meant to be intimidated. It was intentional, of course. If he wasn't so out of sorts, he'd probably have found the number of deer heads, antlers, and tusks mounted on the wall behind Mr. Barrett's imposing desk funny.

"Have a seat." Mr. Barrett indicated the single chair opposite his desk before going around the massive wooden desk to sit. He pulled a checkbook from a desk drawer and glanced at Angus. "I'll make the check out to you."

Angus stared around him. He'd never be comfortable in this environment. Impersonal. More a showplace than a home. He sat and tried not to fidget.

"Impressive?" Mr. Barrett nodded, his gaze sweeping the room. "Like you, I've worked hard to get where I am. I respect a hardworking man. A driven man, putting in the sweat equity and time to ensure their success, is rare nowadays. But it takes a shrewd businessman to recognize a golden opportunity and grab it, before that opportunity passes them by." Mr. Barrett ripped the check out and held it toward him.

He took the check, read the number, and almost fell out of his chair. Something hard and cold settled in the pit of his stomach.

"You take that and the guarantee that you'll get more high-dollar clients than you could ever imagine." Mr. Barrett sat back in his chair, his steely eyes hard. "You take that, end things with my daughter, and never speak to her again. That means no further contact with her or her children of any kind. Ever. Everyone comes out ahead." He paused. "Otherwise, you'll head home with your horses and no check. Whatever claim you make on Savannah's children will land you in court. I'll use my arsenal of lawyers to keep things tied up until you're bankrupt, with nothing and no one to show for it."

By the time the man was finished talking, Angus could

hear his blood roaring in his ears. The check was shaking because his hands were shaking. His throat was too tight to breathe, let alone speak. Richard Barrett was trying to pay him off? The man was giving him a seven-figure check to walk away from Savannah and the baby he'd just learned he was having? He set the check on the desk and stood, his mind ping-ponging back and forth until he was dizzy. He kept coming back to one question. Over and over. "Does Savannah know about this?" Did he really want to know the answer?

Mr. Barrett's grin was hard. "What do you think? Let's just say Savannah has entrusted me to...take care of this. It's my job, Angus. I'll always take care of her. What was it you said? Family first? I couldn't agree more." He tapped his fingers on the edge of the desk. "You showing up was unexpected. She's marrying Greg Powell—you met him— that's all arranged. He's a good man. He cares about Savannah a great deal. He'll take care of her and their family in a way you never could." He patted the edge of his desk. "You need some time to think it over?"

Hell no. The only thing he needed time for was to climb over the damn desk and knock the smug smile off Richard Barrett's condescending face.

"I want you to think long and hard about what I'm saying here. You're a decent man. I can see that. You might feel obligated to do right by her." Barrett used air quotes around the word *right*. "But that would take away any future she has. She's meant for more than being a wife and mother. She's got aspirations and dreams. She wants to make a difference in the world. You can't give her that. And the children? Here, they'll have the best schools. Travel. You name it. Their lives won't begin and end with a ranch full of horses. A real father would want to give their children the world, not limit their opportunities."

Richard Barrett was evil. A bastard. So why the hell did the man's words make some sort of twisted sense? The man wasn't lying. He did want what was best for his child—

There was a knock on his office door, followed by Lana Barrett saying, "Richard, darling, lunch is ready."

Angus couldn't move. He was frozen. His hands, white-knuckled, gripped the arms of the chair. If he let go, he couldn't be accountable for his actions. He was fuming. Raging. Breaking.

"On my way." Richard stood and came around the desk. "Join us for lunch when you're ready. Judge Frye is keen on getting a horse for his daughter. I'm sure you have just the right one." He patted Angus on the shoulder and left, the click of the door echoing in the deafening silence of the room.

Angus stared straight ahead, past the antlers and tusks and glass-eyed deer heads out the window to the bright green fields beyond. Green fields—because they were watered. Because nothing here was real or natural. Because there was enough money to make things how Barrett wanted them, not how things were meant to be.

Did that include Savannah?

Barrett said as much. He was taking care of it for her—it, as in him. But, dammit, last night she'd said she'd wanted to talk to him. She'd come to his room to talk to him. She'd wanted him…and she'd made love to him.

It didn't add up. The girl he'd spent the night with had poured her heart and soul out. Her constant pursuit of perfection and her fear of failure—because of her father. She was a romantic and wanted the white picket fence and all that and believed loyalty was important. Meaning, she wouldn't have slept with him if she was engaged to Greg Powell.

If the girl he'd spent the night with had only lied about her name. What if it had all been a lie?

Before he went off half-cocked, he needed to calm down. Was he seriously considering taking the check and the opportunity Richard Barrett was offering him? How could he walk away and pretend he wasn't going to be a father? It went against everything he stood for. Family was everything.

Then there was Savannah. This talk they needed to have. If there was even the slightest chance that he and Savannah could be a family, they owed it to the kid to try, didn't they?

If Barrett did what he said with the whole possible financial ruin thing, it would make things a lot harder for him, for Savannah, and their family.

Damn Richard Barrett.

He stood, his gaze landing on the check. He'd never seen that big a number in his life. If he worked hard every day for the rest of his life, he'd never earn that number. Few could. Richard Barrett hadn't even blinked.

He pulled his phone from his pocket and dialed his brother, Dougal.

"Hello?" Dougal answered. "Do I need to come bail you out?"

"The day's still young." Angus ran his hand over his head. "I don't think you can get me out of this."

"Talk." Dougal wasn't a big talker.

"You remember the girl? The Rustler's Five concert?"

"The one you haven't stopped talking about?" Dougal sighed. "Lemme guess, you ran into her."

Angus chuckled. "And she's pregnant."

The line went completely silent.

"Her dad, our big client, Richard Barrett, offered me, us, two and half million dollars and business referrals if

I walk away." He swallowed, his anger choking off his words. Until now, he'd been too shocked to fully appreciate the full offensiveness of the man's proposition.

Still silence.

"I didn't knock him on his ass," he ground out, imagining just how gratifying that would have been.

"You didn't?" His brother was pissed. It took a lot to get Dougal pissed. "I'm impressed."

"He made it pretty damn clear business would suffer if I didn't take his offer. He's a real sonofabitch." It helped talking through it. Sort of. His anger had been in check before.

"What are you going to do?" Dougal's voice was pitched low with anger.

He knew. It was easy. He wasn't that man. "I can't walk away." He ran his hand over his head. "I need to talk to Savannah. Hopefully, she'll be more reasonable than Barrett."

Dougal grumbled something under his breath. "Away from the father."

Angus nodded, taking in the view again. "Our way of life is likely to be an adjustment for her." She'd grown up with maids and every material thing at her fingertips. He and Dougal still burned toast and drank two-day-old coffee warmed in the microwave. There was dog hair on the furniture and his favorite recliner had duct tape around the arm to hide the hole his little dog, Gertie, had made when she was a chew-happy puppy.

"Don't start getting ahead of yourself. Talk to her first." Dougal sighed. "I shoulda come with you."

"I'll be home soon enough." Angus took a deep breath. "How's Willow doing?"

"She's fine. She's a tough ol' girl." The only time Dougal sounded that gentle was when he was talking about his big black Lab, Willow. She'd been out with Dougal, clearing brush, and chased a rabbit into a clump of cactus—getting a snout full of needles and one close to her eye. The vet said she'd heal up fine, but Angus told Dougal to stay home anyway—his brother would be too worried about the dog to be of much use.

Angus was quick to offer up reassurance. "Like you said, she's tough."

"That she is." He cleared his throat. "Don't let that bastard rattle you. You do what you know is right and I'll back you."

Angus breathed out a sigh of relief. It wasn't a surprise to hear Dougal say as much, but he'd needed to hear it all the same—especially if his actions did impact their livelihood. "See you tomorrow."

"Yep." And Dougal hung up.

Angus shoved his phone into his back pocket. How the hell was he supposed to sit through lunch without causing a scene? He'd never been one to sit on what he was feeling. Hell, working with Barrett and his friends this morning had been hard enough—worrying over Savannah, the pregnancy, and all that was left unsaid. That was before Barrett had gone and showed his true colors.

He ran his hand through his hair, took a deep breath, and let himself out of Barrett's office. He followed the rumble of conversation down the hall, but couldn't bring himself to go inside. If he was going to keep a cool head, he'd be wise to keep his distance from Richard Barrett—for now, anyway.

Lana Barrett came around the end of the hallway, saw him, and stopped. She gave him a long, thorough inspection—one that made him suspect she knew exactly what was going on—before she asked, "Not hungry, Mr. McCarrick?"

"I was taught to clean up before sitting down at the table. Especially a table as nicely set as yours, ma'am."

He hesitated, wishing Savannah had shared more about her mother.

"I appreciate that, Mr. McCarrick. Manners are overlooked too often these days." She didn't reach for the door or move; she was still studying him.

He tested the water. "Is there something you want to ask me, ma'am? I'm an open book."

"I do have a question, Mr. McCarrick, but it might be a bit personal." She waited for him to nod. "My husband talked to you about what I told him?"

He hesitated. "And that would be?"

She lowered her voice. "That you are the biological father of my grandchild?"

He nodded.

"And, what, exactly, did he say?" She crossed her arms over her chest.

Well, damn. "He made it clear what my options were." He wasn't sure how to go on. For all he knew, Mrs. Barrett had been the one to tell her husband what to say. She didn't come across that way, but Angus wasn't feeling all that confident in his people-reading skills.

"Let me guess, my way or the highway? My husband usually gets what he wants." Her eyes, so like Savannah's, narrowed.

Not this time. Of course, it wasn't up to him. That was why he needed to talk to Savannah. Alone. To know what she wanted. He hoped like hell she'd give them a chance.

She went back to studying him. "I've never seen my daughter light up the way she did when she first saw you, Mr. McCarrick. I'd like to think well of you."

"I'd like that, too, ma'am." He hoped like hell he wasn't making a mistake as he went on, speaking from the heart. "I'd like to do right by Savannah—by my baby—if she'll have me."

CHAPTER FIVE

"Your daddy says we should be expecting a wedding invitation soon?" Judge Frye whispered.

Savannah had years of experience when it came to keeping her features blank but pleasant. "Oh? That's news to me, Judge." She hoped her smile wasn't as brittle as it felt. "Normally, that means an engagement."

He chuckled. "We're all expecting you and Powell Junior to marry, naturally."

Naturally.

"You two have been thick as thieves since you were both knee-high to a grasshopper." He kept on chuckling. "That boy needs to hurry up before some other fella comes along and catches your eye."

Not likely. How many men would be excited to court and marry a pregnant woman? A woman pregnant with triplets, no less? She had yet to see how the babies' father was going to react to the fact there was three of them— after just finding out he was going to be a father... For the fifth time, her gaze swept the table. Still no Angus.

"Greg is a dear friend." Which was true. "Would you like more potato salad?" She held her breath and offered the carnival glass serving dish. The smell wasn't sitting right with her stomach. Then again, not much did.

"Don't mind if I do." Judge Frye took the dish and added a large serving to his plate.

Thanks to Momma, she'd had breakfast in her room.

While she'd appreciated the time to herself, she'd missed a chance to see Angus. Seeing him was key. She had no idea what he was thinking or feeling after Chelsea had dropped the news on him. Now he was nowhere to be found and she couldn't help but worry. Well, add to her worries. Worrying was all she'd done since she'd come home from her doctor's office with a black-and-white set of grainy ultrasound photos and a bottle of prenatal vitamins.

Momma came and went, dishes were cleared, and new courses brought in, Chelsea kept testing Dad's patience, and just when Savannah had almost given up hope, Angus walked in. *Finally.*

"Sorry I'm late." Angus took a seat next to Chelsea. "Didn't feel right sitting down at such a fine table without cleaning up first."

"I'll have a plate made up for you." Momma stood and left, all smiles.

Her attempts not to stare at him were an utter failure.

He was so handsome. Sitting among her father's friends, he stood out. He didn't spend his days with trainers and stylists and wearing high-dollar clothes to fit a part. He earned his physical prowess through hard work—he was confident in his own skin and his abilities and, oh, so sexy. Just thinking about the touch of his hands on her sent a shiver along her skin.

"Your wife is quite the hostess. And as lovely as ever." Judge Frye lifted his cut-glass iced-tea tumbler in honor of their mother.

"I'm a lucky man," Dad agreed, his gaze falling briefly on Angus.

Savannah didn't miss the look. It wasn't a good look. It was hard—and full of judgment. The kind of look she'd seen on her father's face when he was discussing something unpleasant. It set a jagged knot in her throat and her stomach churning.

"How did it go with the horses?" Chelsea shot Angus a dazzling smile. "Was Dad a difficult student?"

"It went well." Angus smiled back. "Your father knows how to handle himself. No fear—a horse can sense that. They're intuitive animals." He leaned back as Momma set a food-laden plate on the table before him. "Thank you. I hadn't meant for you to go to any trouble, Mrs. Barrett."

So sweet and considerate. That was Angus. Angus, who wasn't looking her way.

"No trouble at all." Momma returned to her seat. "Richard's father used to say hard work deserves a good meal."

"My mother would agree with that." Angus ate with gusto—never once acknowledging Savannah.

All she needed was some sign. The teeniest hint as to what he was thinking would help. Or had last night's news so upset him that he couldn't look at her? Maybe he'd pack up his things and go? That would make things easier. *And 100 percent awful.* She speared a green bean on her plate, but couldn't bring herself to eat it.

Conversation drifted from upcoming charity events to football stats and more. Try as she might, Savannah couldn't concentrate on any of it. She smiled and nodded when there was a pause, but for all she knew smiling and nodding was the last thing she should be doing. When dessert was over, her patience was at an end.

Thankfully, Chelsea's twin senses must have been tingling, because she was up and announcing, "Momma, Savannah and I have a mani-pedi to get to. You gentlemen enjoy your afternoon."

This was news to her, but she didn't argue.

It took fifteen minutes for the three of them to extract themselves from the dining room, but Chelsea was a woman on a mission.

"Crap on a cracker, those men can talk." Chelsea was shaking her head.

"Chelsea, that's not very nice." But Momma was smiling.

Chelsea snorted. "Momma, if you think that was bad, be happy I didn't say what I was really thinking."

"It did seem like the longest lunch." Savannah glanced back at the dining room door, feeling a flicker of guilt for leaving Angus to fend for himself.

"Poor Angus McCarrick will earn whatever connections he makes before he leaves tomorrow." Chelsea voiced what she was thinking.

"Don't you worry about Mr. McCarrick." Momma looked quite pleased with herself. "I sense he's made of sturdy stock."

"You do?" Maybe it was the way her father had been sizing up Angus, but Savannah was picking up on a few things herself.

"What are you up to?" Chelsea tugged the both of them into the small study and carefully closed the door behind them.

"Whatever do you mean?" Momma's brows rose but her cheeks were stained pink.

Savannah sat, her nerves too frayed to hold back a second longer. "Momma, you know. I know you know."

"I suspected. You don't get sick, Pickle. You've been so tired. And you've been wearing looser clothes." Momma sat opposite her. "And then I overheard the two of you talking. I know."

"Shit." Chelsea perched on the coffee table between them.

"And Dad knows?" Savannah forced the words out.

"He does." Momma's smile faltered then. "I... I panicked. I'm sorry. I should have talked to you two first. I was just so...so surprised."

"*Wait*. Dad knows? Whoa, whoa, whoa. How is Angus alive?" Chelsea leaned forward, staring at their mother in shock.

"Let's not worry about your father for the moment." Momma patted Chelsea's knee before turning to Savannah. "What I really want to know is what you want, sweet girl. What's in your heart?"

Savannah held her breath, her mother's question pressing in until she blurted out, "I don't know. I don't. But I want the babies."

"Babies?" Momma's eyes widened.

"Three." Chelsea held up three fingers—on both hands. "One, two, three."

"Yes. I see." Momma blinked. "Goodness. Are you all right? Are they all right?"

"Yes. So far, we are all good." Savannah took a deep breath. "I want them very much. I'm happy I'm expecting and that I'm out of the first trimester and they're safe." She cradled her stomach. "But I don't know what's best for them or me or if I'll be a good mother. And how can you tell me not to worry about Dad? He's... Dad. He's already telling people to expect a *wedding invitation* for Greg and me."

Momma reached up and tucked a strand of hair behind Savannah's ear. "Sweetie, let's back up. You being happy is the best place to start."

"And what do you mean you don't know if you'll be a good mother? You've been mothering me since we were in the womb." Chelsea snorted.

Savannah shot her sister a look.

"Huh, I guess that's not exactly comforting?" Chelsea giggled. "It's not your fault I'm compelled to rebel against Dad."

"And you do it so well, sweetie." Momma smiled at Chelsea.

That had all three of them laughing.

"Your sister and I will go get a mani-pedi. You go on out to the barn until you get a chance to talk to Angus. He'll be packing up to head home tomorrow." She shook her head. "Call me old-fashioned, but I believe the two of you need to work through what's best for all of you. Not me, not your father, not Chelsea, or Greg. We might all think we have the best of intentions, but this is one of those times when only you and Angus have any say-so in what happens next. And, whatever that is, I will support your decision. No matter what your father says or does. You hear me?" She drew Savannah into a strong embrace.

"Who knew you were such a badass, Momma?" Chelsea hugged them, too. "You know you can count on me, Pickle."

Savannah held on to the two people closest to her heart. Until now, she'd felt alone and lost. Then again, until now, Momma had tended to hold her peace and follow Dad's lead. She was so glad her mother had chosen now to speak up.

"Now, we'll all leave together." Momma stood, smoothing out the front of her houndstooth-print wool skirt. "As soon as you're ready."

Savannah grabbed her purse and left with them. They dropped her at the barn and headed off into town while she settled into the hayloft to jot notes for her talk with Angus. She wanted to be clearheaded and well-spoken when he showed up looking all manly and irresistible. Whatever else was between them, the attraction was undeniable. Or was it? Maybe learning she was pregnant had killed his desire. He hadn't spared her a single glance through lunch. *Stop.* There was no point speculating what he was or wasn't thinking. Until she spoke to him, all she was doing was making things worse. *I'll find out the truth soon enough.*

Angus sat on a hay bale, legs propped up, whittling on a piece of wood, biding his time. He'd packed up his saddle and tack. The trailer had been washed. He'd made sure the wheels were good and checked all the gauges on the truck, too. He'd run out of things to occupy himself with, but he wouldn't wake Savannah. She was too peaceful. She needed sleep. She and the baby. His mother used to go on and on about how hard her pregnancies had been on her—if she was sleeping, she needed it. He'd wait.

He was flipping through the newest *Ranch & Farm* catalog for the third time when she finally yawned and rubbed her eyes.

"Angus?" She sat up then, eyes wide and startled.

"Hey, hey." He dropped the catalog. "Didn't mean to scare you."

"No, you didn't. I was waiting for you." She blinked, running a hand over her hair.

"You were? That's a relief." It was, too. He was clinging to the hope that Richard Barrett had said all he'd said to scare Angus off—that he hadn't been speaking for Savannah.

"Believe it or not, I don't normally take a nap in the barn." Damn, but he could look at that smile all day.

"I would." He stood and moved to her side, sitting on the blanket she'd spread out over the hay. "As haylofts go, this is pretty comfy."

"Is it?" She sounded nervous.

He *was* nervous. "I'm guessing you want to talk?"

His eyes met hers. "About…the baby." He stumbled over the word.

"Babies," she whispered.

His heart, already clipping along at above average rate, skidded to a halt. "Come again?"

"Babies." She spoke a little louder now but there was a definite waver in her voice. "More than one. Three, actually."

"Three?" He'd never squeaked before. Not once. The word definitely resembled a squeak. He cleared his throat and tried again. "Three." Three was a hell of a lot more than one. Or two. He had two hands. Three meant he'd be outnumbered. It was pretty damn terrifying. "Three," he murmured again.

She nodded, her smile fading. "Does it make a difference?"

"No. It's a surprise. All of this… But, no." He rubbed his hands on his thighs to stop himself from reaching for her. "Not at all."

She stared at his hands long and hard. "I… I thought maybe you'd panicked and left—"

"Oh, I am panicking." He chuckled. "Trust me. But I figure we're in the same boat there."

She nodded.

They were quiet then. It was an easy silence. The horses knickered and snorted below. The ranch hands were talking somewhere a way off. The call of a dove and a finch or two sang from the nearby oaks. After a time, his heart wasn't about to launch itself out of his chest.

"I guess I should talk first?" Savannah's eyes met his. "I'm not certain where to start or what to say. I've been trying to figure out what's the best, the right, thing to do."

He nodded. "And I wasn't part of that equation until now."

"It's not that I didn't want you to be." She turned a bit

so she was facing him. "I didn't know where to start or how to look for Gus with the kind eyes and strong shoulders." She shrugged.

Strong shoulders and kind eyes, huh? Is that how she thought of him? He could live with that. "But you would have looked for me? If you'd known my name?" Her answer was important to him.

She didn't hesitate. "Of course. You have every right to know and be a part of...this. If that's what you want. I'd never force you to... I'd understand if you don't."

He could breathe easier now.

"Is that what you want?" She was looking nervous again.

"I'm not trying to dodge the question, Savannah. But I'd like to know what you want, first. You told me you don't have your thoughts and wishes taken into consideration all that often. Now that I've met your father, I see what you mean." He paused. "No disrespect to him..." Hell, he had nothing but disrespect for her father but he didn't want to influence her.

"That's very considerate of you. He is a man of strong opinions."

Her father was a pile of cow shit, but he'd keep that to himself. The less Barrett was involved in this conversation, the better. "I think this is one of those times when your opinion comes first." He waited, crossing his arms over his chest.

"I was told I'd never have children—not without medical intervention. And even then, it was unlikely. I was devastated. I want a big family. I've always wanted a big family." She shook her head. "Anyway, I went to the doctor last month expecting the worst. And then I found out I was going to be a mother. It was such a surprise. The best surprise." She was all but glowing now, her smile so big it warmed him through and through. "It's a gift, you know? I'll try to be the best mother I can be." Her joy was palpable. And beautiful. "But I guess I'd always assumed babies, if there were any, would come after I'd found my… husband. Or partner. It's what I want. The whole package deal—a husband, kids, all that. Well, what I wanted."

Did she realize she'd taken his hand? "I get that. I think that's what most people want." He glanced down at their hands, noting how silky-soft and small hers was. His was big and coarse and rough. The contrast was stark.

"We're strangers," she whispered.

"Almost." He ran his thumb along her wrist. Her shiver set him on fire. "I know a few things about you."

Her words were halting. "But our lives are so different."

Which was true. "I do have a question."

She nodded.

"It's been said a time or two that there's already someone special in your life." Namely, Greg Powell. "Is this true?"

Her hand pulled free and she stood. "Are you… I wouldn't sleep with *you* if I was involved with someone else." Savannah Barrett, angry, was a sight to see. She was fuming, staring at him with such contempt.

He was smiling as he stood. "Good." Richard Barrett was a dick.

"You… Are you…" She sputtered. "Are you involved? I'm not interested in being the other woman."

"I would never ask you to be. There are a few things I consider unforgivable, Savannah. Cheating is one." He paused. "I was told you were marrying Junior Powell. I figured I'd clear that up."

"Oh. *Oh.*" Her features smoothed. "And, you're not… you don't have a someone special?"

"No. Lifelong bachelor." *Shit.* He hadn't meant to say

that. Not when he knew what needed to be done. "Well...
Now, I guess I do. I have three very special someone spe-
cials." He nodded at her stomach. "I want to be a part of
their lives."

Savannah stared up at him. "You would?"

"If that's what you want?" He sighed. "We can figure
this out, together. We are in this together, after all. I want
to do right by you—by my babies. I meant it when I said
family comes first."

"What does that mean?" It was a whisper.

"It means..." What? He couldn't give her the picture-
perfect family she wanted. He didn't love her. She didn't
love him. "Come home with me. Let's do the right thing."
It was hard to say what came next. "Let's get married.
Try to make it work for them." He heard how unsteady
he sounded, but there was no help for it. Marriage hadn't
been part of his five-year plan—if ever. He liked his life
as it was. *Now that's all going to change.*

"Marriage?" She didn't look happy. Not one little bit.

He pressed his hand to her stomach. "We're a family
now." It was that simple.

"I... I don't want to get married because I'm pregnant,
Angus." Her hand pressed over his, the swell of her stomach filling his palm. "I get that you want to do the right
thing, but I want the real thing. Us, getting married now,
ensures that won't happen."

Which wasn't what he wanted to hear. He didn't *want*
to get married. But no matter what happened, he didn't
want his kids thinking they didn't give it their all to be a
family. No matter what Barrett said or did, Angus had to
live with himself and that outweighed any threat the man
had thrown at him. "Where does that leave us?"

"On the same team. You want to be involved. I want

you to be involved. We…we co-parent?" She looked just as uncertain as he felt.

"Co-parent?" He shifted from one foot to the next. "Can we co-parent at my place?" He was pretty damn sure Barrett would make it impossible if she stayed here.

"I think that sounds like a good idea." It was a small smile, but it was a smile. She held out her hand. "Shake?" Her gaze drifted across his mouth.

He grinned. "I'd prefer a kiss." These babies weren't the only thing that bonded them. There was desire, too. A hell of a lot of it.

She smiled. "Deal." She slid her arms around his neck and stood on tiptoe. "Will we co-parent with benefits? Like friends with benefits?"

"I'm open to negotiations." He chuckled. "We are the ones setting the rules, aren't we?"

"Yes." It was a light kiss. "Yes, we are." There was no denying her hunger for him. She melted against him and he welcomed it.

He didn't know what the future looked like, but they were in it together. He'd do his best by her, his best by their children, and listen to and respect her wishes. Respect wasn't love, but it was something. And, if they were going to stand a chance, the sooner they started building a foundation, the better.

CHAPTER SIX

ANGUS WANTED TO do the right thing. She should be happy. She should have expected as much. He was a good guy. He'd done the honorable thing and proposed. And it made her want to cry. This wasn't how she'd pictured her proposal. Of course, she hadn't pictured being pregnant with triplets when she was proposed to, either.

But he was kissing her now—which was enough to short-circuit any real thought beyond the feel of his mouth on hers and his hands firm against her back. She'd never been this happily consumed by touch before. Not just physical, either. All he had to do was look at her and she was a boneless mass of quivering want. She should be embarrassed. Instead, she held on and enjoyed the scratch of his facial hair.

When the kissing stopped, he held her close. His thickly muscled arms felt just right around her. And, for the first time since she'd left the doctor's office, it was easier to breathe.

"This went really well." Her words were muffled against his chest.

"You were expecting something different?" His tone was low and soothing.

"I didn't know what to expect."

He held her away from him, his auburn brow furrowing.

"Okay, fine, I was expecting you to pack your bags and leave." She winced.

"I'm glad to disappoint you." He was frowning now, his arms sliding from her waist. "It does sting to hear how you thought I was going to react."

She held on to his arm. "It's not a reflection on you. More me, really." She backpedaled furiously. "I wouldn't blame you for leaving. Between learning I was pregnant, which is a lot, and my dad with his 'all about the Barrett family' speech at dinner, being significant and blah, blah, blah. How he has a specific future in mind for me—"

"Like you marrying Powell Junior." Angus was watching her. "Or someone like him. Not like me."

"Like that, yes. Which has nothing to do with you." She went on. "It's him. He's...he's so caught up in the way *he* sees things. *His* plans. I was worried he'd talk to you before I could and, I don't know, get you to see things his way? He tends to get what he wants." She winced again. "I'm making him sound like some sort of mafia kingpin or something."

"Or something." The corner of his mouth kicked up. "Mafia kingpin, huh?"

She rolled her eyes. "I don't know what the right term is. Obviously."

"How would your father convince me to do what he wanted?" Angus was watching her closely.

"Maybe he'd make you an offer you can't refuse sort of thing?" She knew it was a bad joke, but she was only partly teasing. "I'm kidding. Sort of." She took a deep breath. "I don't know. I don't want to know. He's a jerk, but he is my dad."

Angus's expression softened then.

Her hand caught his. "I'm still not sure that came out right, Angus. I didn't mean to imply anything about you. I'm sorry."

"Like you said, we're near strangers. It'll take time for

us to figure each other out." His eyes crinkled from his smile. "Words are easy. Actions are what matter."

And just like that, he was sexier than ever. *Is that possible?* It would seem so. She resisted the urge to fan herself.

"What?" One brow cocked. "What's that look mean?"

"Look?" She blew out a deep breath.

"That look." He pointed at her. "The one you're wearing right now."

Normally, she was good at hiding her feelings, so his calling her out caught her off guard. "Honestly?"

"Always." He nodded. "That's something else. I'd rather hear the truth, even if it's not easy to hear or say. Agreed?"

She nodded. *Don't say it.* She couldn't say it. People didn't actually say things like, "I think you...you are incredibly...sexy." And, yet, now she'd said it. Her cheeks were on fire.

"Oh?" He ran his finger along her lower lip. "Well, since we're being honest... Every time I look at you, I want you more."

She leaned into his touch. "We have that in common." The idea of falling into the hay with him right then and there sounded oh-so appealing.

"We do." He shook his head, but he was grinning. "As much as I'd like to kiss you, I think there's more talking to be done first."

"There is?" She'd rather do some kissing.

"Deciding we want to give this a chance is one thing. How we go about it is another." He cleared his throat, his own cheeks pinkening. "I'd really like us to get married, Savannah."

She opened her mouth to argue, but he kept going.

"If we're committed to making this work, then we should do it right." He said it as if it was the next obvious step.

There it was again. That word. *Right*. It set a lump in her throat. Why did the word have to be so *wrong*? "But marriage is…" Forever. Permanent. Legal.

"A commitment." He ran his fingers through his hair. "I don't want you, or anyone, thinking this is a game or some temporary thing. If we go into it thinking that, it's not real. I have every intention of being there for my kid—kids. I want them to know we gave it our all. They deserve that."

She was reevaluating his sexy status all over again. As in, confirming he was the sexiest man in the known universe—and probably beyond. Men didn't talk this way. At least, she'd never encountered one that did. Angus spoke his mind in a way that stirred her body and her heart. He made a powerful argument. "I can't, Angus. We can't. We can do right by our kids without sacrificing any chance of future happiness. A future that includes real love."

The muscle in his jaw clenched tight.

"I understand what you're saying. I do. But what if we get married and you meet the love of your life? Or I meet the man of my dreams? Then what? We let that opportunity pass us by because we're doing the right thing? I can't do that, Angus. I don't think it's wrong to want to be loved."

His nod was reluctant.

"You should want the same. You said your parents were happily married."

"They were," he murmured. "But I hadn't thought about getting married, Savannah. I never thought I was the marrying type. I like being a bachelor." He shrugged.

Which made his willingness to marry her all the sweeter. She was more than a little overcome. The last twenty-four hours had been one long roller-coaster ride of emotions. Up and around, upside-down and backward. Every once in a while, she knew which way was up. Now was not one of those moments. It took effort to get the words out. "I will not marry you, Angus McCarrick." She swallowed, so nervous she was shaking. "Because you don't want to get married, and I want to marry for love. And, just because we're going to be parents, doesn't mean we have to give up on what we want."

"You're one stubborn woman." But there was a reluctant smile on his face.

"I'll take that as a compliment." She was still shaking, but she smiled back at him. "So, no marrying. Yes to going home with you so we can get to know each other and figure out this whole co-parenting thing."

"I believe you said something about co-parenting with benefits?" He was grinning now.

"I did." Her cheeks were hot. "I can't believe I said that." Further proof that he brought out her wild side.

"I'm glad you said it." He ran his fingers along her cheek. "No debating that one."

She shivered from the touch, leaning into him. "We're good? We have a plan?" Why did her voice waver? This was what she wanted.

He nodded and stepped closer, pulling her back into his arms. "It's going to be okay, Savannah." He ran his hand down her back. "Like you said, we're in this together. A team. Whatever happens, it will be okay."

She rested her head against his chest. His heartbeat was steady and strong—like his arms around her waist. It'd be all too easy to get used to this. Straightforward communication. Honesty. Strength. But they'd have to be strong enough to stand up to her father. As terrifying as that was, what choice did they have?

She glanced at her phone to check the time. "Time's almost up. Chelsea and Momma covered for me so I could talk to you without Dad interfering. I'm supposed to be getting a mani-pedi with them." She eased from his hold.

"Chelsea's loving all the spylike stuff." She took a deep breath. Momma would probably be on his side—disappointed that there were no wedding bells in the imminent future. She'd make her understand. Chelsea would support her. But would that really help? Her brain was already spinning. "Are we leaving in the morning?"

"I'm packed and ready." He nodded. "If you think you need more time—"

"No. I'll be ready to go. We can tell him, everyone, tonight at dinner?" She hoped having the whole family present would help rein in her father's reaction. Her eyes were stinging then. It was too much to hope her father would support their decision. Unlike Momma, he should be thrilled they weren't planning a wedding. "Going with you will give us the time to figure things out on our own. Dad... Well, you know Dad."

"He might not want to hear it, but this isn't about him." He tilted her chin up. "This is what you want?"

Without a doubt. "It is."

The crunch of tire on gravel was unmistakable.

Angus let her go and peered through the hayloft door. "Looks like your ride is here."

She ran a hand over her hair and smoothed her champagne-colored tunic over her long, stretchy straight skirt. "Any hay anywhere? I don't want Chelsea's imagination running away with her."

The corner of his mouth quirked up again. He made a slow circle around her, plucking one piece of straw from her hair. "You look beautiful." He pressed a hand to her stomach again. "I'll see you all soon."

The sight of his hand on her stomach had her eyes stinging again. He was right. Maybe everything would be okay. She stood on tiptoe, kissed his cheek, and hurried down the stairs and out the barn door to her sister's waiting SUV.

"How did it go?" Chelsea asked the moment she'd closed her door.

"It went well." She blew out a deep breath. "I'm going home with him tomorrow."

"No shit?" Chelsea gasped.

"Chelsea, please." But Momma sounded pleased. "Is that all? And where is home? How far away will you be?"

"I don't know." They'd been so focused on coming up with a plan that the details had slipped by. "I'll find out. But, yes, that's it, Momma. For now."

Momma's sigh was disappointed.

"Probably a good idea to get out of town." Chelsea glanced at her in the rearview mirror. "You're not going to be able to hide your baby bump for long."

"What about Christmas?" Momma's voice was tight. "That's only two weeks away."

"I know." And she was sad she'd miss the holidays with her family. "But I'm going with Angus tomorrow. It's for the best. In case Dad—"

"Blows his top? Loses his cool? Explodes?" Chelsea stopped. "Sorry."

"That's very sensible, Savannah." Momma reached around to take her hand. "We can talk and check in over Skype or whatever. It won't be the same as having you here, but I respect your decision."

Thankfully, Momma sounded calm and resigned. Chelsea was Chelsea. And Angus was being about as perfect as a man could be. If her luck held, Dad would see that this was what she wanted and respect that. She stared out the window, her spirits sinking. Her father had never respected her wants or wishes. What made her think he'd start now?

ANGUS SURVEYED HIS appearance in the mirror for a final time. He hadn't intended to take extra care trimming up his beard, starching his shirt and jeans, and making sure his boots were oiled up, but he was glad now. He didn't give a damn what Richard Barrett thought of him; he'd lost the right to Angus's respect the minute he'd pulled out his checkbook. But he respected Lana Barrett, Chelsea, and Savannah—and he was staying under the man's roof.

Tonight was important. He wanted to look like a man capable of providing for Savannah and the babies. Not on the level that Barrett could but, dammit all, she and their kids would never want for a thing. It was important Savannah's family knew as much.

No matter what Barrett said or did, Angus was determined to keep his temper in check. Barrett could protest and rail, but this was about Savannah and his children and their future. As long as he remembered that, Angus would have no problem keeping his cool.

Of course, it couldn't just be the family that night. Pete Powell and the not fiancé, Greg, were already sipping drinks and making small talk with Richard and Chelsea. Lana saw him and offered him a beer, giving him a bright, encouraging smile. But it was Savannah that drew his eye. She looked every bit Texas royalty. Maybe getting married was a bad idea. How would they have been able to make it work?

"Angus." Richard gave him a tight smile. "Glad you could join us for one last meal."

"I appreciate the hospitality." He patted his stomach. "Pretty sure I've put on a pound or two from the food."

"Whatever." Chelsea snorted. "I bet you have a six pack. Or an eight pack."

"Well, that's not awkward." Savannah shot her sister a look.

Chelsea shrugged. "What? I'm just saying what we're all thinking."

"No." Greg Powell shook his head. "No offense, Angus, but I wasn't thinking about your abs."

"No offense taken." At this point, he was pretty sure bringing up Savannah's pregnancy would be less awkward than their current conversation.

"Let's sit down to eat, shall we?" Lana waved them to the table. "Try to behave, Chelsea."

"We could talk about the weather?" Chelsea mumbled, winking at Angus as she sat next to him. "How long does it take you to get home?"

"About six hours." And he was ready to get home, with Savannah, away from the tension and judgment that clouded the air of the Barrett dining room.

"You travel a lot?" Powell Senior asked.

"No." He thanked the maid that filled his glass with iced tea. "A lot of clients like to come out to the ranch, take a tour, and pick up their horses. When we deliver, we try to set up several stops all at once, and my brother and I take turns."

"That sounds efficient." Lana placed her napkin in her lap.

"Work smarter, not harder." Angus repeated one of his grandfather's favorite sayings.

"A sound philosophy," Powell Senior agreed.

"Is your brother married?" Lana asked.

"No, ma'am. It's just the two of us." For now.

"A bachelor pad, eh?" Barrett shot him a narrow-eyed look.

"I hope you're all hungry." Lana glanced around the table. "Chef prepared grilled snapper, mushroom risotto, and a spinach and bacon salad."

"It smells delicious." Greg sat back as a plate was set before him.

It did and Angus was starving. But the food on the

plate had been arranged with such care that he almost felt guilty eating it. Another reminder of what Savannah was used to. Not just food on a plate, more like art on a plate.

"Daniella, our chef, knows her way around the kitchen." Barrett leaned forward and picked up his fork. "She should, for what we're paying her."

And there it is. Barrett never missed an opportunity to slide money into the conversation.

"Pickle?" Chelsea whispered, her tone pulling Angus's full attention to Savannah.

Her skin was green. "I'm good." She took a sip of tea. Then another. She wasn't good and she wasn't fooling anyone.

"Not a fan of snapper?" Barrett asked around a mouthful of food. "You're the one that's always saying we need to eat healthy and now you're not going to eat it?"

Savannah took another sip of tea and set her glass down, eyeing her plate with trepidation. Now she was green and sweating.

"You don't look so good." Angus didn't give a rat's ass what anyone else thought.

"I'm fine." She gave him a reassuring smile.

"You need a minute?" Chelsea was up, pulling Savannah's chair back.

"Sit down, Chelsea. Savannah said she's fine." Barrett waved his fork at her.

"I think you need to make an appointment with the eye doctor, Dad. All anyone needs to do is look at her to see she's *not* okay." Chelsea didn't bat an eye.

Angus couldn't help but admire Chelsea's spirit. And her loyalty to her sister.

"That's enough, Chelsea." Barrett set his fork down. "If Savannah needs to excuse herself, she can excuse herself. She's old enough to make her own decisions."

Finally, one thing he and Barrett could agree on.

"Speaking of which." Savannah patted her upper lip and chin with her linen napkin. "I have some news." She looked at him.

Here we go. Angus smiled and gave her a nod. Now was as good a time as any.

Barrett must have seen the exchange because there was an unmistakable warning to his words. "Whatever it is can wait until our guests leave and we can discuss it privately."

"We're all family here." Chelsea smiled, perching on the arm of Savannah's chair and taking her sister's hand.

"Chelsea," Barrett barked. "Did I ask for your opinion? Stay out of it."

"Richard, dear, please stay calm." Lana glanced at her daughters.

"Angus and I are leaving." The words burst out of her. "I'm going with him tomorrow."

It was deathly quiet in the room. No one moved.

"Over my dead body." Barrett sat back in his chair, his face going a deep red. "I don't know what you're think-ing, Savannah. If he wants to marry you, you know why? You're rich. Texas is a 50/50 state. It's a win-win for him." He drew in a deep breath. "I'm assuming your hor-mones have clouded your judgment." He pointed, more like jabbed, his finger in Angus's direction. "I'll say this once. You cannot and will not marry *this* man."

Savannah winced at the ferocity of her father's words.

"Way to be a dick, Dad." Chelsea was staring at her father, mouth open.

Angus was stunned. Barrett was going to slander him that way? After the bastard had tried to pay him off? He couldn't sit there and say nothing. "While I under-stand your concerns, Mr. Barrett, Savannah and I have discussed this—"

"Stop talking." Barrett's voice was low and harsh. "I don't want to hear you speak. Not now, not ever. Get out of my house."

"Richard." Lana stood. "Be reasonable."

"I am the only person being reasonable here, Lana." Barrett glared at his wife.

"Maybe we should leave you to sort this out on your own." Pete Powell sat his napkin on the table.

"No need." Barrett picked up his fork. "This discussion is over. McCarrick, you have five minutes to leave or I'll call the police."

Angus was shaking with anger as he stood, but he kept his peace. Savannah was stuck in the middle of this. He needed to be strong for her—not wasting time thinking about putting the smug sonofabitch in his place. Leaving was the right call. There was no changing the man's mind. Not now, at least.

"Angus, wait." Savannah came around the table to his side. "I'm coming with you."

He held his hand out, offering her a reassuring smile as she took it.

"Dad, I'm sorry, but this isn't about you." Savannah's hand was shaking in his. "This is about me and Angus… and our babies."

Barrett was up, slamming his hands down on the table with such force everyone jumped. "No, you're not, Savannah. Getting you pregnant doesn't make him a father. I guarantee you, he can't give you and your baby the best. Whatever this is—" he gestured between them "—it won't last. You'll wind up alone. You can count on it. You know I'm right."

Angus was seething, fuming, but Barrett was making enough of a scene without him adding more drama to it.

"I'll take care of them." The reassurance was for her, no one else.

"Get out." Barrett hit the table again. "Dammit. I'm calling the police." He pulled his phone from his pocket.

"Dad, what the hell is wrong with you?" Chelsea moved to put a hand on her mother's shoulder.

"Let's go." Savannah tugged him to the door, trembling so badly he slid his arm around her waist.

"If you walk out that door, you're no longer my daughter." Barrett sucked in a deep breath. "I mean it, Savannah. I won't bail you out when this falls apart. This is your last chance to make the right choice."

Angus stared at the man in shock. He'd known he was an asshole, but this? This was unforgivable.

"Richard. What are you doing?" Lana was shaking her head. "Don't do this."

"I won't stand by and support our daughter throwing away her life." Barrett looked at him with pure scorn.

Damn the man. Damn him for putting Savannah in this position. He was the stubborn ass laying down the law without any regard for Savannah's feelings. Now he was throwing her out like a piece of trash? His selfishness was breaking his daughter's heart and Angus hated the man for it.

Lana Barrett burst into tears.

"I..." Savannah was clinging to his hand, leaning into him. Every breath was ragged and uneven. "I'm sorry, Momma. Chels." She looked around the table. "I apologize for the drama, Mr. Powell. Greg."

"You don't need to apologize for a thing," Angus murmured. "You're doing great."

Barrett moved quickly, coming around the table with a guttural roar. It was pure instinct that had Angus pushing Savannah behind him. He had just enough time to brace for the solid punch Barrett landed against his jaw. His head snapped back, pain shooting along up the side of his face, but he stood his ground. No matter how strong the urge was to flatten the sonofabitch, he wouldn't strike back. For Savannah.

"Mr. Barrett." Greg Powell was between them, placing both hands on Richard Barrett's chest. "Sir."

"Dad!" Chelsea sounded pissed.

"Richard." Lana Barrett had a hand pressed to her chest, her voice trembling. "How could you?"

But all that mattered was Savannah. She was staring up at him with tears in her eyes. "Are you okay?" It hurt to smile, but she needed it so he did. "We should go."

Angus steered her from the dining room, down the hall, and out the front door. It was only when they were in his truck that her tears came. He slid over on the seat, pulled her into his lap and held her close so she could cry herself out. Her grief cut deep. Family was family. They were supposed to stand by you, no matter what.

He rocked her gently, wishing he could fix this. "He spoke out of anger. He'll regret it." Damn fool.

"I... I..." She sobbed.

"I've got you." He pressed a kiss to her temple. Barrett had just made things a hell of a lot less complicated, as he'd left Savannah with no choice but him. "*We* are a family now, Savannah. I'll always have your back." He meant it, too. Savannah and his babies. "Let's go home."

CHAPTER SEVEN

SAVANNAH WAS EXHAUSTED. Her eyelids felt heavy and her head ached. It was quiet—no rhythmic road sounds or Angus humming. She was in a soft bed. Angus's scent. She rolled over, burying her face in the pillow as her hand searched for him. The bed was empty so she forced her eyes open.

Light came from an open door on the far side of the room. A completely unfamiliar room.

Angus was sound asleep in a large recliner beside the bed. His head was cocked back and his mouth was open, his low snore steady. He wore a white undershirt and boxers, his bare feet propped on the edge of the bed. A quilt draped over his legs and pooled on the floor beneath him.

Either her eyes were playing tricks on her or the quilt moved. She leaned closer to the edge of the bed. The blanket moved again. A dog? The scruffy black head emerged from under a fold in the blanket. It was a little dog. Terrier-mix, from the look of it. It had wiry black hair and a tail that curled back over itself. Ears perked up, the dog cocked its head to one side and stared up at her. It had an underbite, one tooth sticking out playfully. The dog whined, standing and stretching so the blanket slid off.

"Who are you?" Savannah whispered, smiling at the frantic wag of the little dog's tail.

"Gertie." Angus's voice was low.

Gertie leaped onto Angus's lap, the tail wagging at light speed.

"I didn't mean to wake you," she whispered.

"I was awake." He yawned. "Sort of."

"I'm guessing we're here? Your home?" she whispered again, smiling at Gertie's attempts to cover Angus's face with doggie kisses.

"Our home." He smiled at her, scratching Gertie behind the ear. His hand all but dwarfed the little dog's head. "Gertie wanted to be the first to welcome you."

The last thing she remembered was Angus tucking his coat around her. She'd been dozing in the truck, the dark road and his humming soothing her to sleep. "You carried me in?" And she'd slept through it?

"You weigh less than a sack of feed." He chuckled, patting Gertie. "And you snore."

"I do not." She didn't, did she?

"You don't." He chuckled. "Hold up." He leaned over and turned on the bedside lamp, a soft light illuminating the room. "Hi."

She blinked, her eyes adjusting. "Hi." Unlike Angus, she was still wearing the clothes she'd left home in. The only clothes she now owned. A crushing weight landed on her chest as every single one of her father's words replayed. Her head hurt. After her sob-fest, she probably had mascara down her face. "I must look like a wreck."

He shook his head. "Beautiful. As always." One thickly muscled arm was tucked beneath his head and pulled his white undershirt tight across his sculpted chest.

He was the one that was beautiful. All she had to do was look at him and she was aching for him. Being hot and bothered over Angus was a vast improvement to being sad. "Bathroom?" She sat up, hoping he didn't see her *look* this time.

"Through there. I'll show you." Gertie refused to move.

"It's all good." She slid off the bed and hurried to the door. "You and Gertie catch up." She closed the bathroom door.

A zebra has fewer stripes than I do. Her reflection was worse than she could have imagined. There were tear tracks and smudges from where she'd wiped and patted and dabbed and made it ten times worse. She looked terrible. She looked sad.

An image of her father, red-faced and with a clenched jaw, had her gripping the bathroom counter. She knew he'd be upset, but nothing could have prepared her for his fury. Nothing. The pressure against her chest almost brought her to her knees. He might be grumpy, arrogant, and a stubborn ass, but at the end of the day, he was her father. He'd said she wasn't welcome back.

You're no longer my daughter.

She could never go home again. She had no home.

It hurt to breathe.

Momma. Chelsea. She didn't even have her phone. There was no way to reach out to them and the distance seemed endless.

"Savannah?" Angus knocked.

"Uh-huh." Savannah took another unsteady breath. Her head hurt from crying. If she kept it up, she'd make herself sick. Poor Angus had dealt with more than his fair share of tears.

"There are towels in the cabinet if you want a shower."

"Sounds good." She sounded pathetic. Maybe a shower would help her feel better?

"It's almost six. How do you take your coffee?" It sounded like he was drumming his fingertips on the door.

She opened the door. "Cream and sugar, please." The

concern on his handsome face only increased the urge to cry.

His brown eyes swept over her. "Tell me what to do."

She shrugged, swallowing down the building sob. But Gertie's frantic whining, a few yips, and her paw pressing against Savannah's foot distracted her. When she looked down, the little dog was sitting at her feet, patting her leg with one paw.

"Gertie." Angus grinned. "She's sensitive. Always has been. She can tell when a person is upset. She likes to cheer them up."

"Me, too." Savannah smiled down at the dog.

Gertie stood on her back legs until Angus reached for her. "Come on." Gertie leaped up into his arms. "You worried about Savannah, too, baby girl?" Angus smiled at Gertie's little whine. "I know. I know. I love you, too."

Savannah's heart melted. "She is precious." Which was an understatement.

"She's a mess." Clearly, Angus adored the little dog. "Gertie, you help me take care of Savannah. She's your momma now."

Gertie cocked her head to one side, leaning forward in Angus's arms to snuffle the hand Savannah offered. A few sniffs and she bathed Savannah's hand with kisses. The dog was leaning so far out of Angus's arms that Savannah wound up holding the wriggling bundle of fur. "I'm happy to meet you, too, Gertie."

"Traitor." Angus chuckled. "I can't hold it against her, though. She's got good taste."

Gertie smelled Savannah's cheek and neck and chest, never still.

Angus shook his head. "Come on, now. Let's give Savannah a chance to shower."

Gertie looked at him, then Savannah. With a grunt,

the dog flopped onto her back in Savannah's arms—like a baby. Savannah laughed, absolutely charmed.

"Yeah, I know you know you're adorable." He sighed.

Savannah cooed, "Aren't you the most precious thing ever?" She carried the dog back into the bedroom and sat on the edge of the bed, cradling Gertie with one arm and rubbing the little dog's tummy with the other hand. "How can I resist?"

"Watch out. If she senses you're a softie, she'll expect you to carry her around like that 24/7." Angus leaned against the door frame.

"What's wrong with that?" Savannah asked, Gertie's little eyes watching her. "Daddy should carry you around, always."

Gertie's tail picked up speed again.

"All right." Angus was shaking his head. "You two are going to be trouble." Gertie grunted again, the tip of her tongue sticking out of her mouth. "Let's go make Savannah some coffee, Gertie. Let's go." He patted his thigh.

Gertie stretched, jumped from Savannah's arms, and trotted out of the bedroom.

Savannah giggled.

"I like the sound of that. You, happy." Angus patted his hand against the door. "Have a good shower." And then he was gone.

It was really hard for her to focus on anything other than Angus when he was near her. He was so…so Angus. She'd never met anyone like him. She'd certainly never had a man affect her the way Angus did. Now that he was gone, she could properly inspect her surroundings. This was his bedroom. *My bedroom. Our bedroom.*

The king-size bed was comfy. The head and footboard resembled wide, darkly stained fence pickets. Four over-size pillows, soft sheets, and what looked to be a handmade quilt with a log cabin print. From a family member, maybe? She stood and smoothed the covers, fluffing the pillows until she was happy with the result.

An antique chest of drawers sat on the opposite wall with a large mission-style mirror mounted above it. The side tables and quilt trunk under the window were all older and weathered, but full of character. There was only one piece of art—a beautiful painting of a palomino horse, running. All-in-all, the room was welcoming and comfy.

The bathroom was clean and minimal. No bath, which she'd miss, but a perfectly serviceable shower that would do the job. She turned on the shower, stripped off her clothes, and stood under the warm water. The soap smelled like Angus. Woodsy. Fresh. A hint of mint. Invigorating. She lathered up, scrubbing her face free of mascara and tears.

No more tears. No more sadness. No more thinking of her father or his hateful words. This was a fresh start—she needed to go into it with a positive attitude. She owed it to Angus and the babies. She rubbed soap over her stomach. "We're home, babies. Just me, you, and your daddy."

ANGUS PULLED TWO mugs from the cabinet. "Sugar we've got." He opened the refrigerator and glanced at Gertie, who was following his every move. "Think milk will do?"

Gertie whimpered.

"Talking to Gertie again?" Dougal came into the kitchen, yawning. "How late did you get in?" Willow, Dougal's black Lab, came trailing after him.

Gertie immediately trotted to Willow, stood on her hind legs, and launched herself at Willow. Willow sat, unfazed by Gertie's playful attack.

"After midnight." Angus shook his head as Dougal took the cup of coffee he'd poured.

"What?" Dougal took a sip. "Two cups." He frowned. "I got the coffeepot ready last night. So, I think what you should be saying is you're welcome."

"Two cups." He nodded at the hall. "She's in the shower."

"Oh." Dougal's brows rose. "Right. How'd it go?"

"Other than leaving without a check for the horses I left behind for fear he'd find a way to land my ass in jail? Bad." Angus gave his brother a very abbreviated version.

"So, you're saying Richard Barrett is an even bigger piece of shit than we'd originally thought?" Dougal's brows were furrowed and his jaw locked.

"Pretty much." Angus pulled another mug from the cabinet. "But she doesn't need to hear that. She needs me on her side, not bad-mouthing her father."

"You're a better man than me." Dougal took another sip of coffee. "What now?"

"Give her a day or two to rest." Angus added one teaspoon of sugar, paused, then added another. "Stress is bad for pregnancy."

"Yep." Dougal nodded. "Might have heard that a time or two in the last year or so."

In the last couple of years, their closest friends had all married and become parents. It had been interesting to see their group of self-professed bachelors turn into doting husbands and adoring fathers. For Angus, it had been confirmation that he wasn't the marrying type. The amount of stress, constant worrying over the well-being of someone else, losing all of their time to another person or people wasn't something Angus could get on board with. He and Dougal got on fine. Of course, he was there for his family and friends, but at the end of the day, he was accountable only to himself.

Dougal was the opposite. He'd grown up with the love

and support of two devoted parents. He wanted the same. A wife and passel of little McCarricks of his own. He'd be a lucky man if he found someone who would put up with his grumpy-ass nature. Dougal had a big heart, but his lack of subtlety and general surliness tended to be too much for most women to look beyond.

What he wanted sort of faded into the background when he thought about Savannah and what she'd been through yesterday. Her own father. Richard Barrett was a bastard through and through. He felt for Savannah.

Savannah, who deserved a good cup of coffee to start her day. He poured a splash of milk into the coffee—then a little more. On top, he added a healthy dollop of whipped cream.

"What the hell are you doing?" Dougal eyed the mug.

"Making her coffee." He shrugged.

"That's not a *coffee*. I don't know what that is." Dougal chuckled and sipped his coffee.

"We don't have cream." Angus nodded at the mostly empty refrigerator. "We don't have much of anything."

"True." Dougal poured himself another cup of coffee. "I guess there's gonna be more than a few changes around here?"

"Not on my account, I hope." Savannah came into the kitchen. "Sorry for the attire." She was wearing the robe Angus's mother had bought for him two Christmases ago—a robe he'd hung on the back of the bathroom door but never worn. She was swallowed in the navy-blue fluffy fabric. "Savannah Barrett." She held her hand out. "You must be Dougal?"

"Yes, ma'am." Dougal shook her hand. "Welcome."

"I made you coffee." Angus handed her the mug, the whipped cream wobbling.

"I didn't know you were a barista." Savannah took the mug. "Thank you."

"I had to improvise." Angus explained, watching as she took a sip.

"It's yummy." She took another sip. "So… What does a day on McCarrick Ranch look like?"

"Up around six." Angus nodded at the clock. It was five fifty. "Coffee." He lifted his mug. "Dougal and I go down to the barns, make sure the guys are up and moving."

"How many employees do you have?" She perched on one of the bar stools.

"Two full-time, two part-time." Dougal leaned against the kitchen counter.

"They've been with us forever so we're more like family. Jack and Harvey might pop in anytime. Jack's got a mile-long beard he takes seriously." Angus chuckled. "He's won a couple of beard awards."

"I didn't know that was a thing." Savannah smiled.

"Speaking of, you're looking a little scruffy yourself. Thinking about entering a competition?" Angus teased his brother.

"Ha ha. Very funny." Dougal sat on the stool next to her. "Don't ask Jack about it. You'll get stuck listening to him tell you about beard grooming for hours."

Savannah laughed. "I'll remember that."

"Then there's Harvey. He's bald and clean-shaven, so you won't mix them up." Angus poured himself another cup of coffee. "He doesn't say much, either. But we all come up to the house for lunch once or twice a week, so you'll meet them."

"I guess I need to wash my clothes." Savannah glanced down at her robe.

Because the only clothing she owned was what she had been wearing yesterday. Barrett was a shit. "Dougal's got things covered here today. We can go into town, get some shopping done."

"Really?" Savannah glanced between the two brothers. "I don't want to get in the way."

"No, ma'am. I'm the one that runs the place, anyway." Dougal shot Angus a look. "He's too busy starching his shirts and jeans and looking pretty."

Savannah laughed again. "He does always look nice." Her gaze met his before sweeping over him. "Normally."

Angus and Dougal both laughed then.

"I'll make sure to put on clothes before we go into town." Angus shook his head. "You'll like Granite Falls. It's a pretty little town. Even prettier when it's all spruced up for Christmas."

"I love Christmas. Making cookies and decorating the tree and helping with the local toy drive." Savannah's smile faltered. "This year, I'll have to make new traditions."

Angus exchanged a look with his brother. "We'll do Christmas up right this year." He and Dougal didn't do much to celebrate unless their mother and aunt were coming to stay. They knew how to make the holidays special— and were characters to boot.

Savannah finished her coffee. "I can make breakfast if you like? I'm not much of a cook, outside of cookies, but I can boil an egg and make some toast?"

"We can eat in town," Angus offered. "Pretty sure they'll have a decent cup of coffee for you, too."

Gertie circled Savannah's stool, whining.

"Looks like you've already made a friend." Dougal nodded. "My Willow's on the shy side of things, so don't expect her to jump into your arms or make a fuss like that little rat."

"Don't go hurting her feelings, Dougal," Angus sighed, shaking his head.

Savannah slipped off her stool and stooped to pet Gertie. "She's not a rat. She's a princess."

Dougal snorted.

Gertie rolled onto her back for tummy scratches.

"Yeah, real modest, too." Dougal set his mug down on the marble counter. "I'm gonna head out. You two have fun. If I think of something we need, I'll send you a text."

Angus nodded his thanks, making a mental list of all the things he'd need to get. Clothes for Savannah took top priority. A tree, some decorations, and food were a close second. But first, he needed to call in the cavalry. His mother and aunt. Savannah would appreciate having family around. He knew without a doubt his mother and aunt would welcome Savannah with open arms. They couldn't replace her family, but it might ease her homesickness some. And give her some semblance of a happy Christmas.

Guilt wasn't an emotion Angus was familiar with. Until now. Barrett might have been the one to force Savannah's hand, but he was partly responsible. If it wasn't for him, and his and Savannah's night together, she'd still be with her family and enjoying their holiday traditions.

She'd had to give up everything—because of him. He'd do his damnedest to make sure she didn't regret it.

CHAPTER EIGHT

GRANITE FALLS WAS like something out of a storybook. Main Street was lined with garland and candy-colored light-wrapped lampposts. Silver tinsel stars, bells, and snowmen hung from white-icicle-bedecked storefront eaves, and a massive Christmas tree stood, straight and tall, on the lawn of the courthouse. She'd visited several small towns in the Hill Country, but she was certain nothing was as picturesque as Granite Falls. This charming little town was her new home—for now.

"I wouldn't be surprised to round the corner and see Santa." Savannah wandered along the brick sidewalk, admiring the touches of Christmas everywhere. "All that's missing is the snow."

"Well, that's a rarity in these parts. A day or two of ice, maybe. But a real snow? Not likely." Angus glanced her way, like he was waiting for something.

"That's Texas for you. I think we've only had snow once, maybe twice, on Christmas. I'm not one for the cold so it's fine by me." She took a moment to inspect the street. "It's a lovely town."

"Christmas has always been a big deal in Granite Falls." He pointed out several winter and holiday scenes arranged in the picture windows lining the street. "Ever since I can remember, there's a storefront window competition. They take their decorating seriously."

"What's the prize?" Savannah paused in front of one window.

"Bragging rights, mostly." Angus chuckled. "The Granite Falls Family Grocer and the Main Street Antiques & Resale Shop can get pretty worked up over it. It always seems to come down to the two of them." He pointed at the next shop. "As you can see."

Savannah did see. "Oh, my." A small train circled a mini Christmas village while automated reindeer turned their heads and stomped their hooves. In the next window, Mrs. Claus sat knitting and rocking in a rocking chair while the mechanical elves wrapped gifts in shiny wrapping paper. "It's something."

"Morning, Angus." A man stepped outside. "Morning, ma'am."

"Dean." Angus nodded. "This is Savannah. Savannah, Dean Hodges owns this shop."

"It's nice to meet you." Savannah shook hands with the man. "I was admiring your decorations. It's so…so festive."

"Thank you. I can't take any credit for it. My mother takes care of the windows every year." He leaned forward to whisper. "Don't tell her I said so, but I think she goes overboard." He shrugged, smiling. "It makes her happy, so I'm not complaining. What brings you to Granite Falls?"

She wasn't sure what to say. This was Angus's home, and she didn't want to say or do anything—

"I guess you could say she's here for me." Angus took her hand. He seemed genuinely proud—and it warmed her heart through.

"Aren't you the lucky man?" Dean shook his head, but smiled. "Welcome to Granite Falls, Savannah."

"Thank you."

"Savannah's things have been waylaid so you got any

suggestions where we can get her outfitted? This is a first for me."

She'd never heard a shopping expedition referred to as being outfitted.

"We've got some things in here. They're a little on the designer end of things. At least, that's what my mother thinks. They're more for the senior crowd." Dean rubbed his chin, scanning Main Street. "I'd go down Austin Street. There's a handful of shops for women—mostly touristy stuff, though. You know, coming through for the rodeos or one of the festivals." He shook his head. "I can't guarantee you'll find something you like. Good luck."

The next stop was The Coffee Shop. As they stood in line waiting to place their order, Savannah realized how hungry she was. Nothing beat the smell of freshly brewed coffee—except maybe freshly baked goodies. There was a wide selection of kolaches, muffins, pastries, doughnuts, and several kinds of decorated Christmas cookies on display in the glass front counter. Her stomach grumbled.

Angus glanced at her, grinning. "I'm hungry, too. I'm tempted to get one of everything."

"Don't you dare. Or I'll have to help you eat them." She nudged him.

"You're eating for four." He nudged back.

She rolled her eyes. "I'll eat one. Maybe two. But that's all."

They got their order and found a small café table next to the front window.

Her delectable pecan roast latte was far more palatable than Angus's attempt this morning. Not that she'd ever say as much. "If you have work to do, I can shop on my own." Savannah had seen him check his watch more than once.

"I'd rather show you around and get you settled." Angus

sat back in the chair. "With Christmas so close, things will be pretty slow until after the new year."

"If you're sure."

"I am." He unwrapped the pastries and put them on their plates. "Now eat."

She devoured the blueberry cream cheese Danish. "Oh, that was dangerously delicious."

Angus chuckled. "If I remember correctly, you've got a job? Do you need to let them know you've moved?"

She nodded, then shook her head. "I did." She pulled the wrapper off her gingerbread muffin. "I'm involved with several charities—charity work is important to me. But my day job was working for my father. Mostly press stuff—you know, for the Cougars football team. I also kept his schedule organized, meetings, events, that sort of thing." She managed a smile. "While he didn't specifically say as much, I assume I'm now unemployed. Is it wrong that I feel just the tiniest bit amused, imagining how lost he'll be without me to keep him on schedule?"

"Not wrong at all." Angus wasn't smiling anymore. His jaw was clenched, and his eyes had narrowed to slits. And, for some reason, he looked sexier than ever.

She tucked a strand of hair behind her ear. "I'll find something useful to do in Granite Falls." She split the muffin in half. "First, I need to find a doctor for me and the babies."

His expression softened instantly. "I can make a few calls, if you like? A couple of my friends are new parents. They'd probably know where to start."

"Yes, please." Having inside information on doctors would help but… "Will this cause you trouble? I mean, gossip and teasing? People talk, I know."

"Trouble? No. Gossip? Who cares." He shrugged. "We had some good luck, running into Dean. He'll make sure everyone in town knows you're here. Dean's mother is like the town crier."

"And that's a good thing?" She looked confused.

"It is." He was studying her with those brown eyes of his. "Why wouldn't I want everyone to know you're mine?"

The way he was looking at her had her insides melting. She should point out that she wasn't his, but the words got stuck in her throat. If Angus loved her and she loved him, she wouldn't mind being his.

"Hell, if I had it my way, we'd march on down to city hall and make it official." He picked up a sausage kolach. "I know you're against it, but maybe think about it. Savannah, after what happened with your father, I don't want you worrying about where to go or taking care of yourself and the babies. Let me help take care of you—of all of you. It's the least I can do."

Savannah wiped her fingertips on a napkin, her throat so tight she couldn't speak. Not that she had any words. Since she'd left with Angus, there'd been an underlying panic twisting her gut. She and Angus hadn't talked about how long she'd stay. Now she was here—with no place else to go. "I appreciate that, Angus. I know this isn't exactly what we'd talked about, but I don't have any place to go." She sniffed. Without Angus's kindness, her situation was pretty bleak. Pregnant and homeless and, for all intents and purposes, alone. As good as Angus was being to her, they were practically strangers. "But I'll do what I can around the place. I don't want to be a burden." Not that she knew much about horses or actual working ranches.

Angus studied her for a long moment. "I'll take you up on that—help get things more festive around the place." He paused. "But you should rest and take care of yourself and the babies. That's most important, don't you think?

Take some time to figure out what you might want to do, a ways down the road, even. It'd be nice if it includes me and the babies, but I'll support you."

She laughed. "I'll try to pencil you all in."

He laughed, too. It was a rich and gruff sound that had her toes curling in her ankle boots. "You're making that face again." He sounded amused.

"I don't know what you're talking about." She turned her attention to her mostly pulverized muffin. Before she could think through her question, it was out there. "Why were you sleeping in the chair?"

It was silent.

She dared to look at him.

His jaw was rigid and there was a fire blazing in his eyes. "It would have been wrong. You'd had a hell of a night. I figured you needed sleep." He cleared his throat. "If I'd been in bed with you, I'm not sure either of us would have slept."

Warmth bloomed in her cheeks. It was all too easy imagining what would have happened. But he was right. She was a mess of emotions. Her poor heart ached for love—and Angus had made it pretty clear he wasn't interested in love. She was too fragile; it would be easy to confuse attraction for real affection. And that would lead to more heartache. "Thank you. I think you're right. It's been so much." She broke off. "I don't think... We shouldn't... Not for now."

His nod was tight. "Whatever you want, Savannah."

It wasn't what she *wanted*. She wanted Angus. But she had to protect herself—she had to be strong. "Thank you. For everything." His gentle smile stirred up all the want she needed to lock away. Wanting Angus McCarrick was oh-so easy. Something told her loving him would be, too.

"WE WILL BE there tomorrow." His mother's excitement was palpable. "It's Angus, Nola." She said to his hard-of-hearing aunt Nola, who wasn't on the phone. "Yes, it's Angus. And he has news. He's going to be a father." It wasn't uncommon for his mother to have more than one conversation at a time. "A father. Yes, a girl. And she's pregnant, Nola. I'm going to be a nanna."

Angus grinned. "Thanks, Ma. She could use some family support." Talking to his mother took some of the worry off his shoulders. "We knew her father wasn't going to like me being in the picture but disowning her—"

"Well, he's cut his nose off to spite his face. What sort of fool chases off his daughter and grandbabies." A pause. "Her daddy did, that's who. I know, Nola, but we can't call him that in front of Savannah, you hear?"

"What did Aunt Nola call him?" Angus loved how Aunt Nola didn't beat around the bush.

"I'm not repeating it. But it's another way of saying dumb donkey."

"*Dumbass* isn't so bad, Ma." Angus chuckled. "And it's a pretty spot-on description of the man."

His mother giggled. "Poor little thing."

"All things considering, she's holding up pretty well. She's tough." But he suspected she was struggling far more than she let on. "Right now, she's taking a nap." Their shopping had been mostly a bust. She'd found some pajamas that had room to grow and some stretchy pants and a shirt that looked two sizes too big for her. But that was about it. By the time they'd gotten home, she was wiped out.

"Good. Growing babies is a lot of work. Heavens to Betsy, growing three at once?" His mother clicked her tongue. "She needs to get all the rest she can while she can." A pause. "Nola, we're gonna have to put off our

cruise to the Bahamas so we can be there when those babies come home." Pause. "Yes, babies. She's having three."

There was a muffled exclamation.

"Nola, that mouth of yours." His mother sighed.

Angus chuckled. "Thanks for coming, Ma. I want her
to make some new happy memories."

"We'll make sure of that." His mother was good at
showering love on people. Savannah needed that. "Nola
and I will spoil all of you. Is the tree up?"

Angus ran his fingers through his hair. "Nope. It's
pretty much a blank slate."

"You boys." His mother sighed. "You make sure there's
a tree ready and waiting to be decorated. We'll take care
of the rest."

"Yes, ma'am." He listened as she rattled off a list of
things she needed him to pick up before hanging up.

"She give you a to-do list a mile long?" Dougal sat on
the opposite side of the kitchen table, a laptop open in
front of him.

"More like a half a mile." Angus sat back. "I know
Ma's a lot, and she and Nola were doing their own thing
this Christmas, but I appreciate you not fighting me on
this and letting them come spend the holidays with us."

"I get it. We're not exactly a barrel of laughs. Ma and
Aunt Nola will definitely energize the place. Savannah's
had a tough go and all." Dougal scratched the back of his
head. "But it might be the right time for me to clean out
the back shed."

"We need to get a tree." Angus rested both elbows on
the table.

"Want me to cut down a cedar?"

"Nah, Aunt Nola is allergic, remember?" Angus would
never forget that Christmas. Poor Aunt Nola's eyes almost
swelled shut. He and Dougal had dragged the tree out

while his mother had done her best to remove all traces of the tree from inside the house, but Nola had sneezed and wheezed until New Year's.

"Right." Dougal closed the laptop. "I'll head into town and see if there's anything at the Family Grocer's." The business line started ringing. "McCarrick Cutting Horses." Dougal listened, his gaze shifting to Angus. "I—" Dougal closed his mouth while whoever was on the phone kept talking. "Yes, ma'am, I—" Dougal sighed. "Ma'am, this is his brother." He held the phone out. "It's for you."

"Hello?"

"Angus? It's Chelsea."

"Hey there." He winked at Dougal.

"How is she? Are you two all right? I was calling and calling and thought she didn't want to talk to us. Then I found her phone." Chelsea paused. "Is she around? I'd really like to talk to her."

"She's sleeping. But I'll wake her up. She'll want to talk to you." Angus stood and headed down the hall. "How are things there?"

"A frigging nightmare. Momma's cried so much she's made herself sick so we're at the urgent care clinic. She says she doesn't want to go home. I think she might actually divorce my dad over this." Chelsea paused. "Which was sort of why I was calling."

"Go on." Angus had a sneaking suspicion where this was going.

"Can Momma and I come spend Christmas with you? I swear, if I have to look at Dad's face one more time…" She trailed off. "I'm worried about Momma, too. We've never spent Christmas apart—me, Momma, and Pickle, I mean. In case you were wondering, Momma does not agree with Dad or what he's done."

"I know." He stopped outside his bedroom door. "You're

both welcome, of course. But I'd rather state troopers didn't show up to arrest me after your father accuses me of kidnapping you all."

Chelsea's laugh was flat. "No, we're telling him we're going to see Uncle Gene. Dad hates Momma's brother, they don't talk, so it'll be fine."

Maybe Richard Barrett didn't understand the way family was supposed to work after all.

"You have no idea what a relief this is, Angus. Seriously. Everything is falling apart here. Which serves Dad right. Dumbass. Anyway, I'm so worried about her."

He opened the door and smiled. Savannah was curled up on her side, sleeping. Gertie was balled up against Savannah's stomach and Willow lay across the foot of the bed.

"What are you two doing in here?" he whispered.

"Who is where?" Chelsea asked.

"The dogs. They've dumped Dougal and me for your sister." He chuckled as both dogs' tails thumped in greeting.

"Sister?" Savannah yawned.

"Yep. It's Chelsea." He handed her the phone and sat on the edge of the bed.

"Chels?" she gushed. "I know. I left my phone. Are you okay? Is Momma okay?" There was a long pause as she listened.

Angus was torn between giving her privacy and being there in case she needed him.

"How sick?" Savannah sat up. "Poor Momma." Gertie immediately wriggled her way onto Savannah's lap and curled into a fluffy ball. "She's brokenhearted." She scratched Gertie behind the ear. "I think we all are." There was another long pause. This time, she was looking his way. "When will you be here?" She sounded so damn happy he had to smile. "Really? Sounds good, Chels.

Please tell Momma everything is okay and I'll see you all soon." She laughed. "Kisses back. I love you." She set the phone beside her and burst into tears.

"Hey, hey." It was the last thing he'd expected. "What's wrong?"

"You're so sweet, Angus. You've had, what, three days to get used to the idea of being a father and had to deal with all of this on top of that. My family. My father. Me, coming here. Now my mother and my sister are invading. And it's Christmas." She sobbed. "It's all so horrible."

"Is it?" Tears were one thing that made him feel useless. "I didn't think we were doing all that bad." He pulled a handkerchief from his pocket and dabbed her cheeks.

"No. No." She grabbed his arms. "Not *you*. You're wonderful. Everything else. I mean, not the babies. The babies are wonderful." She sniffed. "Mostly, my family. My father. I'm so ashamed and embarrassed. The things he said were awful."

"They were." But he couldn't leave it at that. She was hurting. She needed comfort. "He was in shock and angry. People say things when they're in a state."

"You're so…so…kind. After all the things he said. How can you be so generous?"

"Believe me, it's taking effort." He shook his head, wiping away an errant tear from her face. "There's no point in wasting energy on something—or someone—that can't be changed."

She drew in a wavering breath, studying him closely. "I can't help but feel like…like I dumped all of this on you and made you take me in. And…and you've been so nice to me the whole time." She shook her head, sniffing.

"Gertie." He scooched the dog aside so he could get closer to Savannah. He couldn't take it if she started crying again. "You didn't make me do anything. As I recall, I was very willing." He pressed his hand against her stomach.

She gave him a watery smile. "Oh." She rested her hand atop his and pressed. "Can you feel that?"

He did. The slightest movement. So faint he closed his eyes to concentrate. "Barely." He chuckled. "Someone saying hello?" She was smiling at him when he opened his eyes.

She nodded. "You don't mind Momma and Chelsea coming to stay?"

"Nope." He kept his hand against her stomach. "I hope you don't mind my mother and aunt coming, too. They want to meet you and welcome you to the family."

"Really?" Her smile grew. "I can't wait to meet your mom. And your aunt."

"My aunt is a handful. I might need to apologize for her now." He was only half-kidding.

"You've met Chelsea." Savannah shrugged. "It sounds like there will be a houseful for Christmas. Is Dougal okay with this?"

"Dougal is fine with it." He smoothed a strand of hair behind her ear. "It's Christmas, after all. The more the merrier."

"I'm sorry I get so emotional. I'm fine, and then, all of a sudden, I'm crying." She wiped at her cheeks with the back of her hand. "I guess it's part of the joy of pregnancy."

"You're doing a great job." Pregnant or not, she had plenty of good reasons to be emotional right now.

"It helps knowing you're in this with me, Angus. You're a good man." She took his hand in hers as her gaze locked with his. "Thank you."

The way she was looking at him scared the shit out of him. He liked living his life day by day, focusing on what was right in front of him, and doing what he pleased. He didn't relish the idea of being beholden to anyone or missing what he didn't have. But Savannah was changing that and he didn't know how to feel about it. Until now, he'd been perfectly content with one goal: making sure McCarrick Cutting Horses was the top operation in the Southern states. Anything beyond that hadn't really mattered. But now… Now he wasn't so sure that was true.

He was going to be a father. A father of three. He had a family to take care of, plans to be made, and hope for a future…one he'd never known he wanted. With Savannah.

CHAPTER NINE

"YOU ARE THE prettiest thing I have ever laid eyes on." Orla McCarrick announced the minute she walked through the front door. She held both of Savannah's hands, not bothering to hide the thorough head-to-toe inspection she was making. "Sharp eyes and the sweetest smile. I'm tickled pink." She patted Savannah's cheek. "I do declare, Angus, you've done well for yourself."

"That's very kind of you." Savannah's relief was instant. Since Angus had announced his mother and aunt were coming, she'd been worried. Their situation wasn't exactly traditional. A lot of moms might not be pleased to learn their son was in the predicament Angus was in.

"Honest." Angus winked at her. "Ma's always honest."

"So am I. When are you going to shave off that beard? You look like a redneck caveman." Nola Cruz peered over her coke-bottle-thick glasses at Angus, shaking her head in disapproval.

Savannah hadn't meant to laugh, but the redneck caveman comment was too funny.

"Savannah, this is my aunt Nola. Nola, don't go running Savannah off now." Angus shook his head, but he was smiling. "If you don't like mine, you're going to hate Dougal's."

"Is he hiding somewhere?" Nola asked. "I think I scare the boy."

"You scare everyone, Aunt Nola." Angus kissed his aunt on the cheek in greeting.

"Smart-ass." But Nola was chuckling.

"Nola." Orla's disappointment was obvious. "Well, there goes a positive first impression." She looked at Savannah as she said, "You'll have to excuse her. She cusses like a sailor."

"I was married to one for thirty years. Don't blame me for picking up some of the lingo." Nola cackled. "Welcome to the family, Savannah."

"Thank you." Savannah shook the woman's hand. She couldn't wait for Chelsea and her mother to get here. Nola and Chelsea, together? That would be all sorts of fun.

"Where is Dougal?" Orla looked around the great room. "Land sakes, son, the place is short on holiday cheer. There's only six days until Christmas Eve. Six." She took off her coat and hung it in the foyer closet. She was barely five feet tall, but she had an energy that more than made up for it. "You know the red storage boxes have all the Christmas things in them."

Angus nodded. "I was getting them out when you pulled up."

Orla shook her head. "I'll tell you now, Savannah, you'll have your work cut out for you. The boys are just like their father. I'd have to make that man take time off for holidays and celebrations—and even then, I was lucky if he managed a whole day without wandering down to the barn. You might as well start putting your foot down now."

"Especially with those babies coming," Nola added. "You're going to need all hands on deck."

"My father is the same way." It slipped out before Savannah realized she'd said it.

Now all three of them were regarding her with sympathy and concern.

"Angus says your momma and sister are joining us? I'm so glad to hear it. Christmas is a time for family, I always say." Orla surprised Savannah by hugging her.

She hugged the tiny woman back. "I agree."

Orla patted her back. "Good." She stepped back. "Now. Where is the Christmas tree you promised me?"

"Dougal had to drive to Forrest Knoll." Angus ran his fingers through his hair. "They're all out in town."

"Because you waited so long," Orla chimed in.

"I got it, Ma." Angus chuckled. "Go easy on me, will ya? The last week has been an adventure." The way his brown eyes swept over her left Savannah aching.

Having separate bedrooms was the right thing—they both agreed on that. But that didn't mean she hadn't spent last night in bed, missing the stroke of hands on her skin, and the strain of his body against hers had her breathless.

"I'm not complaining." His gaze never left her face.

"I should think not." Orla glanced back and forth between the two of them. "You get a pass on the no decorations. This time."

"But next time, I expect to walk in to a Christmas wonderland." Nola rolled her eyes. "Just like your ma likes."

"Thank you." He hugged his mother, then his aunt. "I'll go get the red tubs."

"That's my boy." Orla waved him down the hallway. "Now, Savannah, you tell Nola and I what you need to make this Christmas special."

Savannah was so touched by the woman's offer. "It already is."

"Oh, now, that's hogwash." Nola wagged her finger at Savannah. "I saw an article in *Texas Monthly* that showed how fancy and posh your place was at Christmas. We might not be able to match that, but, with your mother and sister coming, we need to do something."

Savannah was laughing again.

"She did use the Google." Orla nodded. "Your family home is a showplace. I have to say, even when I've been at my decorating pinnacle, I never managed to make this place look that grand."

"You want to know a secret?" Savannah whispered. "We hire people to decorate. Momma does work with a designer for the layout, but that's about it. A whole team comes in for two straight days after Thanksgiving."

Orla and Nola exchanged a look.

"I can't remember the last time I decorated a Christmas tree. The most Christmas-y thing I do is bake cookies. But I do that well—decorate them, too. And it always makes me happy." Even with a chef on staff, she insisted on making cookies herself. And cleaning up the residual mess she inevitably left from her efforts.

"That we can do." Orla took her hand and led her to the kitchen. "Cookies are always a heartfelt welcome present, too. We'll make some and go calling so you can meet the good folk of Granite Falls."

"Some of them are good." Nola snorted. "Others..." She shrugged. "They don't deserve cookies."

"Nola Ann." Orla scolded.

Nola was a riot. The back-and-forth between the sisters had Savannah in stitches. They'd welcomed her into the family without hesitation, gone out of their way to put her at her ease, and wanted to make her holiday special. It didn't fill the hole her father had put in her heart, but it did ease the pain.

They'd almost reached the kitchen when the front door opened and Dougal came in, dragging a massive tree behind him. "A little help," he called out.

"Is it big enough?" Nola asked.

"It was all they had left." Dougal dropped the tree and

crossed the room, scooping up Nola in a bear hug. "Good to see you, Aunt Nola."

"Get that scruffy thing out of my face." Nola batted at Dougal's full beard. "You got any wildlife living in there?"

"Not that I've noticed." Dougal released her and scooped up his mother next, giving her a spin. "Ma. You getting shorter?"

"Dougal." Orla giggled. "It's more like you're getting taller."

"What are you, seven feet by now?" Nola arranged her thick glasses and clicked her tongue. "That beard is an eyesore."

"I told you." Angus rounded the corner carrying two large red storage bins. "Mine looks downright refined now, doesn't it, Aunt Nola?"

"I wouldn't go that far." Nola shook her head. "But it's trimmed up nice without all that bushiness hanging off your chin. You need me to buy you a razor, Dougal? Now I know what to get you for Christmas."

"I'd rather have some new socks." Dougal winked. "Give me a hand, will ya, Angus? The damn tree's more fit for Rockefeller Center, but we'll make it fit."

"We'll have to wait on the baking just a bit. You sit, darlin'." Orla waved Savannah into one of the leather recliners. "We'll need to supervise or they'll never get it right."

Dougal and Angus both shot their mother an offended look.

"I'm going to end up with a stomachache from all the laughing." Savannah was laughing all over again.

"Good. That's good." Orla patted her shoulder. "Laughter is good for those babies. If their momma is happy, they know it. And they're happy, too."

Savannah sat back in the recliner, Gertie appearing out of nowhere to wedge herself into the chair beside her. She patted the little dog while poor Dougal and Angus turned the tree one way, then the other, then back again. Nola and Orla preferred different sides and neither was willing to concede to the other. Dougal sat on the stone hearth while they argued, but Angus came to sit on the arm of her recliner.

"Were did you come from?" He scratched behind Gertie's ear. "Why do I get the feeling I'm being replaced."

Gertie yawned and settled her head on Savannah's lap.

"They're a pair, aren't they?" Angus shook his head, watching his mother and aunt walk around the tree, arguing.

"I like them." She smiled up at him.

"That's good to hear. 'Cause you're stuck with them through the holidays. All of us." He shook his head as the women kept up their back-and-forth on the right side of the tree.

She liked the sound of that. *Us.* Being a part of that us. She was happy. Really, truly happy. It had only been a couple of days since she'd arrived here, but it was enough to make a difference. Being here felt safe. There were still things that needed to be worked out, but right here and now, she was happy. The babies seemed happy, too, wiggling in her tummy. She placed his hand on her stomach. "I think they like your mom and aunt, too."

"I think they like it when you laugh." This was a new Angus look, one she wasn't sure how to decipher. He swallowed, his gaze falling to where his hand rested on her stomach.

The more time she spent with Angus, the more she cared about him. Despite all her best efforts, it was impossible not to feel something. And she was feeling all the feels for the handsome, burly man next to her. It felt a lot like the way she'd imagined falling in love would feel. Which was bad. Really, really bad. Especially since Angus had only ever said he wanted her. Was it too much to hope that she might affect his heart as much as she affected his body?

"How are you holding up?" Angus stood on the top of the ladder, sliding the cord onto the hook along the roof's eave.

"I haven't snapped yet." Dougal uncoiled another strand of outdoor lights.

"They've only been here six hours." Angus stifled a laugh.

"It's been a hell of a long six hours." Dougal glared up at his brother. "It'd be easier if Aunt Nola didn't keep poking about my beard." He ran a hand over the length of his facial hair.

"It's Aunt Nola. What did you expect?" Angus connected the new strand of lights Dougal handed him and went back to hanging them. "She's all about being cleanshaven, like Uncle Clyde was."

"Poor Uncle Clyde." Dougal sighed.

Angus laughed. Uncle Clyde had adored his wife. "I don't think Uncle Clyde ever lost sleep over being beardless." As far as Angus remembered, they'd had a good, long marriage.

"We'll never know now, will we?" Dougal snapped back.

"You gonna make it?" Angus paused, staring down at his brother. "Lana and Chelsea will be here tomorrow. Lana's on the quiet side, but Chelsea's like a younger version of Nola."

Dougal groaned. "Why'd you have to go and tell me that?"

"I figured I owed you a warning." Angus went back to hanging lights. "I appreciate the effort you're putting in."

"It's not right, what Savannah's father did. I can't imagine Pa ever doing something so…mean. He had his fits now and then, but he never used hateful words. You can't take that crap back."

Angus agreed. Choose Your Words Carefully. It was a motto he tried to live by. He'd swallowed plenty of choice words when Richard Barrett had gone on his tirade, but he'd managed to keep his mouth shut. If, no when, the man got his senses back, he didn't want to make that reconciliation more challenging than it was likely to be.

"You think he'll come after her?" Dougal asked. "Try to take her home?"

"I don't know." Angus climbed down and moved the ladder over. "Part of me hopes he does, for Savannah. An apology would go a long way. Though I'm not sure a man like Barrett ever apologizes or admits when he is wrong." He shrugged. "The other part is still tempted to land him on his ass."

"I don't envy you that. Having that rat bastard for a father-in-law."

"We're not getting married." One perk to her refusing his marriage proposal.

"That's just stupid." Dougal steadied the ladder while Angus climbed back up. "That light is upside down." He pointed at the one bulb pointed in the opposite direction from the rest. "You'll get an earful about it so you might as well fix it now."

Angus climbed down the ladder, dragged it back to where it was a moment ago, climbed back up, and fixed the bulb. "Good?"

Dougal gave him a thumbs-up. "I've been meaning to tell you we got a call from the Ramirez family in Dallas." He waited until Angus was on the ground before going on. "The January delivery."

"Five horses? I remember." Angus nodded. "It's a pretty penny."

"They canceled. Something about changing their mind." Dougal scratched his chin.

"Dammit." Mr. Ramirez served on the Fort Worth Rodeo board—the same board Richard Barrett chaired. The chances of this being a coincidence were slim to none. Barrett had said he'd do this. It looked like he was following through.

"Any others we should worry about? Other referrals from Barrett?" Dougal helped him move the ladder down.

"None that I can think of." He was done talking and thinking about Barrett. He switched gears. There was nothing his brother loved more than competing in one of the cutting horse shows. Dougal could talk about it for hours. "Still planning on competing in Arizona? Last I saw, it was a decent purse."

"I'm going." He glanced at the house. "Might be the only chance I have for some peace and quiet."

"I don't think they're planning on staying until the babies are born." Angus frowned. "At least, I hope not. And they're not due until April. I think. I don't know how it works with triplets."

"Triplets." Dougal shook his head. "You're not scared?"

"Hell, yes." Angus climbed up the ladder. "I've never been so scared." His entire world was changing—there was a lot to be scared about.

"What are you scared of?" Their mother came out the front door, closing it behind her.

"You can't leave Savannah alone with Aunt Nola, Ma." Dougal pointed at the door. "She's liable to sneak out the back door and never be seen again."

"Oh, Dougal, she's not so bad." She waved Dougal's comments aside. "What's got you scared, Angus?" She took the steps down the front porch and came out into the yard, turning to assess their handiwork.

"Up to your standards?" Angus asked, lights in hand. "Tell me now, before I get even further."

"It looks great." She smiled. "Now stop dodging the question and tell me what's got you scared."

"What do you think?" Dougal nodded at the house.

She smiled. "You two seem pretty sweet on each other. That's a good place to start, if you ask me. There's no reason to be scared."

No reason? To start with, he *was* sweet on Savannah. He'd never been sweet on anyone before. Hell, more than sweet on her. It scared him how hard and fast he was falling for her. It scared him that this was turning into something more than doing the right thing. All of which was none of his mother's business. While he'd grown up with his family's unfailing support, they'd never been ones to talk about their feelings. "Nerves, I guess. Screwing up. That sort of thing."

"Nerves are to be expected, Angus." His mother's quick reassurance didn't help. "You've always had good instincts. As long as you two communicate, you'll figure it all out."

Dougal rolled his eyes. "It's that easy?" Somehow, he always said what Angus was thinking.

"It's only as hard as you make it." Ma put her hands on her hips.

"That's another pearl of wisdom, there." Dougal chuckled.

"All right, you two. I appreciate the support." He went back to hanging lights. "Almost done."

"Good. Then both of you can come in and help decorate cookies." Ma clapped her hands together. "We've made about six dozen."

"I've got some work to do." Dougal shielded his eyes

as he looked up at Angus. "Someone has to keep this place running."

"Remember that when you go to eat one." Ma wagged a finger at him before heading back inside.

"I'll eat as many damn cookies as I want to," Dougal mumbled, slinging another roll of lights onto his shoulder.

Angus laughed.

By the time the lights were strung, the sun was low in the sky and Dougal was officially out of patience. He headed for the barn while Angus went inside to check on Savannah.

The kitchen smelled delicious but resembled a battlefield.

On the table, cut-out gingerbread and sugar cookies were piled high on an assortment of festive trays. Aunt Nola sat at the head of the table sound asleep—head back, mouth open, and snoring up a storm.

Gertie and Willow were in a pile under the kitchen table.

Savannah was wearing an apron and a fine coating of flour, humming along to the Christmas carols coming from the radio.

Ma was pouring candy into bowls on the kitchen counter.

"Think you got enough candy?" Angus peered into the bowls.

"Is something missing?" His mother frowned.

"I'm kidding." He shook his head. "What's all this for?"

"A gingerbread house." Savannah announced it with pure glee. "We're making one."

"She's never made one from scratch before." Ma was almost as excited as Savannah.

Angus sat on one of the barstools. "One year, we made a gingerbread castle."

"A castle?" Savannah's eyes went round. "I'm happy with a tiny cottage."

"I don't think Ma has ever made a tiny gingerbread house." Angus popped a chocolate-covered candy into his mouth.

"I didn't say *tiny*." His mother gave Savannah's shoulders a squeeze. "But we can make it a cottage."

It'd been a long time since he appreciated all the time and effort his mother spent to make the holidays special. Watching Savannah with his mother made him feel like a kid again. She was completely caught up in every little thing his mother did, nodding and standing at the ready to offer help.

"You want to make sure the frosting is thick so it'll hold the walls up." Ma laid down a thick stripe of white frosting. "Then you set up the house frame. Here are the walls." She pointed at the four sides of baked gingerbread. "Go ahead."

Savannah was so excited she almost dropped the gingerbread wall. "That would have been bad."

"Sugar, don't you sweat the small stuff. We can always bake more." His mother gave her shoulders another squeeze.

Angus could swear Savannah was holding her breath when she placed each wall—as if she was expecting them to topple over onto one another. They didn't. When she piped frosting between the cookie walls to cement them together, she was painstakingly slow.

"I've never seen anyone make such perfectly straight lines." His mother turned the stoneware lazy Susan to check the forming structure from all angles. "I mean perfect."

Savannah was beaming with pride.

"You got straight As in school, didn't you?" Angus ate another candy.

"I did." She glanced at him. "I was valedictorian of my class, too. High school and college."

"I knew it. Brains and beauty." He winked at her.

"I like understanding how things work. And getting things right," she explained. "There's something very gratifying about cooking. It's a lot like chemistry. I was good at Chemistry so I'd like to think I'd be a decent cook."

"You don't know?" his mother asked, filling the piping bag full of more frosting.

"No." She sounded so disappointed. "We have a chef. Two, actually. Daniella and Becky. They're both lovely, but the kitchen was their territory. I can boil an egg and make toast and bake cookies. But that's about it."

Thankfully, his mother didn't bat an eye. "Well, we can fix that. My meemaw expressed love through her cooking. Meaning, we were all a little soft around the middle. All of her recipes are good, hearty meals without a whole lot of fuss. I'd be happy to teach them to you. If you're interested, that is."

"I am." Savannah nodded.

"As long as you pace yourself." Angus didn't want to discourage her enthusiasm, but the little reading he'd done on a multiple pregnancy said to eat well, drink plenty of water, take walks, and rest.

Both the women were staring at him now.

"I will, I promise." Savannah's smile was sweeter than the candy he was eating.

"Savannah has a doctor's appointment tomorrow." His mother glanced back and forth between them. "I'm sure it'll put both your minds at ease."

It hadn't been easy to get Savannah in before the holidays, but due to the high-risk nature of her pregnancy, they'd squeezed her in. He didn't like how the term *high-risk* was used to describe her pregnancy, but it was standard for multiples. At least, that was what the nurse told them.

"And then your mother and sister will be here tomorrow afternoon." His mother twisted the piping bag closed and offered it to Savannah. "Tomorrow will be a big day. A good day."

Angus settled in as Savannah carefully attached the roof to the house. She was concentrating so hard that the tip of her tongue was sticking out of the corner of her mouth. It was the cutest damn thing she'd ever done. Today, at least. Every day, he found some new quirk or expression of hers that had him smiling like a damn fool. Not that he minded. Not in the least.

CHAPTER TEN

"I'VE WASHED MY hands at least a half a dozen times and I still smell like frosting and gingerbread." She stretched. She was tired but content. "Then again, we did use a ton of both on the gingerbread house." Which she was ridiculously happy about. "It does looks pretty, doesn't it?"

"It's the prettiest gingerbread house I've ever seen." Angus sat on one of the bar stools that lined the long bar separating the kitchen from the great room. A laptop was open on the bar countertop in front of him and a plate of cookies sat beside that. He bit into an iced Christmas cookie, then used it to point at the gingerbread cottage. "I'm having a hard time believing you never made one before."

Savannah untied the apron, walked to the oversize pantry, and hung the apron on the hook inside—next to a collection of aprons. Orla and Nola had been so kind to let her come in and make such a mess. And they hadn't blinked an eye when she asked them about which cleansers and soaps to use in the dishwasher and on the marble countertops. She was mortified at her lack of basic common kitchen cleaning know-how and determined to learn to make up for it. Most people didn't have maids and chefs. She was now one of them.

"You know, I guess I have done it once before." She remembered the fancy children's event her parents had taken her and Chelsea to. She couldn't remember what charity it was—only that she'd been excited to decorate cookies.

"The truth comes out." He grinned. "It fell apart?"

She closed the pantry and frowned at him. "No. I remember it was a charity event we went to, as a family. I can't remember which charity." She paused, thinking, then shrugged. "It doesn't matter. Anyway, Chelsea and I were dressed up in these fancy white dresses. Mine had a red velvet bow and Chelsea's was green."

Angus was listening closely.

"I was so excited because I love to decorate cookies—"

"I sort of picked up on that today." He nodded at the cookies.

She smiled. "Anyway, it wasn't really a gingerbread house. It was a kit. One of those boxes that comes with everything. Cardboard-flavored cookies, prepackaged hard-as-rock decorating candy, and frosting that likely has a hundred-year shelf life."

"My mouth is watering." He finished off his cookie.

"Exactly. It doesn't really count. Then Chelsea started a gumdrop fight and our dresses got ruined and Dad was so mad he didn't talk to us all the way home." She shrugged.

"I can see why you'd remember it." He shook his head. "Chelsea's a piece of work."

"She is. And I wouldn't have her any other way." Savannah surveyed the day's accomplishments with pride. A tray of gingerbread boys and girls with Red Hots buttons and raisin eyes. Two plates of sugar cookies with detailed frosting work and sprinkles. Peppermint double chocolate chip cookies with peppermint she'd broken herself. Raspberry and apricot thumbprint cookies. And shortbread—chocolate-dipped, plain, and lemon. "This was fun."

"I can tell." Angus was grinning.

"Oh?" She put her hands on her hips, waiting.

"You've got some flour, right…here." He pointed from her head to her toes.

"Do I really?" She reached up to smooth a hand over her hair.

He slipped off the stool and came around the bar into the kitchen. "Hold up." He ran the corner of a clean kitchen towel under the tap and approached her. "This might take a minute."

She laughed.

He stepped closer, running the towel along her cheek. "You smell good to me. Delicious, even." His smile was devilishly tempting.

She giggled, then covered her mouth. "You have to behave."

His gaze moved over her face, lingering on her lips. "Says who?" He dropped a kiss on her nose.

Her chest folded in on itself. "I do. Your mother is down the hall. And your aunt." She squeaked as his lips traveled along her neck.

"They're sawing logs, I guarantee it. They both turn into pumpkins at nine." He sucked her earlobe into his mouth.

"Angus." She shivered, pressing her hands against his chest. If he kept that up, she'd never be able to resist him. Her body rebelled at the thought, but her mind was standing firm. "I… I thought we agreed we weren't going to—"

"Kiss?" He stopped kissing her. "Okay. No more kissing." He went back to wiping the flour from her face.

He was adorable. She could almost picture a little boy with the same concentration on his face. Or a little girl with his wide, clear eyes. She could imagine Angus playing with them and wearing that smile. This face. The warm brown eyes to the strong jaw. "We are going to have really beautiful babies."

He paused, a slow smile spreading across his face. "Yes, we are." He leaned back against the counter behind him. "You have a preference? Boys or girls?"

"Healthy." That was all that mattered. "You?"

"I wouldn't mind a little girl that looked like her mother." Then he shook his head. "Nope. Never mind. I don't think I'm cut out to be a little girl's father."

"Why not?" Savannah was surprised by the gruffness in his voice.

"I… I'd be worried all the damn time." He ran his hand along the back of his neck. "I'd have to wrap her in bubble wrap and get her a guard dog to keep the boys away—"

Savannah laughed. "Oh, Angus."

"What?" He looked downright afraid now. "Dammit all. I hadn't stopped to think…" He shook his head again.

She stepped forward and slid her arms around his waist. "Boys or girls or some of each, it will be a challenge."

His heart was thundering beneath her ear.

"But we will figure it out." She glanced up at him. "We will. Okay?"

He ran his hand down her back and buried his face against her neck. "Give me a minute."

She was in no hurry. The sound of his heart was strong and solid and comforting. It wasn't the first time she'd felt true happiness since she'd arrived here. "Angus?"

"Hmm?" He didn't move.

"I know I've said it before, but thank you. For all that you've done for me. For us. We've invaded your life and you've made room for us, and acted like it was no big deal. I know it is."

He lifted his head then, searching out her gaze. "You're wrong, Savannah." He opened his mouth, then paused. "You haven't invaded, you… This is your home now." He had that look again, one that made her heart skip before picking up speed. "I know what you gave up when you chose to give us a chance. Having you, and them—" he glanced at her belly "—here is a damn big deal. I'll try harder to make sure you know that."

She wasn't sure what to say then. It was tempting to say more, to tell him that he was making himself at home in her heart, but the words wouldn't come. It wasn't fair to lay that on him on top of everything else. Her father's accusation that her hormones were affecting her emotions and decisions still lingered. If what she was feeling for Angus was colored by her pregnancy, she didn't want to say something she'd regret. They'd been honest with each other from the start. They'd agreed to try to be the family their children deserved. For now, that was more than enough.

The hunger in his gaze had her thoughts taking an immediate detour.

"You're so damn beautiful." His words were hoarse and raw.

Her lungs emptied and a bone-deep shudder ran the length of her spine. It was so new, this power he had over her. At times, like now, she was dizzy from it. Lucky for her, his arms kept her steady. She tore her gaze from his and drew in a deep breath. "I'm… I'm getting fat."

He cocked an eyebrow and released her. He scratched his chin, glanced at her again, then dropped to his knees. "Tell your momma she's supposed to be making room for you three." One big hand caressed the swell of her stomach. "It's not fat. It's all baby." He lifted her shirt, speaking to her stomach now. "Tomorrow, the doctor will tell her that, you'll see. I can't wait to see you three growing big and strong. Your momma will be more beautiful than ever because she's making you." He kissed her stomach three times. "I'll make sure to check in every night so you can tell me how things are going." He rested his head against her stomach and closed his eyes.

It seemed natural to run her fingers through his thick auburn hair. His close-cropped beard was rough against her skin, but she didn't mind. This was precious and intimate. This great, burly man on his knees, talking to his babies in her stomach. Her heart was so full. When the gentle roll in her belly made Angus chuckle and say, "There you are," she laughed, too.

When he looked up at her, her heart all but beat free of her chest. This was real—it had to be. What was bonding her to this man was solid and it wasn't just these babies. She did love him. She loved Angus McCarrick. The father of her babies. The man who said he wasn't the marrying kind.

"You're the doctor?" Angus stared at the man. Dr. Leland Wurtz was a lot younger than Angus had been expecting. He was more handsome than Angus had expected, too.

"Yes." Dr. Wurtz smiled. "Were you expecting my mother? She's still practicing, but I take on multiple and high-risk births." He waited, scanning Savannah's chart. "Savannah is considered high-risk, but I can see if my mother has room in her client list."

"No, of course not," Savannah answered quickly.

Angus felt like an ass then. He wasn't the pregnant one. She was the one wearing a hospital gown with a cold white sheet draped over her lap, looking anxious.

"You're certain?" Dr. Wurtz asked him.

"Absolutely," Angus murmured.

"Not a problem." Dr. Wurtz sat on his stool. "Let's start with the basics." He referred to her chart. "It looks like you're about four months along?"

Savannah nodded.

"How are you feeling? Any complaints or concerns?" Dr. Wurtz set aside her chart.

"Not really. I'm tired and nauseous a lot of the time, but I know that's normal." She shrugged.

"What have you observed, Dad?" Dr. Wurtz turned to him. "Any concerns or observations?"

Dad. Right, *he* was Dad. He had a million questions, but one thing mattered more than all the rest. "I just want to know that Savannah and the babies are all healthy."

"Understandable." Dr. Wurtz nodded. "Let's find out. We're going to do a quick external ultrasound. We should be able to see all three babies and their heartbeats. In a few weeks, we'll get you set up to have a longer ultrasound. We'll check growth rate and the babies' weight then. Might even be able to see if you're having boys or girls or some of both. Let's set you back a little."

The moment he saw Savannah's face, he moved to her side. He wasn't the only one anxious about this visit. A surge of protectiveness rolled over him as he took her hand. She needed him to be strong for her. And, dammit, that was what he'd do.

Angus had plenty of experience with pregnancy—when it came to horses. This was entirely different. The swell of Savannah's belly was covered in gel before the young doctor pressed the ultrasound transducer over her skin. On the monitor, shades of black, white, and gray appeared.

Savannah turned her head to look at the screen, her hand tightening on his when the first rapid thump-thump of a baby's heartbeat could be heard. The doc nodded, pointing at the screen. "One." He clicked a few buttons before moving the transducer down and to the left. "Two." Another heartbeat, a few more clicks on the keyboard. He moved the machine around, then back up. It took a minute. "Three. That one's shy." He sat back, smiling, and he typed in a few numbers.

Angus appreciated the heartbeat, but he was having a dickens of a time determining what was on the screen. He saw some shadows and movements, but not a lot that resembled a baby. Dr. Wurtz was pleased, though, and that was what mattered.

"Strong heartbeats. All of them." The doctor nodded, wiped off Savannah's belly, and wheeled the ultrasound cart back against the wall.

"That's good." Savannah sighed.

Angus helped her smooth her gown and sheet back into place. He needed to do something, dammit.

"It is." Dr. Wurtz sat on his stool again. "A few things. It's important you're eating enough. On average, we say to add about three hundred calories a day when you're expecting one baby. I'm not saying you need to add nine hundred calories a day, but you do need to up your caloric intake. For your height and build, your weight is on the low end."

"I'll try." Savannah wrinkled up her nose. "I'm still having a hard time with smells and throwing up."

"If it gets really bad, we might need to put you on some medication. Right now, taking your prenatal vitamins and making good, healthy dietary choices are key." He sat back. "Because you're carrying multiples, it's likely you'll experience stronger symptoms than someone carrying a singleton."

"Lucky you." Angus smiled down at her. "Anything else we should do? Or shouldn't do? Any restrictions? That sort of thing."

"Not really. I wouldn't take up training for a marathon or kickboxing, but a daily walk is a good idea." He picked up her chart. "I'm sure your last OB went over this with you, but there are a few increased risks with carrying multiples. Premature labor is one. With triplets, we'd like you to make it to thirty-two weeks. At least. Taking care of yourself won't guarantee you won't have any bed rest, but it's the best thing you can do for you and the babies. Finally, it's very important to reduce stress. Your body is already going through so much without adding the toll stress can take." He waited for them both to nod. "Good. I'd like to see you every two weeks—starting after your sonogram. We'll set that for twenty weeks. Any other questions?" Dr. Wurtz waited, then said his goodbyes.

When they left, they had an appointment card for their sonogram and a large Welcome Baby tote bag full of pregnancy and new baby items.

"You like him?" Savannah strapped her seat belt on.

"I do." Angus started the truck. "I guess I was expecting someone older." Less good-looking. He backed the truck out of the parking lot and navigated his way back to Main Street.

"Younger means he's up-to-date on all the newest and best techniques, right?" She rubbed a hand over her belly. "I'm going to get really big, aren't I?"

Angus grinned. "Probably."

"And that makes you smile?" She shook her head. "I already look big."

"Not according to the doc. As a matter of fact, I'm thinking about running into The Coffee Shop to pick up some more of those pastries you liked so much." He glanced her way. "I'll take that as a yes."

Savannah leaned back against the seat. "I did like them. And I didn't throw them up. If it's not out of the way—"

"Nothing is out of the way in Granite Falls, Savannah." He pointed down the street. "It's right there."

"Okay, then I'd love a pastry or two."

He was thinking more like a dozen. They did have company coming, after all. He parked in front of the shop. "I'll be back."

"I'll be here." She yawned, her head propped against the headrest. "I'll try to stay awake."

"Don't fight it. You heard the doc. Sleep." He rested his hand on her stomach. "Let her sleep."

She was smiling when he left her.

He heard his name called out as soon as he stepped inside the shop. There, huddled over cups of coffee and empty plates, sat his friends since childhood. Town veterinarian Buzz Lafferty, and the three Mitchell brothers—Hayden, Kyle, and John.

"You four sitting here thinking up trouble?" He glanced out the shop's picture window at his truck. He could make out Savannah, curled up on the front seat.

"From what I hear, you're the only one causing trouble." John Mitchell stood. "Gonna be a father, eh? Welcome to the club." He shook Angus's hand.

"When do we get to meet her?" Kyle Mitchell pointed out the window at his truck. "Or should we go introduce ourselves?"

"I'll get around to it. I haven't had time to catch my breath, let alone take her around meeting everyone." He ran a hand along the back of his neck. "We just came from a doctor's appointment."

"How'd it go? Like Dr. Wurtz?" Hayden Mitchell asked. "He took good care of Lizzie when she was pregnant."

"It went well. Three strong heartbeats for three babies." He appreciated that all four of his friends had the same reaction—a slow headshake. "Thanks again for the recommendation."

"Three?" John blew out a low whistle. "That's something."

"Go big or go home, I guess." Kyle laughed.

"I guess." Angus laughed, too. "I better get food and take her home."

"Duty calls." Hayden nodded. "If you need anything, let us know. We've got hand-me-downs by the box, if you're interested."

"So do we." Kyle raised his hand.

"Same here." Buzz nodded. "Boxes and boxes."

"I appreciate that. I'll let Savannah know." He'd grown up with these men and was glad he could still call them friends. There was a comfort in knowing they'd all been through what he was facing—well, close enough. Once things were more settled, he'd make sure Savannah got to know them and their families, too. "I'll see you."

Savannah was sound asleep when he got back to the truck. He put the box of pastries on the back seat, buckled in, and made the drive from town to the ranch. Winter, as mild as it was, had robbed the trees of most of their leaves and turned the grass to muted tones of brown and gray. Even so, Angus admired the scenery. The Hill Country was beautiful country—more so in the spring when the wildflowers were blooming. But spring was still months out yet. And with spring came the babies and a whole new set of challenges and changes. Good challenges. Good changes. All things to look forward to.

He glanced over at Savannah, his head sifting through the information Dr. Wurtz had mentioned. She needed to eat more and take care of herself. Which meant his job was to make sure both of those things happened. His mother had said today would calm his fears and make him feel better. Instead, alarming words like *premature birth*, *bedrest*, *complications*, *gestational diabetes*, and *high-risk* had him more on edge than ever. Not that he'd let on. All he could do was read the pregnancy book the good doctor had sent home with them so he'd know what to expect, what to look for, and how to make this as easy on Savannah and the babies as possible. If they were okay, he'd be okay. It was that simple. When that had come to be, he wasn't exactly sure. In less than a week, his reason for being had changed entirely. Did he have a real understanding of what was coming? Nope. Was he worried he'd screw something up? Absolutely. Was he concerned about Savannah and the babies' health? Hell, yes. Did he regret bringing her home or…falling in love with her? The realization was a lightning bolt to the chest. Shocking. Confusing. But true. He did. He loved Savannah. He took a deep breath. No regrets. Not in the slightest. He was happy she was pregnant—happy she was his. In time, he hoped she'd feel the same way.

CHAPTER ELEVEN

"Biscuits." Savannah secured the apron behind her. It had been a while since she'd been this excited. The kitchen had always been off-limits to her. Today, she was being welcomed and encouraged to try her hand at cooking. Orla and Nola, her teachers for the day, both felt biscuits were a solid starter recipe. Savannah was up for anything.

"Light and fluffy." Orla was putting bowls and measuring cups, spatulas, and canisters of spices on top of the marble countertop. "A good biscuit is the foundation for many a meal."

"That's true." Aunt Nola opened the refrigerator. "Don't forget the butter."

"You don't have to use butter." Orla set the butter aside. "Shortening works just as well. With buttermilk."

"If you want buttermilk biscuits." Nola shook her head, scooting the butter dish back into the middle of the counter. "Mine are lighter, flakier. And delicious."

Angus and Dougal sat on the other side of the counter, finishing off the stacks of pancakes Orla had made for breakfast. Savannah had managed to eat three of them and, so far, her stomach wasn't the least bit upset.

"Nola's biscuits are different than mine." Orla shook her head. "Different. Not better."

"Oh-ho, now who's getting all fired up?" Nola pushed her thick glasses up. "I say we make both and let her decide."

"Oh, come on now." Angus spoke up. "That's not fair, Aunt Nola. You can't put that on Savannah."

"Nope." Dougal mumbled around a mouthful of pancake. "They say they're not competitive, but that's a flat-out lie."

Savannah regarded the two women. "I'd love to try them both if you want to do that much baking. But I don't want to pick which is best."

"It's not too much work." Orla smiled. "We should take turns, though. We're supposed to be teaching her how to cook, Nola. Not judging a biscuit competition."

"Fine by me." Nola snorted. "We both know who makes the best biscuit anyway."

Savannah exchanged a look with Angus. What had she gotten herself into? When Orla and Nola learned she wasn't a cook, they'd been quick to offer her lessons. The idea of cooking lessons had been exciting. First, she'd always wanted to cook. And second, it would give her something to do beyond thinking about the babies and her growing infatuation with Angus. But now that they were all in the kitchen, her enthusiasm was cooling.

"You don't have to do this, Savannah." Angus's smile was sympathetic.

"No, I do want to learn." And she did. "I just don't want to cause any friction." She'd done enough of that lately.

"Ma. Aunt Nola." Angus sighed. "You two behave. Where's that holiday spirit the two of you were going on about?"

"You're right, Angus. I'm sorry, Savannah. We are, as Dougal said, a mite competitive. Both biscuits are delicious and both are handy to know." Orla looked and sounded repentant.

"But mine is better," Nola mumbled, but her smile was one hundred percent mischief.

It wasn't the first time Savannah saw a correlation between Nola and Chelsea. This was how Savannah pictured her sister later in life. Outspoken and stirring the pot. So, basically the same.

"Don't you two have something to do?" Nola peered over her glasses at Angus and Dougal.

"Yep." Dougal was up and gone before Angus could react.

From the little time Savannah had spent with Dougal, it was clear he preferred his peace and quiet. There was nothing peaceful or quiet about Nola.

Angus, however, didn't seem to be in a hurry. "I'll go when you promise to behave *and* not badger Savannah about this morning's doctor's appointment. We want to tell Savannah's mother at the same time."

It had been her request. She didn't want her mother and sister to feel like they were missing out. Hopefully, it wouldn't hurt anyone's feelings.

"I understand." Orla nodded. "And I think it's precious you want to share it all at once. Now." She waved her over. "Let's get started."

Savannah took another quick glance at the ingredients and tools assembled on the counter. "No recipe?"

Orla and Nola both tapped their temples.

"It's all in here." Orla smiled.

"A real Southern chef doesn't write down her secrets." Nola opened the flour. "It's all about keeping the family recipes a secret."

Savannah nodded, her confidence further shaken. No recipe. No notes. No problem. "Okay." She could do this. How hard could it be?

An hour later, Angus had gone out to work, there was a tray of Orla's biscuits in the oven, and Savannah was ready to admit defeat. Her two bowls of dough looked nothing like the dough in Orla's or Nola's bowls. And the two women noticed.

"Hmm?" Nola eyed the lumpy dough.

"I must have forgotten something." Savannah glanced back and forth between the baking powder and baking soda. "Or mixed them up?"

"That shouldn't make the dough look like…this." Nola pointed at her bowl.

"Nola." Orla chastised her. "It's a first attempt."

A terrible first attempt at that. Orla's dough was smooth and creamy. Nola's was rougher, but it didn't have the lumps of flour and butter that hers did. "What should I do?"

Orla and Nola exchanged a look.

"Let's start over." Orla patted her back.

"How about we bake up what Orla and I have made first, have a little snack, and then start again." Nola was already dumping Savannah's botched dough into the trash. "Nothing beats biscuits and honey. Or biscuits and jam."

Savannah's dough hit the bottom of the trash can with a resounding thud. It was biscuit dough. Not brain surgery. And yet, she couldn't manage it. It was enough to leave her deflated. Apparently, the others noticed.

"Don't you fret, sugar." Orla draped an arm around her shoulders. "It was your first try. It'll get better."

"You gotta get back on that horse." Nola nodded, patting her arm. "Shake it off. Have a seat." She pulled one of the kitchen chairs closer to the marble island where they were working. "Get off your feet and give those babies a rest. Those are the only buns in the oven that count."

Savannah was smiling when she sat.

"I remember being pregnant with Joseph. I have five boys, Savannah. Five." Nola was all business. She flipped the dough onto the well-floured counter. "And every time

I got pregnant, my ankles would swell up like tree trunks. Big ol' things."

"I remember that." Orla laughed when her sister shot her a look of outrage. "My ankles were just the same."

Savannah looked down at her ankles. Was this something else she had to look forward to?

"Does Angus always hover that much?" Nola asked her, using a round cookie cutter to cut out biscuits.

"Hover?" Orla sounded offended. "He's only looking out for her. This might surprise you, Nola, but sometimes you say things that shouldn't be said."

Nola chuckled. "Guilty."

Savannah laughed. And it felt good.

"I'll say one thing, I've never seen my nephew so… protective." Nola rolled up the remainder of the dough.

Protective. Supportive. Generous. "He has been amazing." Which was one of the reasons she found him so irresistible.

"So, you don't mind him hovering?" Nola asked, assessing her with a mischievous grin.

Savannah's cheeks were blazing hot, an irrepressible smile spreading across her face.

Orla set the pan down and hugged her. "I can't tell you how happy this makes me. All of it." She held Savannah away from her, her warm gaze locked with hers. "You. The babies. My boy finding someone. And seeing you light up when you think about him. That's all a mother wants for her child—happiness. You'll understand that soon enough." She patted her shoulders and let her go.

Savannah's chest compressed and her eyes stung. If only it was that simple.

"Don't you worry." Orla patted her cheek. "It will all work out just fine."

"Just like your next batch of biscuits." Nola put her tray

of biscuits into the oven. "But first, let's eat some of Orla's perfectly-acceptable-if-not-perfect biscuits."

Savannah listened to the two of them carry on and enjoyed a pretty-close-to-perfect biscuit. Two biscuits in and she was feeling ready to try baking again.

"That's something else you have in common with Angus." Orla toasted her with a biscuit. "You don't give up. That'll serve you well in life. Especially when it comes to motherhood."

Motherhood. Her hand settled on her stomach and she took a deep, calming breath. She would be a good mother. A mother that could make homemade biscuits for her kids.

ANGUS SAT ON the top rung of pipe fence, watching a herd of young horses. They were full of energy, pawing the earth and tossing their manes.

"They look good." Dougal climbed up beside him.

"They should. We've worked hard to get here." And Angus was proud of the stock they were producing.

"We have." Dougal tipped his hat forward and scratched the back of his head. "I don't remember the last time I had a day off."

Angus pushed him. "There's no such thing as a day off in ranching." It was something their father said on a regular basis. He'd instilled a strong work ethic in them. If they didn't get up and do what needed doing, animals would suffer and the whole operation could hit a snag. Ranching was a lifestyle and Angus wouldn't have it any other way.

He hoped it wasn't too big a change for Savannah. On top of all the other changes. Try as he might, Dr. Wurtz's warnings cycled through his head again. Was he wrong to have left her with his mother and Aunt Nola? They could be a lot. But she probably wouldn't appreciate him following her around everywhere. Dougal sure as hell wouldn't appreciate him shirking his duties around the ranch to play Savannah's full-time shadow, either.

"Hello?" Dougal waved his hand in front of Angus's face.

"What?"

Dougal pushed him then. "Where'd you go?"

"Nowhere." He reached up and adjusted his cowboy hat against the breeze. "Is it my imagination or are we getting a cold snap?"

"It's your imagination." Dougal pointed at a pretty little roan. "That one, that filly over there."

Angus nodded. He'd noticed the animal. "She's got a good gait. Light on her feet." He pulled out his phone and made a quick note. He'd keep his eye on her.

"That one, too." Dougal nodded at a dapple-gray filly running along the far side of the pasture.

Angus studied the horse, then added it to his watch list. "We should start working with them in the spring."

"Yep." Dougal agreed. "Didn't you have a doctor's appointment this morning?" He glanced his way. "Is that what's eating you?"

Angus glanced at his brother. "Nothing's eating at me."

"Well, that's a pile of horse shit." Dougal shook his head.

Angus chuckled.

Every horse in the field turned his way, their ears pivoting in his direction.

"Everything okay? With Savannah and the babies?" Dougal's tone was gruff.

"They're fine." Angus took off his hat and leaned forward. "Good."

"Well, that's something, isn't it?" Dougal clapped him on the shoulder.

"It is." Angus slowly turned the hat, working the leather

band back onto the crown of his well-worn brown felt cowboy hat. "I don't know what the hell I'm doing."

Dougal made a noncommittal sound.

"The doctor said some things that scared the shit out
of me." That was it. He was scared for her and the babies.
And there was nothing he could do. "This is a high-risk
pregnancy—"

"What the hell does that mean?" Dougal was frowning.

"It means there's a higher risk of complications." He
ran his fingers through his hair.

"Okay." Dougal blew out a long, slow breath. "Well,
shit."

Angus chuckled. "Exactly. I don't want Savannah or the
babies to be at risk." He spun his hat in his hands. "And I
sure as hell don't like feeling...useless."

"You are pretty damn useless." Dougal shoved him
again.

"Thanks." Angus put his hat back on and sat up. "You're
a real ball of sunshine."

Dougal's eyes narrowed and he shook his head. "I'm listening to your sorry ass, aren't I? That's about all I can do."

Angus felt like an ass. "Sorry."

"You should be. You're sitting there, thinking the worst.
That's me, not you." Dougal slid off the fence. "The doc
said good things, right? So, knock it off. Savannah doesn't
need any of that mopey shit, either."

Angus nodded. "You're right."

"I'm what?" Dougal froze, cupping his hand around his
ear. "Say that again."

Angus laughed, emphasizing each word. "You are
right."

"Damn." Dougal pulled his phone from his pocket. "I'm
putting that on the calendar."

"You should. I doubt it'll happen again." Angus jumped off the fence. "I'm gonna go back up to the house."

"Probably a good idea. Savannah probably needs rescuing from Ma and Aunt Nola by now." He shook his head. "I'm going to help Jack with that damn tractor. Again."

"Good luck." Angus headed back to the barn before he could tease his brother about the "damn tractor." Dougal had a hate-hate relationship with the machine. It was a perfectly good tractor—until Dougal used it. Every time he used it, something went wrong.

By the time he'd made it to the house, he was feeling more like himself. Dougal's advice was solid. Focus on the good. For all the warnings the doc had given them, he'd said all was well. That was good. No, that was great. He'd focus on that and make sure Savannah didn't pick up on his worries.

"Hey, Willow." He stooped on the back porch, scratching the Lab behind the ear. "You holding down the fort?"

Willow stood and stretched.

"Wanna go inside and see what they're up to?" he asked the dog, who was keeping pace at his side. He opened the back door and was greeted with laughter. "Sounds like they're having a good time." Which was a relief.

Gertie was a bullet, running across the room to leap into his arms.

"Hey, baby girl." He cradled the wriggling dog against his chest. "Let's go see Savannah."

"And then I heard this thump-thump overhead." His mother was talking and laughing. "And I looked at my husband and asked, 'Where is Angus?'"

He came around the corner to find Savannah perched on the edge of a kitchen chair, listening intently.

"He jumped up and ran outside. 'I left the ladder up,' he said." His mother started laughing again. "I ran outside, too, but I knew it was Angus on the roof. He was a little mountain goat. Sure enough, there he was. No fear. Just his red curly hair blowing in the breeze and his diaper slipping off."

Savannah shook her head.

"What can I say, I like living on the edge." Angus shrugged.

"You liked keeping your father and me on our toes." His mother wagged her finger at him.

"What about you, Savannah?" Aunt Nola was cleaning up. "Did you get into any mischief when you were a little thing?"

Savannah wrinkled up her nose. "Not quite like that but... I was in ballet when I was about five. I was going to play a dancing flower—"

"And I bet you were precious." Ma was beaming at her.

"I didn't like ballet." She shook her head. "I didn't want to be a dancing flower or perform in front of an audience. If I was going to have to, I wanted to take my stuffed dog, Chance, with me. I took him everywhere." She sighed. "When the lights went down, our ballet teacher set us up on the stage, took Chance with her, and then the music started and the lights went up and I took one look at the audience and started sobbing."

His mother and Aunt Nola both "aww'd" over her story.

"I sat in the middle of the stage through the whole song, sobbing, while everyone else danced around me."

"That's sad." He didn't like the mental picture it conjured up. Little Savannah, sobbing for her toy under the bright lights. "There's no reason you couldn't have danced with Chance."

Savannah turned a huge smile his way. "My teacher said it would ruin the performance. Which I managed to do anyway."

"Chelsea, on the other hand, was aways up to something." Savannah shook her head. "She still is. I can't wait for you to meet her," she said to Ma and Aunt Nola.

Which was a reminder that Savannah's mother and sister were coming. Today.

"Is there anything I need to do to get their room ready for them?" Angus asked. Unfortunately, they were down to one guest room. Which meant Lana and Chelsea would have to room together.

"All set." His mother gave him a reassuring smile. "No need to worry."

Easy for his mother to say. She hadn't seen the Barrett home—or how the family lived. Now he was expecting Lana Barrett to share a bed with her daughter.

"Why are you making that face?" Aunt Nola wiped her hands on the kitchen towel.

"I'm not making a face." He forced himself to smile. "All good. I should probably go wash up before they get here."

"Go on. We're making lunch." Aunt Nola shooed him away.

Angus glanced at Savannah—Savannah, who was studying him. So much for not adding to her stress. He headed from the kitchen, kicking himself. He needed to be more careful.

"Angus?" Savannah had followed him. "Is everything okay?"

"Yes." He smiled again.

"Are you regretting inviting my mom and sister?" Her gaze locked with his.

"No." He swallowed. "I'm... Well, it's not exactly what they're used to, is it? What you're used to, for that matter."

Savannah's brow furrowed. "Angus." Her hand gripped his arm. "Your home is lovely. Your family is lovely. *You've* made it possible for us to be together for the holidays after…" She broke off, blinking rapidly.

Dammit. He drew her into his arms. "You should be with your family during the holidays. That's what the holidays are for." He ran his hand down her back, savoring the feel of her. She felt so right in his arms. It felt so right to have her here.

"I only hope Chelsea doesn't do or say something that's too… Chelsea." She laughed.

His hold eased on her. "She can't compare to Nola." He was glad she was smiling again.

"Don't let her hear you say that. She'll consider it a challenge." She stepped away from him, but her gaze landed on his lips. And she was wearing that look. He swallowed.

"I'll go shower." He cleared his throat.

She nodded, still staring at his mouth.

"Savannah." His voice was all longing. He wanted to kiss her. Ached to feel the softness of her lips beneath his.

Her eyes met his and he all but groaned. The hunger on her face set him on fire.

"A cold shower." He spun on his heel and headed for his room.

CHAPTER TWELVE

"I TRIED TO pack as much as I could." Chels pointed at two bulging suitcases Momma was unpacking. "I didn't know what you'd want—you know, what might fit when you're the size of a hot-air balloon," she teased. "It might be my imagination, but you seem a little rounder than when you left." She cocked her head to one side and stared at Savannah's stomach.

"Really?" Savannah smoothed her soft cotton sweatshirt over her stomach.

"No." Chelsea hugged her. "You look exactly the same. A little less stressed—okay, a lot less stressed. Probably from all the sex you're having."

"Chelsea." Momma stopped unpacking and stared at Chelsea.

"Momma." Chelsea sighed. "How else do you think she got pregnant?" She patted Savannah's stomach. "There's no point in being a prude now."

Momma huffed and went back to putting Savannah's things away.

She'd dreamed of Angus every night since she'd arrived. Cuddling Angus. Kissing Angus. Making love to Angus. But the real thing? Not possible. She and Angus had honored their agreement that sex was off the table. It was the smart thing to do, but there were plenty of times throughout the day that she regretted ever suggesting such a thing. There was something about him, something virile and sexy, gentle and tender—basically everything about him appealed to her.

Savannah sat on the edge of the bed. "You don't have to do that, you know."

"I like doing." Momma smiled. "I like feeling useful."

"How are you feeling?" Savannah glanced at Chelsea, suspecting her sister would be more forthcoming than their mother.

Chelsea gave her a so-so hand wobble.

"I'm fine. I'm good." Momma zipped up the now empty suitcase and slid it under the bed. "I'm even better now that I'm here."

"What do you think of the place?" Savannah held her breath. Their mother had been born into wealth and spent every day since waited on, hand and foot. While the McCarrick ranch was by no means rough living, it wasn't what her mother was used to.

"It's charming." Momma stopped to look around the guest room. "Homey."

Chelsea nodded. "Who was the hunky gardener out back? Thick black hair. Wily beard. He could till my garden anytime."

"Chelsea." Momma's cheeks went red.

Chelsea giggled.

Savannah did, too. She couldn't help it.

"Momma, you didn't see those shoulders? I bet he's good with his hands and knows how to plant bulbs like nobody's business."

Momma was more purple now.

"And gives the ground a good soaking, too. To keep everything nice and wet." Chelsea kept laughing, watching their mother the entire time.

Savannah couldn't breathe; she was laughing too hard.

A little peep slipped from Momma, then she was laughing, too. "Chelsea, you are a mess." She sat between them, hugging them close. "Whoever thought gardening had so many euphemisms for…"

"Sex?" Chelsea finished. "Oh, I'm just getting started."

"No." Momma jumped up. "I can't take anymore. My ears will catch fire if you keep that up."

"I missed you two." Savannah sighed.

"Oh, sweet girl." Momma shook her head. "How can I ever apologize for…everything?"

Savannah was up then, taking her mother's hand. "You have nothing to apologize for, Momma. Nothing." She hugged her close. "Now you're here and we get to celebrate Christmas together."

There was a knock on the door. "You three doing okay?" Angus asked. "You need anything?"

"Hey, Angus." Chelsea smiled her mischievous smile. "I need your help. I was asking Savannah who your gardener was."

"Chelsea." Momma let go of Savannah. "Don't you dare."

"Gardener?" Angus scratched his jaw. "Dougal probably. Gardening is how he unwinds."

"A stress reliever, huh?" Chelsea was enjoying herself far too much. "It's important to let all that stress out."

"Exactly." Angus shot Savannah a questioning smile.

Savannah started laughing again. Her sister had no shame.

Angus looked from one to the other. "Do I want to know?"

"No." Momma held up her hands. "Goodness gracious, no."

"And who, exactly, is Dougal?" Chelsea was not about to be deterred.

"My brother." Angus leaned against the door frame. "He's washing up now. You'll meet him at lunch."

"Oh, goody." Chelsea rubbed her hands together. "I'm famished."

Savannah couldn't seem to stop laughing.

"Heaven help me." Momma pressed both hands to her cheeks. "Angus, thank you so much for having us. I hope it wasn't too great an inconvenience."

"You're family, Mrs. Barrett. You're always welcome here." When Angus was sincere, like now, Savannah was torn between adoring him and wanting to do things to him that would mortify her mother.

"You are a dreamboat, aren't you?" Chelsea shook her head. "Would you say you and Dougal are alike?"

Savannah hadn't had much one-on-one time with Dougal. He was more of a loner than Angus. Quieter. She didn't know what he'd do when Chelsea came for him. It would be interesting to watch, that was for sure.

"He's on the gruff side. Not as verbal." Angus shrugged. "But we're brothers so..."

"Oh, the strong, silent type?" Chelsea nodded. "Lovely."

Savannah's cheeks were beginning to hurt from all the smiling and laughing.

"Is there anything we can do to help with lunch?" Momma was edging toward the door, shooting warning glares Chelsea's way.

"No, ma'am. I think it's about ready." Angus cleared his throat. "We keep things casual around here so Ma, Aunt Nola and Harvey and Jack will be joining us."

"Who are Harvey and Jack?" Chelsea checked her reflection in the mirror, running her fingers through her platinum hair.

"Ranch hands. Good men. They've been with us for years—like family, really."

"I'm sure they're lovely gentlemen." Momma seemed calmer now. "Lead the way." She hooked arms with Angus, leaving Savannah and Chelsea to follow.

"Give me the scoop real quick," Chelsea whispered. "Is Dougal available? Straight? Interested?"

"I can't help you, there, Chels. I don't know."

"Too busy with all the sex?" Chelsea nudged her.

"Chelsea, we can hear you." Momma called back. "Please, please lower your voice."

Angus chuckled then.

"You're no fun, Momma." Chelsea didn't bother keeping her voice down. "I'm simply trying to determine whether or not Dougal is available for…private gardening sessions."

Savannah burst out laughing then. She was settling in here just fine, but having her mother and sister here made it really, truly feel like home.

"Gardening doesn't mean…gardening, does it?" Angus asked Savannah once they were taking their seats at the table.

She shook her head. "Not at all." She rolled her eyes. "I think she's just messing with Momma, but you never really know with Chels. I guess we're about to find out."

Angus sat beside her and rubbed his hands together. "She'll keep him on his toes, that's for sure." He, for one, was looking forward to the show.

"You don't think you should warn him?" Savannah's hand covered his.

He liked that she reached for him—as if it was the most natural thing in the world. It was beginning to feel that way. He turned his hand over, threading their fingers together. "Nope. Dougal's a big boy. He can handle it." Maybe.

"I can see a family resemblance." Ma nodded. "Lana, you look like their sister, not their mother."

"You're too kind, Orla. But all the credit goes to my skin cream." Lana smiled.

"Good genes." Aunt Nola used her fork to point at the Barrett women. "Damn good genes."

"That, too," Lana agreed. "My mother still turns heads when she walks into a room."

"Oh, I do, too." Aunt Nola grinned. "And then, when they realize it's me, everyone scatters." She cackled.

Leave it to Aunt Nola to break the ice. Even Harvey and Jack seemed to relax a bit.

Lunch was family style—as was the normal. Angus tried not to think about the elegantly arranged plates and maids hovering to clear dishes that was the norm in the Barrett household. Funny how he'd never been troubled by such thoughts when it was just Savannah. Now that Lana was here, he saw everything through new eyes. The view left him torn.

"This is delicious." Lana took a bite of Aunt Nola's chicken church spaghetti. "It reminds me of something my meemaw used to make."

"She probably did." Ma sounded proud as she went on. "It's an old Southern staple. Chicken, canned mushroom soup, canned cream of chicken soup, spaghetti noodles. That's about it. Easy, cheap, and filling."

Angus winced at the *cheap* comment. Cheap, for his Ma, was a point of pride. The better deals or more coupons, the better. Cheap, for Lana Barrett, likely meant low quality or less than.

"Will you pass the rolls?" Savannah asked.

He was pleased, however, to see her enjoying every bite of her lunch. She took two rolls, slathered them both with butter, and smiled at him—looking a bit sheepish.

"What? I'm hungry." She shrugged.

"Nothing." He added a third roll to her plate. "I'm tickled pink." Her smile brushed aside all else.

"How did the doctor's appointment go?" Nola piped up, completely oblivious to the way Chelsea Barrett was sizing Dougal up.

"You beat me to it, Nola." Ma nodded. "I figured I'd wait to ply you two with questions until we were all together."

"I figured you'd pester Savannah until she cracked." Angus shot Savannah a smile.

Savannah smiled back, looking proud.

"We didn't ask." His mother sighed. "You wanted to wait until her mother and sister were here, so we did."

Angus was impressed—and surprised. His mother and Nola liked to be in the know about everything. "I appreciate it."

"You had an appointment this morning?" Lana's face lit up. "How are the babies?"

Savannah put her half-eaten roll on her plate. "They're fine. Three heartbeats."

"Strong heartbeats," Angus added. To him, the strong bit was important.

"That's good." Dougal served himself another large portion of chicken church spaghetti.

"What else did the doctor say?" Lana asked. "Don't spare a thing."

"We grammas want to know it all," Orla agreed, winking at Lana.

"We're scheduled for the big sonogram in a couple of weeks. They should be able to determine the size and weight of the babies." Angus looked to Savannah for anything he might be missing.

"And, maybe, the sex of the babies." Savannah eyed her roll. "I'm not sure I want to know."

"Nice to have a few surprises." Aunt Nola nodded.

"Not like there hasn't been plenty of those in, oh, the last month or so." Chelsea laughed.

For the first time, Dougal looked her way.

Savannah nudged Angus, hard. He nodded, watching to see what happened next.

Dougal blinked and went back to eating.

Chelsea was shocked.

And Angus almost choked on his food trying not to laugh. He got the feeling Chelsea Barrett didn't often get a brush-off. Not that that was what Dougal was doing. He was a cool character.

"Whatever you decide, of course." Lana Barrett smiled.

Ma hesitated before saying, "But I can see benefits to finding out."

"I can, too," Lana agreed.

"I just wanted to see what you'd say." Savannah smiled. "I don't think I could handle any more surprises. Like Chels said, we've all had more than enough."

"Oh, good." Lana pressed a hand to her heart. "I want to know."

"Right?" Ma giggled. "I can't wait."

"Are you two waiting to get hitched until after the babies are here?" Aunt Nola asked. "I know some folk frown on a pregnant bride, but I say that's hogwash. Plenty of marriages have started with a baby—good strong marriages, too. Nothing to be ashamed of."

And just like that, the table went quiet.

"We're not planning on getting married, Aunt Nola." Angus hoped his aunt would contain herself.

"What?" Nola stopped eating. "What, now? Why the hell not? What sort of nonsense is that?"

"Nola," Ma shushed her. "Eat and mind your own business."

Savannah had almost finished with the third roll, but she stopped and sat back in her chair. There was a green cast to her skin.

Dammit. He'd hoped her liking the food meant she'd tolerate it better. Instead, he'd fed her too much and made her sick. And he suspected his aunt spouting off and speaking her mind didn't help. "You okay?" he whispered.

She nodded, sipping her water. "I need a minute." She excused herself and left the room.

Which brought all conversation to an end.

"Is she okay?" Nola asked. "She's still getting morning sickness?"

"You didn't help, Nola." Ma sighed, shaking her head.

Angus nodded. "The doc says the symptoms a woman has with one baby are more intense with multiples."

"Poor Savannah." Lana put her napkin down and stood. "I'll go."

"Thank you, Lana." Angus was on the verge of following, but he let Lana go. Savannah wasn't feeling well, and she'd probably welcome her mother's care.

Lana gave him a gentle smile and left.

"I only said what we were all thinking." Nola shrugged.

Angus exchanged a long-suffering look with Dougal.

"How is Savannah doing?" Chelsea asked. "I'm no doctor, but she looks awful skinny."

"She needs to up her calorie intake, as tolerated." He left it at that.

"We'll just have to see what agrees with her." Ma stood, clearing plates. "Harvey, Jack, you two want more?"

"You're so quiet, I almost forgot you were sitting there."

Aunt Nola frowned. "What's that mess hanging off your face, Harvey?"

"Watch out, Harvey. Aunt Nola isn't a fan of beards." Dougal shot his aunt a look.

"The lady has the right to her opinion." Harvey smiled. "It's wrong, but that's okay."

Aunt Nola cackled and passed the food.

Ten minutes later, Ma, Chelsea, and Aunt Nola had cleared the table, Harvey and Jack had gone back to the barn, but there was still no sign of Lana or Savannah.

Angus checked his phone as he paced the length of the great room. No messages or phone calls—nothing to distract him from worrying over Savannah.

"You're looking tense." Dougal stood at his side. "You're not saying all there is to be said."

Angus glanced at his brother.

"Talk, dammit. I can see something's eating at you."

"I'm in a tailspin." Angus ran a hand along the back of his neck. "All of this." He shook his head. He didn't even know where to start.

"Is it…bad?" Dougal's voice was low.

"I don't know." No, it wasn't bad. "If… If she weren't pregnant, none of this would be happening. She wouldn't be here." Which wasn't exactly a revelation. He wasn't making a lick of sense.

"Probably not." Dougal waited, his face clouded with confusion.

"*Definitely* not." He shook his head. "It'd be me and you, since Ma and Aunt Nola had made other plans for Christmas this year, and a whole lot of quiet." It sounded pretty damn depressing.

"You mean, back to normal?" Dougal sighed.

He nodded. Normal. Meaning, boring. He couldn't picture going back to that. Lucky for him, he didn't have to.

But there was a hard jagged knot that stayed glued in the pit of his stomach. It was that knot, like a splinter beneath the skin, that he couldn't ignore.

"She wouldn't choose me, Dougal. There's something humbling knowing that, without fate forcing her hand, I wouldn't stand a chance with her." That was it. Now that he knew he loved her, he didn't want to be someone she'd had to settle for. He wanted her to choose him for him. To love him.

"Now you're being stupid." Dougal sighed. "You're gonna let that get in your way? You *do* have her. It shouldn't matter how you got her. If you're happy, if she makes you happy, then be happy. Screw the rest."

"That easy, huh?" Angus chuckled at his brother's straightforward advice.

"It should be." Dougal shook his head. "Damn, Angus, for a man who's got a good head on his shoulders, you're not thinking straight. See what's in front of you. Be happy."

"You're right."

"Of course I am." Dougal was frowning at him. "And if Ma and Aunt Nola weren't here, then there'd be no gingerbread and, dammit, I do like me some gingerbread." He grinned then.

Angus grinned back. "Speaking of seeing what's in front of you. You happen to notice a pretty blonde giving you a certain look at the lunch table?"

Dougal was frowning again. "What the hell are you talking about?"

"I'll take that as a no." It was Angus's turn to sigh now. "Maybe keep your eyes open at dinner? You might like what you see." He clapped his brother on the shoulder and laughed. Dougal might have just knocked some sense into his head, but he had absolutely no awareness of Chelsea Barrett and the numerous times she'd batted her eyelashes his way. For Dougal's sake, it might be best if his brother didn't catch on. Unlike Savannah, Chelsea wasn't exactly long-term relationship material. It'd be a shame for his brother to take an interest only to have his heart broken. Just the thought of losing Savannah put him in a cold-sweated panic. He wouldn't wish that sort of pain on his worst enemy.

CHAPTER THIRTEEN

PLENTY OF MARRIAGES *have started with a baby—good strong marriages, too.*

Nola's no-nonsense words floated through her brain.

She'd thought there was nothing left to upset her stomach, but she was wrong. Nausea kicked in and sent bile flooding her mouth. With a groan, she pushed off the bed and headed back into the bathroom.

She sat on the mat in front of the toilet and leaned against the wall, resting her hands on her stomach. Nola hadn't meant any harm. She asked a question they'd likely get asked over and over again. Why the hell weren't they getting married? *Because I want it all.* Now that answer seemed insufficient somehow.

"Savannah?" Chels called out. "I'm coming to check on you so try not to throw up for a minute, okay?"

She didn't say anything.

"Are you alive?" Chelsea came into the bathroom and sat beside her on the floor. "What can I do?"

Savannah shook her head. "Ugh."

"Where's Momma?"

Savannah shrugged, not trusting herself to speak.

"I'm so sorry, Pickle." She rubbed Savannah's shoulder. "I can only imagine how miserable you feel."

Until Nola sounded off and the throwing up started, she'd been pretty content. Sitting at that table, Savannah had felt like she belonged. Like they were a family. And then she was reminded that they weren't—not really. Not the way she'd pictured her family, anyway. Angus cared for her, but he didn't love her the way she wanted. And without that, could they ever truly be a family? Or was she being ridiculous?

She was exhausted. She swallowed and rested her head on her sister's shoulder.

"Well, Angus's mom and aunt are awesome. That Nola is a hoot—if a little outspoken. I hope I'm half as cool a badass as she is when I'm her age." She rested her head on Savannah's. "Dougal, on the other hand, is completely disinterested. I swear, I have never had anyone look right through me like that. I'm not going to lie, my ego hasn't recovered."

Savannah smiled. "His loss."

"I know. But still. Does he not see what a hottie I am?" Chelsea laughed. "Here I was hoping to have a festive fling. I guess I'll have to get over that. Or give Harvey or Jack another look?"

"No." Savannah shook her head. "Harvey's attachment to his beard is concerning. I don't think Jack has said more than five words to me, but I think he's closer to Momma's age."

"I guess I'll have to jingle my own bells." Chelsea sighed.

Savannah laughed then. "You have a way with words, Chels."

"What can I say? It's a gift." She took Savannah's hand. "Feeling any better?"

She hadn't thought about throwing up for a whole two minutes. "I don't think my stomach is on the spin cycle anymore." Her heart, however, was another matter.

"Distraction. It's a very useful skill."

"Chels…" She took a deep breath.

"Yes, Pickle?" Her sister squeezed her hand.

"I think… I'm so confused." The words were a whisper.

"What do you mean?" Chelsea leaned back enough that Savannah had no choice but to sit up. "About what?"

"I… I…" She broke off. Chelsea was quick to fall in love, she always had been. And it never lasted. That wasn't the sort of love she wanted. She wanted the real deal— with Angus.

But Angus… Her heart hurt. He didn't want to get married. He didn't. He'd only proposed because it was the right thing to do. Doing the right thing was important. Knowing Angus, he'd marry her tomorrow because he still felt that way. She could marry Angus. But would that be enough for her? Would she be happy in a marriage knowing her husband didn't love her with every fiber of his being? Why was she even considering it?

"Pickle?" Chelsea sat forward, her eyes searching. "What's going on? And don't tell me nothing. Twin thing." She tapped her temple.

"Nothing worth talking about." Before she said or did a thing, she was going to think it all through and get some sleep. Once she clued Chelsea in, her sister would be like a dog with a bone. And while she loved her sister's ability to be single-mindedly focused, she wasn't sure she could take that kind of energy at the moment. "I'm tired."

"Um, you know there are three people growing inside of you right this very minute, don't you?" Chelsea's brows rose. "Three." She counted off on her fingers. "I'm tired just thinking about it."

"Will you stay in here with me?" Savannah asked. "I don't snore as loud as Momma. And I've missed you."

"Where did that come from?" Chelsea was back to studying her again. "I don't really want to be in the same room when Angus comes sneaking in for—"

"There won't be any sneaking in." Especially if Chelsea was sharing a bed with her. "Not with Momma here. It's too weird."

"Oh, please tell me you're not serious. You're too young to think like that, Pickle." Chelsea shook her head, disapproving. "Especially when you've got a big, strong, manly man waiting in the wings."

She didn't want to think about *her* big, strong, manly man at the moment. "Chels, please."

Chelsea's eyes narrowed. "You're really not going to tell me what this is about?"

"Like I said, I'm tired and I've missed you." She was pretty sure her sister wasn't going to buy it, but it was all she could come up with at the moment.

"And?"

Savannah shrugged. "That's it."

"You're going to tell me eventually, you know that. You might as well get it out now." Chelsea took her hand again. "I don't like it when you keep secrets from me."

"You keep secrets all the time." She tried to smile.

"Only because I'm afraid I'd shock you so badly you'd never speak to me again." It took a lot to make Chelsea blush, but she was blushing.

Savannah shook her head. "Nothing you could ever do or say would manage that, Chels. I promise." She didn't want to think about their father or all the hateful things he'd said and how it had made her feel. She could never, ever, do something like that to someone she loved.

"I know." Chelsea nodded. "Because you're the best sister anyone could ever wish for."

"I am." Savannah smiled. "Now I think I'm going to crawl to the bed and take a nap."

"Oh, Pickle. I'll crawl with you." She smiled.

"No, no. You need to go make yourself impossible for

Dougal to miss. I have faith in you." Savannah waved her sister aside. "Go on. You know you want to."

Chelsea stood and held out her hand. "You know me so well. Come on, I'll help you to bed. We'll go really, really slowly."

Savannah took her sister's hand and her help to the bed. But once the lights were off and the door was shut, Savannah's mind refused to quiet.

Was Nola right? Was she being nonsensical? Should she set aside the love she craved and accept his marriage proposal? She was having triplets—the idea of doing every day alone was more than a little terrifying. She'd have Angus for her husband, even if she didn't have any claim on his heart. It did, in a practical way, make sense. Nola hadn't exactly been tactful, but she hadn't been wrong.

No. She couldn't do it. She couldn't settle. This was where she had to be now, and she was thankful, but her future wasn't set. Maybe having something more to think of, something beyond the pregnancy and the babies and Angus, would help.

Think, Savannah. She'd had a life before Angus; why was she basing all of her decisions on him now? Co-parenting was a thing. People did it all the time. She and Angus could make it work and she wouldn't have to live every day knowing her husband didn't love her.

Enough.

She was a strong, independent woman. It was time she started acting like it again.

She didn't need her father or her father's money.

She didn't need Angus or his money.

She had her untouched inheritance from her nanna and a perfectly respectable Public Service and Communication degree. She'd been the press secretary for the Austin Cougars football team for almost a decade and served on numerous nonprofit and charitable foundations—it shouldn't be too hard for her to find a decent job. She had Momma and Chelsea, too. She wasn't alone. She would be okay. *I can do this.*

When it came to the babies, things got a little complicated. She took a deep breath. But that's what co-parenting meant, sharing parenting duties. She and Angus would work that part out together. The fact that her heart would break every time she saw him didn't factor into it. This was about giving her babies the best: a mother and father that loved them unconditionally.

ANGUS TIPPED HIS black felt cowboy hat forward and shoved his hands into his coat pockets. The temp had dropped a good ten degrees over the last hour and the wind had a sharp bite to it. He glanced back at Savannah. The tip of her nose was red and her ears weren't covered, but she and Chelsea were laughing and talking—and that made him happy.

"There are over a million lights here on the courthouse lawn." Ma was pointing up into the branches of the trees overhead. "Isn't it beautiful?"

"It is." Lana Barrett was in awe. "It's a Christmas wonderland."

"People drive from all over to see all the lights." Ma nodded. "I think it gets better with each year."

"It's the same." Aunt Nola argued. "Every year, the same thing."

Angus chuckled.

"Nola." Ma sighed. "Well, *I* think it gets prettier every year."

"It's certainly impressive," Lana agreed. "I can't imagine it ever getting old."

Nola snorted. "I'm going for hot chocolate."

"Sounds good." Angus nodded. "Anyone else want some?"

"Me." Chelsea raised her hand. "And Savannah." She turned a dazzling smile on his brother. "What about you, Dougal? Are you a hot chocolate sort of man?"

Dougal blinked at Chelsea. "I'll lend a hand."

Angus turned on his heel before everyone saw him laughing. Either his brother was more clueless than imagined or he was in fact rattled by Chelsea Barrett. He managed to hold on until they were across the street at the hot chocolate stand operated by the high school agriculture club.

"You been kicked in the head recently?" Aunt Nola peered at Dougal over her thick glasses.

"No." Dougal frowned at her.

"You sure?" Aunt Nola's drawn-on eyebrows were almost in her hairline.

"I'm sure." Dougal sighed. "Is there a reason you're asking?"

Aunt Nola shook her head. "Where do I start?"

Angus was in danger of laughing, so he took a sip of hot chocolate. "Damn." He held the cup away. "That is hot."

"Still think I'm the one that's been kicked in the head?" Dougal shot Aunt Nola a look.

"I don't know. I can't account for either of you." Aunt Nola took an insulated cup in each hand. "You're both clueless, as far as I'm concerned. I guess that's why they say youth is wasted on the young." She carried the cups back across the street.

"What was that all about?" Dougal frowned after her. "I wasn't the dumbass surprised that the *hot* chocolate was *hot*."

"But you are the dumbass that has a woman doing her damnedest to catch your eye." Angus pointed at Chelsea with his cup.

"Savannah's sister?" Dougal appeared sincerely shocked.

"I didn't think I'd have to spell it out for you." At this point, Angus figured he might as well lay it all out there. "But yeah, Savannah's sister might have expressed interest in your clueless ass."

"Savannah's sister?" Dougal repeated, scowling across the street at Chelsea. "You mean... The pretty blonde?"

"Savannah's *only* sister." Angus shoved a cup into each of Dougal's hands. At least his brother had noticed Chelsea was pretty—that was something. "Now you know."

Dougal waited for Angus and walked back across the street with him. "Here." He held out a cup for Chelsea.

Chelsea lit up like a Christmas tree. "Thank you, Dougal. That's very sweet of you."

"Um." Dougal stared at her. "Yep." He turned and walked in the other direction.

"There is something wrong with that boy of yours, Orla." Aunt Nola sounded mighty disappointed.

"Is he okay?" Chelsea asked. "What's wrong?"

"Oh..." Angus stared after his brother. "He'll be fine. I think." With Dougal, it was hard to tell. "For you." He gave Savannah her hot chocolate. "Your nose is red. You warm enough?"

"Perfect." She didn't quite meet his gaze. "This is something. They really do this every year? Decorate all these trees?"

"It's right up your alley." Chelsea pointed at the sign. "All the money raised goes to help the local Christmas toy drive."

Savannah perked right up. "Oh, that's lovely."

"They're always looking for volunteers to help when Santa is here." Ma pointed at the empty gazebo. "He is here all day Saturday and Sunday, taking pictures with kids."

."You'd love that." Chelsea sipped her hot chocolate. "Goodnight, that *is* hot."

"That's what I said." Angus nodded. "Be careful, Savannah."

"I see how it is. I get to burn my tongue, she gets a warning." Chelsea stuck her tongue out and pretended to fan it.

"I do like her better." Angus shrugged.

Savannah glanced his way, but her smile faded quickly—and he didn't like it.

"That's fair." Chelsea laughed. "And as it should be. But man, that's, like, scalding hot."

"Maybe you should go warn Dougal." Angus pointed at his brother.

"You think?" Chelsea asked.

Angus nodded. Then he might be able to catch a second or two alone with Savannah.

"I'll be right back." Chelsea made a beeline for his brother.

"Good for her." Aunt Nola chuckled. "A woman who goes after what she wants."

"What are you talking about, Nola?" Ma asked.

"Well, now I see where the boy gets it from," Aunt Nola mumbled.

"Did you see the wishing tree?" Ma led Lana toward the Christmas tree on the far side of the lawn, with Aunt Nola following.

"Hi." Angus nudged Savannah.

"Hi." She seemed wholly focused on blowing on her hot chocolate.

"You good?" He could feel the tension between them. Ever since lunch, she'd seemed set on keeping distance between them.

"Yes." She glanced his way, then back at her cup. "Don't want to burn my mouth."

"Okay." He'd let it go for now. Instead, he moved on to a topic he knew she'd find impossible to resist. "Dougal had no idea Chelsea was interested."

"Really?" Savannah looked in the direction of Chelsea and Dougal. "I love my sister, but she's not exactly subtle."

"Oh, I know. I think everyone *but* Dougal picked up on that." Angus took a careful sip of his hot chocolate.

Chelsea was laughing, her hand resting on Dougal's arm.

"He looks like he's about to bolt." Savannah's head cocked. "Is he okay?"

Angus took a long look at his brother. "I don't know. I've never seen him act like that before." About that time, Dougal spilled his hot chocolate and jumped back. "Ever."

Chelsea stepped forward to blot Dougal's jacket, but Dougal took another step back, tripped over the curb, and fell over backward. All that was visible were his booted feet and Chelsea, looking down at him.

"Oh, damn." Angus chuckled.

"Poor Dougal." But Savannah was giggling. "She's got him all flustered."

"I'd say so." And it was hysterical.

But then Dougal was sitting up, his hand to his head, and Chelsea dropped to her knees, her face going white.

"Angus," Chelsea called out, waving them over.

"Damn." Angus hurried over, his amusement fizzling when he saw blood on his brother's head.

"You poor thing. Oh, Dougal." Chelsea had a hold of Dougal's arm. "I think you might need some stitches."

Angus pulled out his phone and shone a light on his brother's head. The gash wasn't all that long, but it was deep. "Probably wouldn't hurt." He held out his hand and pulled his brother up.

"I'll throw some superglue on it." Dougal wiped at his head. "I don't need anyone coming at me with needles."

He gave his brother a hard look. He was hurting, Angus could tell. But Dougal was a proud man, and falling, in public, was ten times worse than being in pain.

"Your head bounced off the concrete. It hit hard, Dougal. I heard it." Chelsea stopped Dougal from touching his head. "You could have a concussion."

It wasn't funny, but Angus was still tempted to laugh. "Hell, I could call Buzz and he could patch you up."

"Then I'd never hear the end of this." Dougal closed his eyes.

"Oh, that's never gonna happen, anyway," Angus mumbled.

"Angus." Savannah stared at him in shock.

"I can't believe you're teasing your brother." Chelsea looked like an avenging angel. "He is hurt. He's bleeding, for crying out loud."

Dougal was suddenly enjoying this—a whole hell of a lot. The sonofabitch was grinning.

"How are you feeling?" Chelsea had a hold of Dougal's hand now.

"Fine." But then he looked at Chelsea and went all deer-in-the-headlights dazed.

"You don't look so good." Chelsea patted his hand and held it against her chest.

"We should call for help." There was nothing funny about Savannah's disappointment in him.

"He's had worse." Angus pointed at the small grin on Dougal's face. "He's getting a kick out of you two ganging up on me."

"We are not ganging up." Chelsea frowned at him. "We're holding you accountable for unacceptable behavior."

Dougal nodded.

"I'll call 911." Savannah pulled out her phone.

Dougal wasn't smiling then. "Don't call 911." Because that would bring even more attention to what had happened. An ambulance would cause a scene and, in a small town, everyone would know about it. "I'll call Buzz." He glared at Angus.

What the hell? Like this was all my damn fault. Angus glared right back.

"Are you sure?" Savannah hesitated, glancing between Chelsea and Dougal.

"Buzz can take care of him. He's a vet, but he can patch up a cut as well as any doctor. And he's a friend." Angus was finding it less and less funny by the minute.

Dougal was already on his phone. "Buzz." He walked away, his conversation short and too muffled to hear. He called back, "I'm gonna walk over to the clinic."

"I'll go with you," Angus offered.

"I don't need a babysitter." Dougal brushed off his offer. "I'll see you at home." With an awkward nod for Chelsea, he set off down the sidewalk.

"Should he really go alone?" Chelsea was staring after Dougal, concerned.

"He didn't sound like he wanted company." Savannah took her sister's hand. "You can check on him later, Chels. Let's go find Momma." She yawned.

"It's getting late. And colder. We should probably head on home." Angus didn't want Savannah wearing herself out.

From the look they both sent him, he knew he was in the doghouse.

Growing up, he and Dougal had teased each other

through broken bones, chain saw cuts, dislocated limbs, and more. It was what they did. He would have expected Dougal to do the same if their roles had been reversed. He knew better than to try to explain that to them now. When Dougal was patched up and they were all home, they'd all get a good laugh over it. And he could figure out what was worrying Savannah. She didn't need any extra stress. Neither did the babies. The four of them were what mattered most.

CHAPTER FOURTEEN

SAVANNAH HELD HER hands out to the fire. The fireplace was built into the far wall of the great room, all rocks of varying earthy tones and textures. Orla had told her the rocks had all been found on the property and set into the walls to remind the family of their ties to the land. The McCarrick family had a proud heritage and Savannah admired that.

After their eventful visit to the lights on the chilly courtyard square, it was nice to sit in front of the fire and get warm. Dougal arrived home not five minutes after they did with a bandage on his head and surlier than ever—preventing anyone from questioning him or bringing up what had happened.

"Cookies." Aunt Nola carried a large platter of Savannah's decorated cookies into the room and placed them on the large wooden coffee table. "Orla's making her world-famous hot chocolate."

"World-famous?" Dougal asked.

"Isn't that what they say on all those roadside signs? To get you to buy stuff? World-famous?" Aunt Nola shrugged. "Fine. It's damn good hot chocolate is all I meant."

Savannah smiled. Chelsea was right—the woman was a character.

"It's about time we got this tree decorated." Orla carried in a large insulated pitcher.

Her mother followed, carrying a tray stacked high

with ceramic mugs and a bag of mini marshmallows. "Help yourself."

While everyone fixed their hot chocolate, Orla unearthed boxes of family ornaments—each of which seemed to have a story to go along with it. Savannah hung a few, but wound up sitting on the couch with Gertie in her lap. She propped her head on a pillow, loved on the little dog, and watched the tree come to life. There were strands of vivid-colored twinkle lights and bright white lights, too. Glass bulbs, handcrafted ornaments from the boys and small-framed pictures. In years to come, her babies would add to the ornament collection.

Would she be here to see the tree with those additions?

Now wasn't the time to get bogged down with that line of thinking. She'd rather enjoy the moment and the company.

"All done?" Momma stepped back, tilting her head one way, then the other. She'd seemed more invested in decorating the tree than anyone.

"It's lovely." Orla nodded. "You have a good eye, Lana."

Savannah and Chelsea gave two thumbs-up.

This tree looked nothing like the dramatic statement trees she'd grown up having. This tree was a personal reflection of the McCarrick family's love and history. To Savannah's eyes, it was perfect.

"Want some aspirin?" Aunt Nola asked Dougal. "Or a shot of whiskey?"

Dougal shook his head, winced, and said, "No. Thank you."

"It's just like old times." Orla shook her head. "I remember the time the two of you were playing with those yard darts. You remember that, boys?" Orla sat in the rocking chair by the fireplace. "Next thing I know, Dougal comes running in the house saying Angus was dead."

Savannah stopped munching on her cookie. "What happened?"

"Dougal had thrown the dart up and it had come down, smack, right into Angus's head." Orla pointed at the top of her head. "Sticking up like an antenna."

"I gave you boys those darts." Aunt Nola cackled.

"That sounds about right." Dougal sat in front of the fire on the floor. Willow joined him, putting her head in his lap.

Angus rubbed his head. "That one hurt."

"Lucky for him, his hard head kept it from going too deep." Orla picked up her knitting bag and pulled out the project she'd been working on since she'd arrived. "He had to stay in the hospital a few days so the doctors could keep an eye on the swelling. You know, make sure his brain was okay."

"Traumatic brain injury—by yard dart." Dougal chuckled. "That explains it."

Angus pointed at Dougal then. "See?"

Savannah hid her smile by taking another bite of cookie.

"There was always something." Orla took a deep breath. "It's a miracle they both survived childhood. Falling out of trees. Crashing tractors. Trying to ride the bull—how many times? Using gasoline instead of lighter fluid on a brush pile cost them both their eyebrows and eyelashes."

Savannah could picture the two of them, running wild and up to no good.

"And both of them would look you square in the eye and deny they'd done a thing wrong." Orla frowned at both of them. "I think the only reason that changed was because Angus almost died."

"A dart in the head sounds pretty lethal." Chelsea sat

beside her on the leather sofa, spreading a fleece holiday throw over their laps. Gertie stood, stretched, then wedged herself between them and underneath the blanket.

"Not compared to the two of them jousting with pitch-forks." Orla set her knitting aside. "It gets me choked up just thinking about it."

"Don't think about it, Ma." Angus moved to her side. "I'm fine. Dougal's fine. We're all fine." He kissed the top of her head.

"I do have a knot on my head and glue in my hair." Dougal reminded them all.

"Which I don't understand." Nola pushed her glasses up. "It's not like the place wasn't all lit up. You weren't stumbling around in the dark. I was wishing I'd had my sunglasses."

Savannah couldn't help but feel sorry for Dougal. There was no easy answer. She'd watched the odd exchange between Dougal and Chelsea that led to his fall and she still wasn't sure what, exactly, had happened.

"I've never seen anything like it." Momma sat on the fireplace. "The lights, I mean. It was truly breathtaking."

"You're right, Momma." Savannah yawned. Being tired was becoming her new normal. She yawned again—only to find Angus watching her.

Damn him and that smile.

How was she supposed to stop feeling for the man when his smile triggered an instant response in her? Warm and achy and molten. Want. And so much love. What she'd love right at this moment was to be snuggled up against his side—with his strong arms around her.

Don't. She mentally pleaded as he walked to the couch. If she wasn't so tired, she could scare him off with a scowl or something. As it was, she could only watch. *Please, don't.*

He sat on the other side of her. "You going to make it?"
She nodded.

"No one would blame you if you went on to bed." His voice was low and rich.

She hated that she loved the sound of it. "I don't want to miss anything."

His chuckle, a sound she equally loved, had Gertie waking up and wagging her tail.

I know how you feel. Savannah patted the little dog. *At least you know he loves you back.*

"What's wrong?" It was a gruff whisper.

"Nothing." She wouldn't look at him. She couldn't. Thankfully, Gertie decided to put both paws on her chest and give her an abundance of kisses. "Thank you, Gertie."

"I asked her the same thing." Chelsea leaned forward. "And she answered me the same way."

"Huh." Angus shifted so he could see her sister, but Savannah ignored them both.

"Don't worry. I'll get it out of her. Or I'll figure it out. Twin things." Chelsea sounded pleased with herself.

"How does that work, exactly?" Angus reached over and gently moved Gertie off Savannah's chest. "Behave, Gert. Don't stand on your momma."

Oh, no. She was not going to cry. Not again.

"I'm not sure." Chelsea sighed. "Even when we were kids, we had this sort of shorthand thing going on. Probably from being in such close quarters for so long when we were babies." She rested her hand on Savannah's stomach. "I bet these three will have it."

"I guess we'll see." There it was—that undeniable affection lining his every word.

"You realize you're talking over me?" Savannah hadn't

meant to snap, exactly, but she was stressed and tired and sad and done.

"You're free to join in the conversation anytime, you know." Chelsea patted her stomach. "You need another cookie. You're getting all crabby. I'll be back."

"I apologized to Dougal," Angus murmured, draping his arm along the back of the couch. "If that's what's got you upset."

"Why do you think I'm upset?"

"Well, for one thing, you won't look at me." His hand rested on her shoulder. "For another, you're all tense and stiff."

Which was true. "I guess I'm just tired." She closed her eyes. If she pretended to sleep, everyone would leave her alone. Besides, she was tired. Very tired. Between Gertie curled up on her lap, the soft blanket keeping her warm, and Angus's undeniably delicious scent close enough for her to breathe in, it wasn't all that hard to pretend.

At some point, the conversation became a low murmur and she'd shifted against Angus. She knew this because she could hear his strong heartbeat. His fingers were sliding through her hair. And he chuckled. "Come on, Gertie. I like cuddling with Savannah, too," he whispered. "You're gonna have to share, okay?"

Savannah heard Gertie's grunt and smiled.

"I don't know what she's dreaming about, but she's smiling." Angus murmured.

Was this a dream? It could be. If it was, she could burrow into Angus—so she did.

"I'm sure she's dreaming about you and the babies." It was Orla. "She's a lucky girl, Angus, to have you."

"You got it backward, Ma. I'm the lucky one." It was the softest whisper. So soft and tender Savannah knew it had to be a dream.

ANGUS APPLIED THE slightest pressure with his left knee. The horse responded, turning left without missing a step. "Good." He kept his voice low and steady.

"He's coming along." Dougal rested his arms on the top rung of the fence.

"He's smart. Aren't you, Ranger?" Angus patted the horse. With the lightest touch, he used his right ankle. Ranger went backward until Angus stopped. "Good."

After spending a mostly sleepless night, he'd come down to the barn to work off some of his restlessness. Ranger seemed to understand his mood. He'd settled right in, listening closely to each and every command Angus gave him.

"What time did you get down here?" Dougal rested his chin on his arms.

He tipped his cowboy hat forward, keeping the morning sun out of his eyes. "I don't know." If he told his brother he'd been out here since sunrise, Dougal would start asking questions.

"Uh-huh. Are you thinking of coming up for breakfast? Or are you needing a break from all the women, too?"

He didn't need a break. If anything, he needed more time with one woman in particular. Lana and Chelsea Barrett had been here for three nights now—and something had changed. Maybe he'd imagined it but, before everyone had arrived, the two of them had been building something good. He missed that. He missed her.

"I was thinking about going into town today. Doing a little Christmas shopping." Angus had Ranger do a sharp right turn and stop. "Good."

"I don't have to get presents for everyone, do I?" Dougal ran a hand over his beard.

"No." Angus grinned. "I'm only shopping for Savannah."

"Oh." Dougal shrugged. "I guess you have to, being that she's your…what? Your baby mama."

Angus frowned. He didn't like that. But technically, what was she? He walked Ranger to the gate.

"It's true, isn't it?" Dougal's brows went up. "Someone's touchy this morning." He opened the gate and stepped aside.

"I don't want people thinking of her as my baby mama." Angus slid from the saddle, choosing his words with care. "I want her to be my wife. I want people to know she's my wife. Respect her as such. It might seem like a little thing, but to me, it's not."

"And?" Dougal waited.

"She doesn't want to marry me," Angus snapped.

Dougal's brows rose. "Did she give you a reason?"

Angus tugged off his gloves. "She wants to marry for love." He cleared his throat.

"So, what's the problem?" Dougal crossed his arms over his chest. "You love her. I think she likes you well enough?" He paused. "Or not?"

Angus frowned. "I don't know."

"Well, maybe you should find out." Dougal shook his head. "And you say I'm clueless."

Angus chuckled at that. "Fine. I need a favor."

"Go on." Dougal closed the gate.

"You might have noticed Chelsea and Savannah are joined at the hip." He waited, but Dougal only shrugged. "I figure the four of us can go into town and you can keep Chelsea occupied while I get a few things sorted out with Savannah." Like making sure she understood how he felt and, hopefully, hearing she felt the same. Then he'd put a ring on her finger.

"Occupied?" The look Dougal shot him was all suspicion. "What the hell does that mean?"

Angus laughed. "I don't know. Buy her a coffee or a hot chocolate or something. What's your problem with Chelsea, anyway?"

"She makes me nervous." Dougal was scowling. "I don't like it."

If he thought Dougal would explain what that meant, he'd ask. But Dougal was Dougal and only offered up the bare minimum so he left it alone. "I'm asking for an hour. That's all." Angus sighed. "I'll owe you."

"I'll try... I don't know what I'll do with her for an hour." Dougal wasn't happy. "She talks a lot and is always looking at me."

"She likes you." Angus shook his head and put it all out there. "You could just grab her and kiss her and see where that gets you."

Dougal stared at him.

Angus stared right back. "If you're not interested in kissing her, introduce her to Dean—he's a talker and he'd probably take an interest in Chelsea."

Dougal kept on staring at him.

"What?"

"Nothing." Dougal led the way to the barn.

They stowed the tack, brushed and fed Ranger, and made it all the way back to the house without another word. As soon as they opened the back door, they were greeted by the overlapping conversation of the women inside.

"That's another thing," Dougal grumbled. "The constant talking. What's wrong with a little peace and quiet now and then?"

"Guess they've got a lot to say." Angus shrugged, following the voices to the kitchen.

"All the time?" Dougal shook his head. "How is that possible?"

"There you are." Ma was standing behind the kitchen

island. "We just made some gingerbread muffins. Correction, Savannah made them."

"Momma helped, too." Savannah was stacking muffins onto a tray. "I tried to make a casserole, too, but—"

"They didn't need to know that." Aunt Nola shook her head. "All they need to know is you made food for them and they'll be grateful."

"I'm sure they're very grateful." Ma glanced at them. He and Dougal nodded.

"See that, Savannah?" Lana asked.

Savannah glanced up and they nodded again.

"I'm taking notes." Chelsea was sitting at one of the bar stools along the island, an elbow propped up.

"You free to take us into town in a bit?" Aunt Nola didn't drive. Her license had been revoked after a run-in with a police officer. Nola argued the officer was too young to know what they were talking about and that she'd only been going ten miles over the speed limit, not thirty.

"Savannah signed up to work with Santa this weekend. We need to go pick up her elf outfit." Ma was super proud.

"She loves doing charity work. I don't know what the foundation is doing without you there this year." Lana shook her head. "You do so much."

"I'm sure their people will step up." Chelsea hurried to reassure her sister. "You don't need to worry about it."

But Savannah looked like she was worrying about it. As a matter of fact, Savannah looked pale and tired and not like herself. He ignored the rest of the room as he headed straight for her. For three days, he'd kept his opinions to himself, believing everyone was just as in tune with her as he was. Now he was a man on a mission. "Savannah." He stopped at her side, taking both of her hands. "You look tired. Can I ask you to rest? Even for an hour?"

"You haven't eaten yet." Savannah nodded at the tray of muffins.

He grabbed one and took a huge bite. "I'll eat."

She looked up at him, the ghost of a smile on her lips.

"I'll eat the whole damn tray." Angus squeezed her hand. "If you promise you'll lay down for a bit?" He ignored the 'awws' from behind him, waiting for her answer.

"You're not eating them all." Dougal grabbed at least four. "That should do it." He grabbed another two. "Now. The rest are yours."

Angus shoved the rest of the muffin in his mouth, never breaking eye contact.

Her gaze fell from his. "I'm really—"

"I'm sure you are fine, but it'd mean a great deal to me if you'd lay down for a bit. Ma and Aunt Nola, Chelsea and your mom can take care of things for a bit." He wasn't asking. "Dr. Wurtz said you need to take care of yourself to take care of them."

"I'll lay down. For a little bit." She took a slow, deep breath. Her hands slid from his and she untied and removed her apron.

"Thank you." He was glad she wasn't going to fight him on this. Did no one else see the dark circles under her eyes? "Dougal and I can go into town and get whatever you need."

"I can go on my own," Dougal offered. "If you want to keep an eye on her?"

"I don't need anyone keeping an eye on me." Savannah hung her apron in the pantry with the rest of them. "I'm going." She waved, the door swinging closed behind her.

He took a deep breath.

"You're really sweet on my sister, aren't you?" Chelsea was all smiles. "Like this isn't about you knocking her up."

"Oh, Chelsea." Lana pressed a hand to her forehead.

"I'll try again." Chelsea rolled her eyes. "You care about my sister. This isn't just about doing the right thing, here."

Well, damn, he was in the spotlight now.

"He's sweet on her." Dougal answered for him. "He damn near took my head off when I called her his baby mama. I think he's wanting to get married fast because he thinks she'll leave his sorry ass."

Angus shook his head and leveled a glare at his brother. "Unless you want me going around speaking for you, I advise you to go back to being the quiet one."

Dougal shook his head. "Whatever."

He didn't exactly want to pour his heart out to all of them—at least not until he'd told Savannah. At the same time, he wasn't trying to hide anything. "I do want to do the right thing by her and the babies. But I am sweet on her. I was hoping to tell her that and go into town to find her a ring."

Chelsea clapped her hands. "I knew it." She hugged her mother.

"Or you could use Meemaw's ring?" His mother sniffed. "Nola and I both want you to have it. If you want it?"

The family ring. It would mean the world to him. "I'd like that. I think Savannah would, too, knowing how strongly she feels about family."

"See," Dougal muttered, then glanced at Angus. "What? They can see you. It's all over your damn face. It's kinda—"

"The sweetest thing ever," Chelsea finished. "Someday, I hope a man will look like that when he's talking about me."

"The right man will." Lana slid an arm around her waist.

"Listen to your momma." Aunt Nola slapped the top

of the kitchen island. "If he doesn't look and sound like a lovesick fool, you send him packing."

"I hate to admit it, but she's right." Ma chuckled.

"You heard that, right? Aunt Nola calling you a lovesick fool?" Dougal was laughing.

"Yeah, yeah." He didn't care. "I'd appreciate it if you could all keep this to yourselves until I get to talk to Savannah?" He waited for them to nod. "I'm going to go check on her." He'd feel better knowing she was getting some sleep. Still, deep down, he couldn't shake the feeling that something was off. If he ever got a moment alone with her, maybe he'd find out.

CHAPTER FIFTEEN

HER NOSE HAD gone numb a good hour ago. And, underneath the curling top of her green felt elf shoes, it was very likely her toes had frostbite. Not that she minded. How could she? The line of wide-eyed kids waiting for their turn on Santa's lap stretched from beneath the canopy of a million blue-and-white Christmas lights down the courthouse sidewalk and around the corner. She'd make sure to put her feet up and rest when she got home.

"Ho ho ho." Town veterinarian, Buzz Lafferty, was doing an admirable job as Santa. According to Angus, he'd always been loud—which was an asset in their current situation. "Merry Christmas. What's your name?" He regarded the little girl on his lap.

The little girl stared silently up at Buzz—er, Santa, with both awe and a small amount of terror. Her mouth opened, but nothing came out.

"Come on, Frannie." A boy stood at the front of the line. "Tell him what you want."

Frannie nodded, but never looked away from Santa. "Um…"

Savannah stooped beside the little girl. "I bet you'd like a…princess doll?"

Frannie shook her head.

"Some coloring books?" she tried again.

"Nope." Frannie sat up, smiling widely. "I want another bwothah or sistah."

Savannah laughed. So far, she'd heard requests for dinosaurs, big-wheel trucks, and vacations to see Mickey Mouse but this was the first sibling request.

"Frannie." The boy groaned. "You can't ask for that."

"Why not?" Frannie peered up at Santa. "Can I ask for that for Chwistmas?"

Buzz—Santa cleared his throat, shooting a desperate look her way. He was Santa, after all. He was supposed to make the kids happy. But this was a tall request—one Santa had no control over. Savannah didn't envy the poor man.

"Well, now," Santa murmured, stroking his massive fluffy white beard with one gloved hand. "That's a special request, one that only your parents can give you. Santa can't deliver babies."

Good answer. She shifted from one foot to the other.

"Oh." Frannie frowned. "Why not?"

"Um…" Santa cast another look her way.

"There's not room for them in Santa's bag of toys. It's not safe, you see." Savannah hoped the little girl would accept this. "Babies are very fragile."

"I know." Frannie sighed, looking deflated. "Okay. Then can I have a new pair of light-up sneakers?"

She heard Santa's relieved sigh and stood, smiling.

"I will put that on my list." Santa nodded. "Let's smile for the camera."

The photographer took a picture, Savannah helped Frannie from Santa's lap, and the boy hurried up to take his sister's hand.

"Here you go." She handed them each a candy cane. "Merry Christmas."

"Thank you." The boy nudged Frannie.

"Thank you." Frannie smiled. "Is that why the stawk

delivahs babies, Gawwett?" Frannie was asking as they walked away. "Because they'd get squished in Santa's bag?"

"I guess." Garrett led her to a large family group, bundled up on a picnic blanket beneath the illuminated trees.

She suspected Frannie kept her family entertained. She watched, momentarily struck by the smiles and laughter and overall happiness that exuded from the group. She couldn't remember a time when her family had ever enjoyed one another like that. Not unless photographers or reporters were around, that is. Then the Barrett family was the picture-perfect family. A model family was a requirement for her father's career. Whether it was true or not.

"Savannah?" Buzz whispered. "Earth to Elf Savannah. I think you're being relieved."

"Really?" She shivered as another blast of cold air swept across the courthouse lawn. "Oh, good." She turned to find a teen wearing an identical elf outfit and handed off the stocking full of candy canes. "Hope you wore thermal underwear."

"I did." The girl took the stocking.

I wish I had. Now that her shift was over, she couldn't wait to find some hot chocolate and some comfy clothes. Red-and-white-striped tights were festive, but they didn't do much to keep the cold at bay.

She waved goodbye to Santa and headed straight for the hot chocolate booth, texting Chels to let her know she was done. She was almost at the booth when her left stocking snagged on an especially prickly holly branch.

"Ow." She turned, reaching down to remove the branch—and turning so that her right leg snagged as well. "Really?"

"Need help?" The laughter in Angus's voice was insult to injury.

When had he gotten here? "No." She barely glanced his

way. "I can…get it." She pulled the left leg free, leaving a large hole. "Dammit."

"Is Santa okay with that kind of language?" Angus shook his head.

"Santa is very understanding." She freed her right leg without tearing the stocking—but got one of the poky leaves stuck under her thumbnail. "Ow," she murmured, pulling out the dagger-like leaf and sucking on her thumb.

"I can help, you know." At least he wasn't laughing this time.

"You're always helping." And it bothered her.

"And that's a bad thing?" Angus walked along with her.

"That you think I always need help? Yes." She gathered up as much of her pride as she could and headed for the hot chocolate booth. "A large." She rubbed her gloves together. "With extra whipped cream."

"I'll have the same." Angus was regarding her closely. "There's not much else I can do at this point. Offering to help makes me feel like I'm doing something. I'm not, I know it. You're the one carrying our babies. I'm trying to…be here somehow."

Every one of his words had her heart surging with hope. She glanced up at him and instantly regretted it. He looked more delicious than ever. Warm, dark eyes. That strong, stubbled jaw. All cowboy. From his black felt cowboy hat to the well-worn brown boots, there was no denying Angus McCarrick was a very manly man. It wasn't quite so cold now. If anything, she was feeling warm.

Her not-so-subtle inspection earned her a crooked smile. "You're wearing that look."

Of course he'd notice. She'd spent the last few days trying to put distance between them, and now, with one look, she'd let him know she wasn't as indifferent as she'd been trying to be.

"Hold up." The teen boy inside the booth started banging on something. "It'll be just a minute."

Great. She could handle another minute of standing here—as long as she didn't do anything else to embarrass herself, that is.

"What did Frannie ask for?" Angus asked.

"You know Frannie?"

"She belongs to Buzz. Tonight's Santa." He paused. "Actually, Frannie and Garrett are Buzz's wife's younger siblings. But he and Jenna, his wife, adopted them so, yeah, she's his."

Savannah took a minute to make sense of what he'd said. "Oh. Well, that explains why Santa panicked a little." She smiled. "She asked Santa for a new brother or sister."

Angus was laughing then.

It wasn't fair how much she loved to hear him laugh. "He told her that was up to her mom and dad."

"I bet he and Jenna will be having an interesting conversation tonight." He took the hot chocolate. "Thank you." He handed one to her. "That's a lot of whipped cream."

"It's Christmas." She shrugged. And she was tired. Hopefully, the extra sugar would give her a little pick-me-up.

"How'd it go tonight?" He took a slow sip of his hot chocolate—and wound up with whipped cream in his mustache.

"It went well." She grinned, not saying a word about his new frothy adornment.

"Good." He smiled back at her. "I'm glad. You're the prettiest elf I've ever seen. Even if that holly bush did attack you." He tipped his hat back, revealing more of his devilishly handsome face—the whipped cream didn't do a thing to change that.

If anything, the whipped cream drew her attention to

that smile. He had a nice mouth. Full lips. Kissable, even. Tempting.

Her phone vibrated. Chelsea.

Enjoy your bearded cowboy hottie. He's your ride home.

Chelsea texted, adding a string of winky-face emojis at the end. Get it? RIDE home?

She sighed and tucked her phone into her purse.

"Hey there, cowboy. You've got a little something right there." A very pretty blonde approached. "Looks like your mustache has a mustache."

Angus chuckled. "That was why you were smiling?"

"Guilty." She shrugged, feeling big and awkward next to the woman.

"Need a tissue?" The blonde dug through her purse. "Here." She offered him a tissue and regarded Savannah with open curiosity. "Are you going to introduce me, Angus?"

"Cassie Ford, this is Savannah. Savannah, Cassie. She's Buzz's sister."

And she was gorgeous.

"It's so nice to meet you. Finally." Cassie shook her hand. "Sterling is around here somewhere. My husband." She turned, scanning the crowd.

It came on so suddenly, Savannah wasn't sure what was happening. One moment, she was fine. The next, it felt as if all the blood in her body crashed into her feet. A rush of cold followed. And the world began to spin.

"Angus?" she whispered. And the world went dark and silent.

EVERYTHING SHIFTED INTO slow motion.

Savannah's panic-filled voice.

The sheer terror on her face before she went deathly white and she sort of folded in on herself. Some instinct kicked in and he caught her before she hit the ground.

"Savannah?" He ran his hand along the side of her face. "Can you hear me?" *Please, please say something.* He scooped her up.

He was vaguely aware of voices and movement.

Buzz, in full Santa gear, was there, taking her pulse. "She's breathing. Her pulse is okay." But his expression didn't do a thing to put Angus at ease. "I'll drive you to the ER."

He nodded, cradling her close and running to Buzz's truck.

The hospital was at least ten minutes away, but they made it there in half the time.

"Keep it together." Buzz gripped his arm. "We're here."

Angus carried her into the ER. "She's not moving. She collapsed." He couldn't breathe. "Somebody do something." Anything. Dammit, just make her okay.

A nurse emerged. "What happened?"

"I don't know. She's pregnant." He sucked in a deep breath. "Triplets. High-risk."

She nodded, listening to Savannah's chest with her stethoscope. "Let's get her in the back for some tests, shall we?"

Tests? What sort of tests? "What's happening?"

"That's what we need to find out." She waved someone else with scrubs forward. "We're going to take her back."

"Where? I'll take her." Angus wasn't going to leave her.

"Angus." Buzz put a hand on his arm. "You'll get in the way. Let them take care of Savannah. Trust them."

He was just supposed to watch them take her away? Wait? Do nothing? Fear the worst?

"We need to take her now." The ER doctor pointed at

the gurney. "The sooner we do the tests, the sooner we will have answers."

It made sense so he laid her on the gurney. But the minute they wheeled her behind those doors, he couldn't breathe. He bent over, bracing his hands on his knees, and did his best to keep it together.

"Breathe." Buzz placed a hand on his back.

He shook his head.

"Who should I call?" Buzz asked.

Angus ran a hand over his face. "Dougal." Think. "Get him to bring her mom. Sister."

"Will do."

He couldn't concentrate on anything. Buzz made phone calls, got him a cup of coffee, and tried to get him to sit. Angus couldn't sit.

Instead, he paced.

Buzz's phone rang. "It's Jenna."

Angus nodded and sat. There was nothing comforting about a hospital waiting room. Nothing. The massive clock on the wall was a constant reminder that time was moving on and he still didn't know what the hell was happening with Savannah.

He was on the verge of demanding the nurse get him some answers when Dr. Wurtz stepped into the hallway. He was up and met the doctor halfway.

"Is she okay?" Angus had to know. He had to know now.

"She's fine."

He blew out a slow breath and put a hand against the wall to steady himself.

"She fainted." Dr. Wurtz patted his shoulder. "It can happen. She's fine," Dr. Wurtz repeated. "How are you?"

"I've never been that scared in my life." His poor heart

still hadn't recovered. "But if she's okay, that's all that matters." He shook his head. "The babies? They're okay, too?"

Dr. Wurtz nodded. "All three heartbeats are strong and accounted for."

"What happens now?" He straightened, steadier now.

"You can go sit with her, if you like. Let's keep her here for a couple of hours so I can monitor her, and then you can take her home. Sound good?"

"Are you looking for something specific?"

"No." Dr. Wurtz smiled. "But if she has another fainting spell, I'd like to see if there's a cause."

Angus nodded. That made sense. No reason for alarm. He needed to calm down. Doc said she was fine, and there was no reason not to believe the man. *Get it together.* The last thing she needed was him falling apart.

"I'll take you to her." The young doctor led Angus through a set of double doors and down a long hall. He stopped outside a hospital room and knocked. "Someone to see you, Savannah."

The moment Angus saw her face, all his good intentions went out the window. His heart couldn't handle her tears. "Hey." He sat on the bedside, drawing her into his arms. "You're okay. They're okay."

She clung to him. "I was so scared." Her words were muffled against his shoulder. "I didn't know what was happening."

"Doc says it happens sometimes." He spoke softly. "But if you can help it, I'd be okay with that never happening again."

Her laugh was unsteady.

Dr. Wurtz chuckled. "I've got a patient in labor upstairs. I'll check back in a bit."

"Thank you, Doc," Angus called out, too caught up in

Savannah to say more. She felt so damn good in his arms. Even if she was shaking. "What can I do?"

"I can't stop shaking."

He slid onto the bed next to her and pulled her against him. "Warm enough?" There was an extra blanket at the foot of the bed. She nodded, but he pulled the blanket up and tucked it around her anyway. "Better?"

She nodded, resting her head on his chest. "Your heart is going so fast."

"It's slower than it was." He ran a hand over her hair. Touching her helped.

She yawned.

"Dr. Wurtz wants to keep an eye on you for a bit," he murmured, stroking her hair again. "Might as well get some sleep if you can."

"Will you hum something?"

"Hum?" He smiled. "Like what?"

"Anything." She shrugged.

Angus had hummed his way through several of Kenny Rogers's greatest hits when Lana Barrett tiptoed inside.

"She's sleeping," he whispered.

Lana whispered, "Is she okay?"

He nodded. "Fainted."

"Oh. I did that a time or two, with the girls." She pressed a hand to her heart. "My sweet girl." She tucked the blanket up over Savannah's shoulder. "Thank you for taking such good care of her, Angus. It does my heart good to see how well you treat her." She frowned then. "I hope you'll forgive me, but… When I heard that she'd been taken to the hospital, I panicked and called her father."

Well, dammit. Still, he didn't blame the woman. "He is her father."

"He is devastated." She cleared her throat. "I tried to tell him not to come but…"

Angus closed his eyes. "When will he get here?" Savannah didn't need additional stress. And he was pretty sure Richard Barrett was the epitome of additional stress.

"I don't know." She sighed. "Knowing him, as fast as he can. I did tell him he can't come in here and add to her stress. I made it very clear."

"I'm sure he'll do what's best for Savannah and the babies." He didn't believe a word of it. Richard Barrett would do what Richard Barrett wanted to. Angus would do whatever he had to to keep the sonofabitch in check.

CHAPTER SIXTEEN

ALL THE CUDDLING and smiling and tender touches were going to make it impossible when everything fell apart. And it would. Her fainting spell had caused them both concern, but she'd be back on her feet in no time. Which was good—wonderful. She didn't want to be so reliant or needy. But when Angus was close, she was oh, so needy. Her fool heart seemed determined to hold on to him.

"You need anything?" Chelsea sat in a chair at the side of her hospital bed.

"Nope," she said again.

"How are you feeling?" Orla asked.

"Better." And she did, too. But she wasn't exactly moving.

When Dr. Wurtz had come in to release her last night, she'd stood up and her blood pressure had bottomed out. Dizziness had hit her hard and fast. But Angus had been there to prop her back against the elevated bed and murmur all sorts of reassuring things. He hadn't left her side all night. Once Dr. Wurtz had determined what was going on with her blood pressure, she could go home.

"Here." Dougal walked in, thrusting a large brown paper sack at Angus. "Wasn't sure what to get, so…"

"Thanks, Dougal. I'm sure we can find something in here that works." Angus was smiling at her, then.

And Savannah's heart instantly picked up. The heart

monitor only added to her humiliation. Everyone in the room could hear it.

"What's in the bag?" Chelsea set her fashion magazine aside.

"Food your sister will enjoy." Angus handed over the bag. "You need to eat."

"It's not that I didn't want to." She'd actually been hungry when her breakfast tray had been delivered. One sniff set her stomach to churning.

"I almost turned green, too. And I'm not pregnant." Chelsea sat on the foot of her bed. "It was very sweet of your man to go out and find good food for you and the wee ones."

"Ahem." Dougal cleared his throat.

"Okay, it was very sweet of your man to send someone to go and find good food for you and the wee ones," Chelsea corrected, winking at Dougal.

Dougal flushed, backed into the wall, and mumbled something before leaving the room.

"So that's how he broke his head open." Nola glanced Chelsea's way. "It's your fault."

"I guess so. But I give up." Chelsea laughed, holding up her hands. "My pride has taken too many hits."

"His loss." Savannah reached for her sister's hand. "Want one?"

"You pick first." Chels patted her hand. "Otherwise, your man might not like me, either."

"Take at least two pastries," Angus interjected. "Or three."

She shook her head. "Three?"

"You are eating for four, Pickle." Chelsea pointed at her stomach. "Not that I need to remind you of that."

"The doctor did say you needed to eat more." Momma joined in. "We all heard him."

Savannah seriously regretted letting them all invade. Now it wasn't just Angus hovering, it was both mothers, her sister, his aunt, and Dougal—although she suspected he'd pretty much stay out of it.

"He did," Nola agreed. "We'll have you fat and happy in no time."

"I like the sound of that." Angus nodded.

"Okay, okay." She peered into the bag. "Did he buy everything?"

"The bag's not that big." Angus turned. "We don't have any—"

"Here." Dougal returned with a pile of paper plates and napkins. He sank onto the vinyl-covered sofa that ran the length of the wall, looking acutely uncomfortable.

"Thank you, Dougal." Savannah held out the bag. "Do you want one?"

"Those are all for you. All of them." He leaned back and crossed his arms over his chest. "You need to eat."

"You heard the man." Chels pulled the wheeled bed-side table over and put a plate and several napkins on it. "Dive in."

She ate while the mothers discussed the pattern of Orla's knitting project. Once Momma had learned it was a baby blanket, she'd taken a keen interest in learning all about knitting. Orla was all too eager to share the process. Nola, however, was gleefully giggling over the tabloid paper she was reading.

A blueberry muffin and peach streusel later and Savannah was feeling much better.

Until she heard the unmistakable sound of her father's voice.

"Is that Dad?" Chelsea was up, off the bed, staring at their mother. "Momma, what did you do?"

The guilt on their mother's face said it all. "I was so

worried. We all were. I know I shouldn't have involved him, but he is your father."

"According to him, he's not," Chelsea snapped. "Or have you forgotten his parting comments?"

Savannah hadn't.

From the stony set of Angus's jaw, he hadn't, either. Her father had been horrible to her, and the allegation he'd made about Angus had been beyond offensive.

"I'm sure he regrets all of that," Angus murmured, taking her hand. "Are you okay? You're the one that matters here. Not him." He was watching her intently. "I can tell him not to come in."

Would her father listen?

Dougal stood. "I can take care of that."

"Momma, I can't believe you." Chelsea ran a hand over her short platinum locks, a telltale sign that their father's presence stirred up her insecurities, too. "She's not just supposed to eat. She's supposed to avoid stress, remember?"

"I'll go talk to him." Lana stood. "Thank you, Dougal." She left the room.

Everyone fell quiet as an unintelligible conversation took place outside of her room. From the pitch and tone, her father sounded almost agreeable.

"Should we leave?" Orla stood. "I don't want to get into family business. But I sure don't want to leave you without backup."

"Dougal and I will stay." Angus spoke for his braced and ready brother. "You and Aunt Nola can go down to the cafeteria for a bit."

"Everything will be okay, sweetie." Orla patted her foot. "I'm hoping he's come to throw himself at your feet and beg for your forgiveness. He'd be a fool not to."

"I'd like to give the man a piece of my mind," Nola muttered as they left.

"You going to be okay, Chels?" Savannah could see how tense her sister was.

"You don't need to worry about me. Actually, I forbid you to worry about me." Chels came around to the other side of the bed and took her hand. "Angus is right. The only thing that matters here is you."

Chelsea was on one side, Angus on the other, and Dougal stood against the wall at the foot of the bed. "This is what it must feel like to have bodyguards." She tried to tease.

Angus squeezed her hand.

"Except we all love you. Which makes us ten times more dangerous than a hired bodyguard." Chelsea sighed.

She didn't dare risk looking at Angus then; her damn heart monitor was already letting them know she was flustered. Chelsea meant well, but it wasn't true. Angus cared about her well-being and the babies, but he didn't love her. He'd never said anything to lead her on or imply otherwise. She was the one who'd fallen head over heels for the man.

She smoothed the sheet over her stomach.

"Savannah?" Her father didn't sound like her father. He didn't look like his usual, put-together self, either. His hair was a mess. His shirt was rumpled. He hadn't shaved in some time. "You okay, sweet girl?"

She wasn't going to cry. She wasn't. He'd caused enough tears. He didn't deserve any more of hers.

He barely acknowledged Chelsea and entirely ignored Angus as he reached her bedside. "I know you probably don't want me here, but I had to make sure you were okay. I had to see it with my own two eyes."

She took a steadying breath. "I'm fine."

"You're strong." He nodded. "You always have been."

She was feeling anything but strong at the moment. Or fine. She was tired. Tired of pretending to be strong and okay. Nothing was okay. She had a sinking feeling nothing would ever be okay again.

WATCHING RICHARD BARRETT walk into Savannah's hospital room was an exercise in self-control. He didn't want to physically attack the man, for the most part, but he was going to have to make an effort to school his features. One look or smirk or cocked eyebrow could trigger Barrett—just like it had the last time they were all together. Savannah didn't need that. Hell, Savannah didn't need any of this.

Damn Lana for bringing him here, and damn Barrett for coming. The man better have an apology ready to go.

"They taking care of you?" Barrett asked, scanning the monitors and equipment.

"She's getting excellent care." Lana smoothed the sheet over Savannah's feet.

"Good, good." He nodded. "I brought Dr. Garza, just in case. It can't hurt to have a second opinion."

Breathe. He could get upset at the bastard for meddling or be grateful the bastard was trying to give them all peace of mind.

"You think that's necessary?" Lana was studying Savannah.

"She's in the hospital." Barrett's gaze darted his way. "It seems appropriate."

The silence that followed thinned the air in the room until Angus knew he had to speak up. He could do this. "Your call, Savannah. It can't hurt to have a second opinion."

"No." Savannah pleated and unpleated the sheet with her fingers. "I guess not."

Barrett typed something on his phone, then nodded. "Okay. She's coming back now."

Dr. Garza was a middle-aged woman with a gentle smile. She shooed everyone out of the room and closed the door, leaving the hallway crowded and silent. Chelsea didn't last long, heading toward the cafeteria, mumbling something about a drink. Dougal stood, silent and imposing, like a sentinel beside Savannah's door.

He couldn't make out a single word they were saying, but it was impossible to ignore the heated conversation taking place between Lana and Richard. How Lana Barrett could tolerate the man was a mystery he had no interest in solving. She'd taken Savannah's side when it mattered. For Angus, that told him all he needed to know.

He stared up at the fluorescent lights overhead. What he wouldn't give for a walk in the open. Nothing but nature and fresh air. Which reminded him. "I was thinking we could use the tractor to cut a path around the fence line at the house? Give Savannah a level walking trail."

"Easy enough," Dougal agreed.

"A word?" Richard Barrett was standing before him.

"Richard." Lana Barrett's voice rose.

Angus took a deep breath. What more could the man possibly have to say? He didn't have the patience or the self-control to deal with the man.

Dr. Wurtz chose that moment to come around the corner. "Angus." He glanced at the closed door. "I was just coming to check in on Savannah."

"I appreciate that." Angus was about to make introductions, but Barrett beat him to it.

"I'm Savannah's father, Richard Barrett." His inspection of the young doctor wasn't exactly cordial. "And you are?"

"Savannah's doctor." He shook Barrett's hand.

"I see." Barrett's eyes narrowed as he gave the young

doctor a more thorough inspection. "How long have you been practicing medicine?"

"All done." Dr. Garza opened the door. "You can come in now." She saw Dr. Wurtz and offered her hand. "Are you her attending physician?"

"I am." Dr. Wurtz was slightly irritated now. "Perhaps we could have a brief consultation aside?"

"Perhaps we could do the same?" Barrett asked Angus. "Lana can keep Savannah company."

If Barrett was going to push this, he might as well get it over with. "Fine." He followed the man to the end of the hall. A large window looked out on the view of the concrete parking lot below. No trees. No grass. He felt more fenced in than ever. It didn't help his mood.

"Nothing has changed?" Barrett clasped his hands behind his back and stared blindly out the window. "You're still determined to go through with this."

"This?" He wasn't in the mood to make this easy for the man.

"This…this charade of whatever this is." He gestured back down the hall they'd just come from.

"As in take care of Savannah and the babies?"

Barrett closed his eyes, his jaw muscle so tight Angus wondered he didn't hear bone cracking.

"Why are you so dead set against it?" Angus couldn't stop himself. "I know I'm no Greg Powell, but I'm a good man. I will be a good father." And, if she'd have him, he'd try his hardest to be the best damn husband.

Barrett shook his head. "How long have you known my daughter now? Two weeks?"

Angus didn't answer. It wasn't relevant. Dammit, he knew what was in his heart.

"It takes more than two weeks for a banana to go bad. You can't expect me, or any sane person for that matter, to believe you know this is the life you want." Barrett still didn't look at him. "To understand what sort of lifelong commitment this is."

"No offense, Mr. Barrett, but it wouldn't make a difference if it was two weeks or two years. There are no guarantees in life. Or time limits. There's choosing a path and sticking with it. That's what I'm doing." He didn't owe the bastard anything more than that. "I love her. I won't let her down."

Barrett shook his head. "You don't know what that means. If you did, you'd send her back home where she'd have round-the-clock medical care. The best of the best. Dietitians that ensure she's getting the proper nutrients for herself and this pregnancy. She wouldn't be overtired to the point of collapse." When he did look at Angus, it wasn't anger on the man's face, it was fear. "If you really loved her, we wouldn't be having this discussion. You would have called me, not Lana. Your damn pride and selfishness wouldn't stand in the way of giving her the best."

He was so rattled, it took a minute for him to find the right words. "You keep saying if I really love her, I'll do what's best for her. To you, that means I have to give her up." He wasn't going to let the man twist things around. "You could arrange for her to have the best no matter where she is. The doctors, the dietitians, all of it. What's stopping you? You want the best for her, so give it to her. Here. Where she wants to be." He was done. He didn't take kindly to being manipulated or made to feel lower than dirt. "How about we go and hear what the doctors have to say."

"Are you sure that this is still what she wants?" Barrett stopped him in his tracks.

Angus stared at the man. He couldn't decide which was stronger, pity or loathing.

"Let's ask her," Barrett continued. "If she does, I'll take care of everything. Just like I said. But if there's a doubt or hesitation, maybe you should do a little soul-searching."

"Fine." Angus wasn't worried. Anything to shut this man up. He didn't linger a second longer. He headed back to Savannah's room, doing his best to shake off the whole damn conversation.

Savannah was sitting up with her feet dangling off the side of the bed. "What took you so long?"

"What's the news?" He took up his spot at her side and smiled. "You've got some color in your cheeks."

"Is Mr. Barrett..." Dr. Garza paused as Barrett walked into the room. "Now that you're all here. I reviewed Dr. Wurtz's notes and, after my own evaluation of Savannah, I agree with his assessment and plan of treatment."

"We need to continue to monitor Savannah's blood pressure. She should take her time getting up to make sure she's steady on her feet. Eat more frequently, good calorie-dense food, and stay hydrated, too. She's borderline dehydrated. Which is why we've given her some IV fluids." Dr. Wurtz turned to Savannah. "We have her scheduled for a two-week follow-up and will continue to have appointments every two weeks moving forward."

Angus could breathe easier then. "That's good. All good."

"No cause for alarm." She smiled up at him. "And we can go home."

"I'll have her discharge papers signed shortly." Dr. Wurtz nodded. "Do you have any questions or concerns?" He glanced at Savannah's father. "Mr. Barrett?" Barrett shook his hand. "Well, Angus, Savannah, I wish you a Merry Christmas and I'll see you in the New Year. But if you have any concerns, you can call me."

"Thanks, Doc." Angus shook the man's hand.

"I should be heading home, too." Dr. Garza looked at Barrett expectantly. "Tomorrow is Christmas Eve."

"Yes. I'll take you to the helipad." Barrett was torn—it was written all over his face.

"I'll wait in the hall, then." Dr. Garza followed Dr. Wurtz out.

"Are you leaving, Dad? You don't want to wait for Momma? Or Chelsea?"

"I doubt either of them will be too distressed by my leaving." Barrett came to the side of her bed. "I know I said some hard things, Savannah. I crossed a line. I forced your hand and I've regretted that every second since you left."

Angus figured that was as close to an apology as it was going to get. But he waited, knowing there was more to come.

"A lot was said and done out of passion so if something has changed, you're always welcome home." He cleared his throat. "Is this, being here, still what you want?"

Angus almost felt bad for the man.

"I... I don't know." Savannah's answer knocked the air from his lungs. "It's all been so fast."

What was she saying?

"So much has changed." She shrugged, almost apologetically. "I don't know."

"That's okay." Barrett patted her hand. "I understand."

Angus didn't. What the hell was happening? He was glad there was a chair close by. Better to sit than to fall over.

"You think on it." Barrett kissed her temple. "I'd best get Dr. Garza back to her family." He gave her hand a final pat and left.

Angus didn't know if Barrett was gloating or not. He couldn't move. He sat frozen, willing his heart to slow and his lungs to work. He had to breathe. Be calm. They'd promised to be honest with each other and she had. She wasn't sure. That's why she'd been acting so differently. All the times she'd avoided looking at him. The times she'd slide her hand from his. It made sense now. And, damn, did it hurt.

CHAPTER SEVENTEEN

OTHER THAN THE snap and pop of the fire burning, the great room was quiet. She sat, cuddled up with Gertie, wishing she could absorb some holiday spirit from the Christmas tree or the stockings Orla had added only today. Tomorrow was Christmas Eve. It was her favorite time of the year and she'd never been more miserable.

After tossing and turning, she'd given up. Just because she couldn't sleep didn't mean poor Chelsea shouldn't.

She sipped her glass of milk and finished off her second Christmas cookie. The babies approved. There were all sorts of rolls and flutters.

Gertie's head perked up and she stared at Savannah's stomach. She stood, sniffed, and sat again, staring up at Savannah with her head cocked to one side.

"Did they scare you?" She rubbed the dog behind the ear. "They like sugar. Just like their momma." She cradled the dog's head between her hands and pressed a kiss to her nose. "What am I going to do without you, Gertie?"

Gertie gave her a big doggy kiss right on the nose.

"Thank you." Savannah laughed.

"You and Gertie having a midnight snack?" Angus asked as he came into the room.

"Yep." Savannah did her best not to stare, but it was impossible. His hair was ruffled. His white undershirt hugged every muscle of his chest and stomach, and his flannel sleep pants hung dangerously low on his hips. It would be so much easier if she could turn off her feelings. She didn't want to be happy that he was here. She didn't want him to sit by her or smile at her. And she certainly didn't want to ache at the thought of him pulling her into his arms—or how much she wanted to give his low-hanging pants a tug.

"Solving the world's problems?" He didn't sit beside her. He sat in the leather recliner opposite her.

That was good. If she couldn't touch him, she stood a chance of not getting distracted—as Chelsea put it. "No." She reached for the gingerbread cookie. "I guess the triplets gave Gertie a kick or something. She was showing her disapproval."

He chuckled. "I imagine those kicks are only going to get stronger, Gert."

She nibbled on the gingerbread man's leg.

"I heard what you said, about doing without her." He sat back in the chair, holding tightly to the armrests. "I'm guessing you're not staying, then?" His voice was flat.

How could she? The longer she stayed, the more she'd fall in love with him. The more her heart would break when he didn't love her back. Her throat was too tight to speak, so she nodded.

He sat there like a statue. His hands were tightly gripping the arms of the chair. "What changed?" He didn't sound like himself. Was he mad? Shouldn't he be relieved?

She set her cookie aside and took a sip of milk. It did nothing to ease her throat. "I think it all happened so quickly. We both sort of jumped in without really taking a look at the big picture. The idea is nice, but the reality is…different."

"Oh?" He cleared his throat then, his fingers biting into the leather.

"The whole attraction thing clouded things up, I think.

Wanting doesn't last. And it can't sustain a family." She drew in a deep breath.

"I thought we agreed to give it, us, our all?" He sounded a little gruffer then. "We agreed to that."

"Angus…" She propped her head in her hands. "I'm not going to keep you from being their father. You don't need to worry about that. I give you my word."

"I was pretty sure you did that in the barn that night." He was definitely mad.

"We did. We *both* did." She shook her head. "Then things changed."

"What things, Savannah?" He was up, pacing in front of the fire. "I've been turning it over in my mind, and I can't figure out when, exactly, that change happened for you."

"Everything." She blurted it out, covering her face with her hands. She was not going to tell him how she felt. Being rejected would only make this ten times worse. "It doesn't matter, Angus. We'll still make co-parenting work."

Dougal came around the corner—it sounded like he was mumbling something about bears—and went straight to the kitchen. The door opened and closed and he didn't emerge.

"I don't understand, Savannah." Angus stopped pacing then. "What I wanted hasn't changed. It won't."

She stood slowly before she continued. "I'm giving you—both of us—what we want." She marched up to him, her temper flaring, while trying to keep her voice low. The last thing she wanted was the entire family involved. This was something that needed to be settled between the two of them.

"What are you talking about?" He shook his head.

"Just stop. It's okay. I get it. Neither one of us will be… brokenhearted if we call it quits."

"Savannah." He broke off and took a deep breath. "What makes you think you leaving is what I want?"

"Angus, you've never wanted to get married. Not ever. You point-blank told me you enjoyed being a bachelor." She wrapped her arms around herself. "Then everything happened with my dad and you had to take me in. It was so sweet of you. You are so sweet, Angus." She broke off before she could tell him she loved him. "But doing this, playing house, won't give us what we really want. You want space. I want love. Those things aren't compatible. And that's okay." It had to be okay. She couldn't change it. "We were going to be honest with one another. That's what we said."

"Playing house?" He stepped closer to her. "I'm trying to make sense of all this." He took a deep breath. "If I haven't been clear, then let me clear it up. All I want is you and the babies to be safe and looked after. I'm trying here—"

"I know." She sighed. "But it's not enough. Because of the babies, you're stuck with me." She was not going to cry. "I want more than that, Angus. I want to be someone's choice. And being here, settling, is a constant reminder that I'm not. It hurts...so much."

"I'll let you go if that's what you want, but that'll be your choice. Not mine. Every time, I will choose you." He cradled her face. "Dammit, Savannah, I want you. I want you here, with me, until you're old and gray and as obnoxious as Aunt Nola."

"But...you said..." Now she was confused.

"I should have said something, but I didn't know how you felt." His thumb traced along her jaw. "I was scared the only reason you were staying with me was because of the babies."

"Because you..." She broke off then, his words falling into place. "You... You choose me?"

"Always." He nodded. "It'll hurt like hell, but I'll respect whatever *you* choose. Even if it's not me."

She opened her mouth, but words failed her.

"If you need time—" his hands slid from her face "—you take whatever time you need. There's no pressure here. No stress." He shook his head. "Damn, stress is the last thing you need right now." He led her back to the couch. "Sit, put your feet up. I'll get you something to eat."

Dougal emerged from the kitchen, a pie dish in one hand and a carton of chocolate milk in the other. "The bear wake you, too? The damn wall's shaking, I swear it. How a person's supposed to sleep through that, I don't know." He sat in the recliner and started eating pumpkin pie. "Want some?"

Savannah sat and put her feet up, stunned. Gertie jumped up and turned in a few circles before curling up in her lap.

"No. She needs protein." Angus headed into the kitchen.

"To go along with your cookies." Dougal nodded at the remaining cookie. "Can't say that I blame you. They're good."

"Bear?" Savannah was still sifting through the whirlwind in her head. "I didn't think there were bears here."

"Oh, there are. Few and far between, but I was talking about the bear sleeping on the other side of my bedroom wall. Aunt Nola. Snores like a damn grizzly bear. You really didn't hear it out here?" He shook his head. "Gonna start sleeping in here or in the barn if I'm going to get any sleep."

A few minutes later, Angus came back from the kitchen. "It's a ham and cheese croissant from The Coffee Shop." He set the plate on the table. "And water." He handed her the glass. "To keep yourself hydrated."

She took the glass.

"Where did you find that?" Dougal asked.

"I hid it. It's for Savannah." Angus didn't look at his brother.

"I just asked," Dougal huffed. "I did buy them for her."

Angus sat on the coffee table in front of her. "You can ask Dougal, if you don't believe me."

Savannah shook her head.

"You sure?"

"Ask me what?" Dougal yawned.

Savannah shook her head again.

"I'll say one more thing and let you have space." He cleared his throat, leaning closer to her. "Your dad wants you to come home." He ran his fingers through his hair. "I know he'll make sure you're taken care of. If you have to leave, I guess I'd rather you went there. Then I won't worry about you all. I mean, I will..." He stopped. "I love you, Savannah, and I want you to be happy. You deserve to be happy." He pressed a kiss to her forehead and headed back to his room.

"Yeah, go on and sleep," Dougal called after him. "In your nice quiet room." He set the pie plate on the floor and leaned back in the chair.

Savannah went back to staring at the tree, hope and wonder and love rising up until her chest felt like it would burst right open.

"You better eat that or he'll be pissed off." Dougal pointed at her plate. "The only thing on his mind is making sure you eat and drink and sleep." He chuckled. "It's funny, seeing him like this."

Savannah took a bite of the croissant.

"I guess it's good practice for when the babies get here." He yawned and rubbed a hand over his face. "He's going to be insufferable, then."

She smiled, eating more of her croissant. "I'll take it."

"Thank goodness. If you didn't, he'd be like a lost puppy looking for someone to follow around and love all over." He shuddered. "Spare me from ever falling in love."

She laughed then, earning a look from Gertie. "It's not so bad, Dougal. Especially if they love you back. You should try it sometime." She ate the rest of the croissant and cuddled Gertie until long after Dougal was snoring—very bearlike himself—and the sun was starting to come up.

Angus hadn't bothered trying to sleep. It would be pointless anyway. Instead, he'd dressed and planned to head down to the barn. Instead, he'd taken a detour. Savannah was curled up on the couch, sound asleep—Gertie on her hip. He'd shooed Gertie aside, scooped her up, and carried Savannah to his bed. She sighed, rolled over, and buried her face in his pillow.

Damn, but she was pretty. Now all he had to do was get her to listen to doctor's orders and sleep. Of course, he needed to do the same.

He frowned as he tucked the blankets around her. Last night had cleared up a few things, but he'd gone about it all the wrong way. He'd dumped his wants on her long before he'd figured out what she wanted. That was something he'd learned about her—she put everyone else first.

He'd meant it when he said he wanted her to have what she wanted. He wanted her to be happy. He hoped like hell he could make her happy.

He crept out of the bedroom and headed down to the barn. If he couldn't sleep, he might as well find something useful to do.

He turned the horses out into the corral. They ran and jumped, happy to be out of their stalls and have a little freedom. They nickered and whinnied, as if saying their good mornings to one another. He smiled at the thought. Maybe he spent too much time with animals—Dougal more or less fit in that category. Animals were easy to read. People, not so much.

He headed into the barn, hung his coat on a nail, and started cleaning out the stalls. Harvey would be tickled pink to have a day's break and the physical work would do him some good.

It was Christmas Eve and, depending on what Savannah had to say, he had big plans. His meemaw's ring was in his coat pocket, ready to be put on Savannah's finger. But if she said she wanted to go home, he'd try not to beg her to stay. The very idea of her not being here was unbearable. He didn't know what the hell he'd do if that became his reality.

Not going to think about it.

He stabbed at the old hay with the pitchfork and threw himself into his work.

Christmas Eve had always been a big deal. It had been the same for as long as he could remember. All of Pa's favorites. Ma spent the day slow-roasting a turkey. She insisted on making the rolls from scratch, even though Nola swore store-bought rolls tasted just as good. There would be fresh green beans, glazed carrots, and butter-roasted potatoes for sides. And then there'd be the pies. Nola might suggest store-bought rolls, but she'd never forgive a person who served store-bought pie.

He'd have to make sure Ma and Nola didn't let Savannah do too much. She loved that they were giving her the chance to cook, and she was trying so damn hard. He'd managed to eat her undercooked chicken potpie without incident. He'd tried to feed Gertie the meat loaf, but even the dog tucked tail and ran. On both counts, Nola had taken a bite and announced neither was fit for consumption—

scraping them both into the trash. But Savannah had taken it in stride and tried again.

No matter where he started, his thoughts always came back to her.

He pulled his handkerchief from his pocket and wiped the sweat from his face. The sun was up now, shining down so bright he suspected it'd be a warm Christmas Eve. He hoped Savannah wouldn't be too disappointed. She liked a more winter wonderland vibe.

His stomach was growling and he could use a cup of coffee, but he'd rather finish what he started. He took off his flannel shirt and hung it over his coat, then went back to work. He finished the stall and turned to find Savannah watching him.

"I brought you coffee." She held out a steaming mug. "It might not be as hot as you like it." She was in her green-and-red-and-white Christmas print pajamas—one of the things she'd been most excited about the day they'd gone shopping. Her hair was loose and her cheeks were flushed and his heart kicked into overdrive.

"Thank you." He set the pitchfork aside and took the coffee. "You warm enough?"

She nodded.

He sipped the coffee, uncertain. "Feeling okay?"

She nodded, smiling up at him. "Thank you for putting me to bed."

"You didn't look too comfortable on the couch. Plus, Dougal was snoring." Angus shook his head.

"I'm wondering how much of the snoring is Aunt Nola bear and how much is him." Savannah wrapped her arms around herself.

"Here." He pulled his shirt off the nail and handed it to her.

She slipped it on over her nightgown. "Thanks."

Watching her bury her nose in his shirt and smile gave him the courage to say, "If you don't want to talk about last night, just say so."

She looked at him, but her mouth stayed shut.

"I don't want to sway you one way or the other." He cleared his throat and stepped closer to her. "But I realized I didn't say something last night that I should have said a long time ago." He took another step.

She blinked, those big brown eyes watching his every move.

"I love you." He was close enough to touch her. "That's why I want you to choose what makes you happy. Because you being happy will make me happy—even if we're not together."

Her arms wrapped around his waist as she pressed herself against him. "I don't want us to be apart. I love you, Angus McCarrick." The words were almost a sigh. "I don't want to be anywhere other than right here. With you. I was only leaving because I wanted you to be happy."

"Good." He held on to her as if his life depended on it. "For all my big talk, I don't think I could let you go."

She laughed against his chest.

He pressed his nose to the top of her head, savoring her scent with every breath. Everything would be okay now. "Hold on." He moved closer to his coat, but he didn't let her go. "I'd come up with this big plan for tonight." He reached into the coat pocket and found the ring. "After you told me you were staying, which I've been praying for, I was going to lead you to the Christmas tree and drop down on one knee. But I'm not ready to let go of you just yet, so…" He took her hand and held it up. "Will you marry me, Savannah?"

Her smile lit him up from the inside. It was pure joy and love. For him. "I will marry you, Angus."

"Will you marry me? Soon?" he asked, sliding the ring on her finger. "One of the Mitchell brothers is licensed to do weddings…" He stopped. "I understand if you'd rather something big and fancy—"

"I can't think of anything I want more than to be Mrs. McCarrick for New Year's." She stood on tiptoe to kiss him, but paused. "You feel that?"

It was a solid thump against his stomach. "I do." He chuckled.

"They're just saying good morning to their daddy." She stared up at him.

"Something to look forward to every morning." He brushed the lightest kiss against her lips. "And that." He kissed her again. "And having you in my arms. Where you belong."

"I love you, Angus," she breathed. "You've given me everything I've always wanted."

"Damn straight." He pressed a hand against her cheek. "I'll try to make you happy every damn day." He kissed her again, letting his lips cling a little longer.

"Angus." She gasped.

"Mmm?" he murmured, his mouth sealing with hers until she melted into him.

"Don't be mad at me, but…"

He lifted his head. "But what?"

"It's not that I don't want to kiss you—I do." She smiled. "But I'm *really* hungry."

Angus threw back his head and laughed.

"You're not mad?" She laughed, too.

"No, ma'am." He slid his arm around her waist and led her from the barn. "Feeding you and those babies takes priority."

"But after breakfast—"

"There will be a whole lot of kissing." He nodded.

"And then we'll be married tonight." She leaned her head against his chest. "So, I'll be back in our bed."

"I can hardly wait." His heart was thundering. "But I know it's worth waiting for." He pressed a kiss to her temple. "Everything about you is worth waiting for."

"Tell me again that you love me."

"I'll tell you again. You're going to get sick of hearing it."

"I won't. I promise. I love you." There was so much tenderness on her face he didn't doubt it.

"I love you." He kissed her again. "So damn much."

EPILOGUE

"YOU DON'T LOOK like you gave birth six weeks ago." Chelsea hugged her sister. "You look gorgeous."

"You're lying. But I love you anyway." Savannah was exhausted. Even at the end of her pregnancy, she'd never been so tired. Or happy.

"Where are the wee ones?" Chelsea scanned the room. "I was expecting lots of screaming and chaos."

"Angus and Dougal are taking them for a walk. It's part of the daily routine." And it was adorable. Who knew Dougal would be such a pushover when it came to the triplets? "Overall, it hasn't been that bad, really. Orla and Nola and Momma have been amazing." Which was true. The three of them took shifts, making sure Savannah and Angus had time to sleep and bathe and have a minute to themselves—little things that made such a big difference. "Dad's tried, too. I think it's given him a whole new appreciation for Mom."

"That's good. She deserves it. Dad changing diapers. I can't picture *that*."

"Oh, I didn't say he'd changed any diapers. He gets greener than I did when I was pregnant."

Chelsea laughed. "That I can picture. So, are you excited about your date?" She bobbed her eyebrows. "You know, some quality couple time."

"I am." Savannah bobbed her eyebrows right back.

"Look at you, being all naughty." Chelsea laughed. "I approve."

"Well, that can't be good," Dougal said as he walked through the front door. "Chelsea."

"Oh, hush. I'm not here to see you anyway." Chelsea brushed him aside, cooing, "Ooh, they're so big. How did you three muffins get so big in two weeks?"

"Lots of eating and sleeping and loving." Savannah scooped up little Henry from the old-fashioned pram and handed him to Chelsea.

"Don't forget the diapers." Angus chuckled. "So many diapers."

"Who's my favorite nephew? You still look like an old wise man, Henry." Chelsea cradled him close. "I just know you're already full of insightful things to say. When you start talking, that is."

Tabitha squeaked.

"I got you." Dougal picked up the pink-swaddled baby girl. "You're fine."

"They do like this stroller better." Angus smiled as he lifted little Emilia up. She was wriggling and squirming in her blanket. "I guess it's because you're all next to each other. Makes you feel like you did with your momma." He pressed a kiss against the top of Emilia's head.

Savannah hadn't thought it was possible to find her husband more handsome or sexy. The moment he looked at his babies, she knew she'd been wrong. Somehow, some way, Angus got sexier with each passing day. It was the way he loved them. And not just the babies, but her, too. He didn't shy away from showing or verbalizing his love. Nothing made her happier than seeing the joy on his face when he was spending time with them.

"I know that look." Angus was smiling—that devastating smile.

She didn't bother denying it. She was definitely thinking about how nice it was going to be to have a whole night
alone with him. Assuming they could stand being away
from the babies for a whole night. It wasn't that the babies
wouldn't be loved and coddled and more than taken care
of, it was that they hadn't been away from them that long
since they were born.

She leaned against Angus's side, reaching up to tuck
the blanket beneath Emilia's chin. "She's pretty perfect,
isn't she?"

"They all are." Angus kissed her temple. "You did good.
More than good."

"I had a little help." She smiled up at him.

"Okay, you two, the sweetness factor is getting a little
nauseating in here." Chelsea shook her head. "Put poor
Emilia in the bouncy seat. Dougal and I've got this covered. So, shoo."

"Nola's asleep. Orla and Momma should be back from
the store any minute now." Savannah watched Willow take
up her spot beside the bouncy seats. She'd transferred her
devotion to the babies now, following them wherever they
went and alerting the closest adult if they squeaked or
fussed or needed something.

Gertie, on the other hand, still preferred being the baby.
She took every opportunity to claim a lap. Currently, she
was squeezing in between Dougal and Chelsea on the
couch.

Angus finished buckling Tabitha into the bouncy seat
and stood. "Need anything?"

"We've got this. Go on, Pickle." Chelsea didn't even
look up. She was too besotted with Henry.

"I know their schedule." Dougal nodded, patting Tabitha
on the back and using his foot to rock Emilia's bouncy seat.

Angus took her hand. "You going to make it?"

"Are you?" Savannah asked, squeezing his hand.

"A night alone with you?" He scratched his well-groomed beard. "Hell, yes." He pulled her against him to press a gentle kiss against her lips.

"Seriously, guys." Chelsea groaned. "Your bags are in the truck. Go on. Just don't get pregnant again for a while, okay?"

Dougal chuckled then.

"Oh, Chels." Savannah tugged Angus after her. "Bye."

They could hear Dougal and Chelsea laughing as Angus pulled the front door closed behind them.

"Now, where were we?" Angus pulled her close, his kiss more insistent this time.

She melted into him. It had been so long. "It's weird not to have a massive belly separating us."

"I didn't mind the belly." He rested his forehead against hers. "I guess we should hit the road before Ma and Lana get back."

Savannah slipped free of his hold and led him to the truck. "Excellent point. We'd lose a whole hour, at least."

"Why, Mrs. McCarrick, you in a hurry?" He was grinning.

"Only to get there. Then I want to take everything nice and slow." She hopped into the truck's passenger seat. "Is that okay with you, Mr. McCarrick?"

He kissed her once, then again. "It is. I like the way you think, Mrs. McCarrick."

"Good, because you're stuck with me." She counted her blessings every day.

"Damn straight." He kissed her again. "You know I wouldn't have it any other way."

* * * * *

Hill Country Home
Kit Hawthorne

MILLS & BOON

Kit Hawthorne makes her home in south central Texas on her husband's ancestral farm, which has been in the family for seven generations. When not writing, she can be found reading, drawing, sewing, quilting, reupholstering furniture, playing Irish penny whistle, refinishing old wood, cooking huge amounts of food for the pressure canner, or wrangling various dogs, cats, horses, and people.

Dear Reader,

There's a special kind of comfort in those beloved food and drink establishments where the staff know you by name. Over the years I've been blessed with many of these—Gerald's Donut in Oklahoma City, where my grandmother used to take me on weekends; Richard's Restaurant in Harlingen, where I first learned the joy of being a "regular"; and the Starbucks in Lake Dallas where I used to go to write while my daughters were in ballet. Naturally, such places are always finding a way into my stories.

Tito's Bar has been a favourite gathering place for the residents of Limestone Springs all the way back to the first Truly Texas book. A big reason for that is Tito himself. He's always available to listen to people's troubles and offer counsel while serving them drinks.

Jenna's been hanging around for a few books now, too. She's capable and dependable, but nobody knows much about her life before she came to Limestone Springs.

I'm excited to finally bring Tito and Jenna out of the background and give them a love story of their own. I hope you enjoy it.

Kit

DEDICATION

To my mum, who taught me by example
the meaning of grace.

ACKNOWLEDGMENTS

Many thanks to those who answered my
questions about working in restaurants,
breweries and bars, particularly my husband,
Greg, and my daughter Grace. There's a whole
lot that goes on behind the scenes to keep
things running smoothly so customers can
come in and feel comfortable, whether they're
sipping coffee while working on their laptops or
kicking back with a beer and a burger
at the end of a long day.

Thanks also to David Martin for information
about Formula 1 racing and flashy sports cars,
and to my cousin Colby Langford for his help
with police procedure. As always, many
thanks to my critique partners Mary Johnson,
Cheryl Crouch, David Martin, Janalyn Knight,
Willa Blair and Nellie Krauss, and to my editor,
Johanna Raisanen, for their invaluable insight
and encouragement.

CHAPTER ONE

LALO'S KITCHEN WAS really hopping tonight, with every booth and table full and the back patio crammed to capacity. A crowd stood closely packed just inside the glass front of the old downtown building, waiting to be seated. Seemed as though the entire town of Limestone Springs had unanimously selected that evening to dine at Lalo's. Beyond the pass-through, Tito's Bar was doing a brisk business as well.

Jenna Hamlin balanced a loaded tray high above her head as she threaded her way through the crowded room. One of her servers had called in sick that afternoon. Luke, the other manager, had come in on his evening off to pitch in and was now busily bussing tables, but the wait staff was still spread way too thin.

She reached the guy sitting alone at the two-top over by the exposed brick wall and brought her tray down to waist level.

"Here you are, sir," she said, setting the glass in front of him. "One sweet tea. And your loaded nachos should be out in a few minutes."

Her mind was already racing two or three steps ahead. She had two entrées and a basket of cheese curds to deliver to the couple at the next table, and drink orders to take from the party of four that had just been seated in the corner booth. So when the guy asked her a question, it threw her off her rhythm.

She stopped in midstep and turned back around. "I'm sorry?" she asked.

He spoke up, louder this time. "I said, *did you stick your finger in my tea?*"

Then he sat back and smirked.

Slowly his meaning broke over her. He looked so pleased with himself, with his round blue eyes and toothy grin—as if he'd said something clever, as if Jenna ought to be flattered by the suggestion that she could sweeten tea with the touch of her finger.

Jenna had seen this guy before in Lalo's Kitchen. He had one of those names made of initials—C.J. or T.J. or something. He liked to talk, especially to the female wait staff. Only a few days earlier, Jenna had watched Veronica, one of her part-timers, trying desperately to get away from him, a forced smile pasted on her face, as he droned on and on.

I didn't want to be rude, Veronica had told Jenna after finally making her escape. *He is a customer, after all.*

That's why he thinks he can get away with it, Jenna had replied. *He's taking advantage of that customer-is-always-right crap and using the power imbalance to gratify his ego. Don't let him get away with that. Be polite but firm, and if that doesn't work, come get me or Luke, or even Tito from next door. We'll back you up.*

Veronica had looked doubtful. She was young yet, only a senior in high school. Jenna was thirty-two, with years of experience waiting tables and tending bar during college, as well as other experience with men who abused power.

Now was her time to shine, to put all that wisdom into practice.

She gave Sweet Tea Guy a quick, cool smile, just enough to show that she got the joke without implying that she thought it was funny. "No, sir," she said. "Our sweet tea is sweetened with a simple syrup made from cane sugar."

His grin widened. "But why go to all that trouble when you can sweeten it yourself?" He waited a beat, then added, "You know. Because you're so sweet."

Either he was too obtuse to take a hint, or he simply didn't care. It amounted to the same thing.

Jenna pushed down the rising wave of annoyance. She didn't want to appease the guy, but she also didn't want to lose her cool. Getting mad would just give him power over her. She would be polite, unruffled, firm.

"No, sir," she said again. "That wouldn't work, and it wouldn't be sanitary. Is there anything else I can do for you?"

"Well, you can sit down here with me, and smile at me while I drink it," said Sweet Tea Guy. "Make it go down easier."

Jenna didn't dignify this with a reply.

"Enjoy your drink," she said, then turned and walked away.

She delivered the entrées and cheese curds to the other table, took the drink orders at the booth, cleared some dirty dishes and took them to the washing station, narrowly avoiding a collision with Lalo Mendoza, the restaurant's owner. Lalo was the cousin of Tito Mendoza, who owned the bar next door. Like Luke, Lalo had come in this evening to help, but unlike Luke, he was merely getting in the way without contributing anything, standing around with his hands on his hips and a worried expression on his face. Jenna finessed her way past him, then headed back to the break room to check on Halley.

Any time Jenna was at Lalo's Kitchen, Halley was there too—which meant Halley was there for roughly half her waking hours in any given week. Between rush times, when the dining room was mostly empty, Halley sat out front, reading, doing her schoolwork, wiping down tables, wrapping silverware. But whenever the dining room started to fill up, Jenna sent her to the break room, which not only freed up valuable table space but also kept Halley away from obnoxious customers like Sweet Tea Guy.

The situation wasn't ideal, but there were worse alternatives. At age twelve, Halley was legally old enough to stay home by herself while Jenna worked, but there was no way on God's green earth that Jenna was letting Halley get farther away from her than sprinting distance. That was how it had been for the past year and a half, and how it would continue for the foreseeable future.

The building that now housed Lalo's Kitchen had once been a law office, but that had been eight years ago, well before Jenna's time. She'd only ever known it in its present form, beautifully renovated in a pleasant blend of modern comfort and retro style. The exposed brick wall on the left side of the big open dining room continued down a long hallway that made a straight shot to the back of the building, with doorways on the right. Jenna went down the hallway, backing against the wall to make way for Clint, another part-time server, who was carrying a loaded tray to the dining room. She passed the kitchen, where Abel, the cook, was lifting a metal basket of fragrant, glistening sweet potato fries out of the deep fryer. Next came the two restrooms, followed by a third door, topped by a sign that said Employees Only. This led to a passageway connecting Lalo's Kitchen to Tito's Bar, with access to two break rooms, two offices, and a closet of cleaning supplies shared by both businesses.

Jenna entered the passageway, then opened the door to the break room belonging to Lalo's Kitchen.

It was a small but comfortable space, with a narrow

fridge shoehorned in at the end of a wall of efficient cab-
inetry. Leftover cake from Clint's birthday stood on the
counter next to a stack of disposable plates. Another wall
was taken up by two rows of cubbies with employees'
names written on labels in Veronica's pretty hand-letter-
ing script. There was even a cubby for Halley, filled with
schoolbooks, notebooks, sketchbooks and leisure reading.

But Halley herself was nowhere in sight.

Jenna backed up through the Employees Only door,
which hadn't yet shut behind her. The restroom doors were
both slightly ajar, and the lights were off.

She turned the other way, looking down the remainder
of the hallway to the glass back door. She'd never liked that
door. It led to the patio, the space of which was divided by
vine-covered columns and trellises into lots of cozy little
room-like areas. Anyone could slip in from there while
Jenna was occupied in the front and reach the break room
without her ever knowing.

A sound from the passageway made her jump. There
was Halley, coming out of the break room of Tito's Bar,
holding a canned soda in one hand and a paperback book
in the other, with one finger marking her place.

Jenna hadn't had time to build up much of a panic,
but her knees went weak with relief and she had to lean
against a wall.

"What were you doing in there?" she asked, fear sharp-
ening her voice.

Halley tossed back her straight blond hair. "Tito told
me he got me some of those sodas I like, so I went to his
break room to get one."

A quiver of irritation ran down Jenna's spine. She didn't
like for Halley to go into areas that properly belonged to
the bar, at least during business hours. Besides the safety

issues, she felt sensitive about bringing up a child so close to a bar.

Of course, Tito's wasn't really a *bar* bar. Yes, it did have the word *bar* right there in the name—Tito's Bar. But it stood right next to Lalo's Kitchen, with a big pass-through doorway connecting the two businesses about halfway down the connecting wall, which gave it the vibe of a bar and grill, or even a European tavern, rather than a straight-up bar. You could bring your craft beer from Tito's over to your table at Lalo's, or take your burger from Lalo's to your spot at Tito's, and pay for your purchases at either cash register. And as Tito himself often said, people who were willing to pay eight dollars for a beer generally weren't looking to get drunk. Still, the place did sell hard liquor, and have the occasional three-sheets-to-the-wind customer.

"You know, we have a full selection of craft sodas on tap right here in the restaurant that you can drink for free," Jenna said.

Halley shrugged. "I like these ones from H-E-B. Tito got them just for me. But the box they come in is too deep to fit in our break room fridge. So he put them in *his* break room fridge and said I could come get one anytime I want."

"Take a few out at a time and keep them in our fridge," said Jenna. "I don't want you going back and forth between the restaurant and the bar."

"But Tito's fridge is, like, twelve feet away from ours!"

"It's in a different building. Anyway, I don't want you leaving the break room at all without asking me first."

They were rash words, and she knew she'd made a mistake the instant she heard them coming out of her mouth. Halley stared at her in disbelief. "Seriously? You want me to ask permission every time I go to the restroom? That doesn't even make sense. I'd have to leave the break room to begin with before I could find you in the dining room to ask permission. And that's if you're even *in* the dining room. Sometimes you fill in at bartending, which means I'd have to go to the bar to track you down—and you don't want me to go into the bar."

Jenna's head swam. She didn't have time to quibble over semantics; she had to get back to work. But she couldn't walk away without fixing this.

"You don't have to ask permission to go to the restroom," she said. "But for everything else, find me and ask first."

"What do you mean, *everything else*? You just told me to stay out of Tito's break room. Where else am I going to go?"

Jenna sighed. "Look, I know it doesn't seem fair for you to be stuck in the break room for hours on end. But that's how it has to be right now."

"Why?" Halley asked.

"What do you mean, why? You know why. You can't be too careful."

"Yes, you can."

Halley wasn't whining or cajoling. She was as cool and composed as Jenna had been with Sweet Tea Guy.

"*What* did you say?" Jenna asked, putting some starch in her tone, in a last-ditch hope that Halley would back down.

Halley did not back down.

"I said yes, you can. You *can* be too careful. If you're so afraid of crowds that you never leave your house, or so scared of doctors that you refuse to go to the hospital when you're hurt, or so worried about food poisoning that you never eat food and end up starving to death, then you're too careful. I'm just saying."

She was right, of course. It was exactly the sort of thing

Jenna would have said to her own mother at that age, in pretty much the exact same words.

Jenna stared at Halley, and Halley stared right back. When had Halley gotten so *tall*? She was almost eye to eye with Jenna now. It was almost like looking in a mirror. That hair, those cheekbones, that hard set to her chin, were eerily like Jenna's own.

The unflinching gaze of the bright blue eyes, though—that was all Chase.

Jenna drew herself up as tall as she could. "This isn't that and you know it. I just want you safe, Kara. Okay?"

"Halley."

"What?"

"I'm not Kara, I'm Halley."

Jenna shut her eyes. She wanted to scream. What was happening? How had this situation gotten so far outside of her control?

"I know," she said. "I'm sorry. Just be safe, okay, Halley?"

"Okay, Mother," Halley said with a tiny sigh.

She managed to pack a lot of subtext into that sentence, foremost of which was, *You're not my mother.* Halley had never said those words to Jenna, not out loud, but Jenna could feel them in the air.

Halley had started calling Jenna Mother when she was four years old, long before either of them could have possibly suspected that Jenna would one day be her legal guardian. Halley had gone on calling Kara Mom, but by some odd child logic, she'd found this other word that meant the same thing and decided to use it for Jenna. Kara hadn't liked it much, but she hadn't been able to stop Halley from doing it, and eight years later Halley was still calling Jenna Mother. Sometimes the name had a warm, affectionate feel to it. Other times, like now, it sounded formal and stiff.

Halley went to the correct, Jenna-approved break room and closed the door behind her. The whole thing was surreal, as if Jenna were watching herself at that age, shutting her bedroom door in her own mother's face.

Somehow she'd never envisioned Halley going through a back-talking, authority-challenging stage. Halley was supposed to be immune to all that. She'd seen so many ugly things at such an early age that she was supposed to be grateful just to be in a stable environment, and happy to follow the rules because they were there for her protection.

She used to cling to Jenna whenever Kara came to pick her up, her voice shrill with desperation. *No, please! Don't let her take me away. I want to stay with you!*

It had been like ripping her heart out to let Kara pry off those clinging little arms and take Halley back to the house the two of them had shared with Chase—a dank, disorderly, comfortless house full of brooding silences and ugly outbursts.

Halley didn't cling to Jenna anymore. There was no need now that the two of them were together all the time. The stable, peaceful home life with a predictable schedule, no yelling and plenty of food in the fridge was now the everyday life. Maybe it had lost its value now that there was no horrible alternative to compare it to. Maybe it was confining and dull.

That could spell trouble. Halley wasn't even a teenager yet, but she would be soon. And sometimes teenagers did terrible things.

Jenna shook her head hard. What mattered was that she'd gotten Halley far away from the bad stuff. She'd changed their names, covered their tracks and started a whole new life for them several states away. If Halley started giving her a little lip, well, Jenna could deal with that.

She got back to the dining room just in time to see Clint bring Sweet Tea Guy his order of nachos. Sweet Tea Guy didn't look pleased about exchanging Jenna with Clint, but there was nothing he could do about it. In another twenty minutes—half an hour, tops—he'd be gone.

But he didn't leave. And as the evening passed and the crowd thinned, he moved on from sweet tea to beer.

Never mind, Jenna thought as she served and bussed tables. *You can't stay here forever. I can wait you out.*

One of the big TVs was rebroadcasting the Monaco Grand Prix. Jenna's dad used to watch Formula 1 racing, and when she was little she'd watch with him sometimes, curled up next to him in his big armchair. The Monaco Grand Prix was a notorious street circuit race, with very little room for passing, and no room at all for driver error. Jenna watched a red Alfa Romeo careening through the streets, skimming walls and buildings with mere millimeters to spare.

The sight flooded her with memories of another Alfa Romeo, also red, driven by a broodingly handsome boy with his left hand resting carelessly on the steering wheel and his right arm stretched out along the seat back, warm against Jenna's shoulders. That one had been a street car, not a race car, but with enough power in its engine to reach glorious adrenaline-spiking speeds with no trouble at all, hugging the turns of narrow country roads through the Blue Ridge foothills. She'd loved those drives—windows down, music cranked up, the world rushing by as the boy at the wheel gave her that heart-melting James Dean smile. Now the memory made her sick.

She closed out a party of seven, and after they left she saw Luke wiping down Sweet Tea Guy's table. Yay! Gone at last.

"Looks like things are finally calming down," Luke

told her. He was tough-looking, with his strong build and full beard, but with the kindest eyes Jenna had ever seen. "I'm going to head home."

"Okay. Thanks for coming in."

"No problem. Have you finished making out next week's schedule?"

"Not yet. I'll get it sent out tomorrow."

"All right." He started to go, then turned back. "Almost forgot. The chalkboard got messed up tonight. I think someone spilled a beer on it. I know Veronica usually does the chalkboard art, but she's gone home. Do you think Halley might want to give it a go? She's always drawing, and she's really good."

Jenna smiled. "I'll ask her. I'm sure she'll be happy to try her hand."

"Great. See you next week."

As she watched him leave, she sent up a quick prayer of thanksgiving that this most excellent of bosses was back on the job. Some months earlier, Luke had gotten fed up with Lalo's constant micromanaging and undermining and had actually quit without notice, just taken off his apron and walked out the door, right in the middle of a dinner rush. It had been a pretty dramatic thing for mild-mannered Luke to do, but as it turned out, he'd also been dumped by his girl and was at the end of his rope.

That had been the beginning of a busy and stressful time in Jenna's work life. To Lalo's credit, he'd pitched in, doing his best to take over Luke's duties, but he hadn't done them very well. He'd have done better to give Jenna more responsibility to help, which as it turned out was one of the many things Luke had wanted him to do all along, but he hadn't. It was as if Lalo had to prove that he knew best.

Lalo did not know best.

It was sorely trying for Jenna, being lectured on how

to do her job by someone who knew far less than she did about what that job actually entailed. The part-time employees weren't being managed properly; they slacked off, playing fast and loose with the schedule. Afraid to hold them accountable, Lalo tried instead to make them all happy by demanding more from his reliable employees. It was a case of the squeaky wheels getting all the grease, and the smooth-running, reliable wheels having their bearings ground down under excess strain.

Lalo's Kitchen had gone noticeably downhill. Food quality suffered, service got slower and sloppier, and the place always seemed to look dirty. Every day, Jenna heard from longtime customers complaining about the decline. They missed Luke, and his dog, Porter, and the way things had been under his management, and they weren't shy about saying so. Slowly, those longtime customers started dropping away.

Jenna liked to think that the final straw had been when she'd given Lalo her two weeks' notice. She hadn't wanted to leave the place that had been a major factor in bringing her to Limestone Springs to begin with, but it wasn't the same place anymore, and she'd said so. Lalo had replied, *Hold that thought*, and taken out his cell phone and called Luke right then and there, and begged him to come back. Luke had agreed to return only if certain demands were met, one of which was that Jenna get moved up to management. Lalo had complied. Since then, he'd mostly kept out of the way and let his managers manage. The customers had come back as well, revenue went up, and everything was better.

By closing time, Lalo's Kitchen had cleared out completely, and Tito's Bar was mostly empty. Standard policy for both restaurant and bar was to not rush customers out right at closing time. As long as they were behaving themselves, they could stay while the workers cleaned around them, and as long as they weren't drunk, Tito would go on serving them.

Jenna stood in the pass-through between the bar and the restaurant, leaning her shoulder against the casing as she faced the bar. It was quieter now, quiet enough to hear the music being piped into both spaces—a carefully crafted mix of hits and lesser-known favorites from the past few decades. Tito was in charge of playlists, and he took the responsibility very seriously. He knew exactly what to play to foster whichever mood he wanted to cultivate in the customers.

He was standing behind the bar now, slender and straight in his snowy white shirt and black vest, his perfect posture making him appear taller than he was. He always wore black and white at work. Jenna didn't know if he even had any other clothes. Light from the overhead pendant fixture shone on his hair, making it look impossibly glossy, like polished ebony.

His dark eyes swept over his domain. Long tables and benches ran almost the full length of the room. They were empty now except for one stein of beer on the table closest to the pass-through.

Jenna liked Tito's face, with its high forehead and cheekbones tapering to a long chin covered by a neatly trimmed beard, its thick black eyebrows and deep-set dark eyes, its wide, sensitive mouth. It was a thoughtful, intelligent, inquisitive face, with a look of query and searching about it—a responsive, mobile face, capable of being quirked into a rich variety of comical expressions. He was graceful and deliberate in movement, whether pouring a drink or running a damp cloth across the sparkling-clean surface of the bar top. At the end of the night, when he was counting money, he always put on a pair of old-fashioned gold-rimmed spectacles that perched unevenly on the end of his long bony nose, and looked at Jenna over the tops of them with his forehead all wrinkled up.

Everyone liked and trusted Tito. Customers confided in him, spilling out their troubles over their drinks. It was a stereotype, the sympathetic bartender, but justified in his case. There was something about him that inspired confidence, something deeply compassionate but also thoroughly rational, a razor-sharp intellect softened by self-deprecating humor and a sincere interest in other people.

Jenna understood the draw. She felt it herself. It would be so easy to confide in Tito, pouring out the whole messy history of how she and Halley had come to Limestone Springs, sharing the doubts that wracked her day and night, appealing to him for the wisdom and insight she knew he'd be happy to share, if only she'd ask.

But that could never happen. Her secrets had to stay secrets. She had to keep her new life, and Halley's, airtight. She couldn't afford to slip up.

Tito's eyes met Jenna's, and he smiled at her. It was the easy, casual smile of a good friend, but it sent a peculiar flutter through her heart. She smiled back.

She was about to turn around and head back to her own duties when someone appeared just beyond Tito, out of the hallway that ran along the far wall to the restrooms. It was Sweet Tea Guy. He crossed in front of the bar to the table closest to where Jenna was standing, picked up the beer stein and raised it to her, his grin as goofy as ever.

Jenna felt her own smile wilt.

Ordinarily, Jenna liked working closing shifts. She and Halley were both night owls, and homeschooling gave them the freedom to set their own hours. Her favorite time of day was after the last customer had left and the doors had been locked—especially on nights when Tito was closing, too.

And now here was Sweet Tea Guy, refusing to leave, ruining everything, the way inebriated guys always did.

Minutes passed. The part-timers did their end-of-shift cleaning tasks and went home. Luke left for the night, and so did Lalo. And still Sweet Tea Guy sat stubbornly in his spot, clutching his drink, refusing to budge.

Jenna went back to the break room. Halley was sitting on the tiny sofa with a book, her coltish legs bent at sharp angles. She looked up expectantly as the door opened.

"Sorry, you can't come out yet," Jenna said. "Some diehard is out here taking his time. He got a little inappropriate with me earlier, and I don't want you in the dining room until he leaves."

Halley scowled. "Can't you throw him out?"

"Not yet. We'll clean around him for as long as we can and hope he takes the hint and leaves on his own before it comes to that."

Halley let out a long, exasperated sigh—whether at Sweet Tea Guy for being so inconsiderate, or at Jenna for not throwing him out, or at Jenna for being so protective, was impossible to tell.

"It shouldn't be much longer," Jenna said with an optimism she did not feel. "Tito just switched the playlist over to indie pop."

Indie pop, according to Tito, was the genre to play when you wanted lingering customers to wind down and clear out. Ordinarily it worked like a charm, but Jenna suspected Sweet Tea Guy might be a tougher nut to crack.

"Lock the door behind me," she said.

Halley gave her an incredulous look.

"Do it," said Jenna. "I'll come get you when he's gone."

Halley clomped over to the door and pushed it shut.

As soon as she heard the dry click of the lock, Jenna shut her eyes and leaned her forehead against the door, suddenly exhausted.

Then she opened the door to the supply closet and started loading her cleaning cart. A clipboard hung from a hook on the side, with a checklist for all the tasks to be done at closing, and spaces for the closer to initial as each item was completed. Everything was right there, perfectly spelled out with no ambiguity. Luke had designed those checklists, and Jenna loved them.

Her back was to the doorway, but she saw the shadow fall from behind her. She turned. There was Sweet Tea Guy, blocking the exit. His grin was as wide as ever, but its goofiness had been replaced by something else.

"There you are, sweet thing," he said softly. "Let's have a little alone time, you and me."

As come-ons went, this one was pretty bald. It was insulting that he could possibly believe that Jenna or any other woman would take him up on it.

Her heart pounded hard, not with fear but with anger—against him and every other man who'd ever tried to take what wasn't his.

Jenna grabbed the push broom. She was ready to rumble. Sweet Tea Guy was messing with the wrong woman. He had no idea how thrilled she would be to take out her frustrations on someone who so thoroughly deserved it.

But before either of them could make a move, a calm voice spoke from the passageway.

"Sir, this is an employees-only area. We don't allow customers back here."

Jenna couldn't see who'd spoken, but she didn't have to. She would know that voice anywhere. It was rich in timbre, with a smooth, rolling cadence—the kind of voice used by advertisers to sell fine wines or luxury cars.

Sweet Tea Guy didn't even turn his head, just waved a dismissive hand. "It's all right, Tito," he said. "I know this girl. We're having us a little visit. Go on back behind your bar."

"No," Tito said. His voice was still calm, but the pitch had deepened, and he'd dropped the *sir*. "Come on, R.J. We're closed for business now. It's time for you to go home."

R.J. did turn then, shooting a scowl in Tito's direction. He was a big, tall man, probably a good fifty pounds heavier than Tito.

"I'll leave when I'm good and ready," he said. "Now go back to the bar and mind your own business."

"You'll leave now," said Tito.

R.J.'s hands curled into fists, and he lumbered off to the left, out of Jenna's field of vision. She heard the sound of a scuffle, followed by a yelp of surprise. She hurried through the doorway of the closet in time to see R.J. with his arm bent behind him, being frog-marched by the bartender down the passageway and around the corner.

"Hey!" R.J. barked. "What do you think you're doing?"

The break room door opened, and Halley's shocked face peeked out.

"Close the door!" Jenna shouted. "I told you to stay put and keep the door locked!"

Halley did not shut the door. She came out and crept close to Jenna, almost touching but not quite. Together, they followed Tito into the dining room.

"Get your hands off me!" said R.J. "Who do you think you are? Let go!"

He kept hurling abuse at Tito all the way across the dining room to the glass door, finishing up with how he was never going to spend another dime in Tito's Bar or Lalo's Kitchen again.

"Funny, I was just about to suggest that very thing myself," Tito said.

He tossed R.J. outside, shut the door behind him and turned the bolt.

R.J. stood on the sidewalk, rumpled and indignant, glaring at Tito through the glass. There was no trace of a grin now, goofy or otherwise. His face was red and twisted with rage.

Unfazed, Tito took out his phone and snapped R.J.'s picture, then tapped his screen a few times. "I'm adding R.J. to the *do not serve* group text," he said.

He didn't look the least bit rattled or shaken. He certainly didn't look as if he'd just bounced a much larger man out of a bar. He didn't even appear capable of doing such a thing, which was probably part of the reason why he was so successful at it. Customers at Tito's Bar were generally well-behaved, but whenever one of them did need to be removed from the premises, Tito was up to the task. People underestimated him at their peril.

R.J. straightened his shirt in an exaggerated way and walked off down the sidewalk, his steps weaving a bit from side to side.

Tito flipped the sign on the door to the Closed side and turned to face Jenna and Halley. "Sorry about all that," he said, picking up the abandoned beer stein and carrying it behind the bar. "R.J.'s always been a little on the obnoxious side, but tonight's the first time I've seen him cross the line. You all right?"

"I'm fine," said Jenna, but her voice shook a little, and a wave of weakness washed over her. She was still clutching the push broom. She leaned it against the back of a booth, steadied herself and said, "You didn't have to do that, you know. I could have handled it."

The words sounded ungracious in her own ears, but Tito

didn't seem to mind. He glanced at her over the bar top as he poured out the last of R.J.'s drink and said, "Okay."

Then he picked up the dedicated cell phone used for streaming music and started tapping. The strains of indie pop that had been coming through the speakers instantly ceased.

Tito looked at Jenna and smiled. "It's closing time," he said. "And you know what that means."

Jenna knew, all right. The best part of the night was about to begin.

CHAPTER TWO

FROM ACROSS THE ROOM, Tito saw Jenna's lips curve into a smile. There was a kind of sweetness to her face, with its high rounded cheekbones and delicately arched brows, that made her look like a fairy princess. Even her voice was girlishly sweet. But Tito knew better. Jenna was tough as nails, full of sass and snark, with a passion for classic rock and eighties heavy metal bands.

Her green eyes sparkled with mischief. "I'll go get my till," she said. "Don't start without me."

While she hurried back through the pass-through to Lalo's Kitchen, Halley took down a barstool, plonked herself onto it, rested her arms and chin on the bar top and let out a sigh. Over the past few months, Halley had developed a wide repertoire of expressive sighs. This one conveyed exasperation with obnoxious customers and relief that the three of them finally had the place to themselves—feelings that Tito wholeheartedly shared.

He opened his cash register and removed his till. Then he reached under the counter and pulled out a zippered bag, a legal pad and his reading glasses. He set them all on top of the till, along with the music-streaming cellphone, and carried them to the table where R.J. had been sitting.

Jenna came back carrying her own till, set it catty-corner to Tito's and took a seat on the bench across from him. She frowned at Halley when she saw her sitting at the bar. She seemed oddly sensitive at times to the impropriety of keeping a child in close proximity to a bar for hours on end—and yet Lalo's Kitchen had been the first and only place where she'd applied for work after moving to Limestone Springs. Tito knew, because he'd been there the day she'd first showed up, in a Toyota Highlander stuffed to the gills with all the worldly goods they could carry away from wherever it was they'd come from. She hadn't even found a place to stay before coming to Lalo's to get a job.

"I'm just *sitting* here," Halley said before Jenna could say anything. "It's not like I'm having a drink. Tito would lose his liquor license if he served me alcohol."

"Yeah, I'm pretty sure I'd lose my *life* before the Texas Alcoholic Beverage Commission even got wind of it," said Tito. "Your mom would slay me on the spot."

"You've got that right," said Jenna. "Halley, go get the broom and start sweeping."

With another sigh, Halley got up from the barstool and trudged off.

Tito put on his gold-rimmed spectacles and wrapped the flexible wires around the backs of his ears. He'd found the specs in an antique store. They exactly suited his degree of farsightedness, and he thought they looked pretty sharp.

Peering over the tops of the lenses, he saw Jenna staring at him with a half smile on her face.

"What?" he said, a little defensively. Maybe his vintage specs didn't look so sharp after all. Maybe they looked nerdy and pretentious.

"Nothing," Jenna replied. "Whose turn is it to choose the first song?"

Tito handed her the streaming phone. "Yours."

She took the phone, her fingers brushing his. She thought a moment and started tapping.

The opening bars came through the speakers. Tito listened. Keyboard intro, sort of a rough-edged organ sound, upbeat, brisk tempo. Key of D minor. A late seventies, classic rock sort of groove. Not one of the old standbys he heard regularly on retro playlists, and yet there was something familiar about it.

The guitar came in. He knew that riff. Jenna was watching him from across the table, with that half-angelic, half-mischievous grin, and moving to the beat. The words were right on the tip of his tongue…

He snapped his fingers. "'Blue Collar Man,'" he said. "Styx."

"Yesss!" She held up her hand for a high five. Tito raised his own hand, and Jenna smacked it so hard the palm stung.

After that they didn't talk for a while. They were too busy counting money—and singing.

The first verse of the song started right away, and Jenna sang along, loud and clear, nailing the lyrics and hitting every note perfectly. Tito let her take the verses alone—he wasn't 100 percent sure of the words—and came in to harmonize on the choruses.

They laid out all the bills, tallying how many they had of each denomination on their sheets of paper, and stacked their change in columns. Next door in Lalo's Kitchen, Halley was sweeping the floor with the big push broom.

A guitar solo started, giving Jenna a break from singing.

"Nice job," Tito told her. "You're giving Tommy Shaw a real run for his money on those lead vocals."

She chuckled. "Yeah, I like these tenor-range power ballads, because I can belt out the high notes with no trouble at all. It sounds like I'm crushing it, but really it's just that the song was written for a man to sing."

"That's only part of the reason," said Tito. "You've got a great voice, Jenna."

She darted a quick glance at him. "Thanks. So do you."

A brief, awkward silence fell. Then the chorus started back up again, and they both went back to singing.

When the song ended, Tito glanced down at the screen on the streaming phone. It was his turn to choose a song—or he could let the streaming app's suggestion play through. That didn't count as a turn.

The app followed "Blue Collar Man" with "Jet Airliner" by the Steve Miller Band. Tito let it play. He sang lead on this one, with Jenna harmonizing on the choruses.

But when the grainy guitar intro of Pink Floyd's "Wish You Were Here" came on, he quickly picked up the phone and hit Pause.

Jenna frowned. "Why'd you stop it? That's a really good song."

"I know it is. But I—well, it's part of my depression playlist from my late teens and early twenties, and I can't listen to it now without being drawn into the way I felt back then."

He'd never spoken to Jenna about his depression before. Very few people outside of his immediate family even knew about it.

A silence fell. Then Jenna said, "I get that. Music can have powerful emotional associations. I've never been truly depressed, but there's stuff I can't listen to, as well. Pretty much anything from my senior year of high school puts me in a funk that lasts all day. I think that's one reason why I like classic rock so much. The music of my own youth is too…fraught."

"Yeah."

The mood had taken a somber turn all of a sudden. It would be nice if this led to more confiding on Jenna's part, but Tito knew it wouldn't, not with Halley right there with her push broom. Jenna was already looking as if she regretted sharing as much as she had. Tito wanted to bring back her smile—and he knew exactly how to do it.

He started tapping on the streaming phone.

"Let's shake things up a bit," he said. "Same decade, different sound."

The song was "Stayin' Alive" by the Bee Gees. Tito stood up and began to dance to the electric guitar intro, hips swinging and fingers snapping to the opening bars. Over in Lalo's Kitchen, Halley, still sweeping, did a double take.

The intro quickly gave way to the first verse. Tito jumped onto his bench and sang along with Barry in falsetto, then busted into the point move, à la John Travolta. By the time he reached the *ah, ha, ha* part, Halley was laughing so hard she had to hold on to a table for support.

It was fun to make her laugh. She was such a serious kid most of the time. Jenna, meanwhile, had stopped counting money and was watching and listening with her mouth hanging open.

"What's wrong with this kid of yours?" Tito asked Jenna over Halley's shrieks of hilarity. "What's she laughing about? Doesn't she have any culture?"

Jenna slowly shook her head. "I don't think she's ever even been exposed to disco before."

"Then it's high time she learned about it. This is some good stuff."

"Well then, don't stop now!" said Jenna. "Keep singing. And definitely keep dancing."

He did, with unabashed exuberance, to the accompaniment of Halley's gales of laughter and Jenna's dazed stare, until the lyrics faded out at the end of the song.

"Wow," said Jenna. "That was…wow."

Tito stepped down from the bench, dusted it off,

straightened his vest and took his seat again. "Didn't know I was a disco king, did you?" he asked Jenna.

"No," she replied. "No, I did not. Now, give me that phone."

Tito made as if to grab the phone for himself, but Jenna seized it first and hit Pause before the streaming app could start playing another disco song.

"Oh my gosh," Halley gasped from the next room. "What *was* that?"

"Only number ninety-nine of *Rolling Stone*'s '500 Greatest Songs of All Time,'" Tito called out. "'Staying Alive,' by the Bee Gees."

"Disco," said Halley. "I've heard of that. Is that what you listened to when you were a teenager?"

He made an indignant sound. "How old do you think I am? Disco came and went before I was even born."

"And for that," said Jenna, "we should all be deeply thankful."

"Hey," said Tito. "Don't hate on disco. It gets maligned today, but there's a lot to admire in it. Did you even listen to those lyrics? They're about survival, about fighting back against all the stuff that's trying to drag you down."

Jenna was already tapping away on the streaming phone. "That may be, but we're going to listen to Led Zeppelin now."

"But it's Halley's turn to pick a song," said Tito.

Halley waved her arm weakly and shook her head. "Oh, no. You two carry on. I wouldn't want to mess up your awesome retro vibe."

Not surprisingly, Jenna finished counting her money before Tito did. She zipped it into its bag along with the tally sheet and put it in the office for the night. By the time he'd stowed his own money bag in his own office, she'd started mopping the floor on the restaurant side, and Halley had almost finished sweeping in the bar. The restrooms had already been cleaned by part-timers late in their evening shifts.

Tito stood a moment watching Jenna clean the floor while singing another seventies power ballad. She was so enthusiastic about it, expending energy like there was no tomorrow, like a new hire trying to make a good impression, instead of a newly made manager who'd been working here for over a year.

His own bucket stood ready and waiting. Jenna must have wheeled it out and filled it with cleaning solution for him. He went to work.

Whenever Tito and Jenna shared a closing shift, they joined forces, taking care of their floors at the same time, helping each other with their deep cleaning tasks—and singing, always singing. They sounded good together, their vocal timbres blending perfectly. They traded off singing lead and seemed to have almost a sixth sense of what the other was about to do. It energized the closing, making the work fun.

"The chalkboard's messed up," Halley called out from the restaurant side. "And it smells like beer."

"Oh, yeah, I forgot about that," said Jenna. "Luke asked me to ask you if you wanted to try your hand at redoing it."

"Me? Really?"

"Sure. You're a good artist. You've seen Veronica do it before, and you know where she keeps the chalks and things."

Halley took the assignment very seriously, shutting herself in the break room with orders that she was not to be disturbed. That left Jenna and Tito alone.

Jenna had a head start on mopping, so she finished

her side first and came over to the bar to help Tito finish his floor.

"Man, I am worn out," she said. "Look at me. I'm all sweaty."

Tito didn't have to be told to look at her. Her face glistened, and damp tendrils of hair, darkened to a deep gold, curled around her forehead. She had the most beautiful skin, richly tanned and flawlessly clear.

"Singing while we clean probably takes things up a notch," he said. "I don't know if it counts as cardio, but I'm pretty sure we're expanding our lung capacity."

"I believe it. I never get this worn out closing with anyone else."

"You don't sing when you close with other people?" Tito asked, trying to sound casual. He'd wondered this before but hadn't want to ask, thinking it might come off as possessive or needy.

"Oh, you know, just under my breath. It's different when you're with someone who really knows how to harmonize."

He smiled at her as the two of them started rolling their buckets toward the back area of the bar. "It's all that Bach part-writing I had to do in music theory."

"Is that so? I thought you might have formal training."

"Yeah, I minored in music at the University of North Texas, and had a solid band and choir foundation in high school before that. How about you?"

"Just high school band and choir. What instrument did you play?"

"Oboe."

She flashed a grin. "Ha! That's exactly what I would have guessed. You're a classic oboe type."

Tito wasn't sure if this was a compliment. "Anxious and introverted?" he asked. "Temperamental? Neurotic?"

"I was going to say thoughtful and intelligent. It's a hard instrument."

They'd reached the floor drain. Tito held out his hand in an "after you" gesture, and Jenna emptied her dirty mop water and started rinsing her bucket and mop with water from the big spray nozzle.

"So what did you play?" Tito asked. "Wait, don't tell me." He thought about it as he emptied his own mop bucket. Not flute, or clarinet, or any other woodwind. Possibly percussion, but she gave off more of a brass instrument vibe.

"Trumpet," he said at last.

She laughed. "Guilty as charged. Bold and brash, arrogant and loud."

"I was going to say confident, adventurous and extroverted."

As he rinsed and wrung out his mop, Tito silently filed away his newest bits of knowledge about Jenna. She tended to let information slip in the context of music—which bands she'd seen in concert, when she'd seen them, how old she'd been at the time. If he'd wanted, Tito could have Googled past concert schedules and figured out where she'd really come from, or at least narrowed it down. But he'd resisted the temptation. She'd told everyone that she and Halley were from Tennessee, and she must have a good reason for wanting people to believe it.

But it wasn't true.

At least, Tito was 95 percent certain it wasn't true. He'd been observing Jenna for a year and a half now, and she had a tell.

Tito's uncle—Original Tito to longtime patrons old enough to remember the bar's namesake—had been a master at reading people, and he'd passed his skills along to his nephew. From an early age, Young Tito had learned how to tell when someone felt comfortable around him, or fearful or angry, or was lying to him. And for the past nine years, ever since he'd inherited the bar from his uncle, he'd had ample opportunity to put his people-reading skills to work.

A lot of those nonverbal cues were highly individualized, having to do with a deviation from a baseline. Gaze aversion, for instance, wasn't a sure sign of lying. It might mean the person was momentarily distracted, or simply wasn't comfortable with sustained eye contact. In Jenna's case, direct eye contact was the norm. But when she told a lie, her gaze wavered, then turned down and away, and a brief, split-second flash of guilt appeared on her face.

She'd never lied about anything work-related, or given Tito any reason to think she was untrustworthy. But the official story she'd told about her and Halley's lives prior to coming to Limestone Springs had been an invention.

Without actively trying to discover the truth about them, Tito had managed to piece together a few things. He was pretty sure Jenna used to live someplace with mountains, but within easy driving distance of the ocean. She had at least one sister but didn't seem to like talking about her. Her references to her sister had been few and brief and confined to childhood. She spoke of her mother in the present tense and her father in the past tense.

She'd never said a word about Halley's father, which was suggestive in itself. There'd been no wedding band on her hand on the day of her arrival in Limestone Springs, and no imprint or tan line suggesting that she'd recently removed one.

I can't give you any references, she'd told Luke when she'd applied for a job. *But I'm a hard worker, I'm motivated and smart, and if you hire me, you will not regret it.*

She'd looked him straight in the eye when she'd said that, and subsequent events had proven it true. But after

Luke had hired her, and asked for her ID, things had gotten a little dicey. Tito had been around for that, too. She'd handed over a temporary Texas driver's permit and told Luke she'd lost her old license. Then her gaze had wavered and dropped, and a microexpression of guilt had flashed over her face, vanishing almost before Tito had registered it.

Instantly his mind had buzzed with questions and potentialities. Coupled with the lack of work references, the murkiness over the driver's license had seemed significant. Maybe she'd had a new one made after moving from out of state, and hadn't wanted to show the old one. Maybe it had been under a different name. Maybe she didn't want anyone to know where she'd actually come from.

But he'd kept his guesses to himself. And Luke, unsuspicious by nature and struggling to fill the scheduling gaps created by the two servers who'd quit without notice that week, had taken Jenna at her word. Within weeks she'd become his most trusted employee.

So. What was Jenna running from? That was the question that kept Tito awake night after night. Best guess was an abusive ex. She couldn't be in witness protection, or she'd have had a job lined up before moving and a driver's license that wasn't printed on paper.

He wished she would confide in him. He was accustomed to being confided in. But clearly she wasn't ready, and he wouldn't push. He was a patient man. He could wait.

CHAPTER THREE

THEY PUT AWAY their buckets and mops. Jenna took her hair down from its big plastic clip, shook it loose and twisted it up again, performing the whole action with an unconscious grace that made something catch in Tito's throat.

She didn't seem to notice. "What's your deep cleaning task for tonight?" she asked.

"Um…" Tito forced his attention, and his gaze, away from Jenna. "Display wall," he said. "You?"

"Deep fryer."

"Okay. Let's do mine first, since the deep fryer is a dirtier job."

They went behind the bar. Tito climbed the sliding ladder and started handing down liquor bottles to Jenna from the top shelf. Once all the shelves were empty, he'd clean the mirrored wall behind them while she wiped down the bottles.

Before Jenna had come along, Tito had always taken care of this job alone. There weren't many people he trusted to handle the costly bottles or to put them back in their proper positions. You couldn't just stick the bottles up there any which way. You had to think about how often a particular bottle was used, its shape and size, even its color. The arrangement should be practical and convenient, as well as aesthetically pleasing.

He started, as he always did, with the Galliano, whose

ridiculously long, narrow shape required him to keep it high on the top shelf.

"What is it with these weird bottles, anyway?" Jenna asked as she carefully took it from him. "Look at this thing. It's like a baseball bat—difficult to store and clumsy to pour from. How does the manufacturer not realize that?"

"It's a marketing ploy," said Tito. "Every manufacturer wants its product's packaging to be distinctive and memorable."

"Oh, it's memorable, all right," Jenna said. "I remember how irksome it is, and I don't like using it."

"Yeah, they definitely went way too far with that one. And don't even get me started on the 1800 Tequila bottle. A trapezoid? Really? That was the shape they decided to go with? And what's the deal with that wide lid?"

"And the Goldschläger! That chunky rounded base takes up way too much space, and the long neck is so awkward to pour from."

They continued making fun of eccentrically shaped bottles as they worked their way down the display case. Tito was spraying cleaner on the mirrored wall when he heard Jenna chuckling. He looked down and saw her holding a bottle of Kraken spiced rum.

"What's so funny?" he asked.

She held it up. "Who does this remind you of?"

He studied the sturdy bottle with its two rounded side handles. It didn't look like anyone he knew.

"Imagine it with a worried expression on its face," Jenna said.

Tito snapped his fingers. "Haha! It's Lalo! Because he's always standing around with his hands on his hips!"

Jenna flashed a brilliant grin. "Exactly! I knew you'd get it."

A comfortable warmth spread through Tito's chest.

There was no one he had more fun with than Jenna. Their senses of humor just meshed.

Her gaze swept the other bottles for a moment. Then she seized the Green Chartreuse.

"This one is Luke," she said.

Tito looked at the green liqueur in its clear container. "It is," he agreed. "It's got the same calm, woodsy vibe."

"And Luke's always going hiking and camping," Jenna said.

They went on assigning booze bottles to employees on both sides of the pass-through. Some of the matches were simple and readily apparent. Eric, a redheaded bartender, was the red-lidded Luxardo Maraschino. Another bartender, Garrett, who liked wearing bolo ties, was the Avión Extra Añejo Reserva 44, because of the leather cord and pendant around the bottle's neck. Clint, with his broad linebacker's build, was the big square bottle of Disaronno Amaretto.

Others were less cut and dried.

"This one is Veronica," Jenna said, holding up the Crème de Violette. "I can't say why, exactly. It just looks like her."

"Yeah, it does," said Tito.

He picked up the Cointreau, a clear liqueur in an orange bottle, and said, "This one is Halley. Partly because of the coloring, and partly because of the flavor. Slightly sweet, and slightly tart."

"You've got that right," Jenna said dryly. "Let's see. Which one are you?"

She scanned the remaining liquors, pausing for a moment before a bottle of Tito's Handmade Vodka, a craft vodka made in Austin by some enterprising distiller with no connection to Tito Mendoza, or his uncle.

"Hmm," Jenna said. "This would be the obvious choice for you. But it doesn't really look or feel like you."

She went back to searching. Tito watched, anticipation building in him. It seemed deeply important which liquor bottle Jenna Hamlin thought looked and felt like him.

"Ah," she said at last. "Here we go."

She picked up a bottle of Johnnie Walker Black Label and held it up in triumph.

"This is you. Slender, high-class and formal. And the gold matches those cool vintage spectacles of yours."

Tito's heart gave a quick throb that was half pleasure, half pain. There was something in her smile that he'd never seen there before, something more than the friendly regard of a respected coworker. The overhead pendant light shone on her hair, picking out strands of gold as bright as the trim and lettering on the bottle's slanted black label.

"Wow," Tito said. "Thanks."

Then he reached past Jenna and picked up the bottle of Tito's Handmade Vodka.

"And this," he said, "is you."

He didn't offer any explanation. In his mind, the resemblance spoke for itself. The classic shape of the bottle, the textured, cream-colored label with its black print and accents of metallic pink, the glittering pinkish coppery lid—somehow they were all Jenna, in spite of the fact that it was Tito's own name emblazoned in big italic letters. Jenna loved those pink lids with fanatical, unreasoning zeal. Tito had been saving them for her for well over a year now. She said she was going to make something with them someday, some sort of craft project, but she didn't yet know what. For now, she just liked having them.

Her smile deepened. "That's the one I was hoping for," she said.

It doesn't mean anything, Tito told himself. *We're just playing around*. But that wasn't the way it felt.

They put the bottles back on the shelves in pristine order, laughing and joking and singing, then moved on to the deep fryer. They ended the evening sitting on the floor, side by side, sharing a carton of fried okra, which they ate by hand, like popcorn. Sometimes they reached into the carton at the same time and their fingers bumped. The hearty aroma of peanut oil mingled with the sharp scent of cleaning solution, along with a faint hit of mango from Jenna's shampoo.

They talked and talked and talked—about books, music and sad or funny things that had happened to them as kids. Tito never talked as freely or deeply with anyone else as he did with Jenna. Most of the time he had to keep himself in check, to make sure he didn't bore the other person by going off on some wild tangent. But Jenna liked wild tangents. Sitting beside her with their legs stretched out on the nonskid floor mat, Tito felt as if the two of them were inside a bubble, safe from the rest of the world, beyond the reach of the passage of time.

The bubble burst when Halley came and found them.

"There you are," she said. "I finished the chalkboard. Come see what you think of it. I've been looking at it so long, I can't even tell anymore."

If she thought there was anything strange about the sight of Tito and her mother sitting hip to hip on the floor sharing finger food, she didn't say so. Jenna quickly got to her feet, as if she'd been caught doing something not quite respectable, but then held down a hand to Tito. He didn't need help up, but he took her hand anyway.

The chalkboard looked fantastic, with multiple fonts in a variety of sizes, and intricate scrollwork set off with flowers and leaves.

"Wow," said Jenna. "You really went all out. No wonder it took you so long."

"I had to start over a few times," Halley said. "I watched a couple of tutorials on YouTube. I wanted to get it right. I didn't want it to look like something some kid slapped together."

"Well, you succeeded. It looks amazing."

"As good as when Veronica does it?"

"Oh, yes. Definitely."

Halley gave Tito a questioning look.

"I agree," he said. "This is professional-quality chalkboard art right here."

Halley's cheeks turned pink, and she smiled.

Tito took the trash out to the dumpster. When he came back inside, Halley and Jenna had gathered their things to go home. But Halley, freshly energized from her triumph with the chalkboard, didn't seem all that eager to leave.

"How's Bunter?" she asked Tito, clearly stalling for time.

"Sleek and pompous as always," Tito replied.

Jenna looked confused. "Who are you talking about?"

"Tito's cat," Halley said. "You've seen him before, up in his windowsill, looking down at the town, judging everyone."

"Oh, okay," said Jenna. "Yeah, I've seen him. I just didn't realize he'd been named after Lord Peter Wimsey's valet."

"Who's Lord Peter Wimsey?" asked Halley.

"A sleuth in a British detective series from the early twentieth century," Jenna told her. "His manservant helps him solve mysteries. Lord Peter is the second son of a duke, so he's got plenty of money and leisure for his amateur detective hobby without having to work for a living, and without the bother of being a duke himself."

"Oh, he inherits the title eventually," said Tito. "His nephew and older brother both die, and the dukedom passes to Peter."

"Does it really?" asked Jenna. "How does he cope with that?"

It was a golden opportunity, Tito thought, almost too good to be true. Did he dare to take it?

"Finish the series and find out," he said. "I've got a complete set upstairs."

Halley turned an eager face to Jenna. "Can we, please? I want to see Tito's loft again."

Jenna hesitated. Tito held his breath, trying to look as if it didn't matter, but all the while thinking, *please, please*.

"Okay," Jenna said at last. "But just for a few minutes. We don't want to keep Tito up too late, or Bunter, either."

Tito felt silently exultant, leading the two of them up the long staircase with its beadboard siding and worn wooden steps. Old-fashioned sconces, mounted high overhead, lit the way.

They'd only been there once before, a few months back when Halley had started running a fever shortly after the start of Jenna's shift. The restaurant had been shorthanded that day, so Tito had offered to let Halley crash at his second-floor apartment above the bar. Halley had spent the day lying on Tito's sofa, reading books from his shelves, drinking juice from his fridge and petting his cat. The whole thing seemed to have become a treasured memory of hers.

He unlocked the door, opened it wide and stepped back for Jenna and Halley to enter first.

He watched as Jenna checked the place out. She probably hadn't paid much attention when she'd been there before; she'd been focused on taking care of Halley, getting her set up on the sofa with blankets and cushions.

Now, he saw the apartment and its furnishings through her eyes—the efficient but well-proportioned living area with its crown molding and wainscoting, the moss green sofa and single wing chair, the wall of built-in bookshelves running all the way up to the ten-foot ceiling. To the left, Tito's bedroom door stood open, showing a tall dresser, a Windsor chair and a neatly made bed. Tito always made his bed. It was one of those keystone habits that kept him in a good headspace.

"Bunter!" said Halley, running over to him.

The black-and-white tuxedo cat lay stretched out in his usual spot on the windowsill overlooking the street. He turned on hearing his name and graciously accepted Halley's attention.

"Boy, talk about people who look like their pets," said Jenna, following Halley to the windowsill. "I half expect him to start wiping things down with a soft white cloth and offer me a drink."

"We don't look *that* much alike," said Tito. "Bunter is much fatter than I am."

"You have the same facial expression, though. And the same fashion sense." She stroked the cat under the chin. "Where'd he come from, anyway?"

"I found him in an actual dumpster, the one out back, not long after I took over the bar. I was taking out the trash at the end of the night and there he was, a little bag of bones scrounging for his dinner. I took him upstairs and gave him a bath and a can of tuna. He settled right in. I called him Bunter because he was so dignified, and because he looked like a little valet in his black-and-white fur."

"Poor kitty," said Jenna. "He must have been so scared before you found him. I wonder how he came to be there. I wish he could tell you the rest of his story."

Tito didn't answer. He wished the same thing about her.

"Look at this view," said Halley. "Isn't it great? You can see all the way to our house."

"Can you really?" Jenna asked, kneeling down beside her. "Huh, you're right."

Tito crouched behind them both. "Which one is it?"

Jenna pointed. "See that metal roof, right in between the big oak tree and the row of crepe myrtles? That's it. That's our house."

"I didn't know that," said Tito. But he knew it now, and he also knew that he'd never look through this window again without seeking out that metal roof.

Tito's knee brushed the small of Jenna's back, and his gaze slowly shifted to the back of Jenna's head. Crouching so close to her, he could smell that mango shampoo of hers again. A golden tendril had escaped from the gathered mass of her hair, hanging in a loose spiral down the nape of her neck.

"You ought to see this view in the wintertime," said Halley. "It was February when I was here before, and trees on the square were all lit up."

"That must be beautiful," said Jenna without turning around. "I always thought it would be cool to live in a loft."

All in an instant, Tito imagined knocking a hole through the wall on the right, into the space above Lalo's Kitchen, more than doubling his square footage, and giving him enough space to add a bedroom, another bathroom, maybe a home office. He'd thought about it, back when Tony and Alex Reyes of Reyes Boys Construction were renovating the bar and converting the old lawyer's office into a restaurant, but there'd been no need when it was just him living here.

But what if it wasn't just him? What if he had a wife and child? Could he turn the place into a comfortable home for a family?

Jenna turned suddenly, as if she'd sensed his thought, or felt his stare. She looked over her shoulder at him with those clear green eyes, her cheek making a perfect curve against the darkened window. He wanted to cup his hand against that curve, run his thumb lightly over her lips, lower his face to hers and…

She cleared her throat. "Let's find those books," she said. "Then Halley and I can get out of your hair."

Her voice sounded unnaturally bright and chipper.

"Right," said Tito. "Sure."

He stood and walked over to the bookcase, glad for the opportunity to turn his back to her, and hoping she couldn't see how weak and rubbery his legs had gotten all of a sudden.

"Here they are," he said, holding out a hand to a shelf. "The complete set—including all the short stories, and the unfinished novel that was completed by another author after Dorothy Sayers died, and the additional novels that were added to the series by that same author."

"Wow," said Jenna. "I had no idea there were so many. This is exciting. I have a lot of reading ahead of me."

She darted a quick glance at him. "You know, I actually had quite a crush on Lord Peter Wimsey for a while."

"Did you?" Tito asked. "That shows excellent taste."

"I guess it does. If only my judgment was always that good."

"So how far have you read?" Tito asked.

Jenna scanned the titles. "Let's see. I know I read *Strong Poison*, and the one set in Scotland, and the one where Harriet goes to that resort on a holiday and finds a dead body on the beach. I kind of jumped around in the series."

"You read them out of order?" Tito said in mock horror.

She gave him that sweetly mischievous grin. "Yeah, I'm kind of a rebel that way."

Tito reached for a volume. "Have you read *Busman's Honeymoon*? That's the one where Peter buys Harriet a house for a wedding present. They go there for their honeymoon, find a corpse in the cellar and have to solve the murder."

She made an indignant sound. "Peter and Harriet get married? Uh, spoiler alert!"

Tito chuckled. "Oops! Sorry."

"Oh, well. I'm glad to know they end up together. I wasn't sure they ever would. Harriet's pretty gun-shy after her awful ex."

"Yeah, she is. But Peter waits her out, and in the end she takes him."

In the silence that followed, the words seemed to take on great weight and significance. Jenna looked away. Was she embarrassed for him, thinking he'd made a bookish and clumsy attempt at a come-on? Or was she thinking that she, like Harriet, might come to love a very different sort of man from the one who'd hurt her? She'd once had a crush on Lord Peter Wimsey, after all. That meant she wasn't entirely averse to brainy men of average height with a history of mood disorder.

"How about if I just lend you the whole series?" said Tito. "Then you can start at the beginning and read everything in its proper order."

"Okay. Thanks. It'll be nice to have my bedtime reading taken care of that far into the future."

Tito started pulling the books from the shelf. "You like to read in bed?"

"Every night, until my eyelids are too heavy to stay open."

"Even on nights when you work closing shifts? It must be pretty late when you finally turn out the light."

"That's the point. When I shut my eyes, I want to go right to sleep. I don't like to lie there and *think*."

"I get that," Tito said.

Jenna took a few steps back and scanned his shelves. "Wow, you have a lot of philosophy books."

"Yeah, I got my bachelor's in philosophy."

She chuckled. "A philosophy major and a music minor! It's like you were planning to be a bar owner from the start."

He carried the stack of books to his small dining table and took a plastic grocery bag out of the pantry. "Yeah, looking back, there is something inevitable about the whole thing, though I couldn't see it at the time."

Jenna was still looking at his bookcase, her head tilted to the side to read the titles on the spines. "You've got a big mystery section, too. A lot of Golden Age detective stuff. Nero Wolfe, Hercule Poirot…"

Tito set the books inside the bag. "I enjoy a good mystery," he said.

Suddenly Jenna was looking straight at him with those clear green eyes. "Yeah, well, you're something of a mystery yourself."

"Me?" Tito asked. "What's so mysterious about me?"

She walked over and took a seat at his dining table. "Well, for starters, how about the way you bounce obnoxious drunks out of the bar? I've seen you in action, and not just tonight. It's always the same. One minute the guy's making a jackass of himself, and the next minute he's out on the sidewalk, wondering what just happened. No fuss, no broken glassware, no scene. How'd you learn to do that?"

Tito glanced over at Halley. She looked contented enough, sitting on his sofa with Bunter, who was pacing back and forth over her lap, arching his back with delight and rubbing his face against her hand.

He sat down across from Jenna. "You've heard of my uncle, right?"

"Original Tito, yes. The bar's first owner."

"Exactly. I was always close to him. He was my mother's brother, and I take after her side of the family. Uncle Tito was a neat guy. Very intelligent and well-read. Funny, in a subtle way, but with something sad behind it all. He was married once, briefly, but his wife left him only two months into the marriage. She went away and never came back."

"Wow," said Jenna. "Dramatic."

"Yes. She was the love of his life. He never remarried or had any sort of romantic involvement again. He'd always been something of a loner, but now he turned into a hermit. He was in his bar pretty much all the time, or else upstairs in his apartment—this apartment."

"That's so sad."

"Yeah, it is. I didn't really see it at the time, though. It was just how things were. He was always good to me, and friendly to customers. It was only later, after he died, that I realized how lonely he was, and that he was probably clinically depressed."

He looked down, pretending sudden interest in the salt and pepper shakers, spinning first one and then the other ninety degrees, clockwise, over and over. "One day at school—I guess it was around fifth grade—this group of boys was giving me a hard time about something or other, which wasn't an unusual occurrence for me. But then one of them said that Uncle Tito had killed his wife and buried her body in the alley behind the bar. So I lit into them."

He could feel her watching him. "How did it go?"

"Not great. I got a couple of good punches in, but there

were four of them and one of me, and boxing was not part of my skill set. This was back during the days of zero tolerance policies for fighting in school. I actually got suspended. My mom was taking my grandmother to the doctor that day, so my dad had to come pick me up. I had two black eyes and a busted lip, and my shirt was bloody and torn down the front. He asked me what had happened, and…"

He darted a quick glance at her. "Well, you've seen my dad. I think it's safe to say he hasn't lost many fights in his life. I was kind of embarrassed to tell him what happened, but I had to, so I did. He just looked at me with this stunned expression on his face. Then he grinned, and said, *Well, if you're gonna get into fights to defend the honor of your family, I better show you how so you don't get your butt kicked next time.* He took me to Bart's Gym, and Bart taught me everything he thought I needed to know—which turned out to be quite a lot, because Bart has a pretty broad knowledge base in martial arts. I didn't just learn how to fight, I learned how to stop fights from starting—how to block punches, and do wristlocks and armlocks and holds and things. All of which comes in handy when you work in a bar."

He dared to look at her for real then. She was staring right back at him, and smiling. She seemed lit up with admiration and respect.

"Good for your dad," she said. "And good for you, sticking up for your uncle before you knew how to fight. That took a lot of courage."

"Thank you," said Tito.

Jenna's expression turned serious. "I don't know if I've ever told you this, but… I appreciate the way you and Luke look out for your employees, and back us up when customers get obnoxious. A lot of places would expect us—especially the female employees—to just take it, and go along with it, and not risk offending the almighty customer. But not you. So thanks."

Something warm and happy bloomed deep in Tito's chest. "Oh, well, you're very welcome," he said. "Honestly, I never even thought of that as something deserving of gratitude."

"I know," Jenna said. "That's the best part."

A silence fell, long enough to get awkward. Then Jenna said, "So that's how you learned to fight. But how did you come to own the bar? Did you inherit it from your uncle?"

"Yes. He died about nine years ago, and it turned out he'd left the bar entirely to me. I was doing postgrad work in North Texas at the time, and kind of at a loss for what I was going to do once I finished. There's not a lot of demand in the workplace for doctors of philosophy as such. I could always teach, of course, but the thought of being part of a collegiate system and dealing with actual undergraduates, not to mention the whole stupid tenure system, was not something that made me happy. But I wasn't exactly excited to come back to my hometown and work at the bar, either. I took a semester off from school to take stock and see where the bar stood financially. My plan was to hire good management and set myself up to be an absentee owner."

He ran a finger along a groove in the tabletop. "Once I got here, I saw that the place was overdue for some repairs. I hired the Reyes brothers for that. One thing led to another, and before I knew it, we were doing a full-scale renovation. Then the building next door went on the market, and I thought, why not expand? My uncle had left me a fair amount of cash, and the business was in good enough shape for a loan, so I went ahead with it. My cousin Lalo had grown up working in family restaurants, and he'd always wanted a place of his own, so he came in as front man and majority owner on the restaurant. Meanwhile, I was working full time at the bar. I couldn't find anyone I trusted to do as good a job managing the place as I'd do myself, and by that time I'd realized that I actually liked the work a lot. And I definitely wasn't looking forward to returning to school. So I stayed on."

He turned in his seat and pointed to a ragged photo stuck to his fridge. "This is my uncle. It's not a great picture of him, but it's still the best we have of him as an adult. My mom took it one day when he was standing at the bar. She had to act fast before he could run off. He didn't like having his picture taken."

"Ooh, can I see?" Jenna asked.

"Sure," Tito said. He pulled the photo free of its magnet and handed it across the table.

Jenna studied the image of the heavyset man dressed in black and white, with straight dark hair and a neatly trimmed Vandyke beard.

"You look like him a little," she said finally. "He's heavier than you are, and his facial hair is different, but I can see the resemblance in the eyes and the mouth."

She lightly laid a fingertip on the picture, and Tito tingled as if it were his face that she'd touched.

"Have you ever tried a Vandyke?" she asked.

"Briefly. It made my face look too thin. I've tried all sorts of facial hair over the years before deciding that the full beard is my best look."

Jenna looked up at him. "Oh, I don't know. I kind of liked that little Clark Gable mustache you used to have. That was a good look too."

Tito frowned. "How did you know about that mustache?"

"You had it, didn't you?"

"Yes, but that was years ago, way before you came to Limestone Springs."

"Well, you must have given it a second run, because I know I've seen it."

"No. I'm positive I've had a full beard continuously for over five years."

Something in her expression shifted. "Oh. Well then, I guess I must have seen it on social media or something."

For a moment Tito was honestly perplexed. Jenna didn't have any social media accounts—none, zip, nada.

Then her gaze wavered, and she looked down and away.

The whole thing lasted only for a second before she met his eyes again, but Tito saw it and knew what it meant. Jenna was lying.

Now he was more confused than ever. It was one thing for her to lie about her origins, if she had something to hide. It was another thing entirely to lie about when and where she'd seen a mustache that Tito had had for two weeks, almost six years earlier.

What could it mean? Had he and Jenna actually met back then? He searched his memory. The mustache period had been a chaotic time, because it coincided with a late-summer storm that had done a lot of damage in Limestone Springs. Maybe Jenna had passed through town during that time? But if so, he'd have remembered her. He was sure of that. He had a good memory for faces, and hers was one he wouldn't forget.

Jenna stood abruptly and picked up the plastic bag. "Well, thanks for the books. Come on, Halley. It's time to go."

Tito stood too. "I'll walk you to your car."

"You don't have to do that," said Jenna.

She was clearly eager to get away from him now, but he walked her and Halley downstairs and out to the car anyway.

The battered Toyota SUV was parked in the lot behind the back patio. Honeysuckle and trumpet vines cascaded over the fence, filling the warm air with their sweet scent. After a hard winter and a wet spring, a brutal Texas summer had settled in with a vengeance.

"Good night," Jenna said as she climbed into the driver's seat. "Thanks again for the books."

"You're welcome," said Tito. "See you tomorrow."

She gave him a brief smile. "Actually, no. Tomorrow's my day off."

"Oh," he said. Her days off always felt a little blank to him.

She shut the door and drove away. He watched her headlights disappear down the dark street.

CHAPTER FOUR

THE TROUBLE WITH LIES, Jenna thought as she scraped bacon residue from the cast-iron griddle, was that they weren't true. No matter how carefully you constructed your lie, no matter how plausible it sounded in your head, you couldn't turn it into actual fact. That problem was compounded when you had to build a whole network of lies. The longer you fiddled with it, the more you realized just how flimsy it was, and how easily the whole thing could be knocked down by anyone curious enough to go digging and smart enough to put two and two together.

Truth, on the other hand, was unbreakable. It existed on its own with no need for convincing details or time-lines carefully worked out for consistency. It didn't care if you believed it or denied it or laughed at it. The truth simply *was*.

After a year and a half of lies, Jenna had a new appreciation for the beauty and strength of truth.

She ran hot water over the griddle with the spray nozzle, then wiped the surface dry with a paper towel. She'd bought the griddle at a thrift store in Limestone Springs, along with most of her kitchenware, a set of dishes, two table lamps and a decent collection of paperback detective novels. It would have been foolish to pack her own medium-quality household goods into a rented moving trailer for transport from Virginia, so she'd sold what she could, donated the rest, and packed her and Halley's necessities into a Chevy Trailblazer, which she'd traded in for a Toyota Highlander about a third of the way through Tennessee.

Remember this place, Jenna had told Halley over dinner that evening at a Cuban café. *From now on, if anyone asks you where we're from, you tell them we're from Crossville, Tennessee. Practice saying it so you'll be ready. It's true in a way, because we've stayed here overnight.*

And Halley had looked at her from across the table with those big trusting blue eyes, and said okay. And early the next morning, they'd gotten into the Highlander and driven to Texas.

Jenna had chosen their new home based entirely on internet research. She'd decided early on that she wanted to live in a small town in Texas. Her dad had spent some time in Texas as a young man and always spoke fondly of it, and a small town seemed like a good place for a fresh start. She'd liked the look of Limestone Springs, with its pretty downtown area, thriving economy and strong community spirit. But what had really clinched the deal was the old news video about how the residents had come together to help each other in the aftermath of a severe summer hailstorm. Part of the video had been filmed inside Lalo's Kitchen and Tito's Bar, where volunteer firefighters had gathered to rest and regroup, and people whose homes had been damaged had taken shelter. Tito had been there, serving food and drink with an encouraging smile, wearing crisp black and white, and sporting a debonair Clark Gable mustache.

She felt her cheeks grow warm as she wiped the counters. Why, *why* had she mentioned that mustache last night? And once she *had* mentioned it, why hadn't she simply told him truthfully that she'd seen it on that video, instead of telling him that half-baked lie about social media? It was reasonable enough for her to have watched the video at some point. But she hadn't thought fast enough for that. She'd panicked. And she never would have been in that position to begin with if she hadn't felt the need to weigh in on Tito's past facial hair, as if it were any business of hers. The way he'd looked at her after, with that shrewd, intelligent gaze—for one sickening moment she'd thought he was about to call her out on her lies, and unravel her whole fictitious backstory with a single tug.

And if he had, what then? Would she have stonewalled him? Or told him everything? She honestly didn't know.

The funny thing was, Tito was her best friend in Limestone Springs, or anywhere, and he didn't even know it. And if she was being truthful with herself, there was something inside her that wanted him to be more than her best friend—a lot more. But how could she possibly give in to that feeling when her past was so complicated? Yes, theoretically, she could tell him the truth. It wasn't as if she were a spy, or in WITSEC, or had a bounty on her head. Tito wouldn't look down on Halley for being a Latimore from Franklin County. He didn't even know the Latimores. And he certainly wouldn't get in touch with the Latimore clan and tell them where Jenna had taken Chase's daughter.

It might be nice, actually, having another person in on the secret—especially if that other person was Tito, with his clear, logical mind and warm heart.

But once she started, where would she stop? Where would it end? Would she and Tito tell Tito's parents? His brothers? His multitude of cousins? Once the story was let loose, there was no putting it back in the bag, and no predicting how far it would spread. Jenna wouldn't be able to keep track of it anymore. And how could she expect Halley to keep quiet if *she* couldn't be bothered to keep the secret herself?

No. The whole reason they'd left Virginia in the first

place was to put the past behind them and make a fresh start. In order for that to work, their fake backstory had to stay airtight.

She'd have to be more careful from now on. No more going up to Tito's apartment. No more songfests. No more intentionally scheduling herself to close at Lalo's on the nights when she knew he'd be closing at the bar. No more letting down her guard. She couldn't afford to give her heart away to Tito. She couldn't afford to give away anything to anybody.

That wasn't easy in a small, friendly town where everyone knew everyone's business. She understood that now. The very things that had attracted her to Limestone Springs also made it hard to keep her secret. Even Tito. Especially Tito. He saw too much with those deep dark eyes of his.

She rinsed and wrung out her sponge, put it away and started the dishwasher. Its low, steady hum gave her a reassuring sense of things being under control.

In the small living room, Halley sat curled up in the armchair, reading a book and twirling her hair exactly the way Kara used to. Jenna longed to curl up with her own book and a fresh cup of coffee. She'd started the first of Tito's Lord Peter Wimsey books last night, and it was even better than she remembered—smart and funny, like Tito himself. But she still had utilities to pay, another load of laundry to start and next week's work schedule to finalize. And it was already after nine. Lord Peter would have to wait.

She'd always loved detective fiction, but since she and Halley had made their getaway, she'd started to see the stories with fresh eyes—how the killer planned the crime and covered his tracks, and how the detective deconstructed the deceit.

She'd read once that everyone who commits a murder makes twenty-five mistakes, and that anyone who remembers five of them is a genius. She hadn't killed anyone, but she'd erased two past lives, hers and Halley's and she was bound to have made some mistakes along the way.

"Why are you staring at me?" Halley asked.

Her blue eyes were peering at Jenna over the top of her book. Not open and trusting anymore like in Tennessee, but closed off, almost hostile.

"Sorry," said Jenna. "Just zoning out. Remember we have FaceTime with Gigi this morning."

Halley turned back to her book. "I know. Ten o'clock."

Jenna moved a load of darks from the washer to the dryer and started a load of lights. The washer and dryer added their voices to the soothing chorus of major appliances. She quickly sorted the pile of mail and paid her bills.

The small rental house needed a good dusting, but it was tidy. Jenna and Halley didn't have enough possessions to clutter it up, and they weren't home often enough to make a mess. Jenna liked things to be neat and clean, but today the place looked stark and utilitarian in her eyes. She thought of Tito's apartment, with its old woodwork and high ceilings, its bookcase wall and comfy sofa, the big front window with the black-and-white cat resting on the sill, looking out over the town. Tito's personality seemed to have infused every cubic foot of the space.

Remembering that her roof had been visible from Tito's front window, she stole over to her own back window and looked toward downtown. Through the limbs of a neighbor's pecan tree, she could just make out a patch of stonework that she was pretty sure belonged to the top floor of the building that housed the bar, but she couldn't quite see the window. Was Tito down in the bar, getting ready to open at noon? Or upstairs, enjoying a last cup of coffee and a good book? Or standing in the window, staring at her roof?

She checked the time. Two minutes before the hour. She opened her laptop and put the call through.

In the year and a half since leaving Virginia, she'd never once been late with a scheduled FaceTime session with her mom back home. She'd taken herself and Halley halfway across the country, thereby depriving her mother of her older daughter and only granddaughter. She'd also been the means, however unintentionally, of depriving her mother of her younger daughter forever. Being punctual for Face-Time truly was the least Jenna could do.

The face on the screen was thin and worn, with harsh, sharp cheekbones, and eye sockets dark with shadow. Tufts of untidy fair hair stood out in all directions like fluff on a baby chick. Caroline Travers had once been a beautiful woman who'd taken pride in her appearance and made the most of it with pretty clothes and immaculate grooming. Growing up, Jenna had rarely seen her mother without perfectly coiffed hair and full makeup. This woman was a tired old lady, and a stranger.

But her face lit up at the sight of Halley and Jenna, showing a glimmer of past glory.

"Well, hello, Kayla! Hello, Kirsten! How are you? It's so good to see you!"

Jenna tried to ignore a twinge of annoyance. Was it really that difficult to use the new names she'd taken so much trouble to secure for them? Yes, she and Halley were alone in the house, but what if they hadn't been? What if, one day, they *had* to video chat with Caroline when someone else was around?

"Hi, Gigi," said Halley. "How're you?"

Caroline waved off her own well-being with a casual hand. "Fine, fine. What a pretty shirt you have on, Kirsten!"

Halley looked down at her shirt. "Thanks, Gigi."

Jenna's mother leaned forward with an almost hungry expression. "Now tell me everything you've been up to," she said.

Everything Halley had been up to did not amount to much, but Halley gamely made the most of it, telling her grandmother about funny things that had happened at the restaurant, and what she'd been studying in her school-work, and the books she'd been reading. Caroline hung on every word, smiling, nodding, eager for more, her eyes fixed on Halley's face. Was she searching for traces of Kara? There was plenty of Kara to be seen there, along with a hefty dose of Chase.

Chase. The very thought of him soured Jenna's stomach. For the millionth time, she wondered how it was possible that she'd ever been enough of a fool to fall in love with him. All her life, she'd been told to stay away from the Latimores, that they were nothing but trouble and always had been. The whole clan was tainted by deeply entrenched generational problems going back at least two centuries. They'd started making moonshine not long after the American Revolution, and to date, their collective rap sheets included breaking and entering, possession with intent to distribute, assault, public intoxication, DUI, armed robbery and murder. If ever there'd been a Latimore in Franklin County who'd died of natural causes, it had happened too far back for anyone to remember.

And then there was Chase. Tragically handsome, sensitive and intelligent. A victim of circumstance, scarred by his awful upbringing, trapped by a reputation he hadn't earned. Jenna—or Kayla, as she'd been called then—was the only one who could see the truth about him, and her love could redeem him. Or so she'd told herself. Eight tumultuous months of covert trysts and heated parental arguments later, she'd realized she'd been wrong and everyone else had been right. Chase really was no good.

It was their first real argument that had opened her eyes. She barely remembered what had started it; some trivial thing or other that Chase had blown way out of proportion, no doubt. What mattered was Chase's reaction. He hadn't hit her, exactly, but he'd taken her roughly by the shoulders and shoved her down onto the pavement, hard, right there in the Dairy Queen parking lot.

She'd watched him stalk off, then gotten shakily to her feet and called her dad and asked him to pick her up. He'd come immediately. She hadn't told him Chase had hurt her—she'd been scared for his own sake of what he'd do to Chase if he knew—and, to her relief, he hadn't pressed for details. It had been enough for him to hear her say that she was through with Chase. So she'd hidden the scraped palms and swollen wrist, and toughed out the pain of a bruised tailbone. A few months later she'd gone off to college, feeling as if she'd woken up from a bizarre fever dream, and congratulating herself on putting the whole ugly episode behind her—only to come home for Thanksgiving and find that her horrible abusive ex was now dating her little sister.

Never in her wildest dreams would she have imagined such a thing. Kara was the obedient daughter, the one who did as she was told without talking back. But somehow Chase had managed to take all that unquestioning compliance and sweet affection and transfer it to himself.

And for that, Jenna had only herself to blame. Throughout her own relationship with Chase, Kara had been her confidant. She'd listened to Jenna's rants about how misunderstood he was—listened and sympathized. She'd gone along to the seedy parties where Jenna and Chase used to meet. Was it really surprising that with Jenna out of the picture, Chase had sunk his claws into Kara?

Kara never had a great moment of realization about Chase the way Jenna had, at least not permanently, and she'd endured worse violence at his hands than Jenna ever had. It made Jenna feel sick to remember her sister's bruises, and the bruised spirit that couldn't or wouldn't break free. Kara had held on to Chase with a tenacity that Jenna had never suspected her quiet, sweet sister possessed. Oh, she'd left him a few times, after Halley was born, when the maternal instinct to protect her child had competed with her loyalty to her man. But she'd always gone back.

Had Kara had any idea how stoned Chase was that terrible day when she'd gotten into the passenger seat of his Alfa Romeo to pick up Halley with him? Had she honestly thought he was competent to drive? Jenna had never had a chance to ask. She couldn't ask Kara anything anymore.

Halley's inflated recitation of her own all-too-sparse activities trailed to an end. An awkward pause fell.

"What else?" Caroline asked.

Give the kid a break, Jenna thought.

But before she could cut in on the conversation and help carry the load, Halley came up with another piece of news. "Gillian's started working at the equine center," she told her grandmother.

"That's nice," said Caroline. "Gillian's your friend that you met at Lalo's, right?" she added—unnecessarily, Jenna thought, since Halley didn't have any other friends to confuse Gillian with.

"Uh-huh," said Halley. "Her dad came to Lalo's a few weeks ago to watch a game, and she and I played Giant Jenga together."

The girls had seen each other once or twice a week since

their first meeting, and only at Lalo's. Gillian's dad, Kevin, was a regular customer, and always brought his daughter with him. Kevin looked a bit young to have a daughter Gillian's age, but Gillian's mother didn't seem to be in the picture, and he appeared to be doing the best he could. There was something befuddled about Kevin, with his rumpled T-shirts and unruly hair standing up all over his head, and a perpetually mystified expression on his face, as if he'd woken up one day to find himself inhabiting his own life without any idea how it had come about. Jenna knew he and Gillian lived in an old farmhouse surrounded by lots of rusty tractors and things. But he was always courteous to the staff at the restaurant and bar, tipped well and never drank past his limit or made himself obnoxious.

Not that any of that mattered, because Halley wasn't going to Gillian's house. Sleepovers, trips to the movies and unsupervised sessions of "hanging out" were out of the question for Halley.

Jenna listened in silence to Halley's recital of Gillian's equestrian adventures, feeling simultaneously guilty and fearful. Guilty because Halley's own life was so limited that she had to live vicariously through book characters and her one and only friend. Fearful because even that one friendship made Halley vulnerable. Halley was smart and savvy, as well as naturally introverted. She thought before she spoke. But she was only twelve years old. Would she manage to keep her lies straight when talking with Gillian? Or would she slip up one day and reveal something that would somehow start a chain reaction that would pull down the whole house of cards that made up her and Jenna's false identities? Maybe Halley had slipped up already, and Jenna didn't know it yet.

Something inside Jenna's chest started to clench. She took a deep breath and forced herself to think of all the chores she had to do once the call ended. She wished she could do them now, and get them checked off, and bury her doubts under the illusion that she had everything under control.

"That equine center," said Caroline. "Isn't that the same place where you went for the barn raising?"

Oh, that barn raising. Jenna shuddered at the memory. It had been a big community-wide affair, with dozens of volunteers showing up to reassemble a salvaged hundred-year-old barn at the equine center. Tito and Lalo had donated beer and food, and Jenna had worked the event for half a day. It should have been fun—and for most of the people there, it had been—but all Jenna could think of the whole time was how many people were there, and how easy it would be for Chase to show up and take Halley. Which was ridiculous, because Chase was in prison, and how would he even know about the barn raising, anyway? It was infuriating, how he was always in Jenna's head, ruining everything.

"Yeah, that's the one," said Halley. "The owner's name is Susana. She's really nice. Gillian was already taking lessons from her before the barn raising. Now she and Susana have worked out a deal where Gillian gets the use of a horse in exchange for feeding him and all the other horses twice a day. She grooms him and takes care of him and gets to ride him whenever she wants. He still boards with Susana, but it's almost like he's her own horse."

"That sounds like a good deal," said her grandmother.

"Yeah, it is. And now Susana's having a horse camp this summer and I want to go."

Jenna's head whipped around. *What* did Halley just say?

Caroline clapped her hands together, and suddenly she didn't look sad and worn anymore. She looked like the mother Jenna remembered.

"Horse camp!" she said. "How exciting! What all do they do there? How long is it? Do you stay overnight?"

"Oh, no, it's just a day camp. Five days, Monday through Friday. You show up early in the morning and eat breakfast there. You learn about grooming and feeding, and how to take care of tack, and Susana gives you horseback riding lessons, and you muck out some stalls and go for a trail ride, and have lunch. That's the first four days. Then on the last day, there's an exhibition for the parents to see everything you've learned. Doesn't that sound like fun?"

"It sounds marvelous! Is Gillian going?"

"Yes. I want to go soooo bad."

She said it without a hint of guile in her voice, and without glancing Jenna's way. Jenna felt her mouth drop open. Why, that little schemer.

"Well, you should!" Caroline said firmly.

Things were escalating fast. It was time for Jenna to take back control of the situation.

"Halley," she said, "go to your room, please. It's my turn to talk to Gigi now."

Halley got up without a word of protest and without seeming troubled by Jenna's stern tone. "Bye, Gigi," she said, waving sweetly. "I love you."

"I love you too, precious."

Jenna waited until Halley's bedroom door shut, then turned to face the screen.

"What?" said her mother. Her smile had been replaced by a wary expression.

"What do you mean, *what*?" said Jenna. "You know *what*. Why did you do that? Why did you give in to her that way? She was obviously trying to get you on her side to force me to say yes."

Her mother lifted her chin. "And why shouldn't you

say yes? Why shouldn't that child go to horse camp if she wants to?"

Jenna sputtered. She didn't even know where to begin.

"If it's a cost issue, I'll pay for it," said her mom.

"You know perfectly well that this isn't about money. It's about Halley's safety. I can't let her spend six hours away from me for five days. Why do you think I home-school her?"

Caroline sighed. "Honey, you've already changed both your names and moved fourteen hundred miles away from home. How much more will it take before you're satisfied?"

The words stung. "I didn't do all that for my own amusement," she said tartly. "I did it for Halley."

She glanced down the hall to make sure Halley's door was closed before going on. "It isn't just about safety, you know. Do you have any idea what it was like for her, after the accident? Having everyone know her as the daughter of the man who got behind the wheel stoned and killed all those people in that wreck? It was bad enough just being connected to that clan. As long as she stayed in Franklin County, she was always going to be a Latimore from Rocky Mount. Even as a ten-year-old she was already suffering from that in school. I didn't want a black cloud following her for the rest of her life. It's bad enough she has to live with the memories."

"I know all that," said Caroline. "But enough is enough, Jenna. She's twelve years old, almost a teenager, and you never let her out of your sight. Sooner or later, she's going to have to be away from you. You can't protect her all her life."

"I can protect her now. She's still a child, and I'm her legal guardian. Protecting her is my responsibility."

Her mother leaned toward the webcam. "But protection isn't all she needs! She needs interests, friendships, activities. She needs to spend time in places other than home and that bar. Week after week, it's the same. I ask her what she's been up to, and all she can come up with is a reading list, some lesson summaries and snatches of secondhand conversations. Does that child do *anything* for fun besides reading?"

"Of course she does! She also listens to music a lot, and sometimes she draws."

Jenna knew how inadequate that sounded even as she said the words. Caroline gave her a look.

"She needs more than that, and you know it. She needs something outdoors and physical—like horse camp."

"It won't stop with horse camp. Next she'll want lessons, then a horse-for-hire arrangement like Gillian's got. Then she'll want to learn barrel racing, and next thing you know, the whole thing will have taken over our lives, practically. Horseback riding is a very engrossing sport."

"All the better! If she's into horses, maybe that'll keep her too busy for...other things."

She didn't have to specify. Other things meant bad boys with flashy sports cars and drug habits.

"But horseback riding has its own set of dangers," Jenna said. "Did I tell you about the legal notice Susana has posted at the entrance to her facility? It's this whole inherent risk thing about how you can't hold the owners liable if you get hurt or killed, because horses are obviously huge, dangerous creatures, and everyone knows it."

"There's inherent risk in *life*, dear!" her mother said, her voice rising. Then, more quietly, "Look, I know you have regrets. I do too. But not all sins are sins of commission. The older I get, the more I understand that. Lost opportunities can be as costly as mistakes. They can turn into resentment and bitterness."

Jenna thought about the new thread of defiance in Halley's attitude. She was getting old enough to evaluate Jenna as a person and find her lacking.

"Let Kirsten go to horse camp," said Caroline. "If you clamp down too hard, you'll lose her. You of all people should know that."

Jenna bristled. "What's that supposed to mean?"

"You know exactly what it means. Part of what attracted you to you-know-who in the first place was that he was forbidden."

Jenna almost smiled then. Her mother couldn't or wouldn't remember to call Halley by her new name, but she always referred to Chase as you-know-who—as if speaking his name aloud would conjure him, or something.

"So what are you saying?" Jenna asked. "That if you and Dad had told me to go ahead and date Chase, he would have lost his mystique, and everything would have turned out fine?"

Her mother flinched at the sound of the name. "No, of course I'm not saying that. But maybe if we'd been better about trusting you to use your own judgment about other things... I don't know. Maybe it would have made a difference."

It was easy to get sucked into the "what-if" game. Every day, Jenna found herself playing out a thousand scenarios of things she could have said or done differently with Kara, and wondering if any of them could have saved her. She knew her parents had done the same thing. Had they been too protective? Not protective enough? What had been the exact combination of things they'd done wrong that had caused their daughter to go down that terrible path?

That game could break you. It had broken Jenna's father. Aortic aneurysm might have been his official cause of death, but Jenna knew he'd died of a broken heart.

She sighed. "I'll think about it," she said.

"Good," said her mother, with a smug smile that seemed to say the matter had already been decided.

CHAPTER FIVE

WHEN JENNA WAS five years old, she wanted to be a princess—and so did Kara, who'd always followed wherever Jenna led. Caroline had reveled in being the mother of two girly girls and encouraged the enthusiasm by providing gorgeous dresses, tiaras, necklaces and sparkly shoes. In those days, there'd even been a real-life princess for a role model, Princess Diana—or, as Caroline had insisted on calling her, Diana, Princess of Wales. Even as little girls, Jenna and Kara had been avid followers of the beautiful blonde princess, starstruck by her grace and glamour, the fancy events and adoring crowds. Her death had left them sad and confused. Princess stories weren't supposed to end that way. A princess might fall into a long enchanted sleep, or take a bite of a poisoned apple that made her *look* dead, but she didn't stay that way. The prince always made her wake up again.

It wasn't until years afterward that Jenna had learned the rest of Diana's story, or at least the parts that had been made public—the desperately unhappy marriage, the constant torment from the paparazzi, the ongoing struggles with mental health. In the end, she'd gotten into a car driven by a man she'd trusted to know what he was doing, and he'd crashed that car into the side of a Paris tunnel, with the speedometer frozen at 121 mph.

A lot of rage had been directed at the paparazzi, who'd stood around taking pictures of the wreck instead of calling for help, and at the driver, whose blood alcohol had come in at three times the legal limit in France. But what could you expect? They were all out for what they could get.

You couldn't count on other people to look out for you and yours. That was on you. You couldn't abdicate responsibility for your own well-being. Some people called that preemptive victim-blaming. Jenna called it healthy self-preservation.

Not surprisingly, that mindset had had a profound effect on her personal life. All of her post-Chase romantic relationships had ended before they'd properly begun. She'd gone on a lot of first dates, and a few second and third dates, always taking her own car to meet the guy and driving herself home afterward, because somewhere along the line, she'd developed a full-blown phobia about being driven by other people. She couldn't actually remember the last time she'd let anyone drive her anywhere.

She'd been told more than once that she had trust issues. Well, of course she did. What was wrong with that? What *was* trust, anyway, but valuing someone else's judgment on at least an equal footing with your own, and surrendering control to that person? She didn't have that with anyone, and she didn't want to. And if that meant no romance for her, well then, so be it. That was the price she paid for security. She'd come to terms with it long ago.

So why was she slowly and laboriously wiping down a table that was already clean, pretending she wasn't keeping a peripheral eye on the conversation Tito was having at the bar with a very pretty woman?

The woman was tall and slender, and professionally dressed in a black pencil skirt, red blouse and black blazer. What was her name? Rosanna? Anastasia? Something multisyllabic and ultrafeminine like that. Jenna had never interacted with her much because she usually sat on the bar side, drinking blackberry mead and chatting with Tito, smiling her wistful smile and looking up at him with her big, sad, beautiful eyes.

Suddenly Tito braced his hands on the bar top, leaned toward the woman and delivered what looked like a pretty serious speech. Jenna couldn't see the woman's face from this angle, but judging from her posture and the set of her head, she was paying close attention.

He finished speaking and gave her an imploring look. She responded with a tiny nod. Tito's chest rose and fell in a sigh, and his lips curved into a gentle smile.

Okay, well, that could mean a lot of things. They could be having an intense conversation about philosophy or theology or...

Tito laid his hand over the woman's hand and gave it a squeeze.

A cold weight settled in Jenna's stomach. She'd never seen him do that before. That warm affection, that flow of heartfelt words—it looked as if Tito had himself a girl.

Well, why shouldn't he? He was a good man with a lot to offer—sensitive, intelligent...handsome. And it wasn't as if Jenna had any claim on him herself. There was no reason for her to feel this way, as if she'd been punched in the solar plexus. No reason at all.

Her own hand had slowed to a stop on the tabletop, still gripping the damp rag. Mechanically, she resumed wiping. *This is good*, she told herself, and tried to believe it. If the sight of Tito with another woman was capable of stirring this much emotional turmoil in her, then it was just as well that he'd been officially taken off the market. Now Jenna wouldn't be tempted.

She walked back behind the counter, rinsed her cleaning rag at the sink and wrung it out. For the past ten days, ever since her slipup about his mustache, she'd been frankly avoiding Tito. She'd purposely scheduled herself not to close with him all of last week and done her best to keep away from him during hours of operation. It felt like a kind of penance. And while it had kept her out of his presence, it certainly hadn't kept him off her mind. If anything, she'd thought about him more than ever. She kept remembering that last Friday night, when they'd cleaned the display case together, and assigned all the different liquor bottles to people, and sat on the floor together eating fried okra by hand out of a shared carton, their fingers bumping occasionally.

Without those late-night songfests and cleaning sessions to look forward to, all the flavor had gone out of life. The thread of attraction that she'd sensed between them had been pleasant, and she'd savored it, even while she'd known she couldn't act on it.

And apparently Tito's half of it had been all in her mind. He didn't feel anything for her. The long talks, the warm smiles, the private jokes—they didn't mean anything special. He was just taking an interest, being kind. Being Tito.

All of which was for the best. Nothing remained now but for her to act natural, and congratulate him on his romantic success, as a good friend would. And the sooner she got it over with, the better. Her avoidance of him was childish and cowardly. Time to rip off that Band-Aid.

The lunch rush was clearing out. She took the tickets to two tables and collected payment from three more. When she next turned her gaze toward the pass-through, she saw something that hit her like an ice pick through the heart.

Tito had come out from behind the bar and taken the blackberry mead woman in his arms.

This wasn't one of those quick, light hugs. This was warm, sincere, intimate.

Jenna actually gasped aloud. Then she spun around and walked blindly toward the back of the building, passing the counter and the kitchen, and finally taking refuge in the restroom.

It was empty. Jenna leaned her back against the door and took several steadying breaths. When her heart rate had returned to something approaching normal, she walked over to the mirror and looked herself in the eye.

She had her hair clipped high on her head, but some tendrils had come loose and were curling around her neck. Her shirt had a grease stain on the front that she hadn't noticed until now. She thought of the blackberry mead woman's impeccable clothes and smooth, sleek hair.

Enough! She had to get a grip. She couldn't keep letting her emotions run away with her like this. She and Tito could never be more than friends. She had to act like she was okay with that until it was true.

She took her hair down, ran her fingers through it and twisted it into a high, tight roll.

"You've got this," she told her reflection. Then she walked out of the restroom and down the hallway.

Out of habit, she scanned the dining room for Halley, but Halley wasn't there. Jenna had a brief moment of panic before remembering that Halley was safe and sound at horse camp—at least, Jenna had dropped her off at horse camp that morning. Whether she was safe and sound remained to be seen. All sorts of things could go wrong with a dozen or so high-spirited children and several huge, hoofed animals—even supposing that Chase stayed in prison where he belonged and didn't bust out and take Halley.

Jenna shut her eyes. Had she done the right thing in letting Halley go to horse camp? Her mother had made a pretty convincing case for giving Halley some freedom now to keep her from rebelling later. But was this the right time, and the right kind of freedom to give? Sometimes she felt as if she were driving on a slick road, trying to keep between the lines, but always in danger of swerving or overcorrecting.

She opened her eyes and let out a sigh. This was going to be a long day.

TITO WATCHED ANNALISA walk out of the bar. Her head was held high and her shoulders were squared, but he knew she felt anything but composed right now. Through the building's glass front he saw her draw herself up before briskly walking away down the sidewalk.

"Pretty girl."

He jumped a little and turned. Jenna had somehow managed to slip behind him with a small bin of the bar's pint glasses. With customers constantly passing back and forth between Lalo's Kitchen and Tito's Bar, sometimes an imbalance of plates, glassware and utensils built up on one side or the other, and the items had to be returned.

Jenna crouched and started transferring the glasses from her bin to the crate on the shelf under the counter. "Sorry," she said. "Didn't mean to startle you."

"That's all right," he said. "I guess I was deep in thought."

It was the first time in days that she'd spoken to him on her own initiative. Ever since the night she and Halley had come up to his apartment after closing, Jenna had been keeping her distance. Now here she was, in his space, on an errand she could easily have delegated to a part-timer.

She had her hair clipped high in a businesslike twist. As she carefully worked the crate back into its space, his gaze lingered on the nape of her neck. It looked strangely vulnerable without the usual escaped tendrils of dark gold hair curving around it.

Suddenly Jenna was on her feet again, facing him, looking him right in the eye. "What's her name?" she asked.

Tito blinked. "What's whose name?"

Jenna jerked her head toward the door. "You know who. That pretty girl who just left."

"Oh, you mean Annalisa?" Tito asked. "Annalisa Cavazos."

"That's right. I remember now. She works somewhere downtown, doesn't she?"

"Yes, at the law office down the block. She's a paralegal."

Jenna nodded. "Well, she's very pretty."

It seemed as if that had already been said, but Tito merely replied, "Yes. Yes, she certainly is."

A brief, awkward pause fell. Something about this whole conversation felt off. What was Jenna doing? Why was she suddenly making forced small talk, after a week of avoiding him? And why was she giving him that knowing, expectant look?

At last she said, "So?"

"So what?" asked Tito.

Impatient sigh. "So are you together?"

A quick shout of laughter escaped him. "*Together?* Annalisa and I? Oh, no, no. She's in love with my brother Javi."

"Ohh," said Jenna, drawing the word out. "Oh, I see. So…are *they* together?"

"Nope. Never have been."

"Well then, what—" Jenna stopped herself. "Sorry, I shouldn't pry."

"It isn't exactly a secret," Tito said. "Annalisa has had a thing for Javi since we were all kids. It's never been reciprocated. And she's finally coming to the conclusion that it's time for her to move on."

"Maybe she'll move on with you."

He gave her a sidewise look. "You seem awfully determined to pair me up with her. Why the sudden interest in my love life?"

Incredibly, Jenna blushed. "I'm just looking out for you, that's all. You're a good guy. Annalisa's a beautiful woman, and she seemed awfully intent on whatever it was that you were saying to her."

"Well, yeah. That's because I was talking about Javi."

Jenna gave him a deep, searching look, and he felt his own face heat up. What was happening here? Was it possible that Jenna was jealous?

He was familiar enough with the emotion of jealousy, but he couldn't recall ever being on the receiving end. Usually he was the one with that burning sensation deep in his chest, watching helplessly as the girl he wanted paid attention to some other guy. Did Jenna actually feel that way about him?

Not for the first time, he wished he could see inside her head.

"People confide in you a lot, don't they?" she asked.

"They do," he said. "Occupational hazard. It's natural to tell your troubles to the guy behind the bar."

"I don't think so," she replied. "I mean, yeah, that's true as far as it goes, but it's more than that with you. You're a good listener—compassionate and empathetic, and smart, and...trustworthy. I'll bet you were the kind of guy who was very popular with girls in high school."

Tito considered this. "If by popular you mean they told me all about the problems they were having with their boyfriends or the guys they liked, and listened to my advice, and told me how caring and emotionally intelligent

I was, and how they ought to date guys like me, and then went right back to the jerks they'd been with before, or took up with other jerks, then yes, I was the most popular guy in school."

Jenna leaned her hip against the backbar as if settling in for a long chat. "That sounds kind of harsh and cynical for you."

"Yeah, I guess it does. I don't actually believe that every guy in the world besides myself is a jerk, but there've been times in my life when it felt that way."

"What about your brother Javi?"

"Oh, he isn't a jerk. He's actually a pretty good guy, just stubborn and clueless."

"Which one is Javi, anyway?" Jenna asked.

"You've never met him. He went west a few years back to work in the oil fields. He's kind of the angry rebel of the Mendoza boys. You know how it is with sibling relationships. We all have these roles, relative to each other, and we all know which one is which, even if we never talk about it. Johnny's the one most like Dad, Eddie's the handsome one, Enrique's the biggest and strongest, Javi's the rebel. It's confining and reductive, but we never fully outgrow it."

Jenna pondered this. "You really think Eddie's the handsome one?"

Tito chuckled. "You've seen him, right?"

"Well, yeah. He's good-looking, if you like that type."

"Tall and muscular, with classic features and perfect hair? That type?"

She waved this off. "It's all a matter of taste. So…which one are you?"

"Isn't it obvious? I'm the runt."

She gave him a playful smile. "I'd have thought you'd be the smart one."

Tito shrugged. "Tomato, tomahto."

"Oh, come on. That's a false equivalence and you know it. Who's being reductive now?"

"I am. That's my whole point."

She tilted her head to the side. "Yeah, I guess that's true."

The return of their old friendly ease felt good. He'd missed this. There was no one he enjoyed talking with more than Jenna. No matter what the subject, no matter how offbeat or abstruse, she could keep up, and more than keep up. She challenged him, stimulated him, kept him on his toes.

"How about you?" he asked. "You have a sister, right? What are your sibling roles?"

He was taking a big chance, prying into that deeply guarded background of hers, but her open curiosity about his love life had made him bold.

Jenna's face seemed to turn in on itself, a thoughtful crease forming between the finely arched brows.

"I'm the tough one," she said at last. "Kara was the sweet one."

There was a sad finality in her tone, which, coupled with her use of past tense, was highly suggestive. Kara was either dead, or irrevocably alienated from Jenna. No wonder Jenna didn't like talking about her.

But she'd answered the question, and spoken her sister's name to Tito for the first time ever. Surely she had to trust him a little, to do that much.

He'd pushed enough for one day. Time for a change of subject.

After a respectful silence, he asked, "How are you enjoying the Lord Peter Wimsey books?"

Jenna's face brightened. "Very much. I finished *Clouds of Witness* last night, and I have *Unnatural Death* on my bedside table, ready to go. And I noticed Halley thumbing through *Whose Body?* the other day, so maybe she'll start reading them too. The diction's pretty advanced for a twelve-year-old, but she's a smart kid, and she can always reread when she's older and catch all the things she missed the first time around. That's what I always did."

"Yeah, me too," said Tito. He scanned the dining room next door. "Speaking of Halley, where is she? I haven't seen her today. Is she in the break room?"

"Halley's at horse camp," Jenna said. Her tone was grim, as if she'd said Halley was in juvenile detention.

"Oh, the one at Susana Vrba's place?"

"That's the one."

"You don't seem very happy about it," Tito said.

"I'm not. But she really wanted to go, and I can't protect her all her life. Or so I've been told."

He was pretty sure it wasn't the dangers of horseback riding that Jenna was worried about, or at least not primarily. She just didn't like having Halley away from her. Most parents of twelve-year-olds would be accustomed to having their kids spend significant chunks of time away from them, but that had never been the case for Jenna and Halley. Tito had never asked Jenna why, and she'd never volunteered information. He knew she wasn't a fussy, fearful person. She wouldn't be as cautious as she was without good reason.

He wished he could reassure her that everything would be okay, but that was impossible when he didn't know the particulars of the situation. He wished he could take her in his arms and tell her he'd protect her and Halley from harm, no matter what it was that threatened them, but that was impossible too.

Instead, he said, "Well, if it makes you feel any better, Roque Fidalgo's helping Susana with that camp, and he knows how to handle himself. I've sparred with him at the gym."

She studied him a moment. He was treading on new ground here, recognizing Jenna's security concerns, tacitly acknowledging the elephant in the room.

"Good to know," she said at last.

"So how long does the camp run?" Tito asked.

"Monday through Friday. Gillian's there, too. I dropped off Halley and Gillian at Susana's place at seven this morning, and Kevin will pick them both up and bring Halley here after they're finished for the day."

"Ah," said Tito, enlightened. "Is that why you're working all morning shifts this week?"

He regretted the words as soon as they were out. They sounded needy, as if she owed him an explanation for not closing with him.

"Mmm-hmm," said Jenna.

Her gaze faltered, darting away from him just for a second before returning to his face.

It happened so quickly that he'd have missed it if he'd looked away himself for even a moment. But he'd seen, and he knew what it meant. Jenna had just lied to him. Which meant that it wasn't because of horse camp, or at least not entirely, that she'd scheduled herself to work shifts that would overlap his by only a few hours. It was like he'd thought before. She was avoiding him.

And unless he missed his guess, it wasn't because she didn't want to be with him. It was because she was afraid of getting too close to him.

She was here with him now, though. She'd sought him out in order to ferret out the details of his relationship with Annalisa. And she'd stuck around afterward just to talk. Which might mean that she'd decided he was worth the risk, or maybe that she couldn't help herself.

Possibilities whirled through his head.

Stop overthinking again, he told himself. *Give it a rest. Stop trying to figure her out.*

But he might as well tell himself to stop breathing.

The front door opened, and a tall, bearded man walked in. He was dressed casually, in jeans and a T-shirt, but his manner and bearing, from his upright posture to the shine on his boots, clearly marked him as a cop. In fact, he was a county constable, which around here covered a wide range of duties, from issuing subpoenas to making arrests.

"Hey, Kowalski," someone called from a table. "Did you catch all the bad guys?"

Kowalski didn't answer. He went straight to the bar and took a seat on his regular stool.

"Give me a shot of Jack Daniel's," he said.

Tito silently poured and set the glass down. Kowalski threw back the shot, asked for another and gazed blankly ahead with the thousand-yard stare common to freshly off-duty law enforcement and trauma nurses.

Tito poured again, still without speaking. He'd known Coby Kowalski for a long time. If he wanted to talk, he'd talk. Until then, Tito would leave him in peace.

"Another," Coby said.

Tito and Jenna exchanged a glance. Coby usually stopped after one shot and moved on to beer. Three shots in quick succession was approaching dangerous territory. On the other hand, he wasn't actually intoxicated yet, so cutting him off would be premature. Tito didn't relish the idea of having to refuse service to a respected member of local law enforcement, but having a drunk cop on his hands wouldn't be so great either.

He filled the shot glass again. He'd play this thing by ear. If necessary, he'd send a discreet text to Rick Henderson, Coby's work partner, and hint that it would be a good idea for him to come to the bar.

Coby cupped his hand loosely around the glass, stared into its amber depths a moment and asked, "Why do battered women stay with their abusers?"

Tito wasn't sure how to answer. As a member of law enforcement, Coby certainly knew far more about the subject than Tito did—which meant that he wasn't seeking information. He just needed the release of talk.

Jenna's presence was an added complication. She could have quietly gone back to Lalo's and left Tito to it, but instead she picked up a cloth and started polishing glasses, clearly stalling. Why? Because she wanted to hear what Tito said? Or because she wanted to contribute an answer herself? Either way, he'd have to tread with extra care. He didn't know for a fact that Jenna was a survivor of abuse herself, but circumstances did seem to point that way.

He forced his attention back to the question. Why *did* battered women stay with their abusers?

Some people, Tito knew, would reply that a better question would be, *Why does society let abusers get away with their abuse?* But Coby wasn't society. He was one man. He was also a cop. If there was anything he could lawfully do about whatever particular situation he had in mind, he'd have done it by now.

"It's a complex issue," Tito said at last. "I think sometimes they're beaten down emotionally and mentally as well as physically. They don't believe it's possible for them to get away—or else they've been gaslit to the point where they think that nothing's really wrong or that the abuse is their fault. From what I've read, abusers tend to be skilled talkers and manipulators. They know how to direct a conversation and make people think what they want them to think."

Coby raised his head, and Tito saw the raw desperation in his eyes. "I wish I could—I wish there was a way to get them away, out of that environment. Once she was out from under his influence, she'd start thinking straight again, right?"

"I don't know," Tito said. He wished he had something better to offer, but false comfort was worse than nothing, even if Coby could believe it.

Then Jenna spoke up.

"Sometimes it's more than gaslighting," she said gently. "Sometimes abusers make threats about what they'll do if the abused person ever leaves—threats to hurt or kill that person, or other people, or animals. And the abused person knows that they aren't empty threats."

Coby looked at her. "Yeah, that's true. It's risky to leave. But it's risky to stay, too. If only she would press charges, at least there'd be something to *do*, something proactive. A way forward. It'd sure be better than waiting around to see what's going to happen next."

"Maybe she needs an exit strategy," Jenna said. "A plan that covers all foreseeable contingencies. That's where a third party can be especially helpful. You might be able to help her get everything in place before she leaves, if she's open to that."

"Yeah, I can do that," Coby said. "But she still has to follow the plan."

"That's right, she does. And you can't make her do that. No matter how much support you give, or how well you prepare, you can't make her press charges, and you can't make her leave."

Coby downed his third shot. He didn't order a fourth, and he didn't speak again.

In the silence that followed, thoughts and questions swirled through Tito's mind. Had Jenna spoken from personal experience? If so, how had she gotten away from her own abuser? Had *she* had an exit strategy? Had someone helped her? What threats had her abuser made that had caused her to run away with her daughter and start over someplace new? What had he done to make them so afraid?

He wished he could do more than wonder. He wanted to help protect them both, make them feel secure. But he couldn't do that unless Jenna let him in.

Through the glass front of the building, he saw a battered Dodge pickup pull into a parking space and shudder to a stop. There was a blonde head in the back seat, bent close to a reddish head. Two young girls having a whispered conference together.

He nudged Jenna. "Isn't that Kevin's truck?"

Jenna sucked in a quick breath, then let it out in a relieved sigh. "Yes, it is," she said. "Halley's back."

She flashed him a quick, bright smile and hurried back to Lalo's Kitchen.

Tito watched as Halley got out of the pickup, waved goodbye to Kevin and Gillian and came through the door, flushed and windblown, with a tired, happy smile. She took a seat at the counter and started chattering away to Jenna. Tito couldn't hear the words, but it looked as if her first day at horse camp had been a good one.

He was glad Jenna had let her go. The kid needed to spend time somewhere other than inside these walls. What good was survival if you didn't truly live?

CHAPTER SIX

JENNA HAD THE driving dream again that night, the one where she was sitting in the passenger seat of an out-of-control car, trying and failing to take hold of the steering wheel. It was a recurring anxiety dream for her; she had it at least once a week. But this time the car was hitched to a horse—plunging, rearing, dragging the car into oncoming traffic, with an infant Halley screaming in her car seat.

All that being the case, her unease on the second day of horse camp was worse than on the first day. Throughout the morning, her thoughts were clouded by dread—and not just of Chase showing up and taking Halley away. All sorts of things could go wrong at horse camp. Halley could get trampled by a horse, or thrown from one, or kicked in the head. Once you started being afraid, there was no end to it.

Jenna left her phone sounds turned on and checked for incoming texts or calls every few minutes or so, ping or no ping. She caught a lot of resentful glances from Veronica, with whom she'd had to take a hard line regarding phone usage during work hours. Jenna knew she was being un-professional and hypocritical, undermining her credibility as a manager, but she couldn't make herself care.

The breakfast crowd cleared out, and preparation for the lunch rush began. Nothing terrible had happened yet, but Jenna's sense of dread only grew. She couldn't shake the feeling that a bomb was about to drop.

When the fateful text finally came, it had nothing to do

with equine catastrophe. It wasn't from Halley or Susana at all. It was from her mom.

Chase is out of prison.

Jenna stood with her phone in her hand, staring down at the screen. She couldn't move, couldn't think. Now that the horrible thing had happened, it didn't seem real.

What do you mean? she typed back.

I mean he's out of prison, came the reply. They released him.

Wake up, wake up, Jenna told herself. She shut her eyes tight, willing herself back into her nice cozy bed at home, with sunlight streaming through the curtains, and the whole day ahead of her, and Chase safely incarcerated.

She opened her eyes. She was still in Lalo's Kitchen, and the terrible words on her phone screen were still there.

How do you know? she asked, grasping after facts in a last attempt to make the thing not real.

Myra told me, her mom answered. She saw it on the Internet. All the Latimores went to meet him at the penitentiary when he got out. They were posting pictures on Instagram.

Jenna felt a sudden plunging sensation, as if the floor had just dropped deep into the earth. Myra was her mother's oldest friend. Jenna didn't like her very much. She was opinionated, officious and overbearing, constantly interfering in things that were none of her business. But she wasn't one to go off half-cocked. Jenna had never known her to get her facts wrong.

How is that possible? Jenna typed. He barely served the minimum sentence! How can he be out so soon?

I don't know, her mother replied. Good behavior? Overcrowding? All I know is, he killed my daughter and now he's a free man.

Jenna raised her head, dimly aware that Veronica was standing in front of her, saying something. Jenna could see her lips moving, but the words were just sounds with no meaning. She didn't know how long Veronica had been there or what she was saying. None of it mattered. Nothing mattered except Halley. Jenna had to find her, *now*, and keep her safe.

Jenna turned her back on Veronica, hurried behind the counter and reached into the space where she kept her purse. It wasn't there. She groped blindly for a while, her heart rate speeding up, before stumbling off toward the break room.

The brick-lined hallway had never looked so long. It was like something out of a nightmare. Her legs felt heavy and slow, as if they had weights strapped to them, and she could almost feel Halley's arms wrapped tight around her neck like when she was little, and hear her voice begging Jenna not to let Kara take her away.

She found her purse on the break room counter. She fumbled inside for her keys, found them, and promptly dropped them on the floor. A whimper escaped her throat, a frightened animal sound. She bent to pick up the keys and whacked her head on the counter, so hard that she saw stars.

Tears of pain stung her eyes. Something hurt deep inside her chest, as if there were some vicious wild creature inside her rib cage, clawing and scrabbling to get out. She was breathing way too fast and couldn't stop. She had lost control of her own body.

What was happening? Was she having a heart attack? Was she actually about to die, here on the break room floor?

She didn't know how long she sat there, alone and hyperventilating. But suddenly, there was Tito, holding her face between his hands, staring her straight in the eye.

"Jenna, listen to me. I want you to focus on your breathing. In through the nose, out through the mouth. In through the nose, out through the mouth."

He was kneeling on the floor in front of her. His hands were warm against her cheeks.

"Breathe," he said. "In through the nose, out through the mouth. Do it with me."

She tried. It took a long time, but gradually her breaths grew longer and steadier.

"That's good," said Tito. "Now hold it a few seconds before you let it out. Do it with me."

She was gripping his arms now. They were lean and strong; she could feel the muscle and sinew through his shirtsleeves. The two of them were breathing together, their faces inches apart, as if Jenna was in labor and Tito was her birthing coach. She kept her gaze locked on his, and he stared right back at her, his eye contact anchoring her in reality.

She was breathing almost normally now, and the pain and constriction in her chest had eased up. Tito smiled and gently rubbed his thumbs under her eyes, wiping away her tears.

Unless Jenna missed her guess, she'd just had a full-blown panic attack—and Tito had known exactly what to do about it. Of course he had.

"Better?" he asked.

She nodded. "I have to go get Halley," she managed to say.

"Why? Is she hurt? Sick?"

Jenna shook her head. The panic, which had subsided to a feeble flutter in her stomach, started to rise again.

"I have to get her," she said. Her voice sounded child-ishly high.

"Okay," said Tito. "But not by yourself. I'll drive you."

Fresh tears welled up in Jenna's eyes. "Thank you," she whispered.

She followed Tito out the back door, through the patio and into the parking lot.

Tito's daily driver was a 1969 Cadillac Eldorado in me-tallic red, a restomod with up-to-date air-conditioning and power steering and the like, but retaining its original dash-board and upholstery in pristine condition. Jenna already knew this. She'd walked past the car in the parking lot just about every day for the past year and a half, and Tito had told her all about the restoration work his father had done on it. But this was her first time inside the vehicle.

The engine started with a low rumble.

"Horse camp?" Tito asked as he pulled out of the park-ing lot.

"Yes," she said.

They drove in silence for a while. Then, all in a rush, Jenna said, "Halley's father is out of prison."

She hadn't consciously decided to tell him that. The words had come out on their own.

"And you're afraid he'll come after you and Halley," Tito said.

"Not me. Just Halley."

He gave her a questioning look. "I mean, he's not thrilled with me," she said. "He's bound to be mad that I took her away. But she's the one he's interested in. If he got hold of her, he wouldn't bother with me."

"Okay. Where was he incarcerated?"

"Green Rock Correctional Center. It's in Southern Vir-ginia."

"And when did he get out?"

She stared blankly at him a moment. "I—I don't know. My mom texted and said he was released, but she didn't say when."

She felt like an idiot. The exact timing of Chase's release was pretty critical information, but she'd lost her head the minute she'd learned that he was free.

She thought of Myra, that wellspring of information. She wasn't at all surprised that the Latimores had chosen to use Instagram to commemorate their felon relative's release from prison, but it did seem odd that Myra followed them on social media. Myra had never had any use for any of that clan. Maybe she just checked up on them once in a while without actually following them, to keep tabs on what they were up to. That sounded like something Myra would do. Nosy, but useful. How often did she check in? Daily? Weekly?

"Text your mom and ask her," Tito said.

Jenna reached for her phone, but it wasn't in her pocket.

A wave of nausea washed over her. "I don't have my phone," she said. "I must have left it at work."

She brought her fists down hard on the dashboard. "How could I have been so *stupid*? Letting my phone out of my sight is unforgivably careless."

Her mom was probably blowing up her phone with texts right now, wondering why Jenna wasn't responding.

"Whoa! Whoa!" said Tito. "Let's dial it back a bit here. I don't think anyone at Lalo's is going to take your phone and do anything nefarious with it."

"It's the principle of the thing. Don't you see? I can't afford to let down my guard. If I do, if I'm careless even one time, then it opens a whole floodgate, and where's it going to end?"

Her voice was rising to a hysterical pitch.

Tito laid a hand on her arm and said calmly, "Well,

there's nothing we can do about your phone right now. So the next question is, does Halley's father know where you are?"

That was the pertinent question, all right. Jenna forced herself to focus on it.

"I hope not," Jenna said. "I took all the precautions I possibly could. When I changed our names, I didn't have to go through the usual public disclosure thing where the new names are printed in the newspaper. Sometimes you're allowed to do it on the sly. It's up to the discretion of the judge, and he was an old friend of my father's."

"That's good," Tito said encouragingly. "What else did you do to cover your tracks?"

"Well, I erased myself from social media. That took some doing. Halley was too young to have her own accounts, of course, but I wasn't. I deleted all my accounts and untagged myself from other people's photos. I didn't want someone in Limestone Springs coming across an old tagged photo of me under a different name."

Tito nodded. "That makes sense. Social media must make it hard to establish a new identity."

"It sure does," Jenna said with a sigh. "And it's hard enough anyway. It's possible to get a new social security number, but that happens at a federal level. And if you do it, then you lose everything that's tied to your old number—credit report, bank accounts, job history, college degrees. You don't get set up with a whole new turnkey identity, with a job and a place to live and all that, unless you're in some high-level witness protection type of deal, which we're not. Or unless you have the money to pay for it through private channels, which I didn't. I had to do the best I could on my own."

"So the social security number you gave Luke when you applied at Lalo's was your original social security number?"

"Yes."

"But you didn't give him any references or job history to go along with it."

She glanced over at him, surprised that he remembered this. "Well, no. I had a fake backstory in place, and it didn't include me working or living in…the place I came from. Still, it would be easy enough for anyone who had my social—like Luke or Lalo, or you—to look up my work and school history and piece things together. I just had to hope none of you would do it."

"Sounds exhausting," Tito said.

"It is," said Jenna.

Downtown Limestone Springs lay behind them now. The land opened up into big residential lots, then into ranches and farms. Jenna suddenly realized she had her right foot pressed against an imaginary accelerator. The speedometer's needle showed that Tito was driving above the speed limit, but not by a lot. She supposed that was smart—getting pulled over would delay them even more— but she had to fight the urge to tell him to floor it.

He handed her his phone. "Look up Chase and see if you can find out when he was released," he said. "That ought to be a matter of public record."

She recoiled at the thought of entering Chase's name into Tito's phone, as if it would pollute the new life with the old. But it was a little late for that now. She steeled herself, typed his name and the prison's name, hit Enter—

And there was Chase's mug shot glaring up at her from the screen.

A fresh wave of nausea rose in her throat. It had been a long time since she'd seen even a digital image of that face. The bright blue eyes were squeezed half shut by swollen purplish bruises, but they still managed to glare defiantly at her. The dark blond hair stood up in disarray as if he'd just tumbled out of bed, and his cheeks and forehead showed dozens of tiny cuts made by slivers of shattered glass in the accident that had killed Jenna's sister. Chase had blown through a red light, and his flashy little Alfa Romeo had been T-boned on the passenger side by an extended-cab pickup. He'd suffered only minor injuries. Kara had never stood a chance.

Jenna swallowed hard and started scrolling.

"Here it is," she said. "He was released yesterday."

"Okay," said Tito. "Well, it sounds to me as if you took every precaution available to you to get yourself and Halley away from him. Given all that, how likely do you think it is that he'll find you at all, much less the day after he was released?"

She didn't answer right away. "I don't know," she said at last. "But Chase is smart. Not book smart, but people smart. I can't afford to take anything for granted where he's concerned."

"All right," Tito said.

They didn't speak again for the rest of the drive. Tito turned on to a country road lined with pecan trees that made a dense green arch overhead. At the end of the road was a driveway that wound past a plain barndominium-style house to a covered arena.

The Cadillac pulled into the driveway and parked near the house—close enough for Jenna to see what was happening in the arena, but not close enough for them to draw attention to themselves.

Halley was in the arena, a helmet over her blond hair, riding a brown horse with a black mane and tail and legs—a bay, according to Jenna's memory of horse books she'd read as a child. Susana was in the arena too, calling out instructions. Other campers stood gathered around outside the fence.

Jenna didn't know much about horsemanship, but she could see how confident and relaxed Halley was. The expression on her face was almost beatific.

"She looks good, doesn't she?" Jenna asked.

"She does," said Tito. "You want to watch a while? Let her finish her ride?"

"I guess there's no harm in that," Jenna said.

He shut off the engine, and a restful silence settled over them both. Jenna scanned the crowd of kids standing at the fence. She recognized Gillian right away, but she didn't know any of the others. It was about 80 percent girls, all young teens or preteens.

If Halley had a normal life, she might be friends with some of those kids. They might see movies and go shopping together, maybe have sleepovers and do each other's hair. But Halley didn't even do those things with Gillian, her one friend of her own age in Limestone Springs. Prior to horse camp, she'd only ever seen Gillian at Lalo's when Gillian's dad happened to bring her there. Even for an introverted kid like Halley, it wasn't much of a social life.

Jenna took a deep breath and let it out. "Okay," she said. "I guess I don't have to take Halley out of camp this very instant. It's possible that I overreacted just a bit. Chase probably isn't hiding behind a clump of cactus waiting to grab her and run. She'd be pretty embarrassed if I made her quit in front of the other kids, and it would be a hard thing to explain to Susana. So I'll just let Halley finish her day and then sleep on it."

"I think that's wise," Tito said.

Jenna turned to face him, admiring the clear-cut lines of his profile against the deep green of the trees outside the window.

"I see what you did here," she said.

Tito glanced at her. "What do you mean?"

"You know what I mean. The way you reasoned through this whole situation with me, asking all the right questions so I'd figure things out on my own. You didn't tell me what to do. You just helped me see it for myself. You're so devious, with your quiet, soothing presence and your irrefutable logic."

The corner of his mouth edged up ever so slightly, but he kept a straight face and said, "I don't know what you're talking about."

She punched him on the shoulder, and he turned to her, smiling broadly now. "You knew what you had to do. You just needed a little help getting there."

"Well, thanks," said Jenna. "You're a good friend, Tito."

They were facing each other now across the bench seat. The tension melted away from Jenna's body, leaving a deep sense of security and peace. She always felt safe with Tito.

He had the most wonderful hair, dark and glossy, fine and thick. It fell over his forehead from a widow's peak, barely skimming his eyebrows. His crisply pressed, snowy white shirt gave off a clean scent of laundry detergent and light starch. Did he iron his shirts and slacks for the week, up in his bachelor apartment above the bar? If so, what did he wear while he did the ironing? Did he even own a pair of jeans? Workout clothes? A bathrobe?

"You don't seem very fazed by the fact that I'm living under an assumed name," she said.

"Oh, I'm not. I've known for a while that you were on the run from something or someone."

She sat up straight. "You have?"

"Sure."

"You never said anything about it."

He shrugged. "Well, no. I figured if you wanted to keep it a secret, that was your business."

"How did you know I wasn't dangerous? A criminal fleeing justice?"

His gaze softened. "You didn't strike me as an unsavory character, and my intuitions tend to be correct."

He was watching her closely, his expression grave. His eyes were a rich warm caramel brown beneath expressive black brows. His face was comfortingly familiar—that long thin nose, that lean jaw beneath the neatly trimmed beard.

His right arm rested along the back of the Cadillac's bench seat, his hand almost touching her shoulder. He had beautiful hands, long and slender and sensitive.

His fingers stretched out a fraction of an inch toward her, then folded back in on themselves. She saw his chest rise and fall in a quick breath. In that moment she knew beyond a doubt that what he felt for her went beyond friendship and being a good guy. He wanted to kiss her, but he wasn't going to, because she was so vulnerable right now and he was too much of a gentleman to take advantage.

But if she were to kiss *him*, he would respond.

The ball was in her court. She had the power to make it happen. Right here and now, she could lay her hand against his cheek and close the distance between them with one swift movement. What would it feel like to kiss him? She wanted to know.

His face was deadly serious now. He moved infinitesimally closer to her. It was going to happen. She was finally going to kiss Tito, right here in the front seat of his classic Cadillac.

Realization washed over her in a cold wave. She was in Tito's *car*. She had gotten into a car with a man and let him drive her—willingly, without a second thought. She had surrendered control—like some sort of princess, letting a man take care of her.

Some change of emotion must have shown in her face, because Tito drew back, his own expression suddenly startled and mortified. Jenna faced forward again and stared at the dashboard. The interior of the car felt cramped and airless. Her heart fluttered in her chest like a trapped bird.

Even as the panic rose, she knew she was making a false equivalence. Tito wasn't the drunk French driver who'd smashed the Mercedes-Benz into the side of the Parisian tunnel, killing himself and Diana and Dodi Fayed. He wasn't Chase, who'd been stoned out of his mind when he'd taken the wheel of his Alfa Romeo to pick up Halley, with Kara in the passenger seat. Tito was a hundred times the man Chase was. She'd known him a year and a half and had never seen him lose control. He was a good man, a trustworthy man. She ached to confide in him, to steal into his arms and let the whole story come pouring out in sweet release.

But then what? Then he would know, and she could never take back the words.

She raised her head, sending her gaze back to the arena, and Halley. Without looking at Tito, she said, "Well, thanks for the ride. I guess we'd better head back."

The words sounded cold and hateful in her own ears, but she didn't have any better ones to offer. The sooner she and Tito both got out of this car and back to work, the better. For a moment neither of them moved or spoke. Then, in a voice that held no trace of confusion or hurt, Tito said, "All right," and backed the Caddy out of Susana's driveway.

Jenna concentrated on her breathing—in through the nose, out through the mouth. When her heart rate had returned to something approaching normal, she forced herself to face some facts. She'd gotten into Tito's car without a moment's hesitation. She'd forgotten to feel afraid—and she couldn't afford to do that again. She'd made it this far by not trusting anyone but herself. She wasn't about to change that now.

"I want you to do me a favor," she said.

Out of the corner of her eye she saw Tito turn and look at her. "Sure," he said. "Anything."

"Please don't talk to Halley about any of this. I don't mean just the fact that we drove out here to pick her up, but, you know…all of it. The whole thing with Chase. And please don't do any internet research on him, or on Halley and me. I know it wouldn't be hard to find the whole story, but I'd appreciate it if you'd leave it alone."

"All right," said Tito, and Jenna knew he meant it. Of course he wouldn't press Halley for information about the abusive ex-con father she'd had to run away from. And he wouldn't press Jenna either, if she didn't want him to. He would be discreet. He would respect her boundaries. He'd go on being the friend and coworker that she needed, and not push for more, because that was the kind of man he was.

A barrier had come down today. Jenna had suffered a hull breach, and things wouldn't be quite the same. She had to preserve the distance she had left, keep a buffer of privacy around herself and Halley. That was the only way to keep them safe.

CHAPTER SEVEN

ALL THROUGH THE ride home that afternoon, Halley chattered away, telling Jenna everything she'd learned in horse camp that day. It was rare for her to be so talkative, so... bubbly. She was such a serious kid, very mature for her age. She'd had to grow up fast.

"Susana says I have a good natural seat," Halley said. "She could hardly believe I'd never had lessons before. She's thinking about opening a class to teach barrel racing. Gillian and I could do that together."

She didn't ask if she could, and Jenna was glad. There was no need to thrash the matter out right now. The barrel-racing class might never happen, or Halley might lose interest in horses altogether.

She waited until Halley had talked herself out and subsided into a contented silence. It was a shame to ruin the mood by saying what had to be said now, but it couldn't be helped. Halley had to know.

Jenna steeled herself, then said, "I have some news."

Halley's head spun around to face her. "Tito asked you out," she guessed, her voice breathless with excitement.

"What? No," said Jenna.

"You asked Tito out," Halley said.

"No! Of course not. Why would you even think that?"

Halley rolled her eyes. "Oh, come on. You two obviously like each other. All those closing-time songfests, the way you look at each other and talk for hours on end. I don't understand why you don't just *go* for it already. The two of you would be great together."

Jenna gripped the steering wheel and stared straight ahead. "Tito," she said firmly, "is a good friend and a respected coworker, and nothing more."

Even as she kept her eyes on the road, she could feel the disbelieving look Halley was giving her from the passenger seat. Halley wasn't fooled.

"*Anyway*," said Jenna, "that isn't the news. The news is that your father is out of prison."

Silence. Jenna stole a glance at her niece. Halley was still swiveled around toward her, but her face had gone blank.

"How?" Halley asked. "I thought he was sentenced to four years."

"He was. But sometimes people get off early for good behavior."

"*Good behavior?*" Halley repeated. "Him?"

"I know," said Jenna. "It doesn't sound like him. But there were probably enough Latimores in prison with him, and enough Latimore shot-callers on the outside, to give him plenty of protection. That would make it possible for him to keep his head down and his nose clean if that was what he wanted to do. And he did want that…because he wants you. And now that he's free—"

"Wait," said Halley. "You're not going to pull me out of horse camp, are you?"

"Well—" Jenna began.

"Oh, please, please let me finish horse camp! I'll be so careful."

Jenna sighed. "Halley, you know your father wants you back. He's angry that I took you away, and that I didn't bring you to visit him in prison. All the other Latimores made sure I knew it, and they're all angry too. As far as he's concerned, he's your father and you belong with him. And he doesn't care if he has to break the law to get you back, as long as he doesn't get caught."

"But he couldn't take me from horse camp! There's such a crowd there. How could he grab me in front of all those people?"

"I admit it doesn't seem like a smart thing to do, but he's crazy enough for anything. He's bold and reckless and smart. We can't afford to take any chances where he's concerned."

Halley turned to face forward again. "It's not fair," she said, her voice thick with tears. "A thousand miles away and he's still ruining my life."

"I know," said Jenna. "I'm sorry."

After a brief silence, Halley tried again. "Please let me finish horse camp, Mother. There are only a few days left, and my dad can't have figured out where we are the second he got out of prison. I'll be super, super careful. Just let me finish camp and I won't ask for anything else."

Jenna didn't answer right away. She could feel herself weakening. Halley didn't often ask for things for herself, and she'd already lost so much that a child ought to have. Was it really necessary for Jenna to take this one thing away from her?

Finally Jenna spoke. "I want you to stay with the group at all times. Stay close to Susana and Roque. Don't ever, *ever* wander off. Got it?"

"Got it," said Halley brightly. "Thank you, Mother."

She reached into her bag and took out a book. Within seconds she was lost to the world, deep in her story, twirling her pale gold hair the way Kara used to. Jenna saw so much of Kara in Halley—in the shape of her face, the tilt of her nose, the aching vulnerability that made Jenna want to shield her from all the wickedness in the world.

But only half of her DNA had come from Kara. The other half was all Chase.

Was Jenna doing the right thing in letting Halley finish horse camp? She wished she could be sure. She wanted to keep Halley safe, and also raise her to be an emotionally healthy adult, in spite of all the trauma she'd experienced at a young age. Was Jenna succeeding? She hoped so, and some days she thought so. Other days, she honestly had no idea.

More and more often, as Halley got older, Jenna found herself completely and utterly perplexed. This single parenting gig was *tough*. She and Halley spent so much time alone together, and sometimes Jenna longed for another perspective. A third person could break up the rut and open the way to meaningful communication—especially a third person with a clear, logical mind and a wise, compassionate heart.

Jenna shook her head hard, impatient with herself. It was a sign of weakness, thinking the solution was a man, wanting to rely on him for stability and strength. Halley was her responsibility, not Tito's, and she'd managed just fine so far. She'd figure it out. She had to.

SELECTING THE RIGHT music was a crucial part of the running of a successful restaurant or bar. You wanted all the songs to fit the overall vibe of the place while also providing a good mix of tempo, energy and valence. You had to take into account the age and background of your customers and provide plenty of material that was familiar to them, but you didn't want to draw too heavily on any one genre or era, because if a customer recognized every song, the music became a distraction rather than a pleasant background.

It was a lot to consider, and Tito did consider it, laboring over his playlists, striving for the proper balance, and changing the lists regularly so they didn't get stale. But right now, with only himself to please, he'd chosen an old personal favorite, a blend of folk rock classics from the sixties and seventies—Jim Croce, Simon & Garfunkel, Carole King. It was an introspective, contemplative playlist. Even the relatively cheerful songs were tinged with melancholy, which perfectly suited the stormy weather outside, as well as Tito's present mood.

If Jenna were here, she'd be mixing it up with Lynyrd Skynyrd or Aerosmith. But this was early Sunday morning. Both Tito's Bar and Lalo's Kitchen were closed until noon. Tito was all alone.

Empty of customers, the two connected spaces felt vast and cavernous. But a phantom Jenna haunted Tito's mind, appearing whichever way he turned—carrying a food-laden tray high above her head, singing classic rock at the top of her lungs while wiping down countertops, frowning in concentration over her laptop as she placed orders from suppliers.

Most of all, he saw her sitting in the front seat of his Cadillac, mascara smeared, eyes red and puffy from crying, looking young and lost and achingly beautiful.

He'd replayed the scene again and again for the past five days. With his arm lying across the back of the seat, his fingers inches from her shoulder, it would have been so easy to take her in his arms. It would have been a perfectly natural move on the part of a good friend. But it would have meant something more to him than comfort and sympathy. And it would have been unconscionably pushy and presumptuous, taking advantage of her at a vulnerable moment to gratify his own desires, even if he'd had reason to think the advance would be a welcome one.

So he'd kept himself still. But then their eyes had met,

and Jenna's gaze had sharpened, and darted down, unbelievably, to his lips. And just for a moment, he'd been joyously certain that the attraction wasn't all on his side, and that she was seriously thinking about kissing him.

Apparently he'd been wrong. The next instant she'd drawn back with a look of what might have been revulsion on her face, and said that they should head back.

Which might mean simply that she was fighting her feelings for him. He could understand that. She'd been hurt, physically and emotionally, by a man she'd presumably loved at one time. She'd worked hard to get away from him and start a new life with her child. She couldn't afford to take another chance on romance. All her energy had to be focused on keeping herself and Halley safe.

Or it might mean that Tito had horribly misinterpreted the whole thing, and Jenna had never wanted to kiss him at all. He was usually good at reading signals, but in this case his feelings might be clouding his judgment, making him see what he wanted to see.

After all, she hadn't even meant to confide in him in the first place. The story had come spilling out of her after her panic attack, leading him to imagine an intimacy that wasn't there—unless, of course, she really was just gun-shy, in which case he needed to be patient.

Now here he was, caught in an endless loop of overthinking and second-guessing deep inside his head, exactly where he did not want to be.

A year and a half ago, Tito had been reconciled to being alone. He'd learned to take satisfaction in other parts of his life. But then Jenna had shown up and upset the delicate equilibrium.

His phone let out a ding. Tito picked it up from the counter, irrationally hoping to see a text from Jenna—a stupid thing to hope for, since the two of them had never texted about anything not work-related, but that was no reason they couldn't start. Their easy in-person banter could translate into a playful back-and-forth, a pleasantly stimulating continuo to tide him over through nonwork hours. It might even turn into more than that. Some people let their guard down while texting in a way that they didn't or couldn't in person.

He had a text, all right, but it wasn't from Jenna. It was from his cousin Lalo.

Lalo's long, convoluted, overly detailed, anxiety-filled message was a poor substitute for a flirtatious interchange with Jenna. He was a pretty good guy overall, conscientious and highly ethical, both excellent qualities in a business partner. But he worried too much, and tended to get in his own way.

Right now he was worrying over some policy of Luke's, and wondering whether he ought to step in and override it. Well, at least he was asking Tito's opinion rather than going behind Luke's back and undermining his authority. That was a step in the right direction.

Tito leaned his hip against the bar top and began to type.

Don't do it. Luke is the manager. Let him manage. He's better at it than you are. That's why you put him in charge. Remember what happened the last time you tried to micromanage him?

I remember, came the reply. I just thought I might sort of nudge him in a different direction. But if you think he's doing the right thing, then I'll stay out of it.

I do think so, answered Tito. Stop worrying.

Even as he hit Send, he knew that was useless advice. Lalo would never stop worrying.

Tito glanced at the Kraken bottle, the one Jenna had said

looked like Lalo, and chuckled. The rounded handles really were a dead ringer for Lalo's fussy, hands-on-hips posture.

Memories of that night, when he and Jenna had cleaned the display shelves together and assigned the different bottles to various employees, washed over him. They'd had such a good time.

Stop it, he told himself.

He exited from the Messages app, double-clicked the Home button and started clearing his tabs, swiping them up and away. Swipe, swipe, swipe—

His finger froze above an image of a man's face, bruised and swollen, facing the camera head-on. It looked like a mug shot. Tito didn't recognize the guy. He tapped the tab to bring it up to full screen.

It *was* a mug shot. And it belonged to one Chase Latimore, lately of Green Rock Correctional Center, in Chatham, Virginia.

A chill ran down Tito's spine. This had to be Jenna's ex. Jenna had used Tito's phone to look up details on his release, and the information was still here.

A pair of bright blue eyes glared at him from the screen. The unflinching gaze, the proud angle of the head, the defiant jut of the jaw—whatever Chase had done to get himself incarcerated, he didn't look sorry for it. The bruising around the eyes, a nasty abrasion on the forehead and a sprinkling of tiny cuts all over the face made Tito wonder. Had Jenna fought back? Or had Chase received these injuries in some incident, like a bar fight, completely unrelated to the offense that had landed him in jail? What exactly *had* landed him in jail? What had he done to Jenna, or to Halley, or to both of them, that had earned him a prison term lasting at least as long as Jenna and Halley had been in Limestone Springs? It had to be a felony offense.

A few minutes of internet research could tell Tito everything—not just Chase's crime, but Jenna's and Halley's old names, and where they came from.

His fingers itched to start tapping. Surely there wasn't any harm in finding out any of these things. But he'd given Jenna his word that he wouldn't go digging for information.

Well, he knew Chase's name, anyway, and what he looked like. That would come in handy if Chase ever did show up in Limestone Springs.

He double-clicked the Home button again and swiped Chase's mug shot away. Then he put his phone in a shallow drawer, picked up a bottle of glass cleaner and a lint-free cloth, and turned his attention to the back bar.

Next to the display case with its mirrored back, another, longer mirror, encased in an ornate Victorian frame, ran most of the width of the wall, reflecting the room in its entirety. Tito had gotten it at auction when doing the renovation years earlier. It was a handsome piece. The dark, carved wood gave off an old-fashioned ambience, and the mirror expanded the visual space while allowing Tito to keep an eye on things when his back was turned—to see who needed a refill, who needed to be cut off, who needed to be bounced.

He climbed the ladder and started cleaning at the top. The mirror was starting to develop some black spots, especially around the edges, evidence of its age, but Tito didn't mind. He liked the effect.

A brisk tapping made him turn around. A woman stood outside the door, silhouetted against the moody gray rain-washed street, peering through the glass with one hand shading her eyes and clutching a big shapeless tote bag.

Tito crossed the floor, unlocked the door and opened it just a crack.

"We're closed," he said in his sternest tone.

She gave him a bright smile. "I know the owner."

Chuckling, he opened the door wide, and she came in and gave him a hug, her bag flopping against him.

"Hey, Mom," he said.

"Hey, baby," said his mother.

Rose Mendoza was small and feisty, with a halo of thick dark curls. Tito alone of his brothers had inherited her slender frame instead of the bull-like build of his father. She set her bag on a long table, in the underside of one of the upturned benches resting there.

"So what have you got in your bag of tricks today?" he asked. All his life, his mother had been hauling around capacious, brightly colored tote bags filled with exercise gear, library books to be returned, packages to mail, stuff to donate to the thrift store, stuff she'd bought at the thrift store while making donations, and food to deliver to people who'd just had a new baby or were recovering from illnesses. This one was patterned with big flowers, and judging from its heft and shape, it was stuffed full.

"Oh, just a few odds and ends. A care package for Javi. This cute little clock I found at the thrift store. Some barbacoa to take to Ellen Rogers—she just had cataract surgery."

As she spoke, she removed the things from the bag and set them in a row on a narrow sliver of tabletop between the two benches.

"No barbacoa for me?" Tito asked, pulling a sad-eyed face.

His mother smiled, then reached into the bag again and drew out another food container.

"This one's for you, baby. Oh, and check out this shirt I got you from the thrift store."

"Nice," he said, taking the shirt from her. It was a button-down, deep blue, with a woven stripe—his size, his style, his cut—and looked brand-new. Rose Mendoza was an expert bargain hunter, her skills honed by decades of bringing up five boys on a small income.

She beamed at him. "Good! You can wear it to the party."

Ah, yes—the Fourth of July party. There was always a party coming up in the Mendoza family. Birthdays, holidays—any excuse to invite all the relatives and half the town over to their tiny house and cook enough food to feed an army.

She was watching him closely. "You're coming, right?"

"Sure, wouldn't miss it," he said with a cheerfulness he didn't feel. He didn't especially want to go but figured he'd better. He'd skipped out on this year's Cinco de Mayo bash and hadn't yet heard the end of it.

"Good! We're going to have a great time. Lots of people you know will be there."

Rose started naming them, focusing on single women around Tito's own age. He recognized quite a few names of female friends from high school who'd confided in him about their wretched relationships once upon a time.

"That's a lot of people, all right," he said. "I'm guessing you'll want some beer kegs for the party?"

"Yes. And some of those what-do-you-call-thems, those jugs that you put the mead in. Grumblers?"

"Growlers," he said. "Come on over to the bar top and we'll get it taken care of."

He took down a barstool for her to sit on, turned down the volume on the music and got her order placed.

"Let me bring some food from Lalo's for the party," he said. "My treat."

She waved her hand. "No, no. Don't worry about that. I can handle the cooking."

"I know you *can*. But it's a lot of food for a lot of people. I don't like to think of you slaving over a hot stove in the middle of the summer in that shoebox of a kitchen."

"My mother's kitchen was smaller than mine, and that didn't stop her."

"I know it didn't. But you work too hard, Mom. You're always taking care of people. I'm worried you're going to wear yourself out."

She gave him a look. "You're a fine one to talk. When's the last time you had a day off?"

"We're closed Sundays mornings until noon. You know that."

She laughed. "Baby, this *is* Sunday! And here you are, working! Do you ever rest at all?"

"Sure I do. I read, watch movies…"

"By yourself."

"No, not by myself," he said, thinking of Bunter.

"Your cat doesn't count. You spend too much time alone, baby."

"I'm with people all day, Mom. I need time alone to recharge."

She gave him a thorough once-over, sizing him up, searching for signs of neglect and strain, as she did every time she saw him.

"You're too thin," she said at last.

"Thanks," he said. "That's nice to hear."

"You know what I mean. Are you eating?"

"Yes, and working out. I've just got your metabolism, remember? I burn it all off. Don't worry about me. I'm fine."

"Are you? Okay, so you go to work, and you go home, which is right upstairs from work, and you go to the gym, which is practically next door to the other two. And I guess you go across the street to H-E-B once in a while to pick up groceries. Do you go anywhere else? Do you ever leave this one-block circuit of yours?"

"I'm not seeing anyone," Tito said, answering the question behind the question. Then, before she could ask, he went on, "My diet is excellent, I never drink more than two alcohol units a day, I'm staying hydrated, I get between seven and eight hours of sleep a night, and my mood is stable."

He tried to look and sound happy and healthy, but he knew she wasn't satisfied, because if he *wasn't* doing any of those things, if he was sliding toward a depressive episode, he would say the same thing.

The recurring bouts of depression that had started in his early teens had been incomprehensible to his father. *What have you got to be depressed about?* Juan had asked—not in a mean way, just honestly baffled. And Tito hadn't had a good answer. He had a loving family, a roof over his head, clothes on his back and plenty of food to eat. He was better off than most of the population of the world. What *did* he have to be depressed about? He didn't know, but the added layer of guilt, and the implication that he should simply count his blessings and snap out of it, didn't help.

Rose had understood a little better, because she'd been through it all before with her brother. Like Young Tito, Original Tito had suffered from several depressive episodes in his teens and early twenties. After that, his depression had appeared to clear up. In reality, as they'd realized after his death, he'd simply gotten better at hiding it.

Uncle Tito had always had a strict policy of not drinking on duty, but the autopsy had told a different story. The coroner's ruling had been congestive heart failure, with advanced cirrhosis of the liver. Uncle Tito had spent most of his waking hours at the bar, which meant he'd either been drinking at work on the sly in defiance of his own policy, or seriously hitting the booze after hours.

Going through her brother's belongings after the funeral, Rose had found old pictures of his ex-wife in the top drawer of his desk, evidence of the one unreasoning passion that he'd never gotten over.

"You're listening to James Taylor," she said now. It sounded like an accusation. Tito knew she was thinking of all the times she'd seen him lying on his bed, staring up at the ceiling while "Fire and Rain" played out of his iPod.

"I'm fine, Mom," said Tito. "Really."

She scrutinized him for another long moment. "If you start to get down, you tell me, okay?"

"Okay," said Tito, trying to look as if he meant it.

She repacked her tote bag and kissed him goodbye. "Fourth of July. Don't forget."

"I won't."

The bar seemed quiet after his mother had gone. He went back to work, cleaning the whole surface of the mirror and dusting the ornate scrollwork on the frame, using cotton swabs to get into the grooves. He wondered what Jenna was doing right now. He wished she was here to tease him about his hippy-dippy music. He wished he had an excuse to text her, or even to call her. In general he preferred texting to talking on the phone, but he liked the sound of Jenna's voice—sweet and girlish, lilting and musical.

But he didn't have an excuse, and he couldn't push her. He had to give her plenty of space. Be patient. Earn her trust.

He caught sight of his own face in the bar mirror. Earn her trust? And then what? What exactly did he think was going to happen here? That she would actually want to be with him?

His reflection stared back at him. In his crisp white shirt and black vest, with his neatly trimmed beard, he looked like a character in an old black-and-white film—a minor character, who existed only as a means to get the hero to talk. Once the hero left the bar, the bartender might as well not exist.

Jim Croce started singing about unrequited love. A cold heavy weight settled in Tito's stomach. He walked over to the music-playing phone, paused the playlist and exited the streaming app. He'd had enough music for one day.

The silence bore down on him. It had substance and mass.

He opened Audible and started scrolling through his library of audiobooks, desperately searching for something that would engage his intellect rather than his emotions. He scrolled desperately through his library. Plenty of abstruse stuff here, history and philosophy, but none of it caught his interest. He settled at last on a Wooster and Jeeves audiobook. Humor, that was what he needed.

He had to stop the downward spiral before it started.

CHAPTER EIGHT

"TITO? YEAH, he's kind of cute, if you like that shy, nerdy, awkward type. But he's too much of a beta for my taste. I'm only attracted to alpha males."

The woman who had just said this astonishing thing had her chin resting on her hand and her eyes narrowed in a shrewd, evaluating expression. She swirled her celery stick through her Bloody Mary in a bored sort of way before languidly lifting it out of the glass and biting into it with a loud crunch.

Jenna, who'd just brought the cocktails to the Bloody Mary woman and her dining companions and was now clearing dishes from a nearby booth, barely contained the urge to let out a derisive snort—not at the crunch, but at the ridiculous words.

There were three of them at the table—the Bloody Mary woman, Annalisa Cavazos and Eliana Mahan, Luke's wife. Bloody Mary had already sunk pretty low in Jenna's estimation because of all the substitutions she'd made in the salad she'd ordered—pumpkin seeds instead of slivered almonds, butternut squash instead of roasted corn, feta instead of mozzarella, extra bell peppers, no guac. Jenna could understand the occasional request to hold the onions or put the dressing on the side, but Bloody Mary's alterations were enough to turn her order into an entirely different dish. If she had that little faith in the cook's judgment, what was she even doing here? Why not go home and fix her own lunch?

"I think Tito is very good-looking," said Annalisa, with a definite undertone of friendly loyalty warming her tone. "He's very intelligent, too, but he doesn't show off. He likes people and cares about them."

"That's what I'm talking about," said Bloody Mary. "He's a beta. He's too nice—and too nice is boring."

She picked up her coaster and started shredding it, the way people sometimes shredded cocktail napkins. Jenna hated it when customers did this. Cocktail napkins were disposable, single-use items, and cheap. But this was a sturdy cardboard coaster, printed with the logo for Lalo's Kitchen on one side and Tito's Bar on the other, and designed to be reusable. Apparently Bloody Mary was the sort of person who liked tearing things, and people, into tiny pieces.

Jenna thought of Tito standing up to the boys who'd insulted his uncle, taking them on in a fight he knew he couldn't win. He'd had ten times more grit in him than all of those little bullies put together, and still did.

She'd finished loading dirty dishes onto her tray. Now she took a seat in the booth and started fiddling with the gerbera daisies in the bud vase, keeping the table in her sight line. Bloody Mary was staring through the pass-through at Tito, who was standing behind the bar in that way he had, slim and upright in his crisp white shirt and black vest, his dark hair slanting across his wide forehead to skim his thick black brows, his gaze sweeping over his domain, alert to anything that needed his attention. Pride and affection for his bar shone in his face.

The truth was that Jenna had been looking at Tito a lot these days, and even when she wasn't watching him, she was deeply aware of his presence, as if there were an invisible thread linking them. Every time they made eye contact, she remembered how she had almost kissed him in the front seat of his Cadillac, and wondered if he was thinking about that, too.

She'd also been avoiding him. She'd let her guard down way too much that day at horse camp. She couldn't let herself get that close to him again. But that didn't stop her from wanting to.

Which made it all the worse to see some celery-munching woman checking him out from across the room, sizing him up like a cut of meat, and a substandard one at that. Who did Bloody Mary think she was? Who was she to pick and choose? The way she talked, you'd have thought Tito was hers for the taking, as if all she had to do was lift a finger and he'd come running. What if *he* didn't want *her*? Wasn't that at least a possibility?

Eliana took a sip of her mint julep. "I don't know what people mean when they talk about alphas and betas," she said. "I know those terms are used in the dog world, but they don't seem to make sense when applied to people. But I do know it's a mistake to assume that nice guys are weak."

Yeah, you tell her, Eliana, Jenna thought. She had been slow to warm up to Eliana, who was the sort of ridiculously beautiful, perfectly put together woman who tended to draw every male eye in the room. Her engagement to Luke had come as a shock to everyone who worked at Lalo's Kitchen. No one had thought it would last. And when Eliana had broken the engagement, Jenna had been outraged on Luke's behalf, and not just because the breakup had been part of the reason Luke had left his job and cleared out of town. But then he'd come back, and married Eliana after all, and anyone could see that Eliana adored him and that he was a very happy man.

Bloody Mary gave Eliana a condescending smile. "Well, of course you *would* say that. You married a beta yourself. Luke *looks* like a roughneck, but he's really a teddy bear. Don't get me wrong. Obviously Luke's a nice person and all that. But he's almost *too* nice and kind. I like a little arrogance in a man. I like a man who says exactly what he thinks and takes exactly what he wants with no apology."

Now Jenna was *really* angry. Bloody Mary would probably like Chase, with his swagger, his domineering air and showy good looks.

"I used to date guys like that," said Eliana. "Multimillionaires, investment bankers, CEOs. Real take-charge types. Then one day I was just done. I realized that being an overbearing, abrasive jerk was not strength. Luke is not just a nice guy. He's a good man, and the strongest man I know."

Then Eliana caught Jenna's eye and gave her a tiny conspiratorial smile as if to say, *You and me, we get it. We know.*

Well! Maybe Eliana was a lot more perceptive than Jenna had realized.

And suddenly Tito was right there at the table, smiling warmly at the three women.

"Hello, ladies," he said. "Enjoying your cocktails?"

A shiver passed through Jenna. That voice of his got her every time, even when he was only saying something like, *We need more soap in the men's room soap dispenser.* It was as rich as chocolate fondue.

"Excellent as always," said Eliana.

"Good," said Tito. He went on chatting with the women. Bloody Mary chatted right back, smiling up at him, being perfectly charming, as if she hadn't been picking him to pieces moments before. It made Jenna feel strangely protective of him.

She had to get away. She slid out of the booth and picked up her tray.

But before she could head back to the kitchen, Tito stepped in front of her, those dark eyes looking straight into hers.

"Can you help me in the bar this afternoon?" he asked. "Garrett called in sick, and I can't get ahold of Sam."

"Okay," Jenna said.

"I'm sorry to ask," said Tito, "but there's no one else to do it."

She often helped out at the bar when Tito was spread thin. Unlike most of the wait staff at Lalo's Kitchen, she was over twenty-one and had actual bartending experience, so she was the natural choice. It had never been an issue before. The fact that Tito was apologizing now meant that he'd noticed that she'd been avoiding him.

"It's no problem, really," she said.

But it was a problem. She couldn't keep any sort of emotional distance from him if she was working with him. She just couldn't. She'd be drawn in the way she always was.

She took her tray of dirty dishes to the kitchen, then headed to the bar. Taking her place beside Tito, Jenna felt lighter than she had in days. Being close to Tito certainly had its dangers, but that didn't stop her from liking it.

DURING THE HOURS when Tito had Jenna working behind the bar with him that day, all of her reserve seemed to melt away. Maybe she thought it wasn't necessary anymore, that she'd made her point and Tito understood that she wasn't interested in him, and now they could go back to being friends. Or maybe it meant something completely different.

He wished he could be one of those stone-faced guys whose hearts were never touched—like his brother Javi. He didn't want to turn into his uncle, dying sad and alone, pining away after someone he could never have. He might be alone, but he didn't have to be sad about it. The key was to manage expectations. He couldn't let himself be tricked into thinking he was special to a woman when really he was just a placeholder, a shoulder to cry on—good enough for now.

More than anything, he hated being made a fool of—having that football pulled out from in front of him for the thousandth time, like Charlie Brown.

But he wasn't Javi. He was himself. He could swear up and down that he was going to be detached and rational, but at the end of the day, he was a romantic. And Jenna drew him more than any other woman he'd ever known. He knew he ought to keep his head level and not be drawn in, but he couldn't. It was too easy to fall into their old patterns of banter.

"I heard a new come-on line today," she told him after the afternoon rush had subsided. "Next door, during breakfast. This guy was squinting up at the menu board overhead like he couldn't read it. I asked him if he needed a paper menu, and he looked me straight in the eye and said, *I already know what's on the menu. Me-N-U.*"

Tito groaned and shook his head. "Oh, that's awful. What did you say?"

"Nothing. What *could* I say in response to such wit?"

Tito thought a moment, then reached under the bar top and took out the pen and spiral notebook he used for counting cash at the end of the night. "You need to start writing down all these clever come-on lines," he said. "We owe it to future generations to preserve these brilliant gems."

Jenna took the pen and clicked it. "Okay, but it's going to be a long list."

As it turned out, she didn't make an actual list. She used a separate scrap of paper for each come-on line, tearing the page in pieces as she went. Tito folded up the scraps and put them inside a small carved box below the display shelf. They quickly went through an entire sheet of paper. Jenna remembered half a dozen right off the top of her head, and Tito reminded her of several more that had been used on her and Veronica.

As she tore the last bit of paper out of the spiral and handed it to Tito, she asked, "That's all I can remember right now. Your turn."

"My turn for what?" Tito replied.

"For writing down all the come-on lines that have been used on you."

"Me? No. That's never been an issue for me."

"Oh, come on. I don't believe that for a minute. Customers must hit on you all the time."

He shook his head. "Sorry to disappoint, but no, they really don't."

"Of course they do. You're just missing the signals. It isn't possible that you've never had a customer come on to you. Look at you. You're good-looking, intelligent, sympathetic, a good listener. Women must eat that up."

Why was she saying this, and being so emphatic about it? Maybe it was her way of building his confidence, of letting him know that although *she* didn't find him attractive, plenty of other women probably did, so he should go find one and forget about her.

Well, he wasn't going to play along.

"No, they really don't, in the bar or in the world at large," he said. "My romantic relationships have been few and brief, usually with me in the role of rebound guy, or fallback guy. The closest thing I've ever heard to a comeon line is, *Tito, will you please take me to homecoming to make my ex jealous?*"

Jenna stared at him. "Are you serious? Someone actually said that to you?"

"Someone actually did."

"And what did you say back? I hope you told her where she could get off."

Tito felt his ears turning red. "Um, I believe my exact words were, *What time should I pick you up?*"

Jenna's jaw dropped open. "No. You didn't! Did you? Did you seriously take this person to homecoming?"

"I seriously did. It worked, too. She and her ex got back together right there at the dance, and I went home alone."

Jenna swatted him on the arm. "Tito! That's terrible."

"I know. But what can I say? I'm a nice guy."

For some reason that made her frown. "Don't call yourself that. You're not just a nice guy. You're a good man. You're smart and attractive and a pillar of the community. Any right-thinking woman would agree."

As a list of merits went, this one didn't reach any great emotional heights, but it was something. It dared him to take a chance.

"Well," Tito said, "if any right-thinking woman ever comes along, she's going to have to take a pretty direct approach. Something like, *Tito, you're an intelligent and respected business owner, a good conversationalist and not bad looking on the whole. And I'd very much like you to take me to dinner this weekend.*"

Jenna studied him a long moment. As her clear green eyes stared into his, his heart went from zero to sixty in three seconds flat. For one glorious, terrifying moment, he thought she was actually going to say those exact words back to him, right now.

But before she could say anything, the front door opened, and a big man with a shaved head and a handlebar mustache swaggered into the bar. "Rigoberto!" the familiar voice called out, in a loud roar like that of a friendly lion.

Jenna turned away, and Tito felt his heart sink down to his knees. The moment was lost.

"Hey, Dad," he said, forcing his voice to sound cheerful.

Juan Mendoza was dressed in his usual work clothes—worn jeans, battered boots and a T-shirt. He was so big that his arms stood out from his sides.

Taking possession of his usual barstool, he looked at his son and said, "How you doing, *huerco*? Working hard or hardly working?"

Then he laughed—as if he'd never heard anything so funny, as if he hadn't been asking that same question every day since his son had come into possession of the bar, and asking it of his brother-in-law every day before that.

It was the sort of question that was impossible to answer, and Tito didn't even try. "A pint of Thirsty Goat?" he asked.

"You know it," said his dad.

Tito filled a pint glass with the amber red ale and set it before his father.

"Thank you, son," said Juan. Then he did an exaggerated double-take at Jenna, as if he'd just noticed her standing there, though Tito was sure he'd seen her from the start.

"Oh, so they got you working the bar today, huh?" he asked in mock surprise. "You keeping this boy of mine on his toes?"

"Nope," said Jenna. "I'm too busy keeping the customers in line."

Juan let out a loud appreciative laugh. "I believe it," he said. Jenna was a great favorite of his. Tito could hardly believe the ease of their banter. She sassed him, stood up to him, and he liked it. Tito had heard him say more than once that she was like the daughter he'd never had.

"How are you today, Juan?" Jenna asked.

Juan took a swallow of beer and braced his thick fore-arms on the bar top. "Oh, can't complain. Me and the boys have been doing some earth-moving work out in Schraeder Lake. We tore down some old fencing, got the brush all cleared and reconfigured the pastures. Now we're digging a big tank."

"What are these tanks I'm always hearing about?" asked Jenna. "Do Texans have giant aquariums in their pastures?"

Tito could see the wheels turning in his father's mind as Juan tried to come up with a mischievous answer. Before Juan could speak, Tito said, "They're stock tanks. Ponds for the stock to drink out of."

Juan scowled. "Oh, man. Why'd you tell her? I was all set to go with that aquarium thing. I could have worked up a whole story."

"Yeah, I'll bet you could," said Jenna. "So, basically, you've been digging a big hole in the ground, huh?"

Juan made a scoffing sound. "There's a whole lot more to it than that. There's a real art to digging a stock tank. You want it to look nice as well as hold water. A real big one like this one we've been working on takes days to make. See, you use the excavated earth to build up the banks, and shape it in a way that harmonizes with the land."

"That does sound fun," said Jenna.

"Yeah, it is. We ought to finish this one tomorrow or the day after. If we ever get any rain again, it'll fill right up, and then the guy is going to stock it with fish, so it actually will be sort of like an aquarium after all, only you won't be able to see the fish because the water won't be clear enough."

He took another drink of beer and turned to his son. "How about you, *huerco*? What've you been up to lately?"

"Well, let's see," said Tito. What *had* he been up to lately? He'd recently started reading a new book about the history of Spain during the High Middle Ages. And the night before, he'd taken a pressure washer to the inside of the empty beer vats and run a chlorine solution down the pipes to keep mold from building up. He'd also disassembled the taps, run a cleaning solution through all the lines and poured boiling water down the drains to prevent mites from breeding in the beer residue. He'd been proud of the work he'd done. It was satisfying to get things sparkling clean and stay on top of the routine maintenance that would keep the bar running right and avoid problems.

But in view of his father's earthmoving, brush-clearing and stock-pond-digging, it all sounded fussy and trivial.

"Oh, you know," he said at last. "Same old, same old."

Juan frowned at him. "You're in a rut, Rigoberto. You need to shake things up. Try something new." Then he looked at Jenna. "Fourth of July's just three days away," he said with an expectant grin.

"That is certainly true," she replied. "You'll get no argument from me there."

He went on grinning. "So? Are you gonna ride the bull?"

She narrowed her eyes at him. "Is that anything like cow tipping? Because I wasn't born yesterday."

Juan let out another appreciative bellow of laughter. "No, no. I'm talking about the party."

Jenna clearly wasn't following. "What party?"

"What party?" Juan repeated. He turned to his son. "You haven't invited this girl to the party?"

"Uh," said Tito.

He didn't have time to get any further. Juan turned back

to Jenna and jerked a thumb in Tito's direction. "Can you believe this guy? He doesn't like parties. Told us to stop throwing him birthday parties when he was still a little boy."

"I was fourteen," said Tito.

Juan ignored this. "*You* like parties, don't you?" he asked Jenna.

"Sure," she said. "I like parties fine."

"Good! Then we'll see you there, Fourth of July. And you can ride the bull."

"I still don't understand about this bull," Jenna said. "What bull are we talking about?"

Juan's eyes twinkled. "Big ole mean Brahma we keep in a pasture. Weighs twenty-five hundred pounds with wicked sharp horns *this big*." He spread his hands three feet apart.

"It's a mechanical bull," said Tito.

His dad let out an exaggerated sigh. "Ah, you're no fun, *huerco*."

"Oh, a *mechanical* bull," said Jenna. "Is that all? Sure, I'll ride."

Juan gave Tito a triumphant look. "There, you hear that? *She's* not scared."

"I'm not scared either," said Tito.

"If you're not scared, then how come you won't ride the bull?"

"Can't I just not want to?" Tito asked. "Why does it have to be about being scared?"

But a voice inside his head said he *was* scared—not of getting hurt, but of looking foolish in front of a crowd, of not measuring up to his father and brothers, of being less than.

"Oh, I know *you're* not scared," said Jenna. "Anyone who's as steely-eyed as you are with belligerent drunks isn't afraid of a little riding toy."

Juan glanced back and forth between Jenna and Tito. For a second Tito thought he was going to take issue with his mechanical bull being called a little riding toy, but instead he demanded, "What belligerent drunks? Who's steely-eyed?"

Jenna answered before Tito could open his mouth. "Your son is steely-eyed, and he chucks belligerent drunks right out of the bar before they know what's happening to them. A couple of weeks ago, this great big guy followed me into a supply closet. Tito put him in some sort of fancy hold, bounced him out of the bar and told him not to come back. He never even raised his voice or looked the least bit flustered. It was impressive. And it wasn't the first time I'd seen him do it, either."

Juan looked at his son with something like awe. Then his face slowly spread into a smile. "How about that? You know, Jenna, he was always scrappy, even when he was a kid. He's the only one of my boys that ever got suspended from school for fighting. He took on a whole gang of punks because they threw some shade on his uncle."

"I believe it," said Jenna.

"So it's all settled," said Juan. "Tito's taking you to the party, and you're both gonna ride the bull. You be sure to bring Halley, too. There'll be lots of other kids there."

He finished his beer and paid his bill, leaving Tito a big tip. After the door shut behind him, Tito turned to Jenna.

"What just happened?" he asked.

Jenna gave him a guilty smile. "I think I just invited myself to your parents' party and volunteered you to ride a mechanical bull. Sorry. I guess I got a little carried away."

"No, no, that's fine. I meant the part where you stood up for me to my dad and told him what a tough guy I am. Where did that come from?"

Jenna shrugged. "I don't know. I guess I get tired of

good guys like you being undervalued. I don't mean your dad doesn't value you," she added quickly.

"No, I get it," said Tito. "He teases. That's his way of showing affection. But, yeah, it does get a little old at times. So…thanks."

"You're welcome," said Jenna.

An awkward silence fell.

"So do you really want to go to the party?" Tito asked.

She thought a moment. "A party," she said. "At your parents' place. How big a guest list are we talking about? More people or fewer than at the barn raising at Susana Vrba's place?"

"Oh, definitely fewer. My parents don't have the space for that big a crowd, though they certainly make the most of the space they have."

"Well, we went to the barn raising," Jenna said. "And nothing terrible happened. But that was before."

Tito knew what she meant. Before Chase got out of prison.

He didn't dare speak. He wanted desperately for her to go, but she had to decide on her own.

Then she looked at him and smiled.

"I told your father I'd go, so I'm sort of honor bound now. And I know Halley would be thrilled by a chance to hang out with someone other than me. We'll go."

Happiness flooded through him, and he felt a goofy smile spread across his face. "Good," he said.

She picked up a damp cloth from the sink and started wiping down the bar top. "I used to love parties," she said. Then she glanced at him and said, "How about you?"

"Oh, I'm definitely going," he said. "I missed Cinco de Mayo. I can't miss Fourth of July too."

"No, that's not what I meant. I meant, is it true that you

don't like parties? Did you really tell your parents to stop throwing parties for your birthday?"

"Oh, that. Yes, it's true, but it wasn't quite the way he said."

She rinsed the cloth and wrung it out. "So how was it?"

Tito picked up a pint glass and started polishing it. "Well, my family's always been big on parties. Between Christmas, New Year's, Cinco de Mayo, Fourth of July, Memorial Day, Labor Day and all the birthdays, there's some sort of celebration going on pretty much every month of the year. My birthday is in July, and so is my brother Eddie's, which made July kind of a busy month for us, party-wise. So we used to celebrate my and Eddie's birthday together, in one big bash, near the end of the month so it didn't get subsumed by the Fourth of July. I didn't mind so much when I was little, but the older I got, the less fun it was to share a party with my better looking, more popular brother. Girls of my age used to angle to get an invitation from me so they could come to the party and spend time with my brothers."

Jenna looked outraged. "That's terrible!"

"Yeah. It got to where I dreaded my birthday. So finally I told my parents that I'd rather skip my half of the party and have a small family celebration instead."

"You could have told them the truth," Jenna said. "Asked for your own party."

Tito shook his head. "It would have been a pretty humiliating thing to admit. Besides, I still wouldn't have known if people were coming because they liked me, or because they liked my brothers. No, it was easier to bow out of the whole thing, and tell my parents I didn't like parties."

He set down the gleaming pint glass and picked up another.

"That's really sad," said Jenna.

"It's all right. It was just the way things were. And it really was a huge relief not to have to share a birthday party with Eddie anymore."

He darted a quick glance at her. "I've never told anyone that before."

"Thank you for telling me," she said.

After another awkward pause, she said, "So what time is the Fourth of July party?"

"All day, but it's come and go. It's cooler earlier in the day, but if you want to see the fireworks, you have to stay late."

"I don't mind the heat," said Jenna. "And I do like fireworks."

"Okay. Maybe arrive around four o'clock, then? There should still be plenty of food left at that point."

"Sounds good."

"All right," said Tito. "Should I pick you up?"

He tried to sound casual, as if it didn't matter, but it did. If she said she'd meet him there, then this wasn't a real date. If she said yes, then…well…maybe.

Jenna seemed to think it was a weighty question as well. She considered a moment, then said, "Sure. That would be great."

A fresh wave of elation washed over him, leaving him weak at the knees.

"Good," said Tito. "Great."

He opened the mini fridge and took out some fresh lemon wedges. He could feel Jenna watching him.

Then she said, "Hey, can I ask you a question?"

That sounded serious.

"All right," Tito said.

She looked gravely at him. "What does *huerco* mean?"

This was so unexpected that he laughed. "Oh! Well… there's not really a direct English translation. The way my father uses it, it means something like kid or brat, with an undertone of someone who's sad or dejected."

Jenna nodded. "I see. What about that other Spanish word he calls you—you know, the one with all the syllables? It's like rolo or rogo-something."

"Rigoberto?"

"That's it! Rigoberto. What does that mean?"

He laughed again. "That's my name! Rigoberto Mendoza."

Her eyes widened. "That's your *name*? You never told me that."

She sounded so indignant about it. "Uh, I'm sorry?" he said.

"You should be. When your given name is Rigoberto, that's the sort of thing you ought to tell people right from the start."

She was a fine one to talk. She had legally changed her own name, and he still didn't know what her original name had been. But that wasn't something he could tease her about, so he said only, "Well, now you know."

"So where does Tito come from?" she asked. "Is it your middle name?"

"No, no. My middle name is Luis. Tito is a diminutive for Rigoberto."

"How do you get Tito out of Rigoberto? That doesn't make any sense."

"It makes as much sense as Bobby being a nickname for Robert, or Billy for William."

"Good point. So I guess you were named after your uncle?"

"Not exactly. My uncle's name was Alberto. Tito is a diminutive of that, too."

"Really? That's wild."

"I know, right? Tito is actually a diminutive for a lot

of different names—Humberto, Roberto, Norberto, Ernesto—basically anything that ends in '-to.'"

Before he knew it, they were deeply involved in a whole discussion of Spanish diminutives and naming conventions. Even more remarkably, Jenna seemed truly interested. Ordinarily Tito had to be careful when talking about some esoteric subject, and cut himself off before boring his listeners to the eye-glazing stage. But Jenna was as voracious for knowledge as he was. It was something he'd noticed about her early in their acquaintance. She just liked knowing things, whether or not she had an immediate use for them. He loved that about her.

By the time Sam showed up for his shift and Jenna went back to Lalo's, Tito's mind was a hopeless agitation of pleasure and suspense, and he still didn't know if the two of them had a date.

CHAPTER NINE

JENNA TOOK AN anxious look in the mirror and cautiously admitted to herself that she was more than usually satisfied with her reflection. Her hair was gathered into an asymmetrical French braid that started at the left, slanted across the back and ended in a thick braid trailing over her right shoulder. Different shades of blonde wove in and out of the braid, from deep gold to streaks of an almost flaxen color. The style was a definite step up from her usual hair clip twist. She'd even put on some makeup—not just her usual quick coat of mascara, but a touch of lip color as well. In keeping with the Fourth of July, she was wearing a red top, blue cutoffs and white Keds. Casual, but pretty. That was the look she was going for. It wasn't as if this was an actual date, after all.

Halley stood behind her, shaping some loose wisps into open curls that framed Jenna's face. Jenna could see her intent expression in the mirror.

"You look great," Halley said. "Tito will be blown away."

Jenna opened her mouth to retort that she wasn't trying to blow Tito away, then shut it, because she wasn't sure it was the truth.

"Thanks," she said instead. "You're a genius with hair."

"I know it," Halley said complacently. "I got in a lot of practice. My mom used to French braid my hair, and she showed me how on that Barbie hairstyling head toy that I used to have when I was little. I learned to do all sorts of hairstyles on that thing."

"I remember," said Jenna.

It was unusual for Halley to voluntarily talk about her mother, or anything from further back than a year and a half in the past. When she did, it was from a certain emotional distance, like a much older person reminiscing about a long-ago childhood. But Halley was a child still. It hadn't been that many years since she'd played with the Barbie hairstyling head, or her sparkly plastic ponies, or her treasured stuffed animals.

Jenna waited to see if Halley would go on reminiscing, but she didn't, and Jenna knew better than to push her.

She picked up a bottle of rose-scented lotion and squirted some into her palm. "There is one thing I wanted to mention before we go," she said. "All our usual rules about identity security still apply. So don't be talking about where we came from or what our names used to be."

She could feel Halley staring at her in the dressing table mirror but kept her own gaze fixed on her hands as she rubbed the lotion into them.

"Of course I won't talk about that," said Halley. "When have I ever?"

"No, I know. But it is a party. There'll be a lot of friendly, curious people there. I just don't want you to get too relaxed and let your guard down."

Long pause. "Why would you even say that? Have you let *your* guard down?"

Jenna squirmed. She was not prepared to tell Halley about her panic attack on the second day of horse camp and the revelations she'd made to Tito in his car. "Not exactly. But Tito is pretty observant. I think he'd be quick to pick up on any inconsistencies."

"So Tito doesn't know?" Halley asked.

"He knows we came to Texas to get away from someone, but he doesn't know the details."

"Well, maybe you should tell him."

Jenna met Halley's gaze in the mirror. "I can't do that."

"Why not?"

"Because the whole point of a secret identity is that it's secret. I worked hard to make a fresh start for us. I can't just throw it all away and blab everything to the first attractive man who comes along."

"Tito isn't the first attractive man to come along. He's Tito."

She said it as if the thing were self-evident, with no further explanation needed. Tito was Tito. His trustworthiness was inherent.

Jenna looked down at the dressing table and started setting bottles and jars in order. "I know. Maybe one day we can tell him, but not yet."

"Okay," said Halley. "So what time will he actually get here? I know he said four, but does that mean he's picking us up at four, or picking us up in time to reach the party at four?"

"I don't know," said Jenna. "We weren't that formal about it. I mean, it's not like this is a *date*. His dad was the one who actually invited me to the party. Tito just volunteered to drive us."

She saw Halley's tolerant little smile in the mirror. Then Halley said with conviction, "He'll be here at ten 'til."

Jenna glanced at the crystal clock on the dressing table. It was already a quarter 'til. A flutter of anticipation rippled through her stomach.

There was nothing left to do but wait. Halley settled herself onto the armchair in the corner of Jenna's room with a book. Jenna stayed at the dressing table, playing with a stack of gold bangles Kara had given her for a teenage birthday, admiring the way the sunlight from the window played on their light, graceful shapes. It had been a long time since she'd worn them. She worked with her hands; she couldn't afford to have thin metal bands clanging around her wrists.

The soft rumble of an engine sounded from the street, and a flash of metallic red passed outside Jenna's bedroom window and pulled into the driveway. The crystal clock read 3:50 on the dot.

She whirled around on the small upholstered bench, dropping the bangles to the floor.

For the past three days she'd been telling herself not to get excited, that she and Tito were simply two friends going to a party together. But now that he was here, her body was betraying her with pounding heart, shallow breathing, shaking hands and weak knees—all of which felt an awful lot like panic. She wanted to run away, and at the same time she couldn't wait to open the door.

She knelt to pick up the bangles. She could feel Halley watching her from her corner.

"Do you want to let him in, or should I do it while you take a minute to calm down?" Halley asked.

Jenna set the bangles back on the dressing table. "I can answer the door," she said huffily.

She forced herself to walk slowly and calmly down the short hallway.

And there he was, Tito Mendoza, on her actual doorstep, in khaki shorts and a button-down shirt in a deep indigo blue that suited him perfectly. The sleeves were rolled up to just above the elbows, carefully casual, but precise. There seemed to be an extra gloss about him today. His dark hair shone like polished wood, and his eyes were brighter than usual. He looked familiar and strange and unbearably handsome.

His eyes did a quick appreciative sweep of her outfit and returned to her face. He gave her an eager smile and said, "Hey."

"Hey," she said.

A painful silence fell. Jenna rushed to fill it. "You look different," she said. "I've never seen you wearing a color before."

"You look different too," he said. "I've never seen your legs."

His smile went a little stiff. "I mean—because you usually wear pants," he said.

"Right," she said. "Yes, that's true. I do."

Wow. They were off to a great start. Was this really the good friend she'd talked with for hours on end on every subject under the sun? She felt her cheeks warming up. Great—now she was blushing.

"Um—come in," she said. "I've just got to get something out of the fridge and we'll be ready to go."

As he came inside, she caught a whiff of scent—something woody, with notes of leather and bergamot. Tito was wearing cologne. She couldn't remember him ever doing that before.

"You didn't have to bring food," he said.

"I know, but we wanted to. Anyway, Halley's the one who made it."

He waited in the living room. When she came back with the cream cheese tart in her arms, she saw him standing at the back window, crouching a little, just as she had after she'd learned that her roof was visible from Tito's apartment.

"Can you see Bunter?" she asked.

He straightened and chuckled. "Not quite. That tree hides the second-story window. But I can see the building."

He raised his eyebrows at the sight of the stars and

stripes tart, with its rows of halved strawberries making the stripes, and blueberries forming the field of blue in the corner, and bits of the cream cheese showing in between like stars.

"Wow," he said. "Halley made this?"

"She did," said Jenna.

Halley hadn't put in an appearance yet. Probably wanted to give Jenna and Tito some time alone. Jenna hoped she wasn't going to be too obvious about expecting the two of them to get together.

"Halley, come on!" she called. "It's time to go."

Halley walked into the living room, wearing a pasted-on smile, and said hi to Tito.

"Hello," he said. "I didn't know you were a pastry chef. Your dessert looks really good."

"Thanks," said Halley.

There was no trace of the usual friendly ease between the three of them. It felt as if they were all meeting for the first time.

"Well, let's go," said Jenna, trying to sound natural and relaxed.

The Eldorado was a coupe. Tito went around to the passenger side, opened the door and tilted the front seat forward. Halley settled into the back seat with the tart, and Tito pushed the seat back in place for Jenna.

This was the second time he'd driven her. He didn't know, had no way of knowing, how significant that was. In the years since her breakup with Chase, when she'd called her dad to pick her up from that Dairy Queen, she'd allowed another person to drive her exactly twice, and both times, that person had been Tito.

And she felt okay about it. Better than okay. She felt great. Even the new awkwardness between them was exciting, because it meant that despite her efforts to the contrary, they were more than friends.

It was a beautiful summer day in the Texas Hill Country. The lots in this older, established neighborhood all had mature trees, mostly oaks and elms and pecans, big enough to shade the lawns and create a lush, leafy canopy over the streets. Several houses were displaying flags, Texan and American, and there was plenty of red, white and blue bunting to be seen.

Jenna and Tito filled the short drive with stilted small talk, taking turns offering remarks about decorations and the weather, until Tito turned into a gravel driveway and said, "This is it."

The place was not what Jenna had expected. For starters, she'd imagined it a lot bigger. She'd figured that people who entertained as often as the Mendozas did must have plenty of space to do it in. Besides, hadn't she heard Juan saying that he'd rented an old horse trailer on the property to Roque Fidalgo, and let him pasture his horse there? This lot looked to be about half an acre—larger than in most modern subdivisions, but hardly big enough to pasture a horse. And she didn't see any horse trailer, just a hodgepodge of outbuildings and a house decidedly on the small side for a family as big as Tito's. A big covered workshop area sheltered Juan's earthmoving equipment, along with a flatbed trailer, a riding lawn mower and several vintage cars in various states of restoration.

The party was in full swing, with guests eating and drinking, laughing and talking. Music was playing from a speaker somewhere, loud enough to hear and enjoy without drowning out conversation. Jenna saw lots of people she recognized—Luke and Eliana, Susana and Roque, Coby Kowalski—and lots more who were strangers. A big tent stood proudly open, showing tables of food and beer kegs within. Tony Reyes, a regular at the restaurant and bar, was wearing a Texas flag apron and manning a grill. Small children played in the grass, and some older kids had a game of cornhole going on.

Tito parked in a shady spot under a pecan tree. "Welcome to Casa Mendoza," he said.

As they were getting out of the car, Jenna saw one of Tito's brothers watching them. It was Eddie, supposedly "the handsome one" of the Mendoza brothers, and the one with whom Tito used to have to share his birthday parties when they were kids. Jenna supposed he was pretty good-looking in a flashy, pretty boy sort of way, but his smile was a little too toothy for her. She'd seen him before at the restaurant and the bar, but hadn't interacted with him beyond bringing him his food.

Tito's mother came to greet them. Jenna had seen her at Lalo's Kitchen as well. Rose was a pretty, vivacious woman, always on the go. Today she was wearing a sundress with stars on a blue field for the bodice and a red-and-white-striped skirt.

"Hi, baby!" she said, kissing Tito on the cheek.

Then she turned to Jenna and Halley. "Hello! So glad you two could make it."

She certainly looked glad. There was an unmistakably hopeful sparkle in her eyes as she glanced between Jenna and her son.

"We're happy to be here," said Jenna as Halley handed her the stars-and-stripes tart and scrambled out of the back seat.

Rose came near to see the tart. "Ooh, how beautiful! I haven't set the desserts out yet. I didn't want them to melt in the heat. Let's take this inside and put it in the fridge."

The house looked as small on the inside as it had on the outside, but comfortable and inviting, with cheerful cushions on the overstuffed sofa and chairs, and bright, colorful prints on the walls. Rose led the way to the tiny kitchen, where desserts covered every available inch of counter space. She opened the fridge door, and Jenna carefully balanced the tart on top of a banana pudding.

Halley had halted in the living room to check out the bookcase. She was standing with her head tilted to the side, reading the titles on the spines.

"They have *The Lord of the Rings*," she told Jenna.

Rose smiled. "Do you like *The Lord of the Rings*?" she asked Halley.

"I love it," said Halley. "It's the ultimate."

"I agree," said Rose. "I reread it about once a year. I first read *The Hobbit* to my boys when Tito was three, and the trilogy after that."

"Wow, that's pretty young," said Jenna.

Rose beamed with pride. "Yes. I wasn't sure if he'd be able to follow, but he did fine. Every evening, right after he got ready for bed, he'd climb onto the sofa and sit there waiting for me, all clean and cozy in his PJs."

Jenna darted a quick glance at Tito. He looked a little sheepish, but he was smiling.

"It was easy to follow the story with you as the reader," he told his mother. "You had a different voice for every character. I could just see it all in my mind."

The bookcase stood next to a hallway, which was crammed with family portraits. Jenna saw one of a young Juan in chaps, boots and a cowboy hat, grinning and holding up a prize belt buckle from a rodeo, right next to one of him in a Marine dress uniform, somber-faced and rigid.

"Quite a contrast," said Jenna, pointing.

Rose saw the direction of Jenna's gaze and chuckled. "Yes. Juan was always an adventurer. He rode bulls for years when the boys were small. He was pretty good, too.

But then he got hurt—not too bad, but enough for me to put my foot down. So he quit riding bulls…and joined the Marines just in time to be sent to Iraq for Desert Storm, which wasn't exactly what I'd had in mind. But he made it back in one piece, and after a while he started his earth-moving business."

Jenna moved slowly down the hallway, eyes roving over the wealth of pictures, tracing resemblances. The older boys all had their father's powerful build, but Tito was made on a smaller scale. Lots of sports shots of them, band and choir pics of him.

He followed her, keeping a couple of paces behind. "I may have gone through a bit of an awkward phase," he said. "One that lasted five to ten years."

"Oh, I don't know," she said. "This one of you in your band shirt posing with the oboe is pretty lit."

He winced. "Ugh, that goofy grin," he said.

Jenna pointed to a photo of a young Tito standing beside his uncle at the bar. "You're not grinning in this one," she said. "You and your uncle have the exact same stony-faced expression. You can really see the resemblance here."

He drew near, leaning in to see, and Jenna caught another whiff of cologne. "Yeah, you can. I remember that day. I was helping him with the deep cleaning at the bar. Mom took that picture when she came to pick me up afterward."

The image quality wasn't great, but there was something about the picture that appealed to Jenna. The unsmiling faces gave it an old-timey vibe. She wondered how the picture would look in black-and-white.

The hallway gallery ended at an open doorway that showed a small bedroom.

"That was my room growing up," Tito said. "I shared with Eddie and Javi."

It must have been a tight fit. Jenna thought of her own childhood bedroom, with its canopy bed and dollhouse and frilly linens, and Kara's similarly girlish room across the hall. She felt a new respect for Tito's parents, raising five boys in a small space, and practicing hospitality as a matter of course.

Halley joined them in the hallway.

"Have you finished scanning the bookshelves?" Jenna asked her with a smile.

"Yes. Can I go find Gillian? I saw her as we were driving in."

"Okay," said Jenna. "Just remember…"

"I know," said Halley. "I will."

They all went outside. Halley headed toward the cornhole game and Rose went to greet some new arrivals.

"Are you hungry?" Tito asked Jenna. "There's plenty to eat—sausage, brisket, ribs, fajitas, burgers, hot dogs, chili. There might even be something resembling vegetable dishes in the tent."

"I'm not really hungry yet," said Jenna. "I want to look around."

"Can I get you a beer, then? I need to go check the kegs anyway."

"Sure. I'll take a 9-Pin Kolsch, if you have it."

"I do. I'll be back in a minute."

Jenna watched him walk away, slender but sturdy, with an air of contained strength in his step and in the set of his head.

He disappeared into the tent, and she turned her attention to the crowd. So many people milling about or standing in groups, talking, eating, drinking, laughing. Ordinarily the presence of such a mass of humanity would have made her nervous, but today it made her feel strangely lonesome. This really was a tight community. She thought of school friends from back home, people she'd assumed she'd be close to forever, and had now lost track of completely. Just as well, since every one of them knew what an idiot she'd been over Chase.

Someone laid a tentative hand on her arm. "Hi! You're Jenna, right?"

It was Annalisa, holding a soft drink in a red, white and blue coozie, and smiling her wistful smile. She wore a white sundress and had her hair piled high in a neat bun.

"I'm Annalisa Cavazos," she said. "It seems strange that we've never really met when I've seen you so many times, but Tito's told me so much about you that I feel as if I already know you."

"He's told me about you, too," said Jenna. "Great party, huh?"

"Oh, yes. The Mendozas are always throwing parties. I've lost count of how many birthdays and holidays I've celebrated with them."

"You've known them a long time?"

"All my life."

There was the wistful smile again. Jenna wondered just how long Annalisa had been in love with Tito's brother Javi.

"Didn't I hear something about Roque Fidalgo living here in an old horse trailer or something, and pasturing his horse here?" she asked.

"Oh, no," said Annalisa. "That wasn't here. That was on The Property."

Jenna could hear the capital letters in the way Annalisa pronounced the words.

"Oh," she said. "So where is The Property?"

"That's a long story," said Annalisa. "Maybe we should sit down."

They found a couple of chairs and settled in.

"The Property is on Highway 281, on the edge of town," Annalisa said. "It's in sort of a middle ground between the residential area and the farms and ranches. Most of the lots in that area are one to ten acres. The Property is a one-acre lot. It's got a big metal barn on it and an old slab foundation for a house that was never built."

"Oh, I know that place," said Jenna. "I've driven by it lots of times. I had no idea it belonged to Tito's family."

"Yes, they've owned it for about twenty-five years. It's all that's left of an old ranch that was here before Limestone Springs was a town. The original owners sold off most of the land over the course of several decades, and the Mendozas bought the last of it. The plan was to build a nice big house with four bedrooms. The younger boys would still have to share, but Johnny, the oldest, would have his own room, and after he left home Enrique would get Johnny's old room, and Eddie would have his and Enrique's old room to himself, and once Eddie left home there'd be just Javi and Tito left, and bedrooms to spare. The boys were all pretty pumped about it. I remember seeing the blueprints of the house spread out on the kitchen table. It would have been nice, really nice."

"So what happened?"

Annalisa took a sip of her drink. "Well, at the time when Mr. Mendoza bought the property and started the house, he was planning to go into business with a friend of his."

"What kind of business?"

"Classic cars. Buying, selling, restoring, servicing."

"That sounds like a perfect fit for Mr. Mendoza," said Jenna. "Didn't he do all the work on Tito's Eldorado?"

"Yes," said Annalisa. "But he couldn't have chosen a worse business partner. Have you ever had any dealings with Carlos Reyes, or heard of him?"

"I don't think so. I know Alex and Tony Reyes from the restaurant and the bar."

"Carlos is their father. He's basically a very charming, very handsome con man. Half the people in town have been burned by him in one way or another. Mr. Mendoza fronted most of the money for the business, and of course he was the one who actually knew about classic cars. Carlos was supposed to be the front man and handle the business end of things. But before they even got started, Carlos cleaned out the business account and left Mr. Mendoza with nothing."

"Oh," said Jenna. "That's awful."

"Yeah. The family never really recovered financially, although they've done well enough in the years since. And they never gave up hope on The Property. Always said they'd finish the house one day just like they'd planned. But between one thing and another, it's never happened."

Jenna thought of friendly, boisterous Mr. Mendoza, with his loud laugh and constant jokes, and Mrs. Mendoza, always cheerful and busy. There was no hint of bitterness in either of them. She never would have guessed they'd suffered such a brutal disappointment.

She and Annalisa chatted awhile longer. She learned that Annalisa was at work on a book about the history of Seguin County, and that she'd already written another book some years earlier about ghost stories of the Texas Hill Country.

"I had no idea you were an author," said Jenna.

Annalisa smiled. "It's not as cool as it sounds. The publisher is a small press, and the books haven't had a wide distribution at all. But I love writing about this area and its history, and sharing that with people."

Tito came back with a 9-Pin Kolsch for Jenna and a Bock-N Röhl for himself. He drew up a chair and joined the conversation. He and Annalisa did most of the talking, reminiscing about people Jenna didn't know and events that she didn't remember. It was restful, listening to them, as the party playlist switched between Tejano music, old country, new country and classic rock. More and more, she loved this community where she'd chosen to make her home. She wanted to be a part of it, the way Tito and Annalisa were.

It had been a long time since she'd had a female friend to confide in. She missed that.

She finished her beer and got to her feet.

"I think it's about time I rode that bull," she said. "Where is it, anyway?"

"In the workshop," said Tito. "I'll take you there."

Annalisa said she was going to get something to eat, so Tito and Jenna went alone.

The mechanical bull looked something like half a barrel on a pole, covered with brown-and-white-spotted cowhide, with a horned head at one end and a rope tail at the other. Inflatable cushions covered the surrounding floor. Tito's brother Eddie was just tumbling off the back end of the bull when Jenna and Tito came in.

Mr. Mendoza sat at a control console. When he saw Jenna, his face lit up.

"Well, look who finally showed up to ride Brush Hog!" he said in his big booming voice. "Took you long enough. I thought you'd chickened out."

"Not a chance," said Jenna. "I'm not scared."

"All right, then! That's what I like to hear. You ready to go?"

"Not yet. I'm just going to observe for a few minutes."

He winked at her. "Smart girl."

Several men took turns on the bull, some of whom Jenna knew from Tito's Bar and Lalo's Kitchen. Tony

Reyes was really good, and so was his brother-in-law, Marcos Ramirez. Now that Jenna knew about Tony's father cheating Mr. Mendoza of his money, it seemed strange for Tony to be here, but Mr. Mendoza didn't seem to hold the sins of the father against the son.

A teenage Mendoza grandson, one of Johnny's boys, did pretty well on the bull, too.

"We'll make a rodeo man of you yet," Juan said to the boy, ruffling his hair.

Then he turned to Jenna. "You ready yet?"

"Ready as I'll ever be," she said.

"Good! Someone show her what to do."

Eddie stepped forward right away, his toothy smile as bright as ever. The man was like a toothpaste ad.

"Are you right-handed or left-handed?" he asked.

"Right," said Jenna.

"Okay. Grab the strap with your left hand—underhanded, like this." He demonstrated with his own left hand, taking the opportunity to flex his biceps. "Then swing yourself onto the back. You'll want to use your right arm for balance. Use your thighs to grip the bull, but stay loose in your hips and spine. Just let the movement flow through you."

"Got it," said Jenna.

She gripped the strap and climbed on, then glanced at Tito. He still had his beer in his hand, and he was smiling. She grinned at him, lifted her arm and nodded at Juan.

The bull pitched forward with a jerk. Jenna leaned back, keeping her seat. Back and forth it went, up and down, while also rotating from side to side. It was a lot to keep track of, and impossible to predict. Better to not overthink it, and just take all the shifts and pitches and turns as they came.

She was in a groove now, and it felt great. Up and down,

back and forth, all around. The bull sped up, and she stayed on. The room whirled around her in a kaleidoscope of floor and ceiling and walls. She couldn't see faces, but she caught an occasional glimpse of Tito's indigo shirt.

When she finally came off, she fell forward, rolling onto her back. The workshop's ceiling, really just the underside of a metal roof, spun overhead.

"Eight seconds!" said Juan.

A face appeared above her. She couldn't make out the features, but the flash of white teeth couldn't be mistaken.

"Are you all right?" Eddie asked.

"I'm fine," Jenna said.

He took her by the hand and helped her up. A wave of applause broke out. She let go of Eddie's hand and raised her arms high. The applause got louder.

She made her way back to Tito, her head still spinning, and stumbled on her last step. He took her arm, holding her steady.

"That was fantastic," he said. "You were smiling the whole time."

"It was fun," she said.

He was still holding her arm, his face glowing with pride and something else. It would be so easy to slide her hand into his right now.

"Rigoberto!" called Juan's voice. "Your turn. Come on, *huerco*. You're not getting out of this any longer. Get on that bull and let's see what you're made of."

Tito's smile went a bit stiff, but he handed his beer to Jenna and said, "Okay."

A chorus of *oohs* made it plain that no one had expected him to go through with it. Jenna watched him walk over to Brush Hog and get on. She felt an anxiety for him that she hadn't felt for herself. She wanted him to do well.

He gripped the strap with his left hand and swung onto

the back, positioning himself as far forward as possible, with his feet in front. Without taking his eyes off the bull's head, he raised his right arm and nodded.

The bull started, slowly at first. Jenna watched as Tito seesawed with its movements, leaning back when the bull pitched forward, and leaning forward when the bull went back. So far, so good.

The bull sped up. Tito stayed on. Jenna couldn't see his face. His arm was almost whipping through the air now as the bull changed direction.

When he finally came off, he slid off the back and rolled onto his side. From his seat at the console, his father roared, "Fifteen seconds! Fifteen seconds!"

Jenna realized she'd been holding her breath. She let it out now. Tony and Marcos were looking at each other with raised eyebrows, clearly surprised and impressed.

Juan left his console, walked over to his son and hefted him to his feet, then gave him a big hug with several whacks on the back.

"Fifteen seconds!" he said again. "I can't believe this! That's better than any of your brothers ever did. You been holding out on me, Rigoberto! All these years, I never knew you had it in you!"

"You ought to go on the circuit!" called Tony.

Tito just grinned. He walked slowly back to Jenna, keeping his feet under him all the way.

"Nice job," Jenna said. "Looks like you're a natural."

He took his beer back. "Must be all that disco dancing," he said.

By sundown, Jenna had sampled more meat dishes and met more people than she could possibly hope to remember. She checked in on Halley every few minutes or so and always found her with Gillian, looking happier and more animated than Jenna had seen her in years. Sometimes there was a Mendoza grandson or two hanging around.

At twilight, the whole crowd gathered to hear Alex Reyes, Tony's brother, read the Declaration of Independence—not just the Preamble, but the whole thing.

Alex was a historical reenactor; Jenna had often seen him at the restaurant in one of his old-fashioned outfits, on his way to or from an event. Usually he was dressed as a freedom fighter from the Texas Revolution, but today he had on eighteenth-century garb. He read well, in a clear, carrying voice. His wife, Lauren, hugely pregnant, listened with a smile, holding Peri, their three-year-old daughter, by the hand.

Jenna felt stirred with pride and gratitude by the beautiful and powerful words. Those brave men and women, daring to break free from a bully, and to start a new kind of life in a new home, and to make a better future for themselves and their children—she identified more strongly with them than she ever had before. No one could show them the way, because no one had ever done it before. They had to blaze their own trail. But they weren't alone. They had allies. They had each other.

She darted a quick glance at Tito. The sight of his stern, solemn profile sent a jolt through her heart, half pleasure, half pain.

"...And for the support of this Declaration," Alex said, "with a firm reliance on the protection of divine Providence, we mutually pledge to each other our Lives, our Fortunes and our sacred Honor."

The silence that followed seemed to have weight and substance. Then someone started singing the national anthem, and the rest joined in.

With its octave-and-a-half vocal range, "The Star-Spangled Banner" was a difficult song to sing well. But Jenna and Tito hit every note.

At the end of the song, people started cheering, and firecrackers went off.

Tito turned to Jenna with a smile. "We're good together, aren't we?" he asked.

She didn't know if he meant their voices, or something else. But she answered, "Yes. Yes, we are."

CHAPTER TEN

IT WAS NEARLY dark now, and Mr. Mendoza was busy setting up what looked like a huge fireworks display, with rockets supported on bricks, and enough space between the different types of fireworks for him to be able to move quickly from one to another. Tito left to check the kegs again, and Jenna went into the tent to get some dessert.

The tent was lavishly decorated with red, white and blue streamers, and rosettes made from ribbons, crepe paper and old newspapers whose edges had been cut with pinking shears. The dessert table held a proud display of trifles, cakes, cookies and pies, mostly with some sort of red, white and blue thing going. Halley's stars-and-stripes tart had already been cut into, and several pieces were missing.

Jenna had just picked up a dessert plate when a man stepped in front of her, and she saw a familiar toothpaste-ad smile.

He pointed both index fingers at her. "It's Jenna, right?"

"That's right," she said. "And you're Eddie."

He held his hands up. "Guilty as charged."

Jenna started filling her plate with cookies. She wasn't particularly eager to prolong the conversation. Ever since learning about the joint birthday parties of his and Tito's childhoods, she'd felt vaguely hostile toward Eddie, though the two of them had never interacted much. The handsome one, indeed. Didn't people have eyes? He was all muscle and teeth. Tito was *much* better looking.

Eddie didn't take the hint. "Have we met before today?" he asked. "You look very familiar to me."

"I work at Lalo's Kitchen," she said.

He snapped his fingers. "That's right! I knew I recognized you from somewhere."

Jenna resisted an urge to roll her eyes. She'd served Eddie his burgers and fries probably a dozen times, but apparently, he'd never really noticed her until today, when she'd put extra effort into her appearance.

"Hey, good job on Brush Hog today," he said. "I was impressed."

The way he said it clearly communicated that for him to be impressed was a huge deal and that Jenna should be deeply flattered.

"Thanks," she said, keeping her tone courteous but cool. "But Tito's time was better than mine."

"Ha ha! Yeah, how about that? Beginner's luck, I guess."

She didn't answer. Tito's success was beginner's luck, but Jenna's was deserving of praise from the great Eddie Mendoza? Please.

A silence passed. Eddie seemed to be waiting for Jenna to fill it, but she didn't. She took a bite of cookie instead.

He gave her a thorough once-over, head to toe, and said, "I'll bet you're a dancer. That's why you did so well on the bull."

"Nope," said Jenna through her mouthful of cookie.

"Are you sure?"

"Pretty sure."

"Well, you look like a dancer. You're so graceful and slim."

This whole flirtatious undertone was...not creepy exactly, but definitely inappropriate to use with a woman who'd come to a party with his brother. Maybe he couldn't help himself. Maybe this was just his default mode with women.

"Let's put it to the test," said Eddie. "We'll go out dancing together, this Saturday, you and me."

Jenna swallowed her bite of cookie. Had he really just asked her out? Was he really this obtuse?

"I don't think that would be a good idea," she said.

"Oh yeah?" he said playfully. "Why not?"

She stared at him a moment.

"You do realize I came here with your brother," she said.

His flirtatious grin morphed into a confused grin. "Who, Tito?"

Now she was *really* angry. "Yes, Tito," she said. "You remember him. Bearded guy. Runs a bar."

"Well, yeah, but—I mean, he just gave you a ride, right? It's not like the two of you are actually in a relationship or anything."

"How do you know? Did you ask him?"

The grin was rapidly melting away now. "Um, no."

"So you made a move on your brother's date, and you didn't even bother to verify first whether they were together?"

Eddie squirmed. "Well, I mean, that's just Tito. He has a lot of women friends, but they're just friends. It doesn't actually *mean* anything."

"Oh, it means something," said Jenna. "It means he's a sensitive, intelligent, compassionate man. He's protective and caring and funny. And I don't know how this has escaped your notice, but he's also extremely handsome. Why is it so out of the question that a woman could find him attractive?"

Eddie's smile was gone now. He raised his hands again, this time in a gesture of surrender, and started backing away. "Okay, okay! Sorry."

Jenna took a deep breath and let it out. Her heart was pounding, and her face felt hot. She had gone into full-on fight-or-flight mode, and now that it was over, the energy was draining from her body, leaving her knees weak.

Had she been overly harsh with Eddie? Maybe. But the guy radiated ego and wouldn't take no for an answer, and it made her mad to hear him underestimate his brother. The words had come spilling out beyond her control. It had felt good to say them. But now that they were out, she couldn't take them back.

THE BEER KEGS were fine, as Tito had figured they would be. He'd been intentionally giving Jenna her space today, fighting his instinct to cling to her like bindweed to a fence post. It was good to see her and Halley relaxing and interacting with people. He hadn't forgotten how tense Jenna had looked at that barn raising at Susana Vrba's place a few months back. If she could relax now in her new community, maybe she could start to put down roots.

He felt as if a weight had been lifted off his shoulders, one that he hadn't known he'd been carrying. His father had been after him for years to ride that mechanical bull, and now he'd done it. And the funny thing was, when he'd finally climbed on, it hadn't been to prove anything. It certainly hadn't been to impress Jenna. He hadn't expected to last more than a few seconds.

But he'd seen the way Jenna had gotten onto the bull herself, how fearless she'd been, and suddenly he'd been fearless too. He had sung disco in front of this woman, and she still seemed to like him. He didn't have to stand on his dignity all the time. He could be himself. He could fall off the bull and it would be okay.

Only he hadn't fallen—at least, not until fifteen seconds in, a more than respectable time.

Maybe there were other chances he could take that would turn into triumphs.

He was just beginning to wonder whether enough time had passed for him to find Jenna again without seeming clingy, when Eddie walked up to him, with an expression on his face that Tito had never seen before.

Tito's first thought was that something terrible had happened. Had someone at the party gotten sick or hurt? Or had Javi had an accident out in the oil fields of West Texas? It had to be something bad for Eddie to look like that.

"What is it?" Tito asked. "What's wrong?"

"I, uh," said Eddie. He cleared his throat and went on, "I want to apologize. I had no idea you and Jenna were together. I never would have imagined—but that's no excuse. I should have verified."

Tito stared. He didn't know what to think, what to say, or what Eddie was talking about. His brother was apologizing to him, and looking thoroughly chastened. It was something that had never happened before.

"Anyway," said Eddie, "I'm sorry."

And he walked away.

Tito stood there a moment, then headed to the dessert table to find Jenna.

She was already coming out of the tent, moving so fast that they almost ran into each other. Her face was flushed, and she looked flustered.

"Hey," said Tito. "I just had a confusing conversation with my brother Eddie."

"Yeah," said Jenna, drawing the word out. "He, um, he asked me out."

"Oh," Tito replied. "And you said…?"

Her eyes flashed. "I said no!"

"Wow," Tito said. "I don't think he's ever been turned down before."

"Yeah, I got the impression it was a first for him. He

had a lot of nerve, coming on to me when I'm clearly here with you."

She looked down at the ground. Her voice was shaking. It matched the shaking inside his own chest.

Tito wished he could watch a replay of the whole episode and hear exactly what Jenna had said to his brother. Had she really told him that she and Tito were…well, together? Eddie seemed to think she had. Was it possible that she'd said it just to get rid of Eddie? No. That wasn't her way. She wouldn't make up a fake boyfriend to get a guy to leave her alone. She had absolutely no problem telling a man to his face that she wasn't interested.

He steeled himself. "Look, Jenna, you have to know by now that I think you're pretty fantastic. And sometimes…sometimes I think maybe there could be something between us. But then I think maybe I'm just fooling myself, seeing what I want to see. Or maybe you do like me but you don't want to act on it because of the whole thing with Chase. And I can't take the uncertainty anymore. So just tell me."

The silence felt unbearably long, though in reality it was probably only a few seconds. Slowly her gaze returned to his.

Then, unbelievably, her hand reached for his.

It was a slight touch, their fingertips barely brushing, but it sent a shock through his entire body.

"Tito," she said, "you're the smartest man I know, and the kindest. You make me laugh and you make me think. I love being with you. I can't take my eyes off you. And I'd very much like you to kiss me right now."

He felt as if he were falling—or was it soaring? But at the same time, he knew he had both feet firmly on the ground. This wasn't a fragile girl, weepy over a breakup with some guy she wasn't over, and looking for something to make her feel better in the short term. This was Jenna, who knew who she was and said what she meant. And she'd just said that she wanted him to kiss her.

He laced his fingers through hers and felt her clasp tighten against his. Then he took a step closer and lowered his lips to hers.

EVERY SENSATION STOOD out in exquisite clarity. The roughness of Tito's beard against Jenna's chin. The whisper-touch of that straight fall of dark hair, brushing against her forehead. She laid a hand against his chest and felt his heart beating fast and strong through his shirt.

Then, at the exact same moment, moved by the same impulse, they put their arms around each other. He was holding her tight now. She could feel how much he wanted this, and it was all mixed up with her own want. She'd been fighting this feeling for so long, and now she'd finally given in, and it was glorious.

Lights burst in brilliant, colorful patterns from beyond her closed eyelids. She heard popping sounds and muted booms and cheers. Part of her was still aware that they were at a party, and making a very public display of affection, but the fireworks and celebratory voices all felt like part of their kiss.

Their lips parted. She opened her eyes and saw Tito's face, so bright with joy that she thought her own heart might burst.

She rested her head against his shoulder and watched the fireworks light the sky.

CHAPTER ELEVEN

FOR THE REST of the evening they stayed close to each other, holding hands, and occasionally stealing behind buildings or shrubs to kiss. Tito felt like a teenager, except that his own teenage years were never this good. People kept smiling at them—Annalisa, Luke, Eliana. Tony Reyes gave him a huge grin and clapped him hard on the shoulder. Rose looked as if she was about to cry with joy, and Juan gave him a wink and a thumbs-up. Halley wasn't quite so obvious about it, but every time she saw them, she grinned.

Around midnight, when the fireworks were all spent and the party showed signs of winding down, Jenna picked up the tart pan, empty now except for a few pastry crumbs, and thanked Tito's parents for the party. They both hugged her, and Halley too, and Rose kissed Tito on the cheek. So did Juan. It felt strange, taking leave of his parents not as his solitary self, but as part of a small group—not his own family, not yet, but it didn't seem that out of the question anymore.

He put on some music for the drive home. No one talked much, but the silence felt good, with Halley in the back seat and Jenna beside him, and Jenna's hand in his, in the middle of the bench seat.

The thing that used to be between them, that barrier by which they'd kept each other at a distance—that was gone. They were being their true selves now, with nothing hidden. Tito felt overwhelmed by the wonder of it all. Jenna knew him—his history of depression, his nerdy sense of humor—and still she'd chosen him. She wanted him—not his brother Eddie, and not the mean ex who'd broken her heart, but him, Tito Mendoza.

He tried to contain his joy, to manage expectations, to be reasonable. It wasn't as if she'd made a vow to him. They'd had one date—assuming this was a date, which by now he was pretty sure it was. Their romantic relationship, if that was what this was, was less than a day old. But the joy kept bursting through his caution, telling him that this time was for real.

When they reached the house, Halley hurried inside with the tart pan, saying all in a rush, "Thanks for the party, Tito. I'm really tired and I'm going to go to bed right away. G'night."

She rushed down the hallway into her room and shut the door.

"Did she just take the tart pan with her to her room?" Tito asked in a low voice.

Jenna was trying to suppress a laugh. "Yes. I guess she really wanted to leave us alone together."

"So...is it safe to assume that she approves?"

Jenna's eyes widened. "Approves? She's been actively gunning for us to get together. She likes you."

"Really?" Something warm and bright bloomed in Tito's chest, swelling his throat shut for a moment. "I'm glad to hear that," he managed to say.

She smiled at him. "Is it so surprising?"

"Well, yes, actually. She's got good reason to be wary where men are concerned, after everything she went through with her father. And aside from that, her approval is worth having. She's a smart kid, and she's *your* kid. I want her to like me."

Jenna's smile stiffened, then slipped away.

Then she said, "Come sit down with me. I need to tell you something."

"Okay," said Tito. He kept his voice level and calm, hiding his sudden unease. Why did Jenna look so grave? Had he said something wrong?

Once they were situated on the sofa, she took his hand in hers.

"I'm not Halley's mother," she said. "I'm her aunt. Her mother was my sister, Kara. After Kara died, I was appointed Halley's legal guardian."

"Oh," said Tito. "I must have misunderstood. I thought Chase was your ex."

Jenna squirmed. "Yes, well…he is. I dated him in high school, during my rebel phase. He was bad news even then, and I knew it. The whole town knew it. All my life, I'd been warned away from him and his entire family. But I thought I was in love, and I thought he loved me. Then… he hurt me. Not seriously, but enough to open my eyes. I broke it off right then and there and never looked back. I thought that was the end of it. But after I went off to college, he took up with my sister."

"Wow," Tito said. "That's a twist."

"Yeah. Physical violence was a deal-breaker for me, but it wasn't for Kara. It was a nightmare, seeing what he put her through, and being unable to convince her that she had to get away from him. Then she had Halley, and I thought surely she'd leave him now that she had a child to protect, but it didn't happen. I'd go through all the arguments, I'd tell her she had to get away from him for Halley's sake, I'd talk myself blue in the face. Sometimes, when things were really bad, she'd say yes, I was right, and that she was going to leave him, but then he'd do his charming repentant act, and back she'd go—over and over and over again."

He rubbed his thumb gently over the back of her hand. "That must have been horrible."

"It was. For our parents, too. I kept Halley with me as much as I could, to try to give her some semblance of a normal life in a healthy environment. At times it felt like she was more my child than Kara's. She even started calling me Mother, all on her own, when she was four years old."

Jenna blinked back tears and swallowed hard. Tito waited.

"Finally, when Halley was ten, Kara said she'd had enough, she was done, she was leaving Chase and not going back. Well, I was thrilled, of course. Kara and Halley moved in with me—I had a nice little three-bedroom house, with plenty of space for us all, and a room already set up for Halley where she used to stay whenever she visited me. I really thought Kara meant it that time. We all did."

She shook her head. "I should have stayed with her, twenty-four seven, to make sure she followed through. But I had a job, a really good job as a business analyst in a software company, making good money. I had a mortgage, responsibilities. I couldn't constantly supervise my sister. And one day while I was paying bills, Kara said she was going out to pick up a few things for her and Halley. I thought she meant shopping—and that's probably what she wanted me to think. But instead she went back to the house she'd shared with Chase and started packing clothes and toys, nothing important, nothing that couldn't be easily replaced."

She glanced at him. "You can probably guess what happened next. Chase came home while Kara was there. He said he was sorry, he loved her, he'd never hurt her again, the whole routine. And she fell for it, like she always did. And she called me to say that she was coming back to my place to pick up Halley and take her back home. And I said… I said, *Over my dead body is that child leaving this house.* And then Chase took the phone away from Kara and cussed me out, and told me that Halley was his child and I had no right to keep her from him, and that he and Kara were coming over right now to pick her up and I'd better not stand in his way. I could tell by the way he talked that he was high on meth. After he hung up, I prayed. I prayed for something, anything, to stop him. And…well…something did. Chase ran a red light, and his sports car got hit by a truck. Kara was killed instantly. Chase didn't even have to go to the emergency room."

Tito remembered Chase's mug shot on his phone—the black eyes, the scraped forehead, the tiny cuts scattered across the face. All consistent with a car accident.

"It wasn't your fault," Tito said. "You know that, don't you?"

Jenna shrugged. "Maybe not the actual accident. But I was the one who brought Chase into our lives to begin with. Kara was…she was different from me. Shy and soft and sweet. She never would have even spoken to Chase if I hadn't gone out with him first. I thought I was so cool, dating a bad boy. And Kara was my best friend. She helped me meet with him in secret, she listened to all the ridiculous arguments I came up with to justify his behavior. I guess it all sank in. And once Chase got his claws in her, he never let her go."

Tito shook his head. "You're taking too much on yourself, Jenna. You're making it sound like everything depended on you, like Kara had no choice in the matter. And that's not true. She was a grown woman and she made her own choices. Blaming yourself for her decisions is pretty egotistical."

She gave him a wry smile. "You want to hear something

even more egotistical? I used to wonder whether Chase got involved with Kara just to get back at me for breaking up with him. If he did, then it was a pretty thorough form of vengeance. Except for one thing."

"Halley?"

Jenna nodded. "Halley was the only good thing to come out of that whole sorry situation. Everything I've done since then has been about keeping her safe. And that meant starting over somewhere far away. Chase's family is as bad as he is, and clannish, too. They were furious when I was made Halley's legal guardian, and they did not hesitate to tell me so. I had my tires slashed, my windows broken, death threats left in my mailbox. I had to get her away from them—and from everyone who knew them. Even as young as Halley was when we moved away, people were already treating her differently because she was a Latimore, like she was no good. Not just other kids, but teachers, too. That's in addition to all the kids who were Latimores themselves. It was hard."

Jenna's head bowed. Suddenly she looked achingly small and vulnerable. Tito put his arms around her, and she nestled against him, her head on his chest.

"Thank you for telling me," he said.

"I'm glad you know," she said. "I've wanted to tell you before, lots of times."

He pressed his lips against her hair. "Why didn't you?"

"It just seemed better to leave all that stuff in the past. Safer and…cleaner, somehow. I wanted us to have a truly clean slate. But maybe that's not possible."

"From what you told me before, it sounds like you did a good job covering your tracks. Maybe it's time to relax a little, and not live in fear all the time."

She was quiet a moment. Then she said softly, "Maybe it is."

"You NEED TO go on a real date," Halley told Jenna. "Just the two of you. Without me."

Jenna parked the car, shut off the ignition and turned to face Halley. "But where would *you* go?" she asked. "I can't go out and leave you on your own."

Halley thought. "Why can't I stay with Tito's parents? They're nice, and they want you and Tito to be together. And Mr. Mendoza is tough. If anyone tries to kidnap me, he'll be there to stop it."

"Kidnap you?" Jenna shuddered. "Why would you even say that?"

"Well, it's what you're worried about, isn't it? It's why you never let me go anywhere. Almost never," she amended, seeing Jenna open her mouth to object.

"Of course I'm worried about it," said Jenna. "I think about it all the time. I just don't like the flippant tone you just used."

"Okay. How's this tone?" Halley laid a hand on Jenna's arm, looked her solemnly in the eye and said gravely, "Mr. Mendoza is a tough man, Mother. If anyone tries to kidnap me, he will surely prevent them from succeeding."

Jenna laughed grudgingly. The idea was tempting. Juan and Rose were such warm, friendly people. They'd be wonderful grandparents, so young and active and full of fun.

But hold on. *Grandparents?* How had she gotten there? She and Tito had had their first kiss not twenty-four hours ago, and she was already planning their future life together?

It was way too soon to think that way. But Tito was so remarkable. Ordinary rules didn't seem to apply to him. Maybe, wonder of wonders, a dream was coming true that she hadn't even dared to dream.

"Besides," Halley went on in a normal tone, "Tito's been teaching me some self-defense moves."

"What? When? I didn't know that."

"It was a few days ago, while you were doing the ordering for the restaurant. He showed me how to break different kinds of holds and told me what to do if anyone ever tried to pick me up and put me in a car and how to get out of a locked trunk. Tito's pretty tough too, you know."

Jenna smiled. "Yes, I know."

"So what do you think?" Halley asked as they got out of the car.

"I think you should curb your enthusiasm," Jenna said. "Tito hasn't even asked me out yet for this just-the-two-of-us date."

They were halfway through the parking lot behind the restaurant when the back door opened and Tito stepped out, all straight and slim and bandboxy in his usual black and white. Jenna's heart leapt into her throat. He wasn't taking out the trash. He was walking toward her, purposefully.

"I'll go inside," Halley said, breaking into a run before Jenna could reply. "Hi, Tito!" she said as she hurried past.

"Hi," he said, but Halley was already gone.

Jenna reached him at the edge of the patio, under the leafy canopy of the vines.

"Hey," she said. "What are you doing out here?"

"I wanted to catch you before you went inside," he replied. "I, uh, I was wondering if you wanted to go to dinner with me Saturday. We're both off that evening. I was thinking maybe we could go to the River Walk, since you haven't seen it. Halley can stay with my parents, if you're okay with that. I already asked them, and they said it's fine. I hope I didn't take too big a liberty there but—"

She kissed him. She could feel his surprised pleasure as his arms went around her, holding her to him.

When the kiss ended, he asked, "Is that a yes?"

His face was so open and eager. He really liked her. He knew her better than anyone in this town, but he was still nervous with her, uncertain. He didn't take her for granted. He wanted to make her happy.

"Yes," she said. She didn't want to let go of him—not now, not ever.

"Good," said Tito. "Then it's a date."

CHAPTER TWELVE

IT DIDN'T TAKE Jenna long to realize that she had nothing to wear for her date with Tito. This wasn't a cookout in his parents' backyard. This was a dressy date—not black tie, but at least a step above her usual jeans-and-a-nice-shirt work attire.

She stole a look at Tito across the pass-through. He looked so polished in his pressed black trousers, snowy white shirt and crisp black vest. He'd even looked polished at the Fourth of July party, and he'd been wearing shorts. And she wanted to look polished, too. She couldn't just mail this in.

She'd owned dressy clothes, once upon a time, but she'd gotten rid of them all when she and Halley had moved to Texas and never replaced them, because she had nowhere fancy to go, and no space to spare for transporting and storing things she didn't need.

Well, she needed them now. And a day and a half was not a lot of time to update her wardrobe.

"Hey, Jenna! Your lunch is ready."

Abel, the cook, had set her cup of creamy yellow to-mato soup on a platter alongside a grilled cheese sandwich.

"Thanks," she said, and took the soup and sandwich to the break room. The lunch rush hadn't started yet, but it would soon, so now was the time for her to eat.

She set her food on the table, took her phone out of her

back pocket, looked at it, set it down, picked it up again and finally began to type.

What's the closest place around here to go clothes shopping?

She hesitated a moment longer before hitting Send. She and Annalisa had exchanged phone numbers last night, and Annalisa was the closest thing to a woman friend that Jenna had in Limestone Springs.

Annalisa's reply came quickly. Why are you asking? Do you have a date???

Jenna smiled. Yes. And I have nothing to wear. And you know how dressy T always is. I want to look nice.

She started on her soup while watching the dancing dots.

What time do you get off work? Annalisa asked.

Eight, Jenna told her. Tomorrow I'm off at 3. And he's picking me up at 4:30.

Hmmm, came the answer. That's pretty tight. That's not enough time to reach New Braunfels, much less San Antonio, and do any meaningful shopping. I would lend you something, but I'm taller than you are, and we're very different style-wise. But let me ask around.

Jenna typed fast. Please don't bother. I don't want it to be a whole thing.

It's no bother, Annalisa responded. You don't want to wear tired old work clothes on a nice date, do you? I'll ask Eliana. She knows everyone.

Jenna wasn't sure how she felt about "everyone" being informed about her date. A little nervous, definitely. But also kind of happy and proud. It was nice, getting drawn into this cozy community where everyone knew every-one's business.

Within minutes, Jenna was part of a group text with Annalisa, Eliana and Lauren Reyes. Messages flew fast, mostly between the others. Jenna soon became too busy with the lunch rush to reply to or even read most of them, but the others seemed perfectly capable of carrying on without her input.

By the time the rush ended, Lauren had arranged to bring three dresses to the restaurant for Jenna to try on. She was the closest to Jenna's height, build and coloring.

She brought her little girl with her. Peri was a beautiful and charming child, with her flaxen curls and dimpled smile. Halley helped look after her while Jenna tried on dresses and looked at them in the restroom's full-length mirror.

"When is the baby due?" Jenna asked as Lauren helped her with the tricky buttons at the back of a gorgeous turquoise dress with a flared skirt.

"Three weeks. My dad will be here next week. He lives in Pennsylvania, but he's moving down here to be closer to the grandkids. He's talked about relocating for years, and now he's finally doing it, and I'm so glad. I'm an only child, and he and I have always been close."

Jenna's throat got tight at the thought of her own widowed mother, fourteen hundred miles away. "I'm an only child too," she said. "At least—I am now."

Lauren's eyes met hers in the mirror. "It's a big responsibility, isn't it?" she asked.

"Yes, it is," Jenna said.

Then Lauren stepped back and gave Jenna a long look. "Okay, this color looks fabulous with your skin and hair," she said.

It did. Jenna imagined the look on Tito's face when he saw her in this dress. Anticipation rose up inside her like champagne bubbles.

"I think this is the one," she said.

"Great! I'll take a picture and put it on the group text.

You and Eliana wear the same size shoe. She'll want to see your dress so she'll know what shoes to bring for you to try on."

"You're all going to an awful lot of trouble," said Jenna.

"It's no problem. We're happy to do it."

Soon after Lauren left, Eliana came by with several pairs of shoes and a cute handbag in creamy leather with silk flowers in turquoise and yellow and pink. Annalisa contributed the jewelry, and Eliana's sister-in-law, Nina, threw in a gold-and-pearl hair clip.

By 4:15 the following afternoon, Jenna was ready and waiting, her stomach fluttering with excitement. She hadn't felt this way in years. She smiled at herself in the mirror. Was that even her, with the sparkling eyes, the dangly earrings, the curled hair?

"You look great," Halley said. "Now go out and have a good time, and don't worry about me."

The Eldorado pulled up in her driveway promptly at 4:30, and Tito came to the front door, wearing a Madras shirt in royal blue, turquoise and yellow. Jenna was absurdly pleased that their colors matched.

"You look beautiful," Tito said. It didn't sound like a rote thing to say, not the way he said it, with shining eyes and a voice rich with feeling.

"Thank you," said Jenna. "It was a group effort. You look very handsome."

"Thanks," said Tito. "It was a solitary effort."

Her fear of being driven seemed to have disappeared, at least when Tito was the driver. He drove Jenna and Halley to his parents' house. Juan was outside with some of his grandsons, the smaller ones, filling trash bags with leftover debris from the Fourth of July party.

"Go on inside, Halley," he said. "Rose will put you to

work. She already put me to work. We've got a party to get ready for."

"Looks to me as if you're still recovering from the last party," Tito said.

"Recovering?" his dad scoffed. "There's nothing to recover from. And when it's time to throw a party, it's time, whether you're ready or not, so you better be ready."

Inside the house, Rose was seated at the dining table with the other two grandsons, the one who'd ridden the bull and another one who looked about ten years old. They were working with stacks of brightly colored papers, cutting them into designs.

"Hey, Halley," said the bull-riding grandson in a surprisingly deep voice.

"Oh, hi, David," said Halley. "I didn't know you were going to be here today."

Judging from her carefully casual tone, Jenna was pretty sure this wasn't true. No wonder Halley had been so quick to suggest that she stay with Tito's parents this evening.

"Come on in!" said Rose. "We're making *papeles picados* for Eddie's birthday party. You can help, Halley. I've heard how artistic you are."

David pulled out the seat next to him at the table, and Halley sat down.

"What are *papeles picados*?" she asked.

"It means punched papers," said Rose. "It's a traditional Mexican folk art. They're used in lots of different celebrations—weddings, quinceañeras, Christmas, Easter, Day of the Dead. You can hang them up individually, or string a bunch of them together and make a banner."

She held up a hot pink rectangle with scalloped edges and a cutout flower design surrounded by hearts and stars and swirls.

"Cool!" said Halley, picking up an X-Acto knife. "Bye, Mother! Bye, Tito! Have a good time!"

"Uh, goodbye," said Jenna. "Remember…"

"I know, I know," said Halley without turning around. "All the usual rules apply."

It was a happy family scene, Rose and the boys and Halley sitting around the table, busy with paper and cutting tools. But a prickle of doubt kept Jenna from thoroughly enjoying it. She had kept herself and Halley free from entanglements for a year and a half. Now they were forming connections—not just to Tito, but to his family, and Gillian and Kevin, and Susana and Roque. Jenna's own budding friendships with Annalisa and Eliana and Lauren were quickly gaining momentum. The three of them had been almost as excited as she was about putting together her outfit for tonight. It was nice. But it was also risky.

"All the usual rules?" Tito asked as he and Jenna walked back to the Cadillac hand in hand.

"What?" Jenna asked.

He jerked his head toward the house. "What Halley just said."

"Oh, right. Yeah, you know. Just standard stuff. But I think I might need to add to the rules if she's going to be spending time around that nephew of yours. What is he, fifteen?"

"Who, David? He's thirteen. He's just a big kid. And my mom has very definite standards of propriety and isn't shy about enforcing them, so don't worry."

Jenna didn't answer. She looked over her shoulder at the house.

Tito stopped walking, and gently pulled her to face him. "Hey," he said. "I'm serious. My parents are good people. They won't let anything happen to Halley."

He looked so earnest and decent and kind, and also fantastically handsome.

She sighed. "It isn't that I don't trust them. It's just—I've been solely responsible for her for so long now. And the world is a dangerous place. There are so many things that can go wrong. I can't possibly even predict them all, much less make any sort of effective defense against them. I know worrying doesn't accomplish anything, but…" She trailed off.

"But it doesn't change the way you feel," Tito said.

"Exactly."

"I get that. Look, you can check in as often as you like. And if at any point in the evening you want to come home, we will—even if it's while we're still on our way to San Antonio."

She laid a hand against his cheek. "Why are you so good?"

He chuckled. "Honestly? I'm so happy to be with you that I'm willing to take you on almost any terms."

"Wow," she said. "That's quite a confession. Are you sure it's safe to tell me that? I might take advantage."

He covered her hand with his own, moved it to his lips and kissed it. "I think I can trust you," he said.

TITO HAD ALWAYS loved the River Walk—the old architecture, the stonework, the winding course of the blue-green water opening upon vista after vista of balconies and bridges and tall old trees. Now he was seeing it through Jenna's eyes, and falling in love with it all over again.

It was a warm evening, but the water always seemed to have a cooling effect, even at this level tucked away below the main part of the city, and the big live oak and bald cypress trees provided plenty of shade. Flagstone-paved pathways curved around sparkling fountains and big flowerbeds bursting with tropical plants, bright and bold with big glossy leaves and extravagant blooms. Restaurants and coffee shops spilled out of their walls into patio seating with tabletop umbrellas. River barges sailed down the waterway, looking like children's toys in their candy tints of turquoise and yellow, pink and red, with elaborate designs cut into their sides.

Jenna twined her arm through his and gave it a squeeze. "Oh, I love this place! It's so vivid. There's so much color and life everywhere you turn."

"I thought you'd like it. I do, too. I love living in a small town, but it's nice to come to the city once in a while."

"Yes. It seems strange that I've never been here before after living in Limestone Springs for a year and a half, but…well, you know."

Tito did know. She'd felt more comfortable staying home where things were familiar and secure. But she was here with him now, while Halley was with his family. It was a profound expression of trust from someone in her situation—even if she had already checked in with Halley several times since they'd driven away.

"You should see it at Christmastime," he said. "The lights, the caroling…"

She gave him a flirty glance. "Are you asking me out? Is that going to be our third date? Christmastime on the River Walk?"

A sharp jolt of joy shot through his chest as he laid his hand over hers. "Oh, I expect our third date to be a lot sooner than Christmastime," he said.

"Good," she replied. "So do I."

She pointed at a passing river barge. "Those boats look like those punched papers your mom was making for Eddie's birthday party," she said. "When is his birthday, anyway?"

"The ninth, but the party won't be until later in the

month. Gives everyone a chance to rest from the Fourth of July."

"And when's your birthday?"

"The tenth. Day after Eddie's."

"That's less than a week away. Have you got any plans?"

"Dinner with the family. I'll make sure to get you an invitation."

"Yeah, you'd better. Maybe that'll be our third date."

"Unless I can convince you to go out with me again before then."

She squeezed his arm again. "You might be able to do that. So where are we eating tonight?"

"You tell me. I didn't make a reservation. We're early enough to beat the main dinner rush, and I thought you'd like to look around and choose a place yourself. All the menus are posted outside the entrances."

They took their time, walking hand in hand alongside the water, occasionally crossing a bridge to get a closer look at what was on the other side.

"Ooh," said Jenna, scanning the menu of Boudro's Texas Bistro. "Prickly pear margaritas, tableside guac, shrimp and grits. Let's eat here."

Tito chuckled. "This is exactly the place I thought you'd choose."

She looked almost startled. "Really? Why?"

"I don't know. It just felt like you, somehow. Sort of traditional and hip at the same time."

"Wow. I had no idea I was so transparent."

"Maybe I'm just very observant," said Tito.

"Oh, I know you are. Should we eat inside or out?"

"Whatever you prefer, my lady."

She thought a moment. "Inside, then. We can take a little break from the heat and then walk around outside some more after dinner, when it's cooler."

Tito could see all the heads turning their way as they followed the hostess to their table. He felt his chest swelling with pride. *That's right*, he thought. *She's with me.*

The interior of the restaurant was deliciously dim and cool. They were seated beside a rough limestone wall. Candlelight glimmered on the glassware and shone on the polished dark wood of the table.

Over prickly pear margaritas, Jenna picked up her phone and did some rapid typing. She waited a moment, watching her screen, then relaxed visibly and smiled.

"Everything all right with Halley?" Tito asked.

She darted a guilty glance across the table. "I'm sorry. I'm being rude."

"Not at all. I told you, I don't mind. So how are things going at Casa Mendoza?"

"Well, it sounds like Halley's having a great time. They've had their dinner, and made about a bazillion of those picado papers, and now they're going to play board games."

She smiled down at the text again. "You know, it's easy for me to forget that Halley needs social interaction, because she's such an introverted kid. Most of the time she's fine with a book and some drawing paper, but she does have *some* social needs. Being around your family is good for her."

Tito's own phone lit up. He checked it and said, "Oh, look. My mom sent pictures."

He leaned across the table with his phone so Jenna could see and scrolled through images of Halley and his nephews holding up finished *papeles picados*. The two of them hunched close together, their heads almost touching, laughing over the pictures.

"Thanks for being so understanding about all this," Jenna said.

"It's no problem," said Tito. "I get it. You just want to protect your child."

The white-shirted waiter returned with a wheeled cart, loaded with avocado and citrus fruit, tomatoes and peppers, garlic and red onion, and fresh cilantro. He chatted with them as he sliced and chopped, juiced and mixed.

Jenna scooped up some guacamole on a chip and took a bite. Her eyes rolled back in her head. "Oh my gosh. This is so *good*. I love my adopted state."

"It loves you too," Tito said before he could stop himself. Jenna looked a little flustered, but he thought he saw a tiny smile.

Toward the end of the meal, Jenna got a text. As she read it, her brow furrowed, and she said, "Hmm."

"What's up?" Tito asked. "Is it Halley?"

"Yes. She says your brother Johnny and his wife are trying to set a date to take their boys to Schlitterbahn early next week, and they want to know if we want to come along with Halley."

Her clear green eyes met his across the table. "What is Schlitterbahn, anyway? I hear people talk about going there, but I don't know what it is."

"It's a water park in New Braunfels. Going there is one of the few outdoor activities that are actually fun to do in South Central Texas in July. Really gorgeous place, fed with unchlorinated water straight from the Comal River, and covered with hundred-year-old trees. It's got slides, tube chutes, wave pools, the works. Even a swim-up bar where you can get a Coke or a bottled water or a glass of wine."

"That sounds amazing. Is it big?"

"Pretty big, yeah. But it's not hard to keep a group together."

Jenna took a deep breath and said, "Let's do it."

Tito set down his fork. "Seriously?"

"Yes. If we can manage to get the same day off from work, and coordinate with Johnny's family."

"I don't think that'll be a problem," said Tito, privately resolving to call in every favor owed to him by the staff of Tito's Bar and Lalo's Kitchen, and maybe add some bribery if necessary.

"Great!" Jenna gave him a sly smile. "So that'll be our third date."

"Yeah. A water park with my brother and his wife and a bunch of kids."

Jenna's smile broadened. "Sounds perfect."

"Yes, it does," said Tito.

CHAPTER THIRTEEN

Tito stood behind the bar, looking out over his establishment in that way he had, alert and watchful, spick-and-span in his black and white, with his head held high and his eyes roving to and fro. Every line of him spoke of his pride and affection for this place.

Jenna took out her phone and snapped his picture.

He turned to her, and his expression softened into a smile.

"What are you doing?" he asked.

"I'm taking a picture of my handsome boyfriend," she said.

His smile brightened, as if being called her boyfriend—and handsome—had made his day. He was so tender and responsive to praise. He really had no idea how much he was valued, by her and everyone else around here.

Suddenly, her thoughts and feelings came together in an idea so perfect that it took her breath away.

"Something wrong?" Tito asked.

"No, nothing's wrong," said Jenna. "I just realized there's something I have to do."

She hurried back to the restaurant and started typing on her phone. Could she pull this off? She didn't have much time, but she didn't have to do it alone.

Her first text was to Luke. He replied within seconds.

That's a great idea. Just tell me the day, and put it on the calendar, but in code.

Next she texted Tito's mother, and Lauren, who had a photography business and the necessary technical know-how, and Annalisa, who'd known Tito all her life, and Eliana, who really knew how to bring a project together.

Within minutes, the Events calendar for Lalo's Kitchen was marked with a new item on the tenth of July, under the cryptic name of "private party."

But that was all she had time for right now. Clint called in sick for his evening shift, and Lalo's Kitchen got slammed with a dinner rush that started early and ended late. Jenna didn't have another chance to work on her plan, or see Tito, until well after nine, when he sought her out.

"Hey," he said. "I have to leave, and I don't know when I'll be back."

"Why? What's wrong?"

"Well, there's this neighbor of my parents', Mrs. Gibson. She's going out of town tomorrow to visit her grandson in Denver, and my mom agreed to take care of her cats while she's away. So my mom went over this evening to get the key to the house, and meet the cats, and see where Mrs. Gibson keeps the cat food. And she found Mrs. Gibson all freaked out because she doesn't have her boarding pass for tomorrow. Her grandson booked the flight for her online and had all the flight information sent to her email address, but it's been so long since she checked her email that she was logged out. She couldn't remember her password, so she had to reset it. And now her printer won't communicate with her computer, possibly because she's had her router replaced since the last time she printed anything, and…you get the idea."

"If she gets the app for the airline, she won't need a physical boarding pass," Jenna said.

"She has a flip phone."

"Ah. Of course."

"Anyway, my mom's been there for I don't know how long trying to sort things out—she spent an hour just clearing the pop-ups and malware from Mrs. Gibson's browser—and she's all done in, so she's asked me to come and take over. I don't know how long I'll be. So the upshot of all that is that I've asked Garrett to close for me tonight."

Jenna reached up and smoothed his hair back from his forehead. "You are such a good man."

Tito shrugged philosophically. "Well, Mrs. Gibson was my kindergarten teacher, and she was very good to me the time I stepped right in the middle of a fire-ant mound on the playground and got stung all over. It's the least I can do."

She gave him a quick kiss. "Aw. Try to get some rest tonight. Remember we're going to Schlitterbahn tomorrow."

"I remember. I'll meet you here at nine in the morning."

They'd planned their trip for a weekday to beat the crowds, and this time there'd actually been enough time for a quick shopping trip for something to wear. Jenna and Halley now had new swimsuits, bags, cover-ups, the works. Halley was doing her best to act cool, but Jenna knew how excited she was. She'd been ecstatic when Jenna had actually agreed to visit such a big public place without raising more than a few security concerns.

Jenna smiled as she cleared a table. Things were happening that she hadn't believed possible even a few weeks ago. She felt as if a whole new world were opening up to her, fresh and bright and full of promise.

TITO SAT AT a small table on the back patio of Lalo's Kitchen, wearing his swim trunks and a black-and-white

T-shirt that had an image on the front of Søren Kierkegaard in sunglasses, the sort of thing people gave as gifts to relatives who'd majored in philosophy. He had a lot of nerdy T-shirts in his closet upstairs, but he rarely had a chance to wear them anywhere other than to the gym, or to bed.

But today was different. Today he was taking Jenna and Halley to Schlitterbahn, which he hadn't visited since he was a kid. As soon as Jenna got back from the bank, the three of them would get into his Cadillac and drive to the water park for a day of recreation.

They'd planned to meet Johnny and his family here and caravan to New Braunfels. While Jenna was making the deposit for the restaurant, Halley was in the break room, working on some chalkboard art. Their bags and towels were behind the counter at Lalo's, ready to go.

The breakfast rush had cleared, leaving him alone on the patio. It was pleasant here, in the semi-enclosed outdoor room closest to the back door, with the sunlight filtering through the grapevine canopy overhead and bees buzzing around the blossoms in the flowerpots. He was a little sleepy from his late night helping Mrs. Gibson, but everything had come out all right, and he'd arranged an Uber to take her to the airport and seen her safely inside the car. It was pleasant to sit in the shade now, and watch the dragonflies flit around on the grapevines, and anticipate the day to come.

He leaned back in his chair and shut his eyes. It felt strange to be going on an outing like this with Johnny's family. Johnny was the oldest of the Mendoza brothers, and the only one who'd married and had kids so far, but now here was Tito with a girlfriend who had a twelve-year-old niece. Maybe, just maybe, Tito would have himself a ready-made family soon.

Footsteps approached. Tito opened his eyes and saw a

man rounding the corner of a vine-covered wooden post, looking around as if he wasn't sure he was in the right place. The guy was wearing sunglasses and had his long blond hair pulled back in a ponytail, and he looked to be around Tito's age. When he saw Tito, he stopped short, and a wide grin spread over his face.

"Are you Tito Mendoza?" he asked, in a tone filled with something like awe.

"I am," said Tito.

The guy walked over to the table and stuck out his hand. "Wow. This is such an honor. I've heard so much about you, and about your bar. You know, you're something of a celebrity in the craft bar community. My name's Jordan, by the way."

"Good to meet you, Jordan," Tito said as he stood and shook hands. He was inclined to like Jordan, with his firm handshake and sensible opinions.

"So I guess this is the back patio of Lalo's Kitchen, right?" Jordan asked.

"That's right. And the bar is right next door."

"Well, the patio is gorgeous, with the trellises and the stone walls and all the plants. It's a perfect indoor-outdoor space. I saw the pictures in that article in *Texas Monthly*, but they don't do it justice."

"Oh, you read that, did you?"

"Yeah. Read all about how you transformed the bar after you inherited it from your uncle, and then developed the restaurant next door. You've really put Limestone Springs on the map."

"Wow, thank you. That's nice of you to say so."

"I'm not just saying it to be nice. It's the truth. I live in Austin, and I don't get to come out this way very often, but today I had some business in Seguin County, and I couldn't pass up the opportunity to zip on over to Limestone Springs and see Tito's Bar and Lalo's Kitchen in person."

"Well, go on in," said Tito. "The restaurant is still serving breakfast."

"I will. I'm going to have one of Abel's omelets, relax, watch a game, wait for some people to call me back. Then at eleven, when the bar opens, you can make me one of your signature cocktails, and I can try some of those locally brewed craft beers."

"Actually, I'm not working today. But the other bartenders will take good care of you."

"Oh." Jordan's face fell. He looked genuinely disappointed. "That's too bad. From what I've heard, half the reason people come to Tito's Bar is Tito himself. Sure I can't change your mind? I'm a good tipper."

Tito shook his head. "Afraid not. I'm spending the day with my girlfriend and her kid."

It was the first time he'd called Jenna his girlfriend out loud, and the words filled him with pride.

"Oh, I see how it is," said Jordan in a teasing tone. "Have you been seeing each other long? Is it serious?"

His friendly interest warmed Tito through. "We've only just started dating," he said, "but I've known her for over a year, and...well, she's really special."

"I'll bet. How old's the kid?"

"Twelve."

"Twelve," Jordan repeated, slowly nodding. "That's such a fun age."

"Yeah, it really is. So how long are you going to be in town? Any chance you could come back to the bar tomorrow? I'll be working then."

"Possibly," said Jordan. "I'm not sure how long my business in this area is going to take. A lot of it depends on other people."

Tito chuckled. "I hear that. Here, let me get you a menu."

He walked over to the wall-mounted rack near the back door and took out a menu.

"Thanks," Jordan said. Then he took off his sunglasses, revealing a pair of startlingly blue eyes.

It wasn't just the memory of Chase's mug shot that made everything click into place. Those were Halley's eyes, too. Tito hadn't noticed the resemblance when he'd first seen Chase's picture, but he saw it now.

He froze with his fingers still gripping the corner of the menu that Jordan—Chase—now held in his hand. Chase met Tito's gaze with those oddly bright blue eyes. His smile didn't fade, but something shifted.

"While you're making up your mind," Tito said in as natural a tone as he could manage, "how about if I go inside and get you some merch? We've got some nice T-shirts and hoodies. Plenty of coozies, too. On the house."

It was the best he could come up with on the spur of the moment. All he could think was that he had to reach that glass door ahead of Chase and bolt it shut, and call the cops, before Chase made it inside.

"That's kind of you, Tito," Chase said. His voice sounded as smooth as ever, but Tito could hear the menace beneath the veneer of charm. "But it's a mite warm out here in the sun. I'll come inside with you and see for myself what good things you've got hidden away inside behind that door."

He made a move to step past Tito, but Tito blocked him, placing himself between Chase and the door. No way Tito could get through the door himself, now that Chase was forewarned, without Chase coming through as well. The door was equipped with a damper that caused it to close slowly and gently, to prevent it from slamming shut and possibly breaking the glass. The best Tito could do now was to stand his ground and keep Chase and himself on this side of the door for as long as possible.

They stood, braced and still, inches apart, like two dogs sizing each other up before a fight. Chase was several inches taller and strongly built, probably a good twenty pounds heavier, but Tito had gotten the better of far bigger men in the past. He knew how to handle himself. Unfortunately, so did Chase. Tito could tell by the way he carried himself.

Amusement flickered in Chase's face. "Now, Tito," he said softly. "Don't go starting something you can't finish, or getting involved in things you don't understand. Be reasonable, for both our sakes."

"Reasonable?" Tito repeated. "Is it reasonable to come halfway across the country to terrorize a child?"

A look of cold rage washed over Chase's face. "Kirsten's *my* child," he said. "Kayla took my baby girl away from me. And I'm going to get her back, whether you like it or not."

Light footsteps came hurrying up. Over Chase's shoulder, Tito saw Halley rounding the wooden post at the corner, just as Chase had done minutes earlier.

"Mother just texted. She's on her w—"

Her words cut off and her mouth dropped open as she saw her father.

"Halley, get inside!" said Tito.

There wasn't time to say more. A blinding pain exploded in his head and everything went dark.

CHAPTER FOURTEEN

At 9:00 a.m. it was already a scorcher of a day, perfect for water slides and wave pools with Halley and Tito. The bright morning sunlight dazzled Jenna's eyes as she stepped out of the dim coolness of the bank. With the morning's deposit made, all she had to do was walk back to the restaurant and put the money pouch away, and they could be on their way.

"Jenna?"

It was Annalisa, in a black pencil skirt, sleeveless blouse and high heels.

"Annalisa! Hi! What are you…"

The question died on her lips as she saw the look on Annalisa's face.

"I came to find you," Annalisa said. "I… I don't know how to tell you this, but—"

The ground seemed to drop away from Jenna's feet. "Tell me," she said. "Is it Halley?"

Annalisa nodded, her chin trembling. "She—oh, Jenna, I saw a man put her in his car and drive away. I tried to reach her, but I didn't make it in time. Jenna, I'm so sorry."

It had come at last, the thing Jenna had been dreading for so long, and now it didn't seem real.

"Did you call the police?" She heard herself ask in a voice that didn't sound like her own.

"Yes, right away. They're coming to Lalo's. Luke said

you'd gone to the bank, so I went after you. I didn't want to tell you on the phone."

Annalisa took her arm and started leading her down the sidewalk toward the restaurant, as if Jenna were injured or infirm. The sharp clicking of Annalisa's heels mingled with the shuffles and slaps of Jenna's new mint-green flip-flops. Halley had a new pair too, pink, with little white flowers on the soles.

It was a short walk from the bank to the restaurant. The bell in the front door of Lalo's Kitchen jingled cheerfully as Annalisa opened it and Jenna walked through.

Tito was sitting in a booth at the back of the room. Veronica stood beside him, her hand on his shoulder, holding a white towel to his chin. Coby Kowalski was pacing nearby, in uniform, speaking into his radio.

"...Caucasian female, age twelve. Blond hair, blue eyes, approximately four feet ten inches tall and ninety pounds. Last seen wearing blue jean cutoffs and a yellow T-shirt."

Jenna pressed both hands to her mouth. Then she balled them into fists and put them back at her sides. Panic was a luxury she couldn't afford. She had to put away her fear, lock it inside a drawer in her mind, and do what had to be done.

Tito raised his head and locked eyes with her across the room. His face looked all wrong—hollow-eyed, and with a swollen, misshapen jaw.

Annalisa steered her toward the back of the room. Jenna let herself be led. Her legs were shaking now, but she made it to the booth and sat down across from Tito. There was blood on the white towel and on the front of his black-and-white graphic T-shirt. The restaurant's first-aid kit stood open on the tabletop, stuffed with gauze pads, ice packs and a variety of bandages.

"How long ago did it happen?" Jenna asked.

"I don't know," said Tito. "A couple of minutes, maybe? I don't know how long I was out."

"You were knocked out?"

"I found him out on the back patio," said Veronica. She looked white and scared. "I heard him yell, and Halley was screaming. She was gone by the time I got there, and Tito was lying there with blood all over him."

Tito took the towel from Veronica and scowled down at it. "I'm fine," he muttered.

"It was about five minutes ago," said Annalisa. "I was taking some documents to my car when I saw the guy forcing Halley into the trunk of his car."

A hot surge of anger flared in Jenna's chest. "The trunk?" she repeated, her voice sharp. "He put her in the *trunk*?"

"She did not go quietly," Annalisa went on. "She yelled and screamed and fought him every inch of the way, Jenna. She almost got free, too."

"Did anyone get the license plate number?" Jenna asked. "Or the make and model of the car?"

"I'm pretty sure it was a Ford," said Annalisa. "Maybe a Taurus? It was gray. I remember the license plate started with XXL—that part stuck in my mind—but I don't know what came after that. I'm sorry."

Coby had just put his radio back on his belt and now joined them at the booth. "It's a 2005 Ford Taurus, gray, with a small dent in the driver's-side door and Arkansas plates, plate number XXL 94R," he said. "Assuming that it's the same car that's been parked on this street off and on for the past two days, with a thirty-to forty-year-old white male inside. I saw it yesterday and the day before, and something about it just struck me wrong, so I made a mental note."

A cold, heavy weight settled in Jenna's stomach. Chase

had been watching Lalo's for *two days*? And she hadn't even *noticed*? How could she have been so careless?

But she already knew the answer. She hadn't noticed because she'd been so happy with her new romance. She'd let her guard down—and now Halley was gone.

Coby pulled up a chair, sat down at the end of the booth and took a pencil and pad of paper from his belt. "Jenna, do you know who this man is?"

Jenna took a deep breath. "His name is Chase Latimore. He's Halley's father."

"Her father?" Coby repeated.

"Yes, but his parental rights have been terminated."

"Is he your ex-husband? Current husband?"

She shook her head. "Ex-brother-in-law."

Coby's pencil came to a stop.

"I'm Halley's legal guardian," Jenna said.

"Not her mother?" Coby asked.

"No. Her mother was my sister, Kara." Jenna looked down at the table. "Kara was killed in a car accident a year and a half ago. Chase was the driver. He was high on meth at the time."

"He went to prison?"

"Yes, for felony DUI. He was a repeat offender, so..."

Coby paused while he caught up on his note-taking, then asked, "Where was he incarcerated?"

"Green Rock Correctional."

"Virginia?"

"Chatham, Virginia, yes. He got out almost three weeks ago."

She heard the words coming out of her mouth, a bit jerkily at times, but coherently.

"Did the accident take place in Virginia?" Coby asked.

"Yes. Rocky Mount."

Coby pocketed his notepad.

"Okay. I'll pass this on to my superiors, and they'll get in touch with authorities in Virginia so we can get an AMBER Alert out as quickly as possible."

"Thank you," said Jenna. She'd been serving Coby burgers and beers for months now, joking around with him. She'd never dealt with him in his law enforcement capacity before. Now she felt humbly grateful for his calm competence.

He got to his feet, took up his radio again and walked away.

Veronica was still standing beside the booth, listening, her eyes round. Now she asked, "Can I get anyone anything? Something to drink?" She looked at Tito. "I'll activate one of these ice packs for your chin."

Tito shook his head. "No, that's okay."

"You really ought to at least get a bandage on it," said Veronica.

"I'm fine," Tito said shortly.

"Go ahead and bring them a couple of waters, please, Veronica," said Annalisa.

Veronica nodded and walked away.

Annalisa turned to Jenna. "Is there anyone you'd like me to call for you?"

There was no one to call but Jenna's mom. All at once, Jenna longed to go to her and lay the whole nightmarish situation at her feet, the way she'd once brought her skinned knees and torn doll dresses, and let her fix everything. But Jenna wasn't a little girl anymore, and her mother wasn't the same confident, energetic thirty-year-old that Jenna remembered from her childhood. Jenna could just see her, all alone in her house in Rocky Mount, going about her day, ignorant of the horrible thing that had just happened. She'd already been deprived of her husband and youngest daughter, with her only remaining relatives now accessible only through an electronic screen. She couldn't take any more tragedy. She just couldn't.

Then Jenna saw Halley's canvas beach bag with the big pink hibiscus printed on the side, lying in a heap on the counter behind the booth. A rolled-up beach towel, blue with yellow polka dots, peeked out at the top, along with a bottle of sunscreen. A floppy straw hat was tossed on top.

The tears came then, in an abrupt, violent storm. Halley had been so excited this morning, packing her bag, braiding her hair and then taking it down and braiding it again, and securing the ends with pink elastics. Now she was trapped in a car, scared and possibly hurt, with a father who'd been nothing but terror and grief to her.

Annalisa rubbed Jenna's shoulder and made soothing noises, and Tito silently pushed the napkin holder across the table to her. Jenna grabbed a fistful of napkins and held them to her face.

"I'm going to call Luke and Eliana," said Annalisa. "And I ought to let my boss know where I am. I'll be back soon."

Jenna didn't answer. She just kept sobbing into her wad of paper napkins.

The police will find her, she told herself. *They'll get her back.*

They had a lot of things working in their favor, including an actual cop who'd made note of the vehicle and its license number. Highway patrol would set up roadblocks, or something. Chase would be caught, and be sent back to jail, and Jenna would get Halley back.

But Chase wasn't like other people. He didn't give up, even when he had no chance of success. He just kept going, no matter what it cost him, no matter who got hurt.

She wanted Tito to come over to her side of the booth and put his arm around her, and tell her everything would be all right. But he just sat there across from her, saying nothing, staring down at the bloody towel in his hands.

Veronica came back with their waters. She set the glasses on the table and melted away again. Jenna blew her nose and gulped some water.

She glanced across the table at Tito, turning her attention to the swollen bruise distorting the clean line of his jaw beneath the neatly trimmed beard.

"Wh-what did he do to you?" she asked.

His shoulder twitched up in a shrug. "Uppercut to the chin. Classic sucker punch. I should have seen it coming, but I didn't."

He looked at her then with haunted eyes. "I'm sorry," he said.

She understood now. Tito was ashamed. That was why he wasn't comforting her. He thought he didn't have the right.

"It's not your fault," she said.

"I should have known better. He played me. Came up to me on the back patio, pretending to be an out-of-towner visiting the restaurant and bar. He knew all about me, and the renovation, and the menu. Acted like he was my biggest fan, and I fell for it. I didn't recognize him until he took his sunglasses off. I saw his mug shot after you looked it up on my phone that day. He clearly knew Halley was inside. From what Coby said, it sounds like he'd been watching the place for a while. I don't know what his plan was."

"He didn't have one," Jenna said with conviction. "He was only getting the lay of the land. He was never one for thinking ahead. He just plunges in. And if an opportunity presents itself, he takes it, and figures out the rest as he goes along."

"Yeah, that sounds about right," said Tito. "By the time I figured out who he really was, it was a little late in the game, and he was already several steps ahead of me. I knew I didn't have time to get inside to protect Halley. All I could hope to do was to keep Chase from going through the glass back door to get to her. I never expected her to come out the other way."

"Which other way?"

"From Luke's office, I think. He has that door that leads to the outside."

Jenna let out a groan. "Oh, right. Yes, I texted her from the bank and asked her to go in there and check something for me."

She took her phone out of her pocket, opened up her text thread with Halley and scrolled through, as if the words might hold some clue that would help her get Halley back. The whole exchange looked so innocent and hopeful now, filled with anticipation for their upcoming day at the water park, the words interspersed with emojis of yellow suns and water droplets.

She set the phone down.

"You should go to the hospital," she told Tito. "You've been concussed."

"I'm fine. I don't even have a headache."

"You don't know that you're fine. You could have brain damage. Head injuries are nothing to mess around with."

"I know. I'll go later. After…"

He didn't finish, but she knew what he'd been about to say. *After Halley's found.* As if it were that simple. Another few minutes, a half hour tops, and she'd be back, and life could go on as it had before. Until then, everything else had to be put on hold.

But how long would it take? And what if it never happened? Jenna had learned by now that things didn't always turn out fine in the end. They hadn't for Kara. Chase had seen to that. And now Chase had Halley.

She shook her head. They *would* get Halley back. They had to. It was only a matter of time. And after that...

After that, what? Chase would go to jail, assuming he was caught. But he'd gone to jail before, and gotten out, and somehow managed to track Jenna and Halley down.

How had he done it? Jenna had worked so hard to shut the door so firmly on the past that she and Halley would never have to see Chase again. But she hadn't done all that she could have done, not by a long shot. And over the past few weeks, she'd let down her guard. She'd listened to that soft, soothing voice that had told her it was okay to relax once in a while, that she didn't have to maintain constant vigilance, that she and Halley could have normal lives, with friends, and fun, and parties, and love. Somewhere along the way, she'd messed up, and Chase had taken advantage of that. He'd found the chink in their armor and exploited it, like he always did.

All of which raised a very disturbing question. Once she did have Halley back safe and sound, what new lengths of precautions and safeguards would Jenna have to go to in order to keep her safe?

CHAPTER FIFTEEN

NOT MANY MINUTES had passed since Chase had tossed Halley into the trunk of the Ford Taurus, but it felt as if a long time had gone by. Annalisa soon returned to Lalo's, as she'd said she would, along with Claudia, her boss. Johnny showed up with his wife and kids, ready to go to the water park, and stuck around after learning what had happened. As word of Halley's abduction spread, more people trickled in. Tito's parents came.

Tito was reminded of the time just after the bad storm a few years back when the restaurant and bar had become gathering places for the community. He'd kept busy then, passing out food and drink and trying to encourage people. Now it was Luke who was feeding everyone, while Tito was being treated as a victim of the crisis. He sat there in his booth, useless—as useless as he'd been when Chase had gotten the drop on him and taken Halley.

Coby reported that the local police had been in touch with authorities in Virginia and Arkansas. They'd learned that the car Chase was driving had been reported stolen in Little Rock. Other than that, no progress had been made.

Tito kept thinking about that time when he'd worked with Halley on self-defense. He'd shown her how to break the most common holds, and even given her some pointers on how to escape from the trunk of a car, should she ever find herself stuffed inside one.

But don't let it come to that, he'd told her. *All your en-*

ergy needs to be focused on not being put into the car to begin with. Have you ever seen how a feral kitten acts when it gets picked up? It goes all out, twisting and clawing and yowling and biting. Be like that. Be a little cat.

From what Annalisa had said, Halley had done everything he'd told her to do, but it hadn't been enough. He hadn't told her that a kidnapping victim's chances of survival plummeted once the victim was inside the abductor's car.

If Tito had been vigilant this morning, Chase never would have had a chance to get hold of Halley to begin with.

He writhed at the memory of himself swallowing Chase's lies, being taken in by his flattery. How could he have been so gullible? He, Tito Mendoza, who prided himself on his people-reading skills, had been thoroughly bested by a small-time lowlife criminal. True, he'd never met the guy before that morning, and the long hair, spiffy clothes and dark sunglasses had gone a long way toward altering his appearance from the mug shot Tito had viewed weeks earlier on his phone's screen. But Tito had known of Chase's existence, his cunning ways, his penchant for violence. He'd known, because Jenna had told him, that Chase was a people-smart charmer. Jenna was the smartest, most capable woman he knew, and Tito had seen how much she feared Chase. He should have been on his guard.

But he hadn't. Chase had gotten to him by appealing to his vanity, and now Chase had Halley and there was nothing Tito could do about it.

The words *chances of survival* kept swirling through his mind. He wanted to believe it wasn't a question of survival. Chase was Halley's *father*. Surely he wouldn't hurt her. But Tito couldn't make any assumptions based on the behavior of normal people. And even if Chase's intent wasn't to harm Halley, he was reckless enough to hurt her without meaning to, through drug-impaired driving or sheer thoughtless stupidity. He'd already proven that.

Had Chase been high when he was smooth-talking Tito on the back patio of Lalo's Kitchen? Was he high now? There was no way to know.

Where were Chase and Halley now? How many miles had they traveled in that Ford Taurus, and in which direction, and at what speed? Tito didn't know any of those things. He'd never felt so powerless in his life.

He was still sitting across the table from Jenna in the back booth. They didn't have much to say to each other, but they'd stayed there, waiting, drawing comfort—at least Tito was—from their nearness.

A cell phone's ringtone went off. Everyone turned toward the sound. It was Coby Kowalski's phone. The room went quiet as Coby picked up and said, "Yeah?"

Tito and Jenna reached for each other's hands across the table. The silence grew and stretched as Coby stood motionless and expressionless with the phone to his ear. Jenna's hands gripped Tito's with white-knuckle intensity.

Coby let out a breath. His eyes shut. What did that mean? Good news or bad?

"Thanks," he said. "I'll pass that along."

The entire crowd seemed to be holding its breath. Coby opened his eyes and ended his call.

"She's safe."

A great sigh went through the restaurant, like a gust of wind. Across the table from him, Jenna drew a quick ragged breath and dropped her head onto their clasped hands.

"Where is she?" Tito asked.

"At the Foxes' place with Kevin and Gillian and Kevin's dad. We have officers at the scene. She's about to be transported to the hospital."

"Hospital?" Jenna repeated. "What's wrong with her?"

"I don't have any details about her condition, except that it's not considered life-threatening. Also, the suspect has been apprehended. He's on his way to the police station."

Jenna let go of Tito's hands and stumbled to her feet, looking dazed and bewildered, as if she'd just woken up. "Okay, okay," she said. "I've got to go to the hospital. Where's my purse?"

"You're in no shape to drive yourself," Tito said. "I'll take you there."

"Oh, no," said Annalisa. "Neither one of you is fit to drive. I'll drive both of you, and while Jenna is with Halley, Tito can get himself a brain scan or something. Two birds, one stone."

HALLEY HAD LOST one of her new pink hair elastics. Her hair had come unbraided on that side, giving her a lopsided appearance that would have been funny under other circumstances. She had scrapes and scratches on her face and limbs, her new T-shirt was torn, and her new cutoffs were stained with spots of what looked like motor oil.

But she was safe, and suffering no worse injuries than what would be expected from escaping from the trunk of a moving car on a state highway. Jenna drank in the sight of her. She felt that she could never get her fill of looking at Halley.

"Tito told me how," she said, bright-eyed with excitement on the exam table in the emergency room, her swollen wrist secured in a splint. "There's a cable on the driver's side that you can pull, if it's that kind of car. You have to feel around under the carpeting and cardboard paneling and stuff until you find it. Then you yank it toward the front of the car, and the trunk opens up."

Jenna spared Tito a quick flash of a smile, and he smiled back. He was sitting on the other side of the exam table. He hadn't gone for his own examination yet. He'd insisted on seeing Halley first.

"Smart girl," he said.

She *was* a smart girl, and a brave girl. But things could have just as easily gone another way.

Over the course of the day, details came to light, and the story of Halley's abduction and escape took shape like a mosaic, pieced together from Halley's own recollections and various enthusiastic witness accounts, as well as from the grudging statement given by Chase himself. Coby Kowalski briefed Jenna in a small meeting room at the hospital, using an official-sounding voice and diction that she'd never heard him use before today.

"To the best of our knowledge," said Coby, "this is what happened. After securing Halley in the trunk, the suspect headed east on Highway 281, where he got stuck behind a farm vehicle which we believe to have been a John Deere cotton harvester, traveling at a speed of twenty-five miles per hour. The driver of the farm vehicle did not pull onto the shoulder, and the highway was busy enough at that time of day to make passing difficult. The suspect, whether out of concern for the welfare of his child in the trunk of the car, or because he didn't want to get pulled over, elected to keep in his lane and tailgate the farm vehicle in hopes that it would move over. Eventually the farm vehicle slowed down in preparation for making a right turn. While this was taking place, Halley was searching for the release cable in the trunk of the car. She found it and pulled it. The trunk popped open and she exited the vehicle."

Jenna shuddered at the thought of Halley jumping out

of a moving car onto a state highway. Even at a speed of twenty-five miles per hour, it was dangerous—but not as dangerous as staying in the trunk of Chase's car.

"The motorist behind the suspect was also traveling at a reduced rate of speed," Coby went on. "She witnessed Halley jumping out of the trunk and immediately applied her brakes and slowed to a stop. She then witnessed Halley roll into a bar ditch, get to her feet and begin to run."

Yeah, I'll bet she did, Jenna thought, tears pricking her eyes. She could just see Halley, with her broken wrist and skinned knees, adrenaline coursing through her little body, temporarily numbing her to pain as she ran with all her might—in flip-flops, no less.

"The motorist called 911 from the shoulder," said Coby. "She saw the suspect's vehicle swerve off the road, where it collided with a concrete culvert near the junction of 281 and Ripke Road. The suspect then exited his vehicle and pursued Halley on foot. Halley recognized the home of Kevin Fox and his daughter Gillian and headed toward it."

The property was conspicuous enough, Jenna knew, with its big, ramshackle house and overgrown field filled with defunct farm machinery.

"Kevin and Gillian were both outdoors with Kevin's father, Ray," Coby continued. "They had been working all morning on getting an old tractor into salable condition and had heard nothing of Halley's abduction. By the time Halley reached them, she was incoherent and out of breath, but Ray and Kevin were able to figure out the essentials of the situation. The suspect was still pursuing Halley at this time. Ray took the girls inside the house, locked the doors and armed himself with a shotgun. Kevin removed a rifle from his truck and began walking toward the suspect."

"*Kevin* did that?" Jenna asked.

"Yes," said Coby.

"Kevin Fox?"

"That's correct."

Jenna sat back in her chair, stunned.

She liked Kevin well enough from her interactions with him at the restaurant and bar, and when they'd carpooled together to get Halley and Gillian to and from horse camp, he'd been punctual and responsible with his end of the deal. But he was so unkempt and bewildered-looking, and a part of Jenna had judged him for that. And here he'd stalked out to meet an unknown miscreant, firearm in hand, to protect her child.

"Did Chase have a gun too?" she asked.

"Yes," said Coby.

"Did Kevin shoot him? Did he shoot Kevin?"

"No. While they were still some distance from each other, a neighbor of Mr. Fox's observed the suspect pursuing Halley. The neighbor ran down the suspect, tackled him from behind and secured him with two lengths of baling wire. He and Mr. Fox then disarmed the suspect and remained with him until police officers arrived on the scene to take him into custody."

Jenna slowly shook her head. To think that Chase had a gun on him all along—

"At this time," Coby continued, "it is unknown whether this weapon was stolen, or provided to the suspect by a friend or family member, or recovered from a private stash. But even if the weapon was not illegally obtained, merely having one in his possession and transporting it was a clear violation of the suspect's parole."

"One in a long list of violations, I would think," said Jenna. "Assault, stealing a car…"

"Driving while revoked, driving without insurance," Coby added. "And, of course, kidnapping is a federal offense, as well as a state crime in Texas."

Jenna let her breath out in a big puff of air. Then she asked, "What does Chase say? How did he track down Halley and me? I—I took a lot of precautions to keep him from finding us."

Coby nodded. "It appears that shortly after his release from prison, Mr. Latimore was shown a video of a barn raising which you and Halley attended. You aren't visible in the video, but Halley is. To date, this video has had over twelve thousand views."

"A video?" Jenna repeated blankly. "Someone took a video of Halley at the barn raising?"

"Halley was not the main subject of the video, but she is visible in it long enough to be recognized. Someone within the suspect's circle of acquaintance viewed the video in connection with a building project he was undertaking. He noticed the resemblance to Halley and mentioned it to one of Mr. Latimore's relatives, who identified Halley from the video and passed it along to the suspect. Mr. Latimore was able to locate the Vrba Equestrian Center through an internet search. He then obtained a large amount of cash from a source which has yet to be determined and took a series of buses west. Upon reaching Arkansas, the suspect stole a car. He then drove to Limestone Springs, where he rented a hotel room and spent several days observing the downtown area. In the barn raising video, Halley was wearing a T-shirt bearing the logo of Lalo's Kitchen, which was also listed as one of the businesses providing food for the event. Once the suspect started keeping an eye on the place, he observed you and Halley in the company of Tito Mendoza. It's believed that he did not have an overarching plan but merely waited for an opportunity and improvised."

Jenna dropped her face in her hands. After all the pains she'd taken—the new home, the carefully crafted new identities—Chase had found them through some video on the internet that she hadn't even realized had been taken. He'd staked the place out for days, and she'd never noticed, because she'd had her heart and head filled with Tito. Months of effort and vigilance, wasted. No matter how long Chase went away for this time, it could never be long enough. He'd get out one day, and come after Halley again.

The knowledge wrenched her heart. The more she came to know this place, the more she saw to love. The history, the landscapes, the people. Mostly the people—especially one of the people. But none of that mattered.

Limestone Springs wasn't safe for her and Halley anymore.

CHAPTER SIXTEEN

TITO WAS PEELING off his Kierkegaard T-shirt when Jenna's ringtone went off on his phone, startling Bunter, who was curled up on the bed near the phone. A tremor of pleasure passed through Tito's heart at the sight of her picture on the lit-up screen. He quickly stepped into his jeans and pulled them up before answering.

"Hey," he said.

"Hey. Where are you?"

"Home. The hospital let me leave after my scan. But I'm just here long enough to change clothes. I've been in swim trunks and a bloody T-shirt all day, and I was ready for a change. Where are you, hospital or police station?"

"Hospital. The police came to me for my interview so I could stay near Halley."

"How is she?"

"Sleeping, finally. They had to give her a pediatric cocktail for sedation. I'm in the hallway outside her room."

"Poor kid. How's the arm?"

"Fractured at the scaphoid, which I've just learned is one of the tiny bones in the wrist. She's got a cast on it now. Apparently the fracture is in the part of the scaphoid bone that has a good blood supply, which helps with the healing."

"Glad to hear it."

"Yeah. How about you?"

"Grade 1 concussion. No caffeine or alcohol, no driving or electronic devices, until I'm cleared for them. Ibuprofen for pain."

He could hear the smile in her voice. "You're on an electronic device right now, you know."

He walked over to his closet, flipped through his shirts and took out the dark blue button-down that Jenna liked. "Yeah, well, I won't tell if you won't. I'll meet you back at the hospital in a few minutes."

"I thought you said no driving."

"Johnny gave me a ride home. He's waiting for me downstairs."

"Oh. Well, don't bother coming back. Stay home and get some rest."

"I don't need to rest. I barely have a headache."

This wasn't entirely true, but he could cope with the pain.

"You had a brain injury. You need to rest."

"I'm not leaving you to deal with all this alone. I want to be with you."

"Well, I'd rather you didn't come, okay?"

Tito slowly laid the shirt on the bed. "What's wrong?"

Jenna's voice rose. "What's wrong? I have a child who was abducted and thrown into the trunk of a car by her criminal father, with physical injuries and a fresh load of trauma to add to all her previous trauma."

Tito didn't answer. He didn't say what he was thinking, which was that Halley was free now, that things could have ended much worse, and that they had much to be thankful for. That was all true, but didn't negate anything Jenna had said. And there had been something almost hostile in her tone, as if Tito were the enemy, which gave him an uneasy premonition about where this conversation was heading.

Then her tone softened. "I'm sorry. You didn't deserve that. You've had a hard day too, and you've been very good to Halley and me. If it wasn't for you, Halley wouldn't have known how to escape from the trunk of a car, and... well, thank you—for that, and your friendship, and just everything."

Tito's knees gave way. He sat down on the edge of his bed and waited.

Jenna sighed. "There's no good way to say this, so I'll just say it. We're leaving, Halley and I, as soon as she's well enough and I figure out where we're going to go."

"You can't be serious," Tito said.

"I'm dead serious. We can't stay here. Limestone Springs isn't safe for us anymore."

Tito ran a hand through his hair and clenched a handful of it. "Jenna, Chase is in jail. He's not going to be set free to go on his merry way. He's going away for a long time."

"So what if he is? He'll be released again, maybe early if he keeps his nose clean. He might even escape. He's crazy enough for anything, and smart, and cunning, and charming, and quick on his feet—not to mention that he's got a whole family tree's worth of crazy relatives who aren't above kidnapping her themselves. I've got to take Halley somewhere that he can never hurt her again."

"Jenna, no. Don't do this."

"I have no choice. You heard how he tracked us down. Through that video at the barn raising. That was all it took. I let my guard down and this was the result."

"You can't prevent things like that from happening! It isn't possible, no matter how careful you are. Not in today's world. Isolating yourself won't keep you safe. Stay here, and let me help protect you and Halley."

"Yeah, well, we've seen how well that worked this time."

Tito's hand dropped to the mattress with a soft thud. He was too stung to reply.

"I'm sorry," Jenna said in a different tone. "I didn't mean that the way it sounded. I know how tough you are. I've seen you in action at the bar, throwing out drunks. But Chase is a special kind of crazy. People like you and me will always be at a disadvantage dealing with people like him, because people like him don't operate according to ordinary logic. We can't possibly predict all the bizarre things he might do."

"All the more reason why you shouldn't try to deal with him on your own. Your problem is that you've been taking care of everything by yourself for so long that you've forgotten how to trust anyone else."

"Don't tell me what my problem is. This is my responsibility and my decision to make."

"And your decision is to keep running? How long can you keep that up? It's time you stopped running and made your stand."

Jenna's voice rose. "Make my stand? How? He took her, Tito. He picked her up and threw her in his car and drove away."

"And she got away from him," Tito reminded her.

"Then he'll escalate next time. Do something more extreme." She let out an impatient sigh. "Look, there's no sense in arguing about it. My mind is made up. And I've got to go now and get back to Halley." She paused. "I'm sorry it has to be this way, Tito. I really am."

He could hear the tremor in her voice. He opened his mouth to say something, anything to stop her, but before he could get a word out, she said, "Goodbye, Tito," and hung up.

He slowly lowered the phone to his lap and looked down at the empty screen. Then he lifted his head and saw himself in the mirror, slumped over, shirtless, blank-eyed, his chin still misshapen from its encounter with Chase's fist and his hair standing on end.

A hoarse meow made him turn. Bunter had crept onto his blue shirt and was busy depositing black and white hairs on it. Tito gently removed him, picked up the shirt, brushed it off and hung it back in the closet.

His head was starting to ache now, and there was a weird tense soreness in his neck and jaw. He thought suddenly of Halley when he'd visited her in the ER, before he'd had his own exam. While Jenna was talking to a nurse, Halley had looked at him with tears glistening on her lashes and said, *Thank you for teaching me how to get out of a locked trunk, Tito. I'm sorry my dad hit you.*

He'd smiled at her and said, *Halley, you have nothing to apologize for. None of this is your fault.*

I know, she'd said. *But he's still my dad.*

True enough, he'd thought, looking at those bright blue eyes, so much like Chase's.

She'd glanced at Jenna, then said, so quietly he almost didn't hear her, *I wish you were my dad.*

I wish that too, he'd replied.

But wishing didn't make it so.

CHAPTER SEVENTEEN

JENNA BROUGHT HALLEY home that evening, along with several pages of care instructions and an appointment card for a follow-up doctor's visit. Halley went to bed early. Jenna stayed in the living room, fully clothed, too keyed up to go to bed. She picked up a book, read the same paragraph over and over without comprehending a word of it, laid it down, scrolled mindlessly through her phone for a few minutes, picked up the book again, laid it back down and got up to check that all the doors and windows were locked.

She fell asleep on the sofa around midnight. An hour or so later, she woke to the sound of Halley screaming in her room. Jenna toppled off the sofa, barked her shin on the coffee table and stumbled down the hall to find Halley, alone in her room, sitting up in bed and staring straight ahead at nothing. Jenna took Halley into her arms, and Halley clung to her like she hadn't done since she was a little girl. Halley didn't say anything—Jenna wasn't sure she'd even woken up—but her cries subsided, and within minutes her eyes were shut and her breathing was soft and regular. Jenna crawled under the covers with her and stayed there for the rest of the night, sleeping fitfully and waking at every sound.

In the morning, she crept out of the room and started making breakfast preparations. She was setting the table when Halley emerged, heavy-eyed and rumpled in her old sleep shorts and oversize T-shirt with Tweety Bird on it, with bandages over her knees, scrapes on her legs and the pristine white plaster cast on her wrist.

"Good morning," Jenna said brightly.

"Morning," said Halley.

"How's the arm?"

"All right. Hurts a little."

"Do you want to take something? I've got ibuprofen right here. The liquid kind, so you don't have to swallow a pill."

"Not now. Maybe later. What are you making?"

"Pancakes with blueberry compote. Your favorite."

She was pushing too hard. She'd have been okay if she'd stopped after the first sentence. Halley didn't have to be reminded what her favorite breakfast was.

Halley gave her a wan smile as she took a seat at the kitchen bar. "Thanks."

"I didn't start cooking them yet," Jenna went on. "Well, I did make the compote, but not the pancakes. I just mixed the batter. That way you can have the pancakes fresh and hot off the griddle."

The sound of her voice was chirpy and annoying in her own ears. She needed to stop talking, now, or Halley was going to clam up.

She forced herself not to speak another word until the first batch of pancakes was done. "There we go," she said. "Now I'll just take these to the table and—"

But Halley had already picked up her plate from the table and brought it over to the bar. "I can just eat here," she said. "Will you hand me the pan with the compote, please?"

"I'll ladle some on for you," Jenna said.

"That's okay. I'll do it myself."

Jenna handed over the pan, and Halley spooned some compote onto her stack of pancakes. Jenna stood a moment, uncertain, before fetching her own plate from the dining table and bringing it to the kitchen.

She filled her plate. Now what? Should she eat at the bar with Halley, or would that be hovering? Maybe she should eat at the table. But wouldn't that be weird, the two of them eating in two different places? Seemed like anything she did at this point was going to be awkward.

She ended up eating in the kitchen, standing with her hip against the counter and wondering how she was ever going to survive Halley's teen years if things were this difficult now. Was it really just seven hours ago that Halley had gratefully accepted comfort from her like the small child she used to be?

Halley was halfway through her pancakes when she glanced at the time on the kitchen clock. "It's late," she said. "Don't you have a breakfast shift?"

"Oh, I'm not working today," Jenna said. "We're staying home and watching movies all day, whatever you want to watch. And we'll snack on popcorn and chips like a couple of couch potatoes."

Halley thought about this. For a moment things hung in the balance. Jenna held her breath. Had she struck the right tone, or was she trying too hard again?

Then Halley smiled. "That sounds perfect," she said.

Jenna smiled back. "Good. You need to take it easy and get your strength back, so you might as well enjoy yourself, right?"

"Yeah. Hey, we should invite Tito."

Jenna hesitated a little too long before saying, "Tito can't come."

"Why? He isn't working, is he? He needs to rest, too."

"Actually, he's supposed to avoid screen usage while his concussion heals."

"Oh," said Halley. "Well, we don't have to watch movies. We can do something else. Maybe play some board games. His parents have some good ones."

"Tito isn't coming over," Jenna said.

"Why?" Halley asked, in a tone that indicated that she had a pretty good idea of what was coming and didn't like it.

Jenna sighed. "I didn't want to tell you this way."

"Tell me what?"

Silence. Then Jenna steeled herself and said, "There's no point in my seeing Tito anymore, because you and I aren't staying in Limestone Springs."

Halley's mouth dropped open. "We're moving? What for?"

"Because the whole point of coming here in the first place was to get away from your father and his family. Now that he's found us, this place isn't safe for us anymore."

"I thought he was going back to prison."

"I certainly hope he is. But he already went once, and he got out, a whole lot sooner than we thought he would. That could happen again."

Halley's pupils dilated, swallowing up the blue of her eyes, and her face went white. For a moment Jenna thought Halley might faint.

She reached across the kitchen counter, grabbed Halley's hand and held it tight. "You don't have to be afraid. I won't let him hurt you again."

Halley jerked her hand away and stood up. "Stop it! Stop treating me like a baby. I don't need you constantly taking care of me and telling me what to do."

"I'm not treating you like a baby, Kara, I just—"

Halley actually stamped her foot, like a toddler throwing a tantrum. "I'm not Kara! I'm me. And I'm not a little kid anymore. I can look out for myself. I got myself out of the trunk of that car, and I don't think you're giving me enough credit for that."

"How can you say that, honey? I'm proud of you for what you did."

"That's the first time I've heard you say so."

"Well, I am. You were brave and smart, and you kept your head in a horrible situation. But you were also very lucky. That big tractor thing that slowed down the traffic, the fact that you were on that exact stretch of road close to a house you recognized, the fact that Kevin happened to be at home and outside—not to mention that weirdly athletic farmer who chased after your dad and knocked him down. Without all those things being in place, this story could have had a very different ending. I'm not trying to devalue what you did. I'm just saying that next time, it might not be enough."

"Maybe it wouldn't have to be enough if we had other people on our side. You aren't the only person who can do things, you know. Other people can be smart and strong too, and they can help us. People like Tito, and Gillian's dad, and that really fast farmer, and Tito's family."

She squared her jaw and glared at Jenna head-on with those bright blue eyes so eerily like Chase's. "Tell me you didn't already break up with him. Did you? Tell me."

"I—I—"

The bright blue eyes filled with tears. Halley didn't look like Chase anymore. She was just herself, a twelve-year-old girl, serious and precocious, but still a child.

She turned and stormed off to her room and slammed the door, leaving Jenna alone in the kitchen, staring at Halley's half-eaten stack of pancakes.

She planted her hands on the counter and hung her head. She was shaking all over, and her stomach was tied in knots. How had she managed to make such a mess of things? All she wanted was to keep Halley safe. Was that so wrong?

She stood there, staring down at the countertop, until her hands steadied and her stomach settled into a dreary calm. Then she took a deep breath and ambled slowly through the dining room, all the way to the back window.

And there was Tito's building, just visible through the limbs of her neighbor's pecan tree. Was Tito inside his apartment right now? Sleeping? Reading? Petting his cat? Thinking of Jenna? Feeling as miserable as she was?

Halley's accusations rang in her ears. Was it really just arrogance that made her take all the responsibility on herself? Tito had said pretty much the same thing. Maybe they were right. If she had told the truth right from the start in her new community, she would have had a lot of people looking out for her and Halley. If Coby Kowalski had known about Chase, then his cop instincts would have made the connection between Halley's recently released ex-con father and the suspicious-looking vehicle parked downtown for several days in a row. Tito might not have gotten hurt, and Halley might not have been taken. Jenna's secrecy hadn't protected Halley or herself. It had only made them more vulnerable.

She rested her forehead against the glass. Something was pulling her, gently but firmly, like an invisible line stretching from here to that old downtown building, connecting her heart to Tito's.

She stood up straight, then walked down the hallway and knocked on Halley's door.

She heard Halley let out a heavy sigh, then ask, "What?"

"Can I come in?" Jenna asked.

"Yes."

Halley was lying on her bed with her back to the door.

Jenna sat down on the edge of the bed. She started to reach for Halley, then drew back her hand and said, "I'm sorry."

Almost before the words were out, Halley had spun around and wound her arms around Jenna's neck and was crying into her shoulder. "I'm sorry too. I shouldn't have been so mean."

Halley's hair was tickling Jenna's face. Jenna smoothed it back.

"You weren't mean," she said. "You were right."

Halley sucked in a quick breath of air and pulled back to look Jenna in the face. "I was?"

"Yes. I was trying to do everything on my own, and I can't. It's too much. I'm not strong enough or smart enough to handle it all."

"You're the smartest, strongest person I know," Halley said, her voice quavering. "You gave up your old job and your old house, and got new names for us, and moved us away from my dad and all the other Latimores. I know you didn't have to do all that, and I'm glad you did, I really am. It's just…it's hard sometimes, knowing you did all that for me. It's like I took everything away from you, and now I have to be enough to make up for it."

Jenna laid a hand against Halley's cheek. "Oh, Halley, you're already enough. You don't have to earn my love. You're mine. You hear me? Nothing will ever change that. I'm sorry if I've put too much pressure on you. I guess I'm just afraid of making a mistake. I have to keep you safe."

Halley sniffled. "It isn't only about me being safe, though. You're afraid I'll turn out like my mom—or my dad."

Jenna wanted to deny it, but she couldn't without lying.

"You're right," she said. "I guess I am afraid of that sometimes."

"Well, you don't have to be. I remember what it was

like when I lived with them. I'm not going to make those same mistakes."

"Okay," Jenna said. "I believe you."

And she did. Of course, Halley would make different mistakes. But there was no help for that, and no sense in trying to predict what those mistakes might be and head them off.

"And speaking of mistakes..." Halley gave Jenna a reproachful look.

"I know," Jenna said. "I messed up."

There was no need to be more specific. They both knew they were talking about Tito.

"Do you think you can get him back?" asked Halley.

"I don't know," said Jenna. "I hope so."

"You *have* to. He's perfect for you."

Jenna smiled. "He is, isn't he? He's really special."

"Call him," said Halley. "Tell him you were wrong and that we're not moving away after all."

"Not so fast," said Jenna. "I haven't actually said we're not moving away."

Halley gave her a sly smile. "Then say it now."

Jenna chuckled. "Okay. We're not moving away. We're staying in Limestone Springs."

Halley squealed, and hugged Jenna so hard the bed bounced. "Now call Tito and tell him you're sorry. Where's your phone?"

"I think it's in the kitchen. Halley, wait!"

But Halley had already bounded off through the door and down the hall.

"Careful!" Jenna called. "Do you want to break your other arm?"

Halley came skipping back and dropped Jenna's phone on the bed in front of her.

"Call him," she said. "Do it!"

Jenna picked up the phone and clicked into recent calls. Tito's number was right there at the top. She could call him right now, just as Halley said, and tell him she was wrong and she wanted him back. And maybe that would be enough for him. But it wasn't enough for her. She wanted to give him more. He deserved more.

Halley stared at her, eyes shining. "What are you waiting for? Go ahead!"

Jenna laid the phone back down. "I have a better idea," she said. "I've been planning a sort of surprise for Tito for a few days now. Something to show him how special he is to me, and to the whole town. I sort of forgot about it after—well, you know, everything. And I don't have much time to pull it together."

"Maybe you don't have to do it all by yourself," Halley said.

"Maybe I don't. In fact, I've got one of the smartest, most capable people I know, right here in this house with me."

Halley grinned. "Then let's get to work."

CHAPTER EIGHTEEN

ONE OF THE bedrock principles of self-defense, Bart had told Tito years ago, was not being around to get hurt. This included defensive moves, like blocking, deflecting and dodging, but it went deeper than that. Whenever possible, you had to prevent a situation from developing or escalating to a point where a punch or kick was thrown in the first place. You had to think ahead, and predict different ways an encounter might go, and be ready to respond—and also keep yourself away from compromising situations, whether that meant staying out of dark alleys in sketchy parts of town, or defusing conflicts before they turned violent.

Tito had taken the lesson to heart. In the years since he'd taken over the bar and started acting as its bouncer, he'd de-escalated a lot of situations, and he'd never once had a surly drunk actually land a blow on him.

But Chase had knocked him out cold with a single punch. A child had been taken by force, and Tito, with his years of training and experience, hadn't been able to do a thing to stop it. As Bart used to say, all the knowledge and skill in the world wouldn't do a bit of good if you didn't put them into practice.

And that was the thought that kept nagging at him now. He'd known better, but he'd still gotten hurt. Just like he'd known better than to believe he and Jenna could have a future together, but had fallen for her anyway. It was the same old story he'd seen playing out all his life. Whatever it was that made a woman want to stay with a man for the long haul, he didn't have. His wounded pride hurt more than his concussed head, but less than his broken heart.

He lay stretched out on his unmade bed, with his feet on the floor and his arms spread wide, staring up at the ceiling. Once in a while he eased his mouth open, slowly and cautiously, trying to work the soreness out of his jaw.

It had been a long day. His mother had brought him food and fussed over him for half an hour or so before taking off again, saying that she had a busy day ahead of her.

Try to get some sleep, she'd said. *You need to rest and heal.*

She hadn't even mentioned the family birthday dinner scheduled for the following evening. Jenna and Halley were supposed to come, but of course that wasn't going to happen now. He'd been dreading telling his mother that, because she would want to know why, and he wasn't ready to talk about the breakup to anyone, especially his family. They all liked Jenna so much. But the fact that Rose hadn't even mentioned the dinner was almost worse. Was it possible she'd forgotten it? Had it been eclipsed by the plans for Eddie's big celebration later in the month?

Rose had at least wished Tito a happy birthday, but almost as an afterthought before breezing out his door. It was all very dissatisfying and strange.

He hauled himself to his feet and started ambling around his apartment for what felt like the millionth time that day. No movies or TV or electronic screens of any kind, the doctor had told him, and no reading either, even from an analog book. Well, what else was there to do? It wasn't as if he could go for a hike. He was pretty much stuck indoors resting until he was cleared for regular activities, but resting wasn't very restful without books or movies, at least once you felt well enough to be out of bed.

He'd tried an audiobook, but it couldn't hold his attention. He'd tried listening to music, but every song he heard had some sort of memory of Jenna attached to it now. He'd already taken two naps today, and he could only pet the cat for so long.

It would be different, of course, if he had company. Someone to talk with and be quiet with. Someone to ask how he was feeling and maybe bring him a glass of juice. But he didn't. He was all alone, with nothing to do but wander aimlessly around, and think, and feel.

This must have been what it was like for Uncle Tito after his wife left. No one to talk to about it, and no one he wanted to talk to at all except the one who'd gone away. Nowhere for the pain to go. Nothing for it to do but swell and grow until it was ready to burn its way out of his chest.

He went into the kitchen, took down a glass and poured some bourbon. He wasn't supposed to drink alcohol while recovering from his head injury, but he had to get some relief. They hadn't even given him any good painkillers, just told him to take ibuprofen or acetaminophen, neither of which could do a thing for the worst pain of all, this feeling of loss that was like a physical ache in his soul.

He picked up the glass, swirled it, set it down, stared a few moments into the amber-colored liquid and picked it up again.

Uncle Tito stared solemnly at him from the photo on the fridge, telling him not to do it, that it wouldn't help, that once he started he wouldn't be able to stop, and once the alcohol wore off he'd have a hangover to deal with, and the thing he'd been trying to bury would still be there, staring him in the face, bigger and stronger than ever.

He set the glass back down, picked it up, set it down, picked it up...and poured the bourbon back into the bottle.

He walked to the living room. Bunter lay in his usual spot on the windowsill, surveying the downtown area. He flicked an ear back when Tito knelt beside him but didn't turn around. Tito stroked the cat's smooth back and gazed in the same direction, at the patch of metal roof just visible through a gap in the trees. Was Jenna there right now, making plans for her next move? Where would she take Halley this time?

If only she would call, and say she'd been wrong, that she'd changed her mind and wanted to be with him. He'd been straining his ears all day, listening for her ringtone, occasionally checking his phone to see if he'd somehow missed a call from her.

His phone was lying on the coffee table right now. He was about to pick it up and check it again when the chime of an incoming text message went off.

He spun around in a clumsy sprawl, nearly whacking his head against the coffee table in his haste to reach his phone.

The message wasn't from Jenna. It was from Lalo.

Never in his life had Tito been more disappointed to hear from his cousin. And the content of the message did nothing to change that feeling.

I need to ask you a favor, it said.

Tito stood a moment, staring at the screen, before typing, What is it?

It's kind of a big favor, Lalo replied.

Tito let out a heavy sigh. He was not in the mood for this. He stood watching the dancing dots, waiting to find out what the favor would be. Maybe Lalo had locked himself out of his office again and needed to borrow Tito's keys. That wasn't a very big favor, but maybe he felt bad about disturbing his freshly concussed cousin who was supposed to be resting.

I need you to come downstairs and tend bar.

"What?" Tito said out loud. He typed, *Why?*

It's a long story, Lalo answered. *But you know we've got that private event booked at the restaurant tonight, and the people want an open bar. Eric was scheduled to work but he called in sick, and Garrett has car trouble.*

"Are you kidding me?" Tito asked his phone screen, louder this time. Eric and Garrett had jumped at the chance to work this event, presumably expecting good tips. The servers at Lalo's had been quick to volunteer as well. All of which had worked out really well, since he and Jenna both wanted off that evening. Jenna had said she was going to take Tito out to dinner for his birthday, just the two of them, in advance of the birthday dinner with Tito's family.

Well, that wasn't happening now.

Jenna can tend bar, Tito thought. But Jenna was home with an injured and traumatized child.

He paced around the living room, seething. Why were things like this always happening to him? Why was he always the one who had to take up everyone else's slack?

Maybe he would just say no. He had every right to. He'd given enough hours of his life to that bar.

But it was his name on the sign above the door. And he'd already rested for the 24 hours the doctor had recommended. At this point, in all honesty, an evening of work would be a pleasant change.

I'll be there in ten minutes, he typed.

Great! Lalo replied. *See you downstairs.*

No mention of the fact that Tito had suffered a brain injury the day before while trying to prevent a kidnapping, or that today was his birthday. Not even a simple thank you.

Tito started to exit from the messaging app, but the dancing dots appeared again, followed by a new message.

Be sure to wear your gold tie bar. This is a classy event.

It took Tito longer than usual to get dressed. Everything felt like a huge effort. He sat on the edge of his bed for a good five minutes, unable to summon the energy to button his shirt.

But he did it at last and made his way downstairs, ready to slip into his place as the guy handing out alcohol, unseen except as part of the background.

The bar seemed unnaturally quiet as he walked down the hallway. Maybe they were still setting up for the event, or maybe the guests hadn't started arriving yet.

But when he entered the room, he saw that it was already packed with people. Tony and Alex Reyes were there, along with their wives and kids. Annalisa and her boss Claudia. Mad Dog McClain and the entire volunteer fire department. The Reyes brothers and their families. Luke and Eliana. Bart. Lalo. Coby Kowalski. Abel from the kitchen. Kevin Fox with his daughter, Gillian, and his dad. Susana Vrba and Roque Fidalgo from the equine center. Eric, looking perfectly healthy, and Garrett. Tito's own parents and brothers.

What the heck? What was happening here? Just what was this event, and why hadn't he been invited?

Everyone was facing him, and smiling at him, no doubt relieved to see that the serving of alcohol would go on as expected. Someone had set up a long buffet table, with plates, flatware and chafing dishes of food neatly laid out.

Standing at the end of the table, in a mango-colored

dress, was Jenna, with Halley at her side. Her eyes met Tito's. He saw her take a deep breath.

Then he saw the banner hanging overhead, painstakingly made of *papeles picados*, each letter a sheet in itself, spelling out *Happy Birthday Tito!*

There was no shout of *surprise*, no throwing of confetti or blowing of noisemakers. Just a familiar loud laugh ringing out, followed by, "You ought to see your face right now, Rigoberto! Come on in, birthday boy, and join the party."

And then his mother's arms were around him, and she was kissing him on the cheek and saying, "Happy birthday, baby!" More people hugged him, or shook his hand, or clapped him on the back.

Lalo grinned as he gripped his hand. "I had you going there, didn't I, cousin? Asking you to come in and work when you were supposed to be taking it easy. You fell for it, too!"

"I can't believe you didn't figure it out!" said Garrett. "We were planning this party right under your nose, on your actual birthday and everything. But Jenna said you'd never suspect it was for you, and she was right."

"Jenna said that?" Tito asked.

"Oh, yeah," said Lalo. "The whole thing was her idea. She's been planning it for days."

Since before she'd broken up with him, then. And now she was following through with it. Why? Out of duty, or friendship, or something more? Why didn't she come over to him right now? He wanted her to, and at the same time he was terrified of what she might say if she did.

Then Lalo started clinking a spoon against a glass. Once the room had quieted down, he held the glass high.

"We're here tonight to honor Tito Mendoza," he said. "Tito is my cousin, business partner and sounding board. I know I'm not the easiest guy in the world to work with—"

lots of agreeing murmurs from the crowd "—but believe me, I'd be a lot worse without Tito to give me reality checks and help me think things through. This place, Lalo's Kitchen, this is my dream. And that man right there—" he pointed at Tito "—he's the one who made it happen. I never could have raised the capital on my own to get a place with as good a location as this one. Being right next door to an established bar, connected to it by a pass-through, gave Lalo's Kitchen a head start and credibility that can't be overestimated. I wouldn't be where I am today without Tito. He took his uncle's legacy, and he made it into something more. So let's all raise glass to him. Happy birthday, Tito."

"Happy birthday," the crowd said, and drank.

Eddie went next. He was looking his best, well dressed, hair perfectly styled, grinning hugely.

"I remember when this guy was born, just one day after *my* fourth birthday," he said, his eyes sweeping the crowd. "Yeah, that's right. Our birthdays are one day apart! Can you believe that? I don't know what my mother was thinking!"

He paused for the crowd to laugh, which it did.

"I didn't get much of a party that year, with a brand-new baby in the house squalling all day and all night," he continued. "Lots of people came over to drop off food and take a look at him, and you know what they told me? They told me how cool it was that I'd gotten a new brother for my birthday. Well, I didn't think much of *that*. I already had three brothers. What did I need with one more?"

He looked at Tito, and his toothy grin softened into an affectionate smile. "I couldn't have been more wrong. Tito is one of a kind, and my life is richer for knowing him.

Happy birthday, little brother. Here's to many more years of separate birthday celebrations for me and you."

"Hear, hear!" Tito called out above the laughter and cheering.

Then Tito's father said, "Quiet down, everyone. My turn."

Holding his stein of beer, he faced his youngest son head-on across the room and spoke in his usual bellow.

"This is a very special occasion, y'all. This is the first time my boy Rigoberto has had a proper birthday party since he was fourteen years old! Can you believe that? He told his mother and me that he didn't like parties, and I believed him. But I might have been wrong about that."

He paused to rub his jaw, then went on, "There might actually be a lot of things about this son of mine that I don't understand. He's kind of a hard one to figure. He's always been his own man. It takes a lot of courage to be different, and Tito's one of the best and most courageous men I know."

He raised his stein high. "Happy birthday, *huerco*!"

The rest of Tito's brothers toasted him as well. Javi gave his toast over FaceTime via Annalisa's iPad, live from West Texas, beer in hand.

Even Marcos Ramirez gave a toast. He was Tony Reyes's brother-in-law and a man of famously few words. He and his wife and son came to the restaurant and bar regularly, but Tito didn't know him very well, despite having gone to high school with him. After graduation, Marcos had joined the Marines. He'd only moved back to Limestone Springs a few years ago. Marcos didn't drink alcohol, so that glass he was holding probably held turmeric ginger tea.

Marcos took a deep breath and squared his shoulders. "I, uh, I'm not one for public speaking, but I'll do my best.

There was a time in my life, not many years back, when I was at a crossroads and not sure what to do. Tito had some words of wisdom for me that pointed me in the right direction, and I've never forgotten that, though I don't think I ever thanked him for it. He and I didn't know each other all that well, even though we went through high school together and graduated the same year. I see now that that was my loss, and I'm glad and honored that Tito is my friend today."

He raised his glass. "Here's to you, man. Happy birthday."

Tito was touched. He didn't even remember ever giving Marcos any advice.

The toasts kept coming. Tony Reyes gave one, followed by Mad Dog McClain, chief of the volunteer fire department, and Coby Kowalski. All of theirs made reference to that late-summer storm a few years back, when Tito and Lalo had provided free food and drink to first responders and to people whose houses had suffered damage.

And then Tito's heart seized up, because it was Jenna's turn.

She stood straight, head high, looking very determined, a little nervous and unbelievably beautiful. Halley watched from nearby, her face shining with excitement.

The crowd quieted down. They'd yelled out some good-natured cross talk during some of the other toasts, but everyone seemed to want to pay close attention to whatever Jenna had to say.

"I think everyone here knows me," she said. "I've been living and working in this town for about a year and a half now, and I've served beer and burgers to most of the people in this room. As recent events have probably made very clear, Halley and I came to Limestone Springs to get a fresh start, away from a dangerous man and some bad history. But what you don't know, what I haven't yet told any-one, is how I chose Limestone Springs in the first place."

She spoke formally, as if she'd planned in advance what she was going to say. She cleared her throat.

"The Texas part was an easy decision," she said. "My father once spent some time here as a young man and often spoke fondly of it. He always wanted to go back one day but never got a chance. And I knew I wanted to live in a small town. It felt safer, somehow. So I Googled best small towns in Texas, and wouldn't you know, Limestone Springs made everyone's top ten."

She tucked a long curl behind one ear. "I liked the look of Limestone Springs, with its prosperous small businesses and beautiful old downtown buildings. I liked the fact that the town had an annual persimmon festival, with a parade and carnival rides and a dance, and a Persimmon Queen and a Persimmon Court, and vendors selling crafts and pastries and jams, and even a guy who put on a persim-mon suit and walked around glad-handing the crowd and posing for pictures."

Several people laughed. Jenna laughed too. Then her expression turned serious again.

"And then," she said, "I saw an old news video about how the people in the town came together to help each other after a late-summer hailstorm. Some of the video was actually shot right here inside Lalo's Kitchen and Tito's Bar. Tony was in that video. You were great on camera, Tony, talking about the community's neighborly spirit and generosity. You even teared up a bit when you said how grateful you were that no one had been seriously hurt."

She turned the full force of her gaze on Tito. His heart was pounding now.

"But what really caught my eye," Jenna said, "was the guy in the background, quietly handing out food and drink to firefighters and volunteers and people who'd been displaced by the storm. A slender guy in a crisp white shirt and black vest, with a gold tie bar, and a little Clark Gable mustache that made him look like a film star from a bygone and classier era."

A surprised murmur rose from the crowd. "That's right," Jenna said sheepishly. "I basically traveled fourteen hundred miles to meet a cute guy I saw on the internet. That sort of thing is usually not a smart move, and in general, I don't recommend it. But in this case, it worked out pretty well."

The crowd laughed but quickly subsided, clearly eager to hear more, as was Tito, who could hardly believe what he was hearing. Was it possible? Could it be true? Had Jenna actually come to Limestone Springs because of him?

"So I came here, and got a job at Lalo's," Jenna said. "I got to know Tito, and found out that he was even better in person than he was on that news video. But I didn't really put down roots here, because I didn't trust anyone enough to share the truth about myself and where I'd come from. That was a mistake, and I want to do better now."

Her chin trembled. Tito swallowed hard over a lump of soreness in his throat. The room was dead silent.

"But enough about me," Jenna said briskly. "We're here tonight to celebrate Tito Mendoza—son, brother, boss, friend, confidant, and so much more." She raised her glass. "Happy birthday, Tito."

"Happy birthday, Tito," the crowd chorused.

Then Juan's voice called out, "Enough with the speechifying. Let's eat!"

CHAPTER NINETEEN

IT TOOK A while for Tito to make his way to Jenna. He had a whole succession of people to get through, all of whom wanted to shake his hand, wish him a happy birthday and tell him how much he and his bar had meant to the community, and to them personally, over the years. It was very gratifying and heartwarming, of course. He'd never realized how much of an impact he'd managed to have on the town, and hearing it made his heart swell. But it took time. And while he was listening and smiling and nodding, another part of him was yearning after Jenna in her mango-colored dress, beautiful and out of reach.

When he finally got free, he had a brief moment of panic because he couldn't see her anymore. Had she left without even speaking to him?

Then suddenly there she was in front of him, holding out a glass.

"Hey there," she said. "I thought you could use some sustenance. It must be thirsty work, getting toasted by half the town."

He took the glass from her, his fingers brushing hers. "Thanks," he said.

"It's just juice," she said. "No alcohol for you."

He sipped it just to have something to do. He didn't even know if he was thirsty anymore. The juice was mango, like her dress.

An awkward silence fell. There was so much Tito

wanted to say, but he couldn't seem to get the words from his brain to his mouth, and Jenna looked anxious.

"I got you a present," she said. "Do you want to open it?"

"Sure," he said.

She led him through the crowd to the bar, and he followed, keeping his gaze fixed on her smooth golden head. Eric and Garrett were busily pouring beer and mixing drinks. And on the bar top was a black box topped with a gold bow.

He set down his juice, opened the lid of the box—

And there was his uncle, looking out at him from a black-and-white photo with a white mat and a gold frame. Uncle Tito was standing behind the bar as it had looked in the eighties, his head held high, gazing out with the watchful expression that Tito remembered so well.

Tito lifted the picture out of the box. "Is this the pic that's on my fridge?" he asked.

"Yes. Your mom gave me the negative."

There was something else in the box, beneath a thin sheet of cushioning foam.

Another picture. Same size, matching frame, also in black-and-white. It was the photo Tito's mother had taken of Tito and his uncle together at the bar.

Tears pricked his eyes. His uncle looked so *young*. So did he, for that matter.

He laid the two pictures side by side on the bar top. "These look amazing," he said.

"Yes, they do," said Jenna. "But are you sure there isn't anything left in the box?"

Sure enough, there was one more framed photo under another sheet of foam. This was an image he'd never seen before. It showed just him, standing behind the bar as it appeared today, with the antique mirror behind him. He had the same upright posture and vigilant expression as his uncle. He'd never seen the resemblance so clearly before now.

It was a good picture, too, probably the best picture he'd ever seen of himself.

"Where did this one come from?" he asked.

"I took it," Jenna said. "Remember?"

And suddenly he did remember. It was the day after the Fourth of July party and his and Jenna's first kiss, when everything had seemed so fresh and full of hope. He remembered seeing her at the pass-through, holding her phone pointed at him, smiling at him. *I'm taking a picture of my handsome boyfriend*, she'd said.

A rush of heat flooded his face and neck.

"I got Lauren Reyes to edit the photos for me," Jenna said.

"She did a great job," said Tito. "The black and white gives them a nice vintage vibe. And the gold frames are perfect."

She smiled. "They look like the Johnnie Walker label," she said. "They look like you."

He let out a shaky laugh. Memories washed over him—of the day when they'd assigned all the liquor bottles to the people they most resembled, and all the other times they'd closed together.

He managed to get control of his voice long enough to say, "They're beautiful. Thank you. Thank you for all of this. The party and…everything."

She shrugged. "I had a lot of help. Everyone was happy to pitch in. They just needed someone to give them the idea. They really love you, you know."

And you? The question was right there, in the air between them, so plain that he didn't need to ask it.

Jenna spoke in a rush. "Tito, I'm sorry for what I said

before, and for all the ways I've held out on you and been less than truthful with you. I was only trying to protect Halley, but I should have realized that I can do that better with you than without you. Everything is better with you than without you."

"So…you're not leaving?" Tito asked.

It seemed unlikely that she was still planning on leaving after she'd just told her story to a roomful of people, but he had to hear her say it.

"I'm not leaving," she said. "You were right. It was arrogant of me to take so much on myself, to think I was stronger on my own and that I was the only one who could take care of Halley."

"It wasn't all arrogance," Tito said. "You've been carrying a heavy load for a long time, and you don't want to make a mistake. That's only natural. And it isn't everyone who'd take on the responsibility of raising their sister's child. I've never heard you speak a single complaint, or a word of regret for the life you left behind. You're the strongest woman I know, Jenna."

She smiled. "Thank you, Tito. That means a lot. But a lot of it really was arrogance. Halley pointed that out to me in no uncertain terms when she found out I was planning to move us away from Limestone Springs. So did you. You were both right, and I was wrong."

"Thank you," said Tito. "That couldn't have been an easy thing to say."

"It wasn't that hard," said Jenna. "I'll admit to any number of character flaws if you'll take me back."

A LOOK OF soft wonder washed over Tito's face. Jenna saw him swallow.

"Take you back?" he repeated in an incredulous voice. "As if there could be any question of that."

Then he laughed, a wonderfully rich laugh, and said in his wonderfully rich voice, "Come here."

He reached for her, and she came to him, resting her cheek against his chest. She felt it expand as he took a deep breath; she felt the rapid beating of his heart and inhaled the clean starchy scent of his shirt.

"You know," he said, "you could have just called and told me you were staying. You didn't have to be so dramatic with the party and everything."

She squirmed. "I know. Maybe I was wrong to wait. But I wanted to do something special for you, to show you how special you are—to me, and to the whole town."

He held her tight for a moment longer. When he finally pulled back and looked at her, his eyes were shining. Slowly, gently, he lowered his face to hers and kissed her.

Someone cheered, but Jenna didn't open her eyes. She just held on to Tito as surges of joy went off like fireworks inside her head.

SHE DIDN'T LEAVE Tito's side for the rest of the evening. He kept her hand tightly clasped in his as if afraid she'd slip away if he let go. They made the rounds of the party together. People smiled at them in an approving sort of way. Some of them said, "It's about time." And quite a few of them said words to the effect that if Chase ever tried to take Halley again, or harassed Jenna in any way, or so much as dared to show his face in Limestone Springs again, he would have a whole town's worth of angry Texans to deal with. By the time the party wound down, Chase's mug shots—the Virginia one and the new one taken a few days earlier at the Limestone Springs police station—had been posted on the *do not serve* group text and circulated to various other local businesses.

Halley appeared to be having a great time. By the end

of the evening, her cast was full of signatures, including a *David M* in bold black letters.

Susana and Roque came by to pay their respects.

"I'm going to go ahead with those barrel-racing lessons," Susana said. "I could do Halley and Gillian in a class together if you're interested—after Halley's out of her cast, of course."

Jenna glanced at Tito and smiled. "That sounds great," she said. "Why don't you go tell her right now?"

She did. Jenna and Tito watched as Halley's eyes lit up. Her squeal of delight carried across the room.

It wasn't even 9:30 p.m. when the guests began to make their goodbyes. Jenna had seen to that ahead of time.

"I didn't want you all worn out," she said. "Don't forget, birthday boy, you're still recovering from a head injury, and you need your rest."

She and Tito walked outside together to send Halley on her way to her first ever sleepover at Gillian's house. They lingered awhile, thanking Kevin for everything he'd done to protect Halley. By the time they went back inside, the food was cleared away. The benches and chairs were upside down on the tables, and Clint and Veronica were mopping. They'd already worked pretty far back, and the middle part of the floors were starting to dry in streaks.

Jenna took off her strappy shoes and tiptoed across to the bar, and the music-streaming cellphone.

"No indie pop tonight," she said. "Just a playlist of old love songs for slow dancing. Plenty of Journey and Guns N' Roses for me, and sixties and seventies stuff for you."

Tito slipped his own shoes off. "I thought the party was over," he said.

"This is the party after the party," Jenna replied.

Jenna held on to Tito, swaying to the music, and let her mind drift and wander. A Bee Gees cover band was coming to New Braunfels. She would take Tito to the concert as a surprise. She wanted to take him to Virginia, too, to meet her mother. She'd look at the schedule tomorrow and figure out some dates. She wanted the trip north to happen sooner than later. Why not? Chase was locked up again, and would be for a long time. There'd be a trial to deal with at some point, but with as many crimes as he'd racked up, and as many credible witnesses as their side had, she was confident that the charges would stick.

They had so much to do, so much to look forward to. Lots of wonderful things seemed possible just now. She felt as light and buoyant as if she could fly.

* * * * *

WESTERN

Rugged men looking for love...

Available Next Month

Sweet-Talkin' Maverick Christy Jeffries
The Cowboy's Second Chance Cheryl Harper

....

Fortune's Baby Claim Michelle Major
The Cowgirl's Homecoming Jeannie Watt

....

LOVE INSPIRED
A Valentine's Day Return Brenda Minton
Their Inseparable Bond Jill Weatherholt
Larger Print

Keep reading for an excerpt of
STAKING A CLAIM
by Janice Maynard — find this story
in the *Texas Cattleman's Club: Ranchers and Rivals*
anthology.

One

Layla Grandin hated funerals. It was bad enough to sit through somber affairs with friends who had lost family members. But today was worse. Today was personal.

Victor Grandin Sr., Layla's beloved grandfather, had been laid to rest.

It wasn't a tragedy in the truest sense of the word. Victor was ninety-three years old when he died. He lived an amazing, fulfilling life. And in the end, he was luckier than most. He literally died with his boots on after suffering a heart attack while on horseback.

There were worse ways to go. But that didn't make Layla's grief any less.

After the well-attended funeral in town, many of Royal's finest citizens had made the trek out to the Grandin ranch to pay their respects. Layla eyed the large gathering with a cynical gaze. The Grandin family was wealthy. Even folks with the best of intentions couldn't help sniffing around when money and inheritance were on the menu. That was the burden of financial privilege. You never knew if people really liked you or if they just wanted something they thought you could give them.

For that very reason, Layla had been lingering in the corner of the room, content to play voyeur. Her newly widowed grandmother Miriam looked frail and distraught, as was to be expected. Layla's father was relishing the role of genial host, embracing his chance to shine now that his larger-than-life parent was out of the picture.

Layla wished with all her heart that her own father cared for her as much as her gruff but loving grandfather had. Unfortunately, Victor Junior was not particularly interested in his female offspring. He was too focused on his only son, Victor the third, better known as Vic. Her father was grooming Vic to take over one day, despite the fact that Layla's older sister, Chelsea, was first in line, followed by Layla.

Chelsea crossed the room in Layla's direction, looking disgruntled. "I am so over this," she said. "I don't think anyone here really cares about Grandfather at all. Some of them probably haven't even met him."

Layla grimaced. "I know what you mean. But at least Vic and Morgan are genuinely upset. Grandy loved all his grandkids."

"You most of all," Chelsea said. "You were the only one who could get away with that nickname."

Layla flushed. She hadn't realized anyone else noticed. As the middle of three girls, and with Vic their father's clear favorite, Layla often felt lost in the crowd.

Suddenly, Layla realized her father was deep in conversation with a man she recognized. She lowered her voice and leaned toward Chelsea. "Why is Daddy cozied up to Bertram Banks? Oh, crap! Why are they looking at me?"

"Who knows? Let's go find out." Chelsea, always the proactive one, took Layla's elbow and steered her across the room. Layla would have much preferred hiding out in the kitchen, but the two men obviously saw them approaching.

When they were in earshot, Layla and Chelsea's dad gave them a big smile. For such a sober day, it might have been a bit too big, in Layla's estimation.

"Here are my two oldest," he said, giving Bertram a wink. "Take your pick."

Chelsea raised an eyebrow. "That sounds a little weird, Dad."

Bertram chuckled. "He didn't mean anything by it."

Layla distrusted the two men's good humor. Both of them were known to manipulate people when the occasion demanded it. Layla had known the Banks family forever. As a kid, she had been a tomboy, running wild and riding horses and dirt bikes with Bertram's twin sons, Jordan and Joshua.

Back then, she was lean and coltish, not at all interested in girly pursuits. She could take whatever the Banks boys dished out. As she grew older, though, she'd developed a terrible crush on Jordan. It was embarrassing to think about now.

"What's going on?" Layla asked.

For once, Chelsea was silent.

Bertram smiled at Layla. This time it seemed genuine. "I have tickets to see Parker Brett in concert tomorrow night."

It was Layla's turn to raise an eyebrow. "Congratulations. I've heard those were impossible to get."

Bertram puffed out his chest. "I know a guy," he said, chuckling. "But the thing is, I've had a conflict arise. Jordan has offered to take you, Layla, you know—to cheer you up. We all know how much you loved your grandfather."

Layla was aghast. Chelsea bit her lip, clearly trying hard not to laugh. She knew all about Layla's fruitless crush.

To be honest, Layla highly doubted that Jordan had volunteered to do anything of the sort. She wasn't even sure he liked country music. "That's sweet of you," she said. "But I don't think I'll feel like going out. This has been an emotional week."

Her father jumped in. "It will do you good, Layla. Everyone knows you've had a crush on Jordan forever."

A split second of stunned silence reverberated between the uncomfortable foursome. *Did he just say that? Oh, yes he did!* Layla felt her face get hot. *Recover, Layla. Quickly! Think!* "When I was a kid, Dad. I've moved on," Layla mumbled.

Chelsea tried to help. "Good grief, Daddy. Layla's had a million boyfriends since then. Even a fiancé." She stopped short, clearly appalled. "Sorry, sis."

Layla forced a smile. Her doomed engagement two years ago was a sore spot, more because it reeked of failure than anything else. "No worries." She faced the duo of late-fifties males. "I'm sure Jordan can find his own date for the concert."

Bertram's expression was bland, suspiciously innocent. "You're it, kiddo. He'll text you the details later tonight."

Layla glanced around the room. "He's not here?"

"He went to the funeral, but he had another commitment this afternoon."

Victor beamed. "So, it's settled. If you two ladies will excuse us, Bertram and I are going to mingle."

When the two men wandered away, Layla groaned. "You have to be kidding me. Why didn't you say something? I needed help."

Chelsea cocked her head, her sisterly smile teasing. "Well, he wasn't wrong. You *have* always had a thing for Jordan Banks. What could it hurt to get out of the house? With you swearing off men after your engagement ended and now Grandfather dying, I think it would do you good. It's just a concert."

Layla couldn't disagree with the logic. "Fine," she said. "But I hope this doesn't put Jordan in a weird spot. I'll have to make sure he knows I'm not pining for him."

"I'm sure he doesn't think that." Chelsea grinned.

Layla had been too tense and upset to eat lunch before the funeral. Now she was starving. Her mother had made arrangements for catered hors d'oeuvres to serve the dozens of guests who showed up for the reception. Judging by the crowd, it might ultimately prove to be two hundred or two fifty. But her mother, Bethany, was an experienced hostess. No one would run out of food.

"Let's get something to eat," Layla said to Chelsea.

"Good idea."

The two sisters filled their plates and retreated to a sunny alcove just off the large living room. Some people might be taken aback by the luxurious, enormous house, but to Layla and Chelsea it was simply home.

From their comfortable seats, they enjoyed the sunshine and the food. Chelsea sighed. "I can't believe it's only four days till May. Summer will be here soon."

Layla's composure wobbled. "Grandy loved the long days and even the heat. Not to mention watermelon and fresh corn. It won't be the same this year." She scanned the crowd. "I guess we should have asked Morgan to join us." Chelsea was thirty-five, Layla thirty-two. Morgan, their baby sister, was still in her twenties.

"She's hanging out with Vic," Chelsea said, stabbing a fat shrimp with her fork. "Did I tell you she sided with Vic over me yesterday? Again."

Vic was third in line, but first in their father's heart and plans.

Chelsea continued, "Every damn time she takes Vic's side. Just once I'd like her to take mine. Still, it's not their fault Daddy thinks I can't handle the ranch eventually. It makes me so angry. I love this ranch as much as anybody. It ought to be me. Or you and me together."

"Well, it won't, so you might as well get used to the idea. Besides, if genetics are any clue, Daddy will live another thirty years. You and I might as well forget about this ranch and find something else to keep us busy."

"True," Chelsea said glumly.

"Look at Mr. Lattimore," Layla said. "He must be grieving terribly, but he's as dignified as ever." Augustus was ninety-six. His wife, Hazel, was at his side speaking to him in a low voice. As a Black family in Royal, Texas, the Lattimores hadn't always had it easy, but they were equally as influential as the Grandins. The only difference was, their patriarch, Augustus, had been forced to give up the reins several years ago because of his struggles with memory issues.

"He and Grandfather were so very close. I wonder

if he understands that Grandfather is gone. They've been friends for decades." Chelsea's comment was wistful.

"His memory comes in flashes, I think. You've seen people like that." The two families were so close the Lattimore kids probably felt sad about losing Grandpa Victor even if he wasn't their blood kin. It would be hard to see the oldest generation begin to pass on, especially since they adored their own grandfather.

Chelsea put her plate on a side table and grimaced. "I hate funerals," she said.

Layla burst out laughing.

Her sister gaped. "Did I say something funny?"

"Not particularly," Layla said, still chuckling. "But I've been thinking the same thing all day. When it's my time to go, just put me in the ground and plant a tree. I don't need people kicking the dirt and fighting over my estate."

"Always assuming you have one."

"Touché." Chelsea's joking comment gave Layla something to ponder. After college, she had spent the last decade pouring her energies into this place. She assisted her mother with frequent entertaining. She helped train horses. And though her father was sometimes dismissive of her expertise, she used her business degree to make sure the family enterprise was solid.

Her grandfather had been proud of her ideas and her knack for understanding the ranching business.

Unfortunately, he was too old-school to ever think a woman could be in charge of anything that didn't involve cooking, cleaning or changing diapers. A woman's place was in the home.

No matter that he had been affectionate and supportive of Layla's thoughts and dreams, he had been forged in the patriarchal environs of Maverick County, and he agreed with his son. The only grandson, Vic, should be next in line to run things when it was Victor Junior's time to hang up his spurs.

Layla was at a crossroads. Her personal life was nonexistent. If Vic was going to be heir to the Grandin ranch, she might as well make a plan for the future. Many of her friends were married and had kids by now. Layla didn't feel any rush.

Her ex-fiancé, Richard, hadn't been too excited about the prospect of starting a family. That should have been a red flag. But Layla had taken his words at face value. He'd said he was concentrating on his career.

Unfortunately, the thing he'd been concentrating on was screwing as many women as possible in the shortest amount of time. The only reason he'd given Layla a ring was that he saw the benefit in allying himself with the Grandin empire.

For Layla, the entire experience had shaken her confidence. How could she trust her own judgment when she had been so wrong about Richard?

Gradually, the crowd thinned. She and Chelsea split up to mingle, to thank people for coming and to say goodbyes. The food tables were demolished. The furniture was askew. By all accounts, the funeral reception was a success. Hazel and Augustus Lattimore were just now being escorted home. Layla's grandmother Miriam looked shaky and exhausted as she headed for her suite.

Fortunately for Layla, Bertram Banks had disappeared half an hour ago. She definitely didn't want to talk to him again. She was already planning how to ditch the concert arrangements.

She had nothing against country music. Jordan would be a fun companion. But she was emotionally wrung out. In some ways, she had never completely processed the trauma from two years ago, and now this, losing her grandfather.

As the room emptied, only the Grandins and Lattimores remained, parents and kids, though the term *kids* was a misnomer. Even Caitlyn, the youngest, was twenty-five. The reception had been advertised as a drop-in from two until five. Now it was almost six.

Layla was about to make her excuses and head to her bedroom when her mother went to answer the doorbell and came back flanked by a uniformed person holding a legal-size envelope.

Oddly, the room fell silent. The young courier looked nervous. "I have a delivery addressed to The Heirs of Victor Grandin Sr.," he said.

Layla's father stepped forward. "That's me. Where do I sign?"

Ben Lattimore, her father's best friend, joined him. "What's up? Kind of late in the day for any kind of official delivery."

Victor nodded absently, breaking the seal on the envelope and extracting the contents. After a moment, he paled. "Someone is pursuing the oil rights to both of our ranches."

"Somebody who?" Chelsea asked, trying to read over Victor's shoulder.

He scanned farther. "Heath Thurston."

Ben frowned. "Why didn't I get a copy?"

"Maybe you did at your house." Victor glared at the document. "It's in incredibly poor taste to deliver this today."

"The timing could be a coincidence." Ben Lattimore was visibly worried. "If this is legit, our properties are in trouble. We're cattle ranchers, damn it. Having somebody search for oil would destroy much of what we've built."

Vic stepped to his father's shoulder. "I thought we didn't have any oil, right? So this is probably all a hoax," he said. "Don't worry about it, Dad. At least not until we investigate."

"That's the ticket," Victor said. "I know a PI—Jonas Shaw." His gaze narrowed. "But I'll start with my mother first."

Layla shook her head. "No, Daddy. She's grief-stricken and so frail right now. We should only involve her if it's absolutely necessary." It was obvious that her father didn't like being opposed. But he nodded tersely.

"I suppose," he said grudgingly. "But *you*…" He pointed at his brother. "I'm going to need cooperation from you, Daniel."

"I'm flying back to Paris tomorrow."

"Not anymore. No one leaves Royal until we meet with our lawyer."

Layla could tell Daniel wanted to argue. But he settled for a muttered protest. "This whole thing smells fishy," he said.

Conversation swelled as the two families broke up into small groups and began to process the bizarre information. Layla was surprised that Heath Thurston would pursue something like this. From what she knew of him, he was an honorable man. But if he and his brother thought they were entitled to the oil rights, maybe they were taking the only logical step.

Still, it was very suspicious that Thurston was claiming oil rights under *both* ranches. What possible claim could he have?

Layla spotted Alexa Lattimore gathering up her purse and light jacket, preparing to leave. Layla had talked to her earlier in the day, but only briefly. "Don't rush off, Alexa. I miss you." The eldest Lattimore daughter hadn't lived in Royal since finishing college.

"I've missed you, too, Layla. I was sorry to hear about your engagement. I wish I could have come home to give you moral support, but things were crazy at work."

Layla sighed. "It's no fun being the subject of Royal's grapevine. I don't think Richard broke my heart, but he definitely dented my pride." She tugged her friend to a nearby sofa. "I wanted to ask you something."

Alexa sat down with a wary expression. "Oh?"

"I was hoping you might think about coming home for a longer visit. I think Caitlyn would love having you around, and besides, it looks like your lawyer skills may be in demand. For both our families."

Alexa chewed her lip, not quite meeting Layla's gaze. "I don't know, Layla. I wanted to pay my respects at your grandfather's funeral, but this was just a quick jaunt. Miami is home now. There's no real place for me in Royal."

"If I know you, Ms. Workaholic, you probably have a million vacation days banked. At least think about it."

"I will," Alexa said.

Even hearing the words, Layla wasn't sure Alexa was telling the truth. Alexa had kept her distance from Royal and didn't seem eager to get involved with an ongoing crisis.

At last, Layla was free to escape to her bedroom and recover from this long, painful day. She stripped off her funeral dress and took a quick shower. After that, she donned comfy black yoga pants and a chunky teal sweater.

When she curled up in her chaise lounge by the window, the tears flowed. She'd been holding them in check all day. Now she sobbed in earnest. She would never see Grandy again, never hear the comfortable rumble of his voice. She had loved him deeply, but perhaps she had never realized just how big a void he filled in her life.

With Grandy gone, she felt adrift.

In the end, she had to wash her face and reapply mascara. The family would be gathering for dinner at seven thirty. It was the Grandin way, and old traditions were hard to break.

Just before she went downstairs at a quarter after, she glanced at her phone. All her family and friends had been at the house today, so there was no real reason to think she might have a text.

But Bertram had said Jordan would text her tonight.

It was dumb to feel hurt and uncertain. She knew Bertram. He was probably, even now, pressuring his son to take Layla to the concert. It was so embarrassing. Bertram would like nothing more than to have one of his sons marry a Grandin daughter. He wasn't picky. He would keep trying if this didn't work out.

The concert was a day away. If Layla hadn't heard from Jordan in the next couple of hours, she was done with this shotgun-date situation. She might have a long-standing crush on Jordan, but honestly,